ALWAYS
CLOSE TO
HOME

DISCARD

Books by Jerry S. Eicher

THE ADAMS COUNTY TRILOGY
Rebecca's Promise
Rebecca's Return
Rebecca's Choice

THE BEILER SISTERS
Holding a Tender Heart
Seeing Your Face Again
Finding Love at Home

EMMA RABER'S DAUGHTER
Katie Opens Her Heart
Katie's Journey to Love
Katie's Forever Promise

FIELDS OF HOME
Missing Your Smile
Following Your Heart
Where Love Grows

HANNAH'S HEART
A Dream for Hannah
A Hope for Hannah
A Baby for Hannah

LAND OF PROMISE
Miriam's Secret
A Blessing for Miriam
Miriam and the Stranger

LITTLE VALLEY SERIES
A Wedding Quilt for Ella
Ella's Wish
Ella Finds Love Again

THE ST. LAWRENCE COUNTY AMISH
A Heart Once Broken
Until I Love Again
Always Close to Home

OTHER STAND-ALONE TITLES
My Amish Childhood
The Amish Family Cookbook
(with Tina Eicher)

ALWAYS CLOSE TO HOME

JERRY S. EICHER

HARVEST HOUSE PUBLISHERS
EUGENE, OREGON

Cover by Garborg Design Works

The author is represented by MacGregor Literary, Inc.

ALWAYS CLOSE TO HOME

Copyright © 2017 Jerry S. Eicher
Published by Harvest House Publishers
Eugene, Oregon 97402
www.harvesthousepublishers.com

ISBN 978-0-7369-6591-0 (pbk.)
ISBN 978-0-7369-6592-7 (eBook)

Library of Congress Cataloging-in-Publication Data
Names: Eicher, Jerry S., author.
Title: Always close to home / Jerry S. Eicher.
Description: Eugene, Oregon : Harvest House Publishers, [2017] | Series: The
   St. Lawrence County Amish ; 3
Identifiers: LCCN 2016026998 (print) | LCCN 2016034144 (ebook) | ISBN
   9780736965910 (softcover) | ISBN 9780736965927 (ebook)
Subjects: LCSH: Mate selection—Fiction. | Twin sisters—Fiction. |
   Amish—Fiction. | BISAC: FICTION / Christian / Romance. | FICTION /
   Christian / Romance. | GSAFD: Christian fiction. | Love stories.
Classification: LCC PS3605.I34 A79 2017 (print) | LCC PS3605.I34 (ebook) |
   DDC 813/.6—dc23
LC record available at https://lccn.loc.gov/2016026998

Printed in the United States of America

16 17 18 19 20 21 22 23 24 / BP-GL / 10 9 8 7 6 5 4 3 2 1

Chapter One

Lydia Mast slipped into her upstairs bedroom in the old farmhouse and closed the door behind her. In the stillness of the room she hesitated, but she heard no footsteps following her in the hallway. And why should she? Her twin, Laura, was busy in the kitchen, and both of her brothers, Nelson and Lester, were in the fields with *Daett*. That only left *Mamm*. But *Mamm* wouldn't sneak around the house—even if she knew her daughter had a letter addressed in a man's hand tucked into her dress pocket.

Lydia was thankful that she, and not Laura, had collected the noon mail at the end of their driveway on Lead Mine Road. Laura would have opened the letter addressed to Lydia, because the twins had few secrets between them. But even Laura didn't know about the great ache Lydia had held in her heart ever since Laura had begun to date John Yoder last year.

Wasn't it about time she dated too? Didn't twins do things together? Why couldn't she have someone special to call her own now that Laura had John?

Laura and John were so in love, and Lydia certainly wished them no ill. She simply wanted to experience that same joy by bringing home a young man from the hymn singings on Sunday evenings. And not just any young man, but none other than the handsome Milton Beiler.

Lydia paused as the vision of Milton's face danced in her mind. Milton barely knew she existed. *Yah*, he had returned her smiles a few times at the Sunday services, but Milton returned all of the single girls' smiles. Even so, she still dared to imagine there was something special in the attention Milton paid her. With such a desire in her heart and with many a prayer on her lips, surely Milton must feel a little of what she felt. Didn't Milton see her spirits lift whenever he was around her? And now, with this letter, had Milton finally noticed her? Who else would write a letter to Lydia Mast and not disclose his return address?

Lydia took a deep breath. She must stay practical and out of dreamland. She must think sensible thoughts because this letter could be from someone else. Some other single man in the community. Didn't most men leave their return addresses off of a courtship proposal? Otherwise they would advertise their intentions to the curious eyes of family members who might see the letter before its arrival in the hands of the intended. *Yah*, this could be from any unmarried man in the community who had taken a fancy to her—someone with whom she didn't share such feelings.

Lydia breathed a quick prayer as she reached into her dress pocket and pressed the smooth paper between her fingertips. "Oh, let it be Milton, dear Lord." She pulled the envelope slowly out of her pocket and studied the handwriting. She had never seen Milton's penmanship, but he had to write better than this. Every letter was malformed, with bends this way and that. How could this be Milton? If she hadn't been so breathless before she would have noticed.

Lydia lowered the letter to hang loose in her hand. How wise she had been to bring the letter up to her room. Disappointment always showed plainly on her face. *Mamm* and Laura would comfort her, but she didn't want sympathy. She wanted Milton to ask her home from the hymn singing.

Why couldn't he? Hadn't she and Laura both decided earlier in the year to end their *rumspringa* time and join the fall baptismal class? *Yah*, she and Laura would say their sacred vows in only a few weeks. Wasn't that a virtue Milton should take into account when he decided on what girl to pick as his *frau*? Most of the other girls her age wouldn't make that choice until next year, or not until they had secured a boyfriend.

Lydia stared down at the letter. And here was another point. Milton wouldn't write a letter! How had she missed that? Milton would speak to her directly if he wished to take her home from the hymn singing. Milton wasn't intimidated by girls. He wouldn't hide behind the printed page.

So what were the other options? Wendell Kaufman, perhaps? But that didn't fit either, even though she had caught Wendell this past Sunday with his gaze fixed on her and a slight smile on his face. She had given him a glare, but the man's smile had only grown broader. Wendell's self-confidence was unbounded.

Not that long ago, Wendell had been determined to win Laura's affections, but she had chosen John. Now Wendell apparently planned to settle for second best, and with such a step down, a letter was all he considered her worthy of. Or perhaps he felt this was the best way to get each word just right so he could slip past her defenses.

Lydia glared at the letter. Whoever this was, it was not Milton, and she must face the first advances from a man with a firm *no*. This wasn't what she had hoped for, but the Lord seemed to have a mind of His own. No doubt she had much to learn and needed the humiliation. Was not humility of spirit always a worthy lesson?

Lydia tore the top off the letter and pulled out the single piece of white paper. She flopped down on the bed quilt and focused on the crooked writing.

"Dear Lydia," she began to read.

> Greetings in the name of the Lord. I can say with King David that His glory fills our lips with many praises. As you've no doubt heard, your Aunt Millie has borne our fifth child last week. Little Moses is healthy and squalling like all the rest did. He'll soon grow out of his colic, I hope, but that is not why I'm writing you. Your cousin Sarah is here for a few days to care for Moses, so that base is covered. What I need help with is my roadside stand this fall. We have an extra acre of pumpkins out, to say nothing of the potato patch and carrots. We are in our third year with the stand, so I'm expecting plenty of *Englisha* people to buy from us again. Could you come live with us and help with the work, at least until Christmas? I would appreciate it very much. I can even pay you some. Not much, but a little. At least more than you'll make working at home.
>
> And we have some handsome young men in our district, and I have hired on one for the season. Just teasing.
>
> Your Uncle Henry

The page slipped from Lydia's hand and fluttered to the bedroom floor. This was not a letter from Wendell or Milton or from any single man, but rather from Uncle Henry in the adjacent district who needed help with his roadside stand. The Lord had said no to her prayers again. When would she learn her lesson? She had best accept this rebuke with all the humility she could muster.

Lydia rose to her feet and retrieved the paper from the floor. She stood again and set her face. Slowly she opened the bedroom door, and with an unsteady step made her way down the stairs.

"What's wrong?" *Mamm* asked as soon as Lydia appeared in the kitchen doorway. *Yah*, nothing could be kept secret from *Mamm*.

"Nothing." Lydia steadied herself on a chair. "Just this." She held out the letter.

Mamm reached for the page, and her eyes raced over the words. "Well, this is surprising news. Do you want to accept the offer?"

"What offer?" Laura asked, stepping closer to snatch the letter from *Mamm*'s hand.

Lydia seated herself on the chair while Laura read quickly and then glanced at her sister. "And I bet you thought this was something else," she teased. "That's why you tried to sneak upstairs with the letter."

"So you knew?" Lydia admitted. "*Yah*, I had proud thoughts, and I was going to turn Wendell Kaufman down if it was him. He's been watching me lately."

"An offer from Wendell Kaufman would be nothing to be ashamed of," *Mamm* said.

Laura sniffed. "I'd turn him down too."

"There's nothing wrong with Wendell," *Mamm* repeated.

"I suppose not," Laura allowed with a shrug. "If it's not Lydia or me he's asking."

"Laura!" *Mamm* warned. "We are to have humble thoughts about ourselves and seek the Lord's will at all times."

"Thank the Lord I have John then!" Laura proclaimed, busying herself with the pot of potatoes simmering on the stove.

Mamm gave Laura a look but didn't say anything more.

"I'm accepting the offer," Lydia said, jumping to her feet. "Maybe it will be *goot* for me."

Laura sent Lydia a sly smile. "Like Uncle Henry said in the letter, they have plenty of handsome young men in his district. In our district, there's no one left since I've taken John."

"Laura!" *Mamm* warned again. "I fear John's attentions have gone to your head. That's not *goot*."

"*Yah, Mamm,*" Laura replied.

Mamm looked worried. "Lydia, are you sure you want to go? This is kind of sudden."

"I'm ready for something sudden," Lydia said. "Don't you think it's about time?"

"Well, I sure do," Laura volunteered.

Mamm silenced her oldest daughter with a sharp look. "That's enough out of you, Laura. Lydia, we'll have to speak with *Daett* about this. If he has no objections, you can accept the offer."

"He'll have no objections," Laura said.

Mamm muttered something but didn't look up from her work at the stove. *Mamm* knew that *Daett* was normally agreeable when they tried new things around the farm. For example, take the gate behind the barn that opened into the pasture. Nelson had fixed the old sagging one with new boards this summer and then announced that the gate needed green paint. Nelson hadn't said anything about bright green, which was the color he had chosen.

Daett had grinned when he saw the final product. "That'll be the first bright-green Mast pasture gate we've ever had," he had said.

Laura gave Lydia a meaningful glance. "I like what Uncle Henry said about hiring a handsome young man. You know what that could mean."

"Hush, girls!" *Mamm* said. "I want my daughters settled on a husband with thoughts of home and *kinner* in their hearts, but you don't have to traipse all over creation for that. The Lord will provide."

"*Mamm*," Lydia protested. "I'm not going to Uncle Henry's because of…" She let the words dangle as she considered that she could ask Uncle Henry to hire Milton. Could she make such a request? Where would she find the nerve? From somewhere. She would have to!

"Okay, *Mamm*," Lydia concurred. "Maybe Laura's partly right, but you know you can trust me. I came back from my *rumspringa* time on my own free will. You have nothing to be concerned about."

Mamm tried to smile. "I'm thankful for that. But I still don't understand why you don't accept Wendell's advances. He's right here in our district, and he's obviously interested in you."

"*Mamm*," Laura chided, "that's an awful thought. Are you forgetting that Wendell pursued me and I wouldn't have him? Now you want Lydia to accept him?"

"I'm sorry," *Mamm* said. "I didn't mean that the way it sounded. I don't expect you to be second best, Lydia, but isn't there something you can do? You're getting older, you know. You do smile at the men, don't you?"

Thankfully Laura came to Lydia's defense. "*Yah*, she does smile at them. You just aren't looking at the right time."

Lydia shook her head. "I'm not taking Wendell, even if he's the only one who seems interested in me."

"Wendell would be better than working for Uncle Henry," *Mamm* said with another weak smile. "Any husband is always better than a job away from one's home and district."

"Lots of unmarried woman take short-term jobs away from home," Lydia protested.

Mamm continued with her work at the stove and didn't respond.

Laura gave Lydia a sympathetic smile.

"We will see what *Daett* says," *Mamm* repeated, oblivious to the signals sent between the two girls. She took a quick look at the kitchen clock. "Hurry up, girls, and get lunch ready. We've been chattering long enough."

Lydia busied herself with setting the table, but her mind was racing. She must be bold and brave. She would tell Uncle Henry she'd come if he'd hire Milton. After all, Milton was Uncle Henry's nephew on his *frau*'s side of the family. That would serve as a *goot* excuse.

Chapter Two

Lydia set the last plate on the kitchen table with the utensils lined up properly on either side. *Daett* and her two brothers would be in any minute now for their lunch of cold cut sandwiches and hot soup.

The pot of potatoes Laura was simmering at one end of the stove was for the meal tomorrow. They would eat at the barn-raising for Deacon William, and the whole Mast family planned to attend. At the other end of the stove, *Mamm* was stirring an equally large batch of a vegetable soup. They would eat their fill today, but there would be plenty left for tomorrow. Any soup that remained from the barn-raising would be brought home and consumed at future lunchtimes. Nothing would be wasted. That rule was never broken.

Lydia straightened the tablecloth as she heard the washroom door rattle and the men's heavy footsteps shuffle inside. They would emerge from their time in front of the washbasin, *Daett*'s beard still dripping and her brothers brushing back their hair with their fingers. Her family always brought a smile to her face. She would miss them when she went to work for Uncle Henry. Nelson and Lester were both handsome young men. Nelson would be even manlier once he said the vows with Emily Byler and allowed his beard to grow. Nelson had snagged a *goot* catch in Emily. Lester was the youngest of the family and a decent young man. When all things were considered, Lydia had much to be thankful for.

She glanced up as Lester came in the door. "Howdy, girls," he called out, his damp hair plastered over his forehead. "Lunch ready?"

"*Yah*, it's ready," Laura grumbled from her pot of potatoes. She slammed the lid down and pushed the container off the hot part of the stove. "That'll simmer while I nourish my exhausted body."

Lester grinned. "You couldn't have worked that hard unless you were sending smiles to John all morning."

"Of course I wasn't," Laura snapped. "And John's smiles cheer me up, if you must know."

"*Sit down*," *Mamm* ordered when Nelson came in. Lester had crept up to the bowl of vegetable soup and craned his neck to look inside. He took a long breath over the pot before he seated himself.

"Satisfactory?" Nelson asked as he pulled out a chair.

"You know *Mamm*'s meals are always satisfactory!" Lester proclaimed. "I was taking a whiff for strength so I wouldn't pass out before we were served lunch."

As Nelson grinned at his brother's attempt at humor, Laura said, "You're both spoiled brats!"

That brought a laugh from Nelson. "You need to keep her away from those potatoes, *Mamm*," he managed in between gulps for air.

Lester sent a dark look Laura's way. "She'd better not throw one at me. Those are hot."

"Then behave yourself," Laura said as she sat down with an exaggerated groan.

"The girl doesn't work hard enough," Lester said.

"Boys, boys," *Mamm* warned. "Enough has been said."

A slight smile lingered on *Mamm*'s face. *Mamm* clearly enjoyed this light banter they often had at mealtimes. Her warnings were as much a part of the mix as everything else. Lester now heeded *Mamm*'s words and settled into his seat, but not before sending a fake smile toward Laura.

Laura made a face at him in response, but *Mamm* didn't notice. She was looking up to greet *Daett* with a bright smile.

"Lunch is waiting, I see," *Daett* responded. He wore a smile of his own and paused for a moment to squeeze *Mamm*'s arm before he took his seat.

Lydia ducked her head at this display of affection between her parents, though she never tired of seeing their love for each other. This was what she desired for herself someday, once she said the vows with a proper young man like Milton. Someone who the Lord—

"Let us pray." *Daett* interrupted Lydia's thoughts. They bowed their heads in silent prayer until *Daett* said, "Amen."

Lester didn't waste any time to holler out, "Soup, please, or I will die of hunger."

Daett grinned and waited until Lester filled his bowl before he took some for himself. That was another thing Lydia loved about her *daett*. He always allowed others first place, even when he didn't have to. Lester wasn't starving, but *Daett* humored him.

"Lydia received a letter today," *Mamm* announced.

Nelson jerked up his head. "For a date? What kind of man would use a letter to ask for a date?"

Laura gave Nelson one of her glares. "It wasn't like that. Uncle Henry wants Lydia to help him with his roadside stand this fall— perhaps up until Christmastime."

"Whoa there," *Daett* said. "Uncle Henry wants Lydia's help?"

"It sounds like it," *Mamm* said. "I told Lydia she has to ask you about it."

Daett glanced across the table. "Does that mean Lydia wants to go?"

"*Yah*," Lydia said, before *Mamm*'s disapproval could be voiced.

But *Daett* still looked at *Mamm*. "You don't think this wise?"

"Lydia should focus on other things, Yost," *Mamm* said. "She still hasn't been asked home from the hymn singing. Besides, it might not be safe. Who knows what all could happen to a young girl out there on her own."

"On her own?" A smile played on *Daett*'s face. "Lydia wouldn't exactly be alone. She'd live with your brother, and—"

"See?" *Mamm* interrupted. "That's exactly my point. She would see *Englisha* people each and every day, and who knows? One of them might take an interest in a young Amish girl."

"*Mamm*!" Lydia exploded. "I'm through with my *rumspringa* time. Haven't I demonstrated that well enough? I'll be baptized in a few weeks."

"Then wait until you're baptized," *Mamm* said. "Henry lives all the way up near Kokomo Corner."

Daett intervened, his tone mild. "Henry will bring Lydia home for the Sunday of her baptism, I'm sure."

"I'll be okay," Lydia insisted. "I'm done with…and…" She didn't have to finish. Her family knew her record.

Despite what *Mamm* had implied, Lydia's *rumspringa* had been a mild affair. Laura and she hadn't even ventured up to Heuvelton, where the bulk of the Amish young people hung out. Nelson had taken them once, but he had also ended his *rumspringa* early. Mostly because of Emily, but also because Nelson wanted what was right. They were a decent family, so why was *Mamm* so fearful?

"It looks as if you've made up your mind then, Yost," *Mamm* said. "All before you've asked further questions."

"I've not made up my mind," *Daett* protested. He took a spoonful of soup. "But I don't think Lydia should be pushed into a relationship she doesn't want here in the district. I don't mind her being at home with us—"

"As an old maid!" Horror filled *Mamm*'s voice. "That's not happening, Yost. And having Lydia trotting all over the country will only make things worse. She'll gain a reputation of being hard up. You can't allow this."

"We'll see." *Daett* busied himself with his soup.

Mamm didn't back down. "It's not as though I don't need help here at home. I need Lydia worse than Henry does with his harebrained ideas. I told him this spring not to plant that acre of pumpkins, but you can't tell him anything. Who knows what he'll have Lydia up to if you give him half a chance?"

"I thought you were trying to get rid of Lydia a moment ago." *Daett* cracked a smile.

"To a decent husband, of course," *Mamm* huffed. "Not to that wild brother of mine."

"He's always seemed decent enough to me," *Daett* teased. "You always had kind words for him when I dated you."

"That was then," *Mamm* shot back. "I had to snag you somehow."

Daett laughed. "I didn't think you were that desperate, Lavina. You turned down Ezra Swartz and Willis Stoll before I asked you home. Henry's okay. It's just Lydia you're worried about."

Mamm appeared ready to protest, but she leaned over to nestle against *Daett*'s shoulder instead. *Daett* as usual had found the heart of the matter quickly. *Mamm* was worried about Lydia and the lack of boys asking to take her home from the hymn singings. Finding a decent husband for Lydia was high on *Mamm*'s list of priorities, right below one's relationship with the Lord Himself.

But *Mamm* was right about Uncle Henry. The man was known for his impulsive ways, even down here in the southern districts. More than one conversation at the Sunday services had centered around Uncle Henry's latest escapade.

"He's got a waterwheel at his place, I heard," one woman proclaimed in horror. "Henry plans to grind his own grain to save money."

"I heard that Henry talked with the milk inspector himself, and persuaded the man into a kinder look at our affairs." At least this was said with gratefulness. "The Lord knows things are difficult enough without the government involved like it is."

"Henry put up a little sign for his roadside stand right on the Heuvelton bridge," another one had said with a laugh. "He brought in a lot of business until the sheriff took it down. At least Henry acted like a real Amish man on that one."

Was that what *Mamm* didn't want? Her daughter exposed to her brother's ways? But no doubt that was only part of the truth. *Mamm*'s real concern was the lack of a decent young man to court her. But how could Lydia control that part of her life? She had sent plenty of smiles Milton's way whenever he looked at her, and she was willing to ask Uncle Henry to hire Milton. What more was she supposed to do?

Thankfully Laura smiled and spoke up. "Lydia does give someone plenty of attention at the Sunday services when she has a chance. It's Milton Beiler, so don't blame her."

"She does?" *Mamm* was all interest. "Milton's a decent man, isn't he?"

Daett shrugged. "As they go, I suppose."

"That's not a very hearty endorsement." *Mamm* gave *Daett* a long look. "Do you know anything about him that we should know? But surely you wouldn't hinder Lydia's chances at marriage, Yost?"

"*Mamm!*" Lydia protested. "Milton hasn't even asked me home." *And won't,* she almost added, but she shouldn't think such dark thoughts. After all, maybe she really could get Uncle Henry to help her out.

"What I've heard is that Milton's thinking about jumping the fence," Lester said. "I just heard of his plan last week. He's not coming back from his *rumspringa.*"

"You don't say!" *Mamm* exclaimed. "Well, that settles that."

Lydia tried to breathe. Was this true? Lester would be one to know. Yet, she couldn't back down this easy. "Men say all sorts of things," she managed. "I still like him, and I'm going to…" She stopped. The plan was for Uncle Henry's ears alone.

"So you do care about the man?" *Mamm* asked.

"*Yah,*" Lydia admitted. She might as well tell the truth.

Mamm glanced at *Daett.* "This doesn't sound *goot,* but—"

"She'll be fine." *Daett* gave Lydia a warm smile. "You need to relax, Lavina. The Lord will take care of things."

"I'm trying," *Mamm* said. "I'm just worried. So I suppose this means you'll be letting Lydia help Henry?"

"I suppose it does," *Daett* said. "The Lord doesn't seem to be opening the doors to a relationship with a young man around here, so maybe Lydia should walk through the door that is open. Doesn't that sound like the right thing?"

Mamm didn't appear convinced, but she kept quiet. Lydia could have hugged *Daett* on the spot. But what if Milton had really made up his mind not to return to the community? She had spoken up in his defense, but maybe Milton was serious about jumping the fence. She couldn't date the man if he was, and neither could she go through with her plan.

Lydia leaned toward Lester. "Is what you said true?" she asked.

"Don't worry about it," Laura said before Lester could answer.

"Even if Milton said that, you never know how things will turn out. Smile at him all you want. That's what I say."

Laura should know, Lydia told herself. She had captured John's attention and likely would have his promise of marriage soon. Lydia's life had taken strange turns today, but she must not allow her emotions to get the best of her. She was getting nowhere with Milton in this district, and *Daett* was apparently going to allow her to accept Uncle Henry's offer. Maybe this all was from the Lord's hand. Didn't He work in strange and mysterious ways?

Chapter Three

The Friday morning sun peeked over the horizon as Laura and *Mamm* emerged from the Mast home with a huge pot of mashed potatoes between them.

"Look, *Mamm*!" Laura gushed as *Mamm* pulled the door shut behind them. "The Lord's glory is showing all around us this morning, and I will see John today at the barn-raising. I'm so full of blessings I could burst."

"It is a beautiful morning," *Mamm* said as they lowered the heavy pot to the porch floor.

The first blaze of sunlight lit the red and gold leaves of the maple trees in the front yard with splashes of bright color. *Mamm* and Laura gazed in wonder at the sight.

"Isn't that just something!" Laura exclaimed. "I do think it's a sign of things to come today. Look, the sunlight is streaming straight through the leaves. We came out just in time. If we'd come out a minute later we'd have missed the most beautiful part. The Lord is blessing us. I can feel it. I think that John might propose to me today at the barn-raising. Wouldn't that be just like him? Right there with all those people around, he could ask me, 'Will you be my *frau*, Laura? My precious and only one?' Oh, *Mamm*, I know it will happen today."

Mamm grunted and reached for the handle of the pot. "Don't get your heart too wrapped up in how it all happens. Just thank the Lord you have a man on the hook and that you're about ready to reel in the line—unlike your sister."

Laura made a face. "*Mamm!* You take all the fun out. It's not mechanical. I'm not reeling John in."

Mamm huffed. "Don't deceive yourself, Laura. You did it quite well. You ought to give your sister lessons on how to capture a man's heart."

"Lydia is a jewel in her own right," Laura scolded.

"But an uncaught jewel," *Mamm* muttered. "Diamonds are useless if they only glitter at the bottom of the ocean."

"That's pearls, *Mamm*," Laura said. "And pearls don't lie around. They grow in clams or oysters or something like that."

"Come on, grab your side of the handle," *Mamm* ordered. "You shouldn't be so educated in the *Englisha* ways. It won't help with housekeeping and raising *kinner*. I've always said Nancy teaches dangerous things in that schoolhouse of hers. I'm glad my *kinner* made it safely past that woman's fancy thinking—all of which comes from never having married. I even heard that Teacher Nancy read a piece in school the other week written by that horrible *Englisha* man, Shakespeare. She read it to the class after lunch, but most of the children couldn't understand a word. Thank the Lord, but what a scandal!"

Laura giggled so hard she almost dropped the pot handle.

"It's not funny!" *Mamm* gave Laura a glare as if she had read the offending piece herself. "The bishop's *frau*, Rose, told me that Deacon William had to make a trip over for a talk with Teacher Nancy.

But Rose said it won't happen again now that Deacon William has spoken some sense into the woman."

"It was only the story of Romeo and Juliet," Laura said as they arrived at the buggy. "Everyone knows that story."

"I don't," *Mamm* declared. "Or didn't until recently. And what an awful ending, from what I heard."

Laura giggled again.

"Stop that and help me lift," *Mamm* scolded.

Laura tried, but she was overcome by the giggles.

"What's so funny now?" *Mamm* demanded.

"Oh, nothing." Laura tried to keep a straight face. "I'd best not tell you how the story really goes."

"If they didn't get married, that's all I need to know," *Mamm* said. "Now lift. That's the kind of thing John will be impressed with."

Laura heaved upward. John seemed much more taken with her smiles than he was with any lifting she had ever done, but *Mamm* didn't need to know that.

"There!" *Mamm* exclaimed. The pot of potatoes fit in perfectly with the large bowl of vegetable soup. "Now for the plates and utensils, and then we can be on our way."

Laura closed the buggy door and followed *Mamm* back to the house. Her face grew warm at the memory of John's light kiss on her cheek this past Sunday evening. She would want another one—a much longer one, if John asked her to marry him today.

When they entered the kitchen, Lydia looked up from packing the large cardboard box on the table. "I'm ready. I think I got everything," she said.

Mamm appeared pleased. "Then let's go."

Laura suppressed her grimace. "Don't be so efficient," Laura whispered as she took a firm grip on her side of the box.

"What did you say?" *Mamm* asked.

Laura shook her head. "Never mind, let's go."

Mamm shrugged, and the twins wrestled the large box out through the front door.

"What did you mean by that?" Lydia asked once they were outside.

Laura pasted on a smile. "Nothing."

"I know that's not true."

"I can't breathe and talk both with this box," Laura gasped.

Lydia kept silent as they made their way across the lawn and slid the box into the front of the buggy. Then her voice cut through Laura's daze. "So tell me now."

What harm was there in telling her sister? Maybe it would help the situation. "Okay," Laura said. "*Mamm* is worried about you. She thinks that I know how to catch men and that I should teach you how—so I just did. Be more womanly, Lydia. Don't be so efficient. Let the soft side of yourself show."

"*Mamm* said that?" Lydia asked.

"No, *I* did. And don't be mad at me." Laura reached over to touch Lydia's arm. "I'm sorry. I shouldn't have interfered."

Lydia's face softened. "I know I'm a failure in *Mamm*'s eyes, but what can I do? It's not easy like *Mamm* thinks it is—at least for me. Do you think men are different today from what they used to be? I mean, *Mamm* snagged *Daett*, and she's not all cuddly and gooey."

Laura giggled at her sister's description.

"Come on, girls," *Mamm* called from the washroom door. "Go get the horse. You can giggle tonight once you're in bed."

"I think everyone has changed since then," Laura said.

"*Yah*, it's a new generation."

"Do you think *Daett* kissed *Mamm* before they were married?" Laura asked.

Lydia took a sharp breath. "Has John kissed you then?"

Laura looked away, but her face betrayed her.

"Oh, Laura," Lydia whispered, before she turned and hurried toward the barn for the horse.

Laura watched her sister disappear. They were of one heart on the inside, even if they were so different in their ways. She should have waited until Lydia had a boyfriend before she yielded to John's advances, but that might have meant John would find someone else. No, she couldn't help it that their ways had parted. Lydia would always be her twin, but they were different people. She was not going to put John off just because...

Mamm's sharp footsteps came up behind her. "Hurry up, Laura. The men left an hour ago."

"They won't need anything to eat until lunchtime, and that's hours away," Laura shot back. "Calm down, *Mamm*."

"With your sharp tongue, how you ever caught John is beyond me," *Mamm* said. "But thank the Lord you did."

"I had several chances at other men," Laura reminded *Mamm*. "I didn't have to take John if I didn't want to."

"I know," *Mamm* huffed. "I just hope John doesn't figure things out before the wedding. Because if he does..." *Mamm* let the sentence hang as Lydia reappeared with their old horse, Tanner, in tow.

"I know how to sew and cook, and I love *kinner!*" Laura said. *Mamm* didn't seem to hear as she lifted the buggy shafts. Lydia expertly twirled Tanner underneath with a twist of her hand on his bridle.

She could handle a horse just as well, Laura told herself, but why bother with the protest? Lydia knew she could, and *Mamm* did too. *Mamm* should complain less and appreciate her daughters more. Laura imagined that if she ever had twins, she would sit and talk with them all day long instead of lecturing them on how to win

husbands and keep house. But *Mamm* was the way she was, and
Laura didn't want to fuss. John loved her and would soon ask her to
be his *frau*. Wasn't that enough blessing for now?

Mamm interrupted Laura's thoughts. "Jump in the buggy and
let's go."

Both girls climbed in, and *Mamm* jiggled the reins. Tanner
tossed his head before taking off.

"I guess we won't be too late," *Mamm* mused. "The sun's not been
up long."

"It'll be okay, *Mamm*," Lydia said. "We'll be there by the time
everyone else arrives."

Mamm didn't relax until they were within sight of Deacon William's place on Old Slate Road right off of Highway 10. Plenty of
buggies were parked in the yard, but there was still a line of them on
the road. *Mamm* pulled back on the reins and old Tanner swished
his tail as they waited for their turn to park in the fields below the
new barn's foundation.

Laura searched the forms of the men scurrying over the site. She
couldn't distinguish faces at this distance, but she was sure John
was there in the mix. He was a hard worker and would have been
among the first to arrive. If *Mamm* thought Laura lacked housekeeping skills, John more than made up for her lack. They would
make a perfect team—once they said the wedding vows. She would
be exactly the *frau* John needed. Laura searched the crowd of men
again as a dreamy smile crept over her face.

The buggy bounced into the field, and they parked beside Bishop
Ezra's *frau*, Rose, who had also just arrived.

"Whoa there," Rose hollered out to her horse in a cheerful voice.
"This horse is awful frisky for an old woman like me."

"I'll help you." Lydia hopped out of the buggy to undo the tugs
while Rose climbed down.

"It's sure a mighty fine morning for building," Rose said as Laura made her way out of the buggy on the other side.

Lydia responded with something Laura couldn't hear. Lydia and Rose chattered away as Laura helped *Mamm* get Tanner out of the shafts. If Lydia could be as carefree around men as she was with Rose this morning, she would have no problem snagging a husband. Maybe she would suggest the point—gently of course—once they were at home again. For now, she wanted to catch a glimpse of John's form among the men. He had to be there somewhere.

"Take Tanner over to the fence," *Mamm* said once the horse was out of the shafts. "Then come help carry the food inside."

Laura did as she was told, and Lydia came right behind her with Rose's horse. They fastened the tie ropes on the fence wire at the same time.

"To a beautiful day and a great barn-raising." Laura glanced toward Lydia with a smile on her face.

"*Yah*," Lydia said. "And I think we'll have plenty of food."

"Think about smiling to Milton," Laura whispered. "Not about the food."

Lydia took a deep breath, and they linked arms to walk back toward the buggies.

Chapter Four

An hour later, Laura took yet another pitcher of lemonade and set it carefully on the small table under the oak tree. At her request, the task had been assigned to her and several of the other unmarried girls. The men had formed lines on both sides of the table, and so far the girls had been able to keep the wait a short one. She had known it would be a full-time job to keep the table stocked with lemonade and water, but she didn't mind. Not with the chance to catch a glimpse of John once in a while when he came through the line.

"*Goot* stuff, this lemonade is," Bishop Ezra said with a twinkle in his eye. He stood off to the side of the line and took another swallow from his glass. "I shouldn't have my second glass already. I haven't worked that hard this morning, but I can't stay away from all these *goot*-looking young women."

A guffaw of laugher from the line of men greeted the words. "You behave yourself now, Bishop," one of the men teased.

Laura gave the elderly man a kind smile. "You're welcome to have as much as you wish," she said. "I'm sure you've worked harder in your lifetime than most of these men have."

A chorus of "That's not fair!" greeted Laura's words.

She smiled and continued to fill the lemonade glasses. John's laugh was what she was waiting to hear, but he had yet to make his appearance at the table. How like him. The man worked much too hard, but that was John. It was one of the reasons she was so in love with him.

"You could at least help pour the lemonade," one of the men teased the bishop. "Make yourself useful, you know."

"I think I'll go carry some boards for the grown men," the bishop shot back. He ambled off to the roar of the men's laughter.

One of the men stepped closer to tease Laura. "Where's that bright young fellow of yours?" He picked up a glass of lemonade but didn't wait for her answer.

"She's speechless," the next man in line said. "That's what happens when you fall in love."

The laugher pealed again, but Laura ignored them. If John didn't come soon, she would go looking for him. Exactly how that would be managed, she didn't know. She wasn't above a march right along the outskirts of the group of working men. She'd find John and hand the glass of lemonade right to him. She'd scold him for not coming sooner.

"Here." Laura handed the dipper to one of the other girls as she grabbed a large glass of lemonade and hurried off.

"Where's she going?" one of the men hollered after Laura.

"I wanted that glass of lemonade," another added.

The sound of their laugher was soon lost to Laura amid the noise of the building project. Huge timbers stood tall in the air as the frame of the barn was raised. Men swarmed everywhere, and Laura was careful to keep a proper distance from their work. She finally caught sight of John on the other side of the barn, bent over a wall frame that was lying on the ground. She skirted even farther around the men at work and approached the spot where John was working. A few feet away she stopped short. There was no sense in hollering to get his attention. John wouldn't hear her. Laura waved her arm, but John stayed bent over with his attention focused on a massive beam. He held a wooden peg and a large mallet in his hands. He looked ready to pound in the peg when Laura finally caught his attention.

John straightened himself as a huge grin spread over his face. Several of the other men noticed and looked in the same direction. Smiles broke out and hands shoved John in her direction. She couldn't hear their words, but she could imagine how the men were teasing John.

"She's come looking for you, John."

"Sounds pretty serious if you ask me."

John was red-faced when he arrived in front of her, and it wasn't from exertion. Laura gave him a shy smile and lifted up the glass of lemonade. "You're surely needing some by now," she said.

"I guess I got a little too busy," he agreed. "But what I needed more was a look at your face." John took the glass and their fingers brushed. She gazed deeply into his eyes, as John's fingers slowly left hers. He lifted the glass of lemonade and took a long sip, and as she looked up at him, he didn't look away. She would hold his hand in marriage someday. She would be his *frau*.

"This is *goot*," he said—but he really meant *she* was *goot*.

She wanted to hold his hand right here in public, but she had best not. Quiet and privacy lay behind a small shed only a short distance away. She had imagined something like this moment all morning. Would John follow her if she led the way?

"This is *goot*," John said again.

"Come," Laura whispered, stepping backward. He hesitated with a quick glance over his shoulder. All the men were back at work, and no one was paying them any attention. Together they approached

the small shed, and Laura stepped under the edge of the roof and out
of sight from the builders. John took another quick glance behind
him before he followed. His head barely fit under the shelter's eaves,
but this would do.

"John," she whispered. "I—"

He silenced her with a touch on her arm. "You brought me a
glass of lemonade," he said, his voice hushed. "I hope it was because
you wanted to see me."

"*Yah*, very much!" she said. "You work so hard."

He grinned.

"Don't work so hard, and be careful out there." She reached up
with both hands to touch his face. The touch of his bristled chin felt
good. "You'll look *goot* in a beard, John."

He grinned again. "I forgot to shave this morning with the
excitement of the day in front of me."

"You're so handsome," she said with a shy look. "Much too handsome, in fact."

"Is this a warning?" he teased. "You're going to send me packing
because I'm too handsome?"

"Oh, John," she whispered, pulling him closer.

His empty arm slipped around Laura's shoulder and he held her
tightly. She leaned into him and tilted her head up. His face edged
closer to hers…and finally their lips touched. After a moment, she
pulled away and sighed. Oh, that this was just the first of many such
moments! Someday she would be in his arms as his *frau*, but this
would have to be *goot* enough for now. She looked up into his face.
"I shouldn't be keeping you, John."

"I'm glad you brought me back here for this," he said. Color
rushed into Laura's face.

His grin broadened. "You're special to me, Laura. You know that,
don't you?"

"*Yah*." She looked away.

He held her tight. "Maybe I *should* get back," he teased, but Laura didn't move. His fingers found her face and she turned to meet his gaze. The teasing look was gone, replaced by a gleam in his eyes. "You are very dear to me," he whispered. She lifted her head again and the bristles brushed her cheeks. She pulled his head down with both hands and their lips touched again.

This time John slowly pulled away. "You're very sweet, Laura," he whispered, his fingers stroking her cheek. "You will be my *frau* someday, won't you?"

Laura caught her breath. "You know I will."

He studied her face for a long time before he bent his head again. Laura clung to him even longer. He finally shook his head. "We should be going back. I could stay here with you all day, but…"

"Of course," she said. She took the empty glass from his hand. "You go out the way we came. I'll go around the other side of the building."

John nodded, and she brushed his lips with her finger before she slipped away and moved quickly along the edge of the crowd. The noise was intense. The men were about to set another of the massive walls in place. The walls looked like spiderwebs once they were off the ground, giant beams interlaced with wooden pins that formed the shell of the building. Already the men had begun to install the cross-webbing on the far side. Laura smiled at the sight of John heading into the crowd of men again. Her gaze followed him, but he didn't return to the wall he had come from. Rather, John headed straight for the spot where the wall was being raised.

"Pull her up, boys, pull her up," Laura heard a foreman shout above the din.

Strong arms strained on the ropes as the men's muscles bulged. John had vanished, but he was somewhere among the men. She had felt his arms around her only moments before. They had been tender then, but now they would be pulling on the ropes with a strength that made her tremble. She was blessed to have such a man's love, and now his promise to wed her. Laura's knees shook as the huge timbers on the wall groaned and moved skyward. She held her breath until she couldn't hold it any longer.

The wall had stopped moving, and the orders increased in volume. She heard a solid yell now. "Pull her, boys, and don't stop now. Pull!"

Once more the wall inched upward until it stood upright. A mighty cheer went up from the men.

"Fasten her tight," the foreman hollered again. "Don't let her get away from you now."

Ladders were pushed upward and leaned against the newly erected wall, held in place by ropes on either side. Laura could see John climbing one of the ladders, his step steady as he moved ever higher.

John was soon on top of the wall with a wooden peg in one hand and a heavy mallet in the other. Laura held her breath again. Surely he would pound in the peg quickly and get down from there. Instead, John stood and walked along the beam. She wanted to scream at him to be careful. Why would he be doing such a daring thing? But maybe it wasn't daring at all. For all she knew, this was a normal part of how a barn was built.

John had both of his hands out as he bent to kneel on the beam. He brought the hammer back to pound away at his wooden peg.

The foreman's voice rose above the noise. "Hold her tight!"

As John pounded away, the wall seemed to shake for a moment. John clung to the timber for a few seconds before he began pounding again. Laura stifled her gasp. She must not be fearful, but this was her promised one up there on the wall. Were all barn-raisings this way? She had never before paid much attention to the men's work on a day like this.

"Don't let her move!" the foreman shouted. Laura looked up to see the wall shaking again. "Get down from there, John, until we get this tightened up," the foreman hollered. Yet instead of moving back toward the ladder, John clung to the wall with both hands. Maybe he couldn't move? But he must. Laura almost forced her way through the crowd toward him, not sure of what *goot* she could do.

Thankfully the shaking calmed down and John whacked the peg again a few times.

"That's *goot* enough," the foreman hollered.

John nodded and stood. He was halfway back to the ladder when the wall began shaking again—violently this time. And without warning, John was catapulted into the air.

The silence swept like a wave over the crowd until Laura heard her own screams. She began to run, only to fall after a few yards. What had happened? Where was John? She opened her mouth to scream again, but nothing came out. The world in front of her slowly drifted into a solid white.

Chapter Five

Moments later Nancy Beiler left the large bowl of carrots on the kitchen table and stepped closer to the window. The chatter of the women's voices still filled the house, but a silence had fallen outside.

"What is it, Nancy?" Deacon William's *frau*, Elizabeth, asked.

"The men have stopped working," Nancy said.

"Really?" Elizabeth stepped closer to peer out of the kitchen window.

Behind Nancy stillness crept into the kitchen, as several more women joined them.

"Something's wrong," Bishop Ezra's *frau*, Rose, said, but Nancy was already halfway out the washroom door.

"Someone must be hurt," she called over her shoulder as she hurried on.

But what could she do if this was true? She knew only the basics of first aid, which she had learned from books and from…She must not think about Charles Wiseman right now. Nancy broke into a run. The double life she had been living these past few months could not be revealed even if there had been a serious injury.

Nancy slowed as she approached the edge of the crowd. "What's happened?" she asked. "Has someone been hurt?"

One of the men turned to her. "*Yah*. John Yoder just fell. Deacon William has gone to call the *Englisha* ambulance."

"I'd best see John then," Nancy said, pushing past him.

Several of the women from the house had followed her, but they stopped at the edge of the crowd. There were girls over by the lemonade table but they stood as if transfixed.

The men parted for Nancy without objection. She was the district's schoolteacher, and she was also an older single woman. Those two characteristics in combination engendered a degree of deference. A respect she had pushed to the limit these last few school terms with her newfangled teaching methods, but she couldn't help herself. There was so much knowledge out there. Ignorance wasn't necessary. She still believed that—even with Deacon William's admonishments fresh in her ear. He had asked her to tone down her fancy *Englisha* lessons, and stick with the basics of reading, writing, and arithmetic.

Nancy stepped between the broad shoulders of two Amish men who were standing with heads bowed in prayer. Prayer was important, *yah*, but how much better would things be if there were a first responder present amongst the Amish. This person could administer aid long before the ambulance arrived from either Heuvelton or Richville.

Nancy stumbled and nearly fell. She caught herself as the thought rang in her ear. What if the ambulance came from Richville? What if Charles was the paramedic on duty? Would he know to pretend he didn't recognize her? Charles was an honest soul if there ever was one. He didn't like the secrecy in their relationship, but he was willing to put up with it. That's just how things were, and he understood.

The question, of course, was how she had become entangled in a secret relationship with an *Englisha* man. She still didn't know. It had just happened. Charles had stopped by the schoolhouse a few months ago after classes were dismissed to ask if a team of paramedics could offer a first-aid lesson to the school. The answer, of course, was no. But the truth was, she shouldn't have spoken with the man at all, let alone for the length of time that she had. Something in her voice or her look must have given her away. Charles had dared to ask her out on a date that first evening. They had spoken like two souls who had found each other in the dark. And yet how could that be? Charles was an *Englisha* man who volunteered his spare time for *goot* causes. She was an Amish schoolteacher who could create a scandal and a half if her innocent dinner with Charles ever became known in the community.

All that was lost in the rush of her emotions as she realized she enjoyed her time with Charles. Enjoyed it immensely. He had been kind and very open with her. His *frau*, Nichole, had died of cancer only a couple of years ago, leaving him with his daughter, Lisa, who had since finished high school and begun college. To have felt an attraction to Charles was bad enough, but if the man had divorced his *frau*, Nancy would have brought things to a halt at once. Part of her wished that Charles *had* divorced Nichole. It would have made things so much easier, and brought her foolish heart to its senses. Now she was falling in love and helpless to do anything about it. Maybe Deacon William had been right. Perhaps this is what came from fancy *Englisha* notions.

Nancy stepped around a large beam and caught sight of Laura Mast ahead of her. Laura was bent over the still form of young John Yoder, sobbing softly with John's hand in hers. Nancy hurried forward. Maybe there was something she could do until the paramedics arrived. She had peppered Charles with questions every time she saw him. That was no way to learn proper first aid, but it was the best she could do.

Laura's sobs rose higher when Nancy knelt beside her. Nancy touched Laura's arm and whispered, "I'm here, dear, and I'll stay with you."

The men kept their distance, seemingly at a loss, as if no one knew what to do with John's still form.

"He dead," Laura cried. "And it's all my fault."

Nancy reached for John's pulse and felt a strong heartbeat. "He's not dead, just badly injured," she said.

Laura's sobs caught. "Why doesn't he move?"

Nancy glanced upward at the high beams and hazarded a guess. "He must have fallen a long way and broken something. But there's still a strong heartbeat."

Laura burst into fresh sobs. "It's all my fault. All of it!"

Nancy ignored Laura to study John's still body. Should he be moved? Charles said the first rule was not to move an injured person if there was a chance of a back injury. And a fall from that height surely could have injured John's back.

One of the men cleared his throat and said, "We must move him since the work must go on. Nancy, can you take Laura back to her *mamm*?"

A protest leaped out of Nancy's mouth. "But you can't move the man! His back may be injured or worse. He has to stay until the paramedics arrive. That's what the *Englisha* say, and they know."

The man looked over his shoulder and said something Nancy couldn't understand. Moments later Deacon William appeared and knelt down beside her.

"Nancy," the deacon said, his tone kind, "I made the phone call to Heuvelton and the ambulance is on its way, but this is a big day of labor and the community can't wait any longer. Let the men move John to a safer place."

Nancy didn't move from her spot beside the fallen form.

Deacon William's face grew sober. "Nancy, this is not the way you should act. The work must go on, and John will be in no worse shape waiting somewhere else. In fact, a move might be much better for him."

Nancy took a deep breath. "As I said, the *Englisha* say not to move a man after a fall. You might further injure nerves or even cut them. Do you want John to never walk again?"

Deacon William frowned. "Nancy, your *Englisha* learning has no place among the people. We trust the Lord to hold John in the palm of His hand. No evil can come nigh him unless the Lord allows it. This is the faith of the community. Now take Laura back and let the men move John to the house. The ambulance men can pick him up there."

Nancy pulled Laura against her with one arm and kept her head low. "I'm going to pray," she whispered.

She didn't look up for approval, but that seemed to work. Deacon William would give her a few seconds to pray, and the ambulance might arrive by then. The longer she held on, the greater the chances that John's future life could be affected for the *goot*.

Nancy's lips moved in silent prayer. "Dear Lord, be with John right now, and keep him safe in Your arms. Give me the courage to do what I know is right. Please let the paramedics hurry and get here…"

As if in direct answer to her plea, the distant wail of a siren interrupted Nancy's prayer. The Lord had heard.

"We will speak more on this later," Deacon William said at Nancy's shoulder. "You take things on yourself that are not yours to take, Nancy. Your choices of late…"

But Nancy was already beyond his caution. If the deacon knew half of what her choices of late had been, he would have much worse things to say. How her conscience lived with itself, she didn't know.

Nancy held Laura tight as the siren wails died down and ambulance bounced into the front yard. Laura clung to Nancy as if she would never let go.

"It's all my fault," Laura repeated.

"What do you mean?"

Laura's shoulders shook. "I kissed John behind the shed not twenty minutes ago and he asked me to marry him. He was thinking about that. He never would have fallen otherwise."

"Hush now!" Nancy ordered, hugging Laura close. "It's not your fault. John is a man, and he's responsible for himself."

"No! I'm to blame."

"Whatever you did, keep it to yourself," Nancy said. "John is still responsible for himself, and that's that."

Laura sniffed, but a fresh cry burst out of her when the paramedics pulled the gurney out of the ambulance. Nancy kept her head down. Two younger attendants in front of them had their backs turned, but neither of them was Charles. An *Englisha* woman hurried toward them, and Nancy recognized her as Wanda Burundi—a longtime paramedic she had met through Charles.

"Nancy!" Wanda's exclamation rose clearly above the men's murmuring noises. "Are you okay? It's good to see you here. Do you want to go in the ambulance to the hospital?"

Nancy tried to smile. "I'm fine." *Hush, Wanda*, she wanted to say, but that was no way to address the woman.

"These men can be thankful you were here this morning," Wanda said in a loud voice. "Looks like nobody moved him. Charles must have taught you well."

Nancy wanted the ground to open up and swallow her. Wanda

carried on with her other duties as the two men with her moved John onto the gurney, but the damage to Nancy's reputation had been done. Deacon William was regarding her with a steady gaze. Clearly the deacon now had more questions than he had before, and there was little she could say to pacify the man.

The paramedics moved John's gurney toward the ambulance, and Nancy came out of her daze to lead Laura over toward him. "You can go with him to the hospital," Nancy whispered in Laura's ear.

"I can?" Laura exclaimed.

"She's his fiancée," Nancy told Wanda once John was settled inside. Already the sounds of the men returning to work rose in the background.

Wanda motioned toward the ambulance door. "Hop in, sweetheart. We're leaving."

"I had best speak with *Mamm*," Laura said at the last moment.

"They'll know where you are," Nancy said. "Wanda will take care of you."

Wanda nodded. "If need be, Charles can drive you home this evening, honey. Nancy knows him."

Laura didn't pay much attention to the instructions, but climbed into the ambulance to stare at John's still form.

"I'll take care of her and him," Wanda said. "I'll tell Charles I saw you."

Please don't, Nancy wanted to say as Wanda hopped into the back of the ambulance. As the vehicle pulled away, Nancy waited, afraid to move.

Deacon William had moved closer to her. "Sounds like you knew the right thing to do."

"*Yah*." Nancy still didn't move. "I hope you don't hold it against me."

"How do you know that woman?"

Nancy turned to face him. "Do we have to speak of this now? We both know I indulge in the search of knowledge more than the community allows, but I have not taught any of the medical things I've learned to my students. I've tried to obey your instructions. Wanda knows me from when I…" Nancy looked away. She couldn't lie. "The truth is, I've been invited to the hospital and I've met some of the paramedics there. They've answered my questions. I admit I wanted to know more things than I do. Is that so wrong, Deacon William?"

"Maybe we had best speak of this another day," Deacon William said. "There is much work that must be done here, and we did have an accident for which you had the right answer." The deacon forced a smile and disappeared into the crowd, but this was not the end of the matter. Nancy was certain of that.

Chapter Six

Later that afternoon, Lydia emptied the last of the dirty dishwater down the drain in Deacon William's home. She straightened her weary back as Bishop Ezra's *frau*, Rose, tugged on her arm.

"Sit down for a bit," the elderly woman ordered. "I'll finish what little there is to do here."

Lydia nodded her thanks and took the offered chair. Tiredness had crept into every part of her body, and still most of the afternoon lay in front of them. Lunch had been served and eaten an hour ago. The men were back to working hard, and the newly constructed barn frame was now covered with siding on one side. John's accident hadn't been forgotten, but the work had to continue.

Lydia sat up straighter in the chair, remembering Laura's tearstained face as she had climbed in the ambulance. Lydia had been disturbed herself, and John wasn't even her boyfriend. How Laura must have felt was difficult to imagine. Lydia's bone-weariness surely must have come from John's accident and not from the day's work. Stress and worry wore the body down much faster than hard labor. She must trust the Lord even when events in life appeared dark. She told herself to practice this virtue more often, and to encourage Laura with the same hope.

Rose's concerned face appeared above Lydia's head. "Are you okay?"

"*Yah*." Lydia tried to smile. "Is there any word from the hospital yet?"

Rose shook her head. "We might not know until tonight. It will take a while for the tests. But your parents will let you know as soon as they can, I'm sure." Rose gave Lydia a quick hug. "We'll be praying for you and for the Yoder family."

"The Lord will help us," Lydia sighed.

Rose smiled her approval. "*Yah*, He will."

Lydia stood and made her way slowly out of the house. Several women in the house gave her looks full of encouragement as she passed by. Everyone in the community was concerned for John and Laura. They knew the couple was serious with their relationship. Some probably expected a wedding next year, and now this had happened.

Lydia pushed the dark thoughts away. She must not imagine the worst. Everything had always gone well for Laura. Surely the Lord would see her twin through this, and John's injuries would be minor. Hopefully just a broken bone or two, and soon things would be back to what they had been for John.

Lydia searched the crowd outside and caught sight of Teacher Nancy near the lemonade table. Only a few men were in the line, and Nancy was in a conversation with Deacon William's *frau*, Elizabeth. Lydia moved closer. Nancy had been there with Laura and John for most of the time after John fell. Maybe Nancy would know how serious John's injuries were.

Lydia waited a few feet away, but she still overheard the conversation between the two women. They made no attempt to hide their words.

"I'm sorry for how things went today after the accident," Nancy was saying. "I meant no disrespect, but I've learned some things from the *Englisha* people that were helpful with John's injuries. I couldn't stand by and do nothing."

"I understand, but you have to be more careful," Elizabeth replied. "William is quite worried about how things are going with you."

Lydia took a step back. She would ask Nancy her question later. This was a conversation she shouldn't hear, even if the two women didn't care. Whatever *Englisha* teaching methods Nancy was in trouble for had helped John, so her sympathies were with Nancy. Besides, she had adored Teacher Nancy since her school years. And it certainly didn't hurt that Nancy was Milton's older sister.

Surely Nancy wouldn't be in any long-term trouble for whatever she had done. As the oldest in the Beiler family, Nancy had always been a model for respect and decorum in the community. Why Nancy had never married had always been a mystery to her. Maybe she ought to bring Nancy up as an example of a successful single woman the next time *Mamm* lectured her on the necessity of marriage. Look at the respect Nancy received.

Lydia moved closer to the crowd of men. She should find Uncle Henry, who had come down with some of the other men from his district to help, and speak with him about the opportunity at his roadside stand. If she needed further motivation, John's accident had provided the impetus. Laura would need extra work around the house to distract herself from the grief of John's accident.

Lydia moved quickly around the edge of the crowd, but she didn't find Uncle Henry's broad back until she had almost circled the barn. He was hammering busily away on the barn siding as Lydia walked up to him and called out, "Uncle Henry?"

His hammer stopped, and a big smile filled his face when he turned around. "If it isn't Lydia herself, my sister's own daughter. How are you doing?"

"As *goot* as can be expected today," Lydia answered.

Uncle Henry dropped his hammer to his side. "*Yah*, it was such a sad thing to happen when everything was going so well. But that's when tragedy often strikes. When we're least expecting it. It's as if the Lord wishes to keep our thoughts on Him and not on our busy lives."

"I suppose so," Lydia allowed. "But I wanted to ask about your letter. Were you serious about me helping with the roadside stand this fall?"

Uncle Henry's face brightened. "*Yah*, of course. Why else would a poor writer like me have gone to all the trouble to send you a letter? Could you even read the thing?"

Lydia laughed in spite of herself. "You write quite well," she said. "Just not straight up and down and in the right places."

Uncle Henry's eyes twinkled. "Were you fooled for a moment? Thinking it was from some beloved's hand?"

"You are so naughty," Lydia scolded.

Uncle Henry laughed. "I couldn't help myself. I had to get a little fun out of that horrible letter writing. So will you say *yah*?"

Lydia lowered her voice and turned red as she forced herself to say the words. "I have one condition. Would you invite Milton Beiler to help with the harvest?"

Uncle Henry appeared shocked, then answered with a sly smile. "Milton?"

Lydia nodded. "But you can't tell him that I asked. I thought that maybe…" Lydia's neck burned, and she fell silent. How had she become so bold and brazen about this?

With his sly smile still in place, Uncle Henry bent close. "Lydia, I'm way ahead of you. Milton's been working for me for two weeks now. Didn't you know? Of course, I didn't dare mention that in the letter, what with your *mamm* sure to read it. She probably had a big enough fit the way it was."

"You know about Milton?" Lydia's face blazed.

Uncle Henry reached out to playfully squeeze Lydia's arm. "Little birdies are everywhere, dear. So it looks like it's a go, *yah*? I can expect you next week? Millie's got the room upstairs ready and waiting. I knew you'd accept." Uncle Henry appeared quite triumphant as he picked up his hammer and went back to work.

In a daze Lydia forced her feet to move away. Uncle Henry knew about Milton and her. Was it possible that Milton himself had asked for Uncle Henry to invite her? Her heart pounded at the thought. Who would have thought that on this day of Laura's sorrow such hope could rise in her own heart. How strange were the ways of the Lord.

Lydia paused as she passed the place where John had fallen earlier, where Laura's heart had been torn in grief. She jumped when she heard a man's voice behind her. "Looking at the same thing I am?"

Lydia whirled about to face Milton. "Why are you sneaking up on me?" she said, clearly flustered. "And how did you know…"

He laughed. "Your Uncle Henry just spoke to me. He told me you'd be joining us this fall at the roadside stand. I'm glad you're coming." Then his face sobered. "I'm sorry about John. What a tough thing to happen."

"*Yah*," Lydia agreed.

"Do you think Laura will stick with him?"

"Stick with him?" Lydia allowed the horror to show on her face. "Of course she will."

Milton didn't appear convinced. "I wasn't there, of course, but Cousin Amos said Laura was guilt-filled after the accident. She kept telling Nancy that it was her fault. That she was to blame for John's fall."

"But why?" Lydia realized she was clutching Milton's arm.

Milton didn't pull back. "I heard that Laura was kissing John behind the shed just moments before the fall." He motioned with his head. "I suppose she thought John was distracted."

Lydia let go of Milton's arm. "But Laura wouldn't do such a thing."

Milton raised his eyebrows. "Really?" They both knew that Laura would do exactly that sort of thing. "Sometimes people disappoint us," Milton muttered, as if he knew all about such things.

Lydia kept silent and held her gaze on the ground. No wonder Laura had been so distraught. John had been seriously injured because of…

"Don't be too hard on your sister," Milton said. "She's in love, and people do foolish things when they're in love."

Warmth crept up Lydia's neck. Did Milton know that she had asked Uncle Henry to hire him for the fall? But how could he? Surely Uncle Henry had kept his mouth shut about the matter. She peeked up at Milton. Thankfully he seemed lost in his own thoughts.

"Well, I'd best be going," she said.

Milton stopped her with a touch on her arm. "I'm glad you're coming this fall to help out, Lydia. Your uncle's been running me like a slave driver."

Lydia took a deep breath. "I'm sure you're teasing me. Uncle Henry's not a slave driver."

When she glanced up at his face, Milton's grin was all the answer she needed.

"I'll be seeing you then," he said. Then he was gone into the crowd.

Lydia caught her breath. Did Milton suspect that she was in love with him? Did he feel some of what she felt? Did his heart beat faster at the thought of the fall spent together on Uncle Henry's farm each day? Milton must, but she couldn't be sure. He wasn't like John, and she wasn't like Laura. Not if being in love meant sneaking kisses behind a shed in the middle of a barn-raising. Now *that* was in love! But she must not compare herself with Laura or Milton with John. Everyone was different. Hopefully she would never have to go through what Laura had gone through this morning.

And what about Milton's question regarding Laura and John? Would Laura still accept John as her husband regardless of his injuries?

Lydia shivered. Surely Laura would remain true to John regardless of how things turned out. That's how Laura was, and Lydia, too, would stand beside Laura as a loyal twin.

Lydia hurried back across the lawn. It was time she helped with the remainder of the work in the house before the day ended. She would drive home soon with the single buggy, since *Mamm*, *Daett*, and Laura were at the hospital. *Mamm* and *Daett* had gone to see to Laura.

Nelson and Lester wouldn't be home until almost dark as they helped complete the barn, so she would have supper ready for them. As she worked, she would think of this fall at Uncle Henry's place, and the *wunderbah* door that had opened for her in the midst of today's tragedy. She would pray and be thankful and find the courage to embrace the opportunity set before her.

Chapter Seven

The next morning Lydia awoke with a start. The clock by the dresser read a few minutes after five. Nelson and Lester would be up to begin the chores soon, and she should get up herself.

At least she felt rested after yesterday's turmoil. She had slept soundly all night and hadn't heard anyone come in the house, but surely by now *Daett* and *Mamm* must be home with Laura.

Lydia lit a kerosene lamp and dressed quickly before creeping across the dark hallway to crack open Laura's bedroom door. She could see by the starlight that no one was under the quilt. So where was Laura? Was she still at the hospital? Were *Mamm* and *Daett* still there too?

Lydia closed Laura's bedroom door, retrieved her kerosene lamp, and made her way downstairs. Poor Laura! This could only mean one thing. John was seriously injured and Laura had stayed at the hospital while she had slept soundly here at home. Why hadn't she felt her twin's grief and been in prayer?

"Forgive me, Lord, and please help us," Lydia whispered. She approached her parents' bedroom door and paused to listen, as the flickering flame of the lamp cast wild shadows on the walls. All remained silent in the bedroom. *Mamm* would have awakened by now, so no one had returned from the hospital. Lydia turned as the stairs behind her creaked and Nelson appeared with sleep-filled eyes.

"They're not back yet," he muttered.

"That must mean…" Lydia paused. "Oh, Nelson. What do you think is wrong? And I slept so soundly all night. How could I?"

Nelson shrugged. "Don't go beating yourself up. We didn't know. They'll send someone soon with information. Maybe they didn't want us to worry."

As if in answer to Nelson's hope, the headlights of a car bounced into the driveway.

"There they are now," Lydia said, hurrying into the kitchen to set the lamp on the table.

Nelson grabbed his coat and bolted out through the washroom door. Lydia hesitated only a moment before she draped her shawl over her shoulders and followed Nelson. The air was brisk, but the dawn had begun to show in the sky. *Mamm's* and Laura's figures were huddled near the car as *Daett* spoke with the driver. Nelson stood a few feet away, his head bowed in silence. Lydia ran past him to embrace Laura.

Laura fell into her arms, her voice trembling. "Oh, Lydia!"

Lydia held her twin tight until the *Englisha* driver had backed up in the driveway and left.

"It's so awful," Laura managed. "John is all—"

"It'll be a while before they know for sure how bad things are," *Mamm* interrupted. "But it was time to come home."

"I didn't want to!" Laura wailed. "John needed me."

"It's for the best." *Mamm* grasped Laura's arm and steered her toward the house. "John isn't conscious yet, and his parents are there. And don't forget, you're not his *frau* yet."

"But I'm his promised one," Laura objected. "And it was all my fault. I told you this."

Mamm opened the front door with her hand still on Laura's arm. Nelson took the chance to hurry off toward the barn. Lydia turned to follow *Mamm* when *Daett's* voice stopped her. "I'm sorry we couldn't get word back sooner. I hope you didn't worry."

"I just woke up minutes ago," Lydia said. "I was feeling quite badly about that. I know I should have been…"

"This is just as well." *Daett's* smile was soft in the dim light. "There was nothing you could have done."

"So how is John?"

"Not *goot*." *Daett's* gaze was fixed on the brightening horizon. "His back is broken and he has a serious concussion. He's still unconscious. Poor Laura has been carrying on all night. I don't understand why she thinks the accident was her fault. She won't say why—or she can't, I'm not sure which."

Lydia looked away. She knew part of the answer, and the other was easy to surmise now that Laura claimed she was John's promised one. How like Laura to manipulate an engagement out of John right under the noses of the working men.

"Do you know why?" *Daett* asked.

"We don't share the same brain," Lydia said.

But *Daett* wasn't deceived. "Perhaps you'd best tell me, Lydia."

She took a deep breath. "Milton Beiler talked to me afterward. He told me that he heard that Laura was kissing John in secret only moments before he fell. Now Laura says she's promised to John. Laura probably figures John was distracted when he fell. And she could be right."

"So that's what's going on." *Daett* stared at the house where *Mamm* and Laura had vanished inside.

"How bad is John?" Lydia asked. "I mean, really?"

Daett sighed. "He will probably never walk again. But don't tell Laura that. We shouldn't destroy what little hope there is. You never know what happens after the doctors have done their thing."

"Can she still marry him if that's true? Will you and *Mamm* let her?"

Daett stroked his lengthy beard. "That's a hard question, Lydia. I suppose the first thing we need to know is, would Laura still want to marry John?"

"Oh, *yah*, she would," Lydia said. "Out of guilt if nothing else. But she does love him very much."

Daett nodded. "That's what I thought. Perhaps this is the Lord's will for Laura."

"A crippled husband?"

"Come." *Daett* took Lydia's arm and led the way toward the house. "Let us not decide things of which we are uncertain. It's better to allow the Lord to light the path clearly before we make our choice."

Lydia pulled back from his touch. "I've decided I'm going to accept Uncle Henry's offer to work for him."

"Now? In the middle of all this trouble?"

Lydia met his gaze. "*Yah*. Am I wrong in going on with my plans?"

Daett smiled. "I think the Lord has shed light on your path, so I would not discourage you. But…" *Daett* hesitated at the front porch step. "Your *mamm* is not well, Lydia. One of the nurses noticed her last night and had a doctor check her vital signs. They were not *goot*. Apparently she has not been well for some time, but she has said nothing."

Alarm filled Lydia's voice. "What's wrong with her?"

"High blood pressure, for one thing. Beyond that, it's hard to say. Your *mamm* is stubborn. She didn't want to submit to any further tests."

"What can we do then?"

"Just pray she'll change her mind," *Daett* said as he opened the front door. Laura looked up from where she was seated on the couch and tried to smile.

Daett seated himself beside her. "Feeling any better now that you're home?"

Laura lowered her head. *Daett* gave Lydia a glance that said, *I want to speak with her alone.* Lydia hurried into the kitchen, where *Mamm* was busy with the breakfast preparations. *Daett's* soft murmur came from the living room behind them as he spoke with Laura. *Daett* would help her sister through this crisis, Lydia told herself.

"How was your night?" *Mamm* asked, her face drawn and weary.

"I slept right through everything," Lydia said. "But you…" Lydia stepped closer to touch *Mamm's* arm. "Are you okay? *Daett* just told me about your health."

Mamm forced a laugh. "I'm the last person anyone should be worrying about right now, what with John lying in that hospital bed broken and bruised. I know the man will never walk again, even if the doctor tried to sound hopeful."

"You should have let a doctor put you through some tests," Lydia said. "Maybe it will help to find out what's wrong."

Mamm huffed. "I don't want anyone poking and prodding me. What are they going to look for? The aches and pains of an old woman? That's like looking for a needle in a haystack. And high blood pressure? Of course I had high blood pressure last night. Anyone would have had high blood pressure under the circumstances."

"But something is wrong. It would be *goot* to know what, so the doctors can help," Lydia urged.

"There's nothing wrong with me that a few hours' sleep and a hard day's work won't fix. Now, help me with breakfast. Your sister won't be worth much today. She'll want to rush back to the hospital, but I'm having none of it. Laura is not staying with John unless one of us is with her. It's not decent."

"But I think John asked Laura to marry him yesterday," Lydia said.

Mamm huffed again. "It doesn't matter. Now, let's get busy."

Lydia pulled out a pan to fry the bacon. Behind them *Daett's* voice rose and fell in the living room, but *Mamm* didn't seem to hear. Lydia opened the firebox to place several more sticks of wood on the fire. *Mamm* was silent, so Lydia left things as they were. She could explain later about her planned move to Uncle Henry's place for the fall.

A few moments later, *Daett* spoke from the kitchen doorway. "I'm leaving for the barn and the chores." He turned to leave but then turned back and asked *Mamm*, "Do you have any idea why that *Englisha* nurse at the hospital seemed to know Teacher Nancy so well?"

"Everyone knows Nancy," *Mamm* responded. "She was just trying to make us feel comfortable with conversation about someone we both knew. That's how the *Englisha* are."

Daett shrugged and left by the washroom door. *Mamm* stirred the pot of oatmeal in silence and then spoke out of the blue. "Did you know that your *daett* once dated Teacher Nancy before we were married?"

Lydia nearly dropped the large fork she was using to stir the bacon. "Teacher Nancy? *Daett*?"

Mamm frowned. "Forget I said that. Their relationship was a long time ago, and your *daett* is a decent man. A long sleepless night has befuddled me."

"Did Teacher Nancy come to the hospital?" Something didn't make sense. *Mamm* wasn't one to blurt out information at random.

"I shouldn't have said anything." *Mamm* bent over to stare at the stove.

"*Mamm*." Lydia stepped closer. "What is wrong?"

Mamm tried to smile. "Nothing is wrong. Just a backache from sitting in that chair all night. Don't pay any attention to me."

Lydia turned back to the bacon pan, but her thoughts wouldn't stop. "Tell me, *Mamm*," she finally said. "I want to know about Nancy and *Daett*."

Mamm shrugged. "At one time Nancy was your *daett's* steady girlfriend. *Daett* broke off the relationship, but he won't talk about it, so I don't know much." She tried to smile again. "Not that I objected—or object now. Your *daett* was more than a decent catch for a girl like me."

Lydia put her arm around *Mamm's* shoulder. "Are you sure you're okay?"

Mamm stood up straighter. "I'm fine. I don't know why I brought this up. I guess I'm just thinking that Laura is going to want to marry John in spite of his condition. And there won't be any talking her out of it. Let's hope John has more sense than she does."

A soft footstep came into the kitchen and Laura spoke. "*Yah*, I will marry John. A promise is a promise."

Mamm stirred the oatmeal and didn't answer.

"I will!" Laura repeated. "And John will have me. Even after—"

"It's whether you will still have him," *Mamm* said. She turned to face Laura. "That's the question. You're emotional right now and not in any shape to make such an important decision. Now, come help with breakfast."

"I'm not abandoning John," Laura said as she sat down at the kitchen table. "Love is forever. That's just the way it is."

"Couples break their engagements all the time," *Mamm* said. "You wouldn't be here if your *daett* hadn't broken his."

Laura appeared befuddled, but Lydia wasn't about to enlighten her twin now.

Laura finally shrugged. "I know what my heart says. I'm sticking with John whatever his condition turns out to be."

The look on *Mamm*'s face said that the conversation was far from over. Lydia took a deep breath and changed the subject. "I'm leaving for Uncle Henry's early next week. I spoke with him yesterday and with *Daett* this morning, and it's decided."

Mamm looked at her for a long moment, but turned back to her oatmeal. That conversation wasn't over either, Lydia knew. But she felt as sure about the matter as Laura apparently did about hers. How things had changed from only a few years ago. Neither of them would have dared challenge *Mamm* back then.

"We will speak of this later," *Mamm* said. "Breakfast must be prepared now. So set the table, Laura."

Her twin wearily stood, and only the tinkering of pots and silverware filled the kitchen as they worked.

Chapter Eight

Laura waited with clasped hands outside of John's hospital room. *Mamm* sat next to her. Laura had wanted to come by herself, but *Mamm* had not allowed it. "It's not seemly," *Mamm* had said.

"But there will be someone from John's family there, too, so I won't exactly be alone with him," Laura had argued. But *Mamm* wouldn't back down.

So here they were—together. When Laura wanted nothing more than to be left alone with John. The words she wanted to say to John were not for anyone's ears but his.

"You can go in now," a nurse said as she approached the two women. "Is this the first time you're seeing him since he regained consciousness?"

"*Yah.*"

"Go ahead then." The nurse motioned toward the doorway.

Laura stood and walked slowly, *Mamm*'s footsteps close behind her.

"*Mamm*, give us some time alone," Laura whispered over her shoulder.

Mamm didn't reply as they entered the room. John was lying on the bed, his face the color of the white sheets. Laura gasped and hurried forward. "John!"

John's sister Clare was seated in the shadows, but Laura ignored her to touch John's pale hand. "John," she tried again. "Are you awake?"

John opened his eyes, but there was no response.

"He's not speaking much," Clare said. "We haven't got a word out of him yet."

"How long has he been conscious?" *Mamm* asked from a few feet away.

Clare shrugged. "I've only been here since around eight. We try to keep someone with him at all times. *Mamm*'s been doing that for the most part. John's still on strong pain medication. The doctors will…"

Laura shut out Clare's words as she squeezed John's hand and whispered, "I'm so sorry about this. It's all my fault. I'm so sorry. I shouldn't have…" She couldn't go on.

How could she say that the kiss she had enjoyed with John behind the shed had been wrong? It simply wasn't, and yet this had been the result.

Laura studied John's face as *Mamm*'s and Clare's voices rose and fell behind her. "Do you know me, John?" she finally asked. A flicker of recognition seemed to cross his face. Laura squeezed his hand and a slight response came. "Can you forgive me?"

John's lips moved and Laura moved closer. "It wasn't your fault," he mouthed. The words were plain enough.

"You'll be better soon," she said. "And everything will be like it was before."

John blinked and seemed to fade away.

"He's been doing that since I got here," Clare said. "Don't take it personally."

Laura looked away. This simply wasn't right. She needed a private conversation with John. But what could be done? *Mamm* wouldn't leave her alone with him, and even if by some miracle *Mamm* disappeared, John appeared to have drifted off to sleep.

Mamm pulled on Laura's elbow. "Come. You can do no more now. He's not able to communicate."

Laura resisted, but the effort was useless. She wouldn't make a scene in front of Clare. Besides, *Mamm* would still win.

As they left the room, *Mamm* paused with her hand still on Laura's elbow. "*Goot* morning, Hilda," *Mamm* said.

Laura looked up to see John's *mamm* approaching.

"*Goot* morning to both of you," Hilda said, her face lined with weariness.

"I thought you had gone home for the day." *Mamm* let go of Laura to slip her arm around Hilda's shoulder, and the two women clung to each other for a moment.

"How is he?" Hilda asked.

"Not *goot*," *Mamm* said. "I think he spoke a few words to Laura though."

Hilda turned to Laura. "I'm glad I didn't go home yet. I'd like to speak to you." Hilda motioned toward the waiting room. "Let's sit down, or my legs will give out on me."

Laura moved toward Hilda, and *Mamm* shrugged and followed them to a row of empty chairs. Hilda sighed as she sat down, and then she looked at Laura. "I don't know where to begin, dear. I know you've been seeing John for quite some time, so we should keep you filled in, although..." Hilda looked away as tears rolled down her cheeks. "I guess I really should just say what needs saying, Laura, and have it done with. You don't want John as your husband in the condition he's in."

"But no!" Laura half-rose from her seat. "I'm promised to him. I love him."

"You are promised to him?" Hilda appeared puzzled. "John never told me. Of course, maybe he wouldn't have, but still…"

"It only happened the day of the barn-raising," *Mamm* said.

Hilda's puzzlement increased. "But how? I mean, the accident happened…" Hilda fixed her gaze on Laura.

Laura looked away. "I suppose I might as well tell you. The accident was my fault. I was tending the lemonade stand and took the opportunity to step away and speak with John for a few moments. He followed me behind the little shed, the one near the building site. We kissed and he asked me to marry him." Laura kept her gaze on the far wall. "I'm sure John fell because his thoughts were on me and our future together. I will certainly still marry John. Even if John never walks again."

"But we have to be practical, dear heart." Hilda reached for Laura's hand. "Even if John did ask you to be his *frau*. That was…" Her voice trailed off.

"*Yah*, I know. Before the accident." Laura forced back the tears. "But nothing has changed, even if I'm sure that John fell because he was thinking about our love…and the kisses we had just shared. How could something so pure and holy become so wrong?"

Hilda sighed. "Your kisses weren't wrong, dear. John obviously loves you. You shouldn't blame yourself. The Lord knows we did our own share of foolishness back when."

"You did?" Laura asked.

Mamm huffed. "Hilda only means the point rhetorically. I'm sure she didn't go kissing Herman behind sheds on barn-raising days."

"Don't be too hard on the girl," Hilda said. "We weren't exactly saints. You snatched Yost up quickly enough after he quarreled with Teacher Nancy. Long before he had time to heal the hurt. And Nancy has never married, so she must have been hurt too. Deeply, I'd say!"

Mamm fell silent, and Hilda squeezed Laura's hand. "See, dear, John might not make it through this. His back is broken in three places. His lung is punctured, and he has fluid on his brain from a severe concussion. Even if John pulls through, he'll never walk again. Not without a miracle, and those don't happen much anymore." Hilda paused as tears streamed down her face.

Laura gasped at the notion that John might not even pull through. "He must get better!" she wailed. "He must!"

Mamm and Hilda both wrapped their arms around her and held her close, one on each side. The sound of her soft sobs filled the waiting room. Several of the *Englisha* people looked their way, but understanding was written on their faces. Others had mourned here before her.

"Even if John lives, I don't want you to marry him," Hilda whispered through Laura's tears. "I couldn't live with myself if I allowed it."

"And I couldn't live without John," Laura insisted as her cries increased.

Heads turned again. "Hush, Laura," said *Mamm*. "We don't carry on like that."

Hilda squeezed Laura's hand again and stood. "Well, I need to be going. I'll peek in and see John for a second first."

As Hilda walked down the hall, *Mamm* turned to Laura. "Hilda is only trying to make things easier for you."

Laura didn't answer. It would be useless.

They found their driver in the parking lot, near where she had dropped them off. Once their neighbor, Mrs. Meyers, had found out about the accident, she had volunteered to do any driving they needed. *Mamm* didn't want to impose on others more than necessary, but the drive up to Ogdensburg by horse and buggy this morning would have taken more time than they had to spare.

"How was he?" Mrs. Meyers asked once they were in the car.

"Conscious for a little bit," *Mamm* said.

Mrs. Meyers gave Laura a sympathetic look. "Any word on the prognosis?"

"I don't know," Laura mumbled, because she didn't. She was not about to repeat the grim conclusions John's *mamm* had drawn without solid evidence.

"He may not make it," *Mamm* said. Laura turned away and looked out the window.

"I'm so sorry," Mrs. Meyers said, sounding close to tears herself.

Laura tried to pull herself together. She was not about to get emotional in front of Mrs. Meyers. "Thank you for your concern. I think he'll be better soon."

There was silence in the car as *Mamm* and Mrs. Meyers exchanged looks. Neither of them said anything, but Laura could hear their thoughts. *She's in denial, too grief-stricken to face the truth.*

Mamm ticked off John's injuries to Mrs. Meyers on the way home, but Laura didn't listen. Maybe she *was* in denial. She preferred to call it hope. Thankfully *Mamm* and Mrs. Meyers kept up a stream of chatter on the drive home, and Laura didn't have to speak.

Mrs. Meyers slowed on Lead Mine Road for the Masts' driveway and turned in. After she came to a stop by the barn, Laura was the first out of the car. "Thanks for the ride," she hollered over her shoulder, hurrying toward the house without waiting for an answer.

Lydia met her at the door with a worried look. "How is John?"

"I'm not talking about it," Laura said. She raced up the stairs and past Lydia's bedroom door, where a suitcase lay open on the bed and appeared fully packed. Life was going on without her, as she hung in limbo with John lying helpless in the hospital. Laura plopped down on her bed and wrapped her face in the quilt.

"It's not your fault," Lydia said from the doorway, having followed her sister upstairs.

Laura sat up to face her. "Lydia, I'm so scared! John's *mamm* said he might not make it. He might die! And she said I can't marry him because he'll be a cripple. I protested, but it all fell on deaf ears."

Lydia sat down on the bed and took Laura in her arms. The two rocked from side to side as soft sobs filled the bedroom.

Laura finally sat up straight. "You don't need to cry. He's not your boyfriend."

"I know," Lydia said. "But I feel what you feel. We've always shared everything, haven't we?"

Laura nodded and stood to retrieve a fresh handkerchief. She wiped her eyes and asked, "What would you do if you were in my shoes?"

Lydia shrugged. "I don't know. I guess if this had happened to Milton—"

"You'd be true to him," Laura interrupted. "You know you would."

"I'd stay true," Lydia said, "if I really loved him to begin with."

Laura nodded. "I do love John, and I'm not walking away. I don't care what anyone says."

"Did you tell John this?"

Laura looked up. "I tried. They wouldn't let me speak with him alone, so I said what I had to say in front of *Mamm* and Clare. But John heard me. I know he did."

"Of course he did!" Lydia moved closer and hugged her sister.

Mamm soon appeared in the doorway. "You're making an awful fuss, Laura," she said. "You're going to have to move past this tragedy.

At some point, it appears childish to carry on so. You'll have to face the truth. Weeping is a proper response for a while, but it must have an end."

Laura stood and dried her tears. *Mamm* was gone when she looked up again, but Lydia stood in the doorway.

"You'll be okay?" Lydia asked.

Laura nodded and tried to smile as she closed the door behind her.

Chapter Nine

Laura sat perched on the low wooden bench along the outer wall of Bishop Ezra's barn. The young folks from the district had arrived at Bishop Ezra's place on a Thursday evening to help harvest the bishop's sweet corn crop. The bishop had planted more than half an acre behind the barn. Several of the boys were still busy outside with the last rows. Brown tassels and green husks lay everywhere on the barn floor, but all that Laura could see was John's pale body lying in the hospital bed in Ogdensburg.

Mamm had gone with her to the hospital today, but John had done little more than blink his eyes when she bent over to whisper what words of comfort she dared. Someday soon she would be brave enough to ask everyone to leave the hospital room, and she'd wrap her arms around John's neck and kiss him with all the love she had in her heart. He'd get better quicker that way, she was sure. John needed her love and she needed him to get better. The Lord had not intended things to turn out this way. How could He with the joy and laughter that had bubbled up in their hearts that morning at the barn-raising? John's kisses had spoken of all the things that were right in life, and this was not right. Darkness had interfered, and now only the Lord could set things right.

Laura forced herself to focus on the freshly picked sweet corn in her lap, as her lips moved silently. "Please help us, dear Lord."

"What did you say?" John's sister Clare leaned closer to ask.

"Nothing." Laura tried to smile. "Just thinking of John. We were up to see him today."

"Praying then?" Clare guessed correctly, her warm smile indicating her approval. "We remember John every day in our family prayers. John is such a dear brother." Tears filled Clare's eyes, and she looked away.

Laura slipped her arm around Clare's shoulder. The hope for miracles must be the desire of the young, but at least now she had someone other than Lydia who shared that hope. *Daett* and *Mamm* were hoping too, but for different things. After the accident, *Mamm's* dream of a marriage for her daughters had become conflicted. John had been a perfect fit for that dream, but now *Mamm* wanted Laura's relationship with him to end so she could move on with life. But Laura knew she must not blame *Mamm* or grow bitter. *Mamm* had never loved John like she did.

Laura forced herself to listen to the conversation of the young girls around her, but it all sounded like static to her ears as the image of John in his hospital bed lingered in her mind. On a night like this, John normally would have been on the seat beside her where Clare was sitting.

Laura wiped away the forming tears and glanced up as Bishop Ezra appeared in the barn door. His long white beard was filled with green corn leaves, and she laughed at the sight along with the rest of the young people. Bishop Ezra smiled and brushed the leaves out, declaring, "I must say, I am happy tonight. This is such a *wunderbah* gift from the Lord that you young people have come to help an old man and woman with their corn patch."

More laughter rippled through the barn.

"I see the trick now," one of the boys teased. "Your sons-in-law also planted on the home farm to play on our sympathies. They knew we wouldn't be over to help with *their* corn patches."

Wide grins spread over the faces of the bishop's two sons-in-law, who were both standing within earshot.

Laura again tuned out the banter. *Yah*, she knew life must go on, but her heart wasn't ready. She wondered if her heart would ever be ready without John.

Clare must have noticed the silence because she reached over to squeeze Laura's hand.

"Thank you," Laura whispered as she busied herself with the corn. She ripped long streams of green husk off the soft yellow centers. A few bugs scurried about in search of new hiding places, and Laura ignored them to toss the husks on the barn floor. If only she could so easily tear away the darkness that had crept over John's life, their problem would be solved—but she couldn't. All she could do was pray. The Lord could touch John and restore him to his former vibrant health. Why would the Lord will otherwise? John had been strong, and honest, and kindhearted, and so alive. There couldn't have been anything wrong with that. She could still feel his arms around her that morning behind the little shed, though the memory seemed years ago now. She would never forget how that felt, even if she were never to feel that strength again. The morning would never come when she would awaken and be unable to remember what his touch felt like. She—

"How are you girls doing tonight?" A man's voice sounded from in front of her, and Laura jerked her head up. Wendell Kaufman, Bishop Ezra's notorious grandson, stood in front of them.

"I'm sorry for John's trouble," Wendell said to both girls. "I hope he's doing well."

"My brother's hanging on," Clare answered.

"*Goot*! Can I sit?" Wendell motioned with his hand.

Laura reluctantly slid over to make room for him. Wendell sat down with his shoulder inches from hers, right where John should have been sitting. Did Wendell realize this? Was he trying to take John's place? Knowing Wendell's reputation, she wouldn't put it past him.

Wendell sent a smile Laura's way. "Have you been up to see John lately?" He reached for a sheaf of corn from Laura's lap and began to strip off the green husk.

"*Mamm* took me today," Laura replied.

"Is he responsive?" Wendell asked with a concerned look.

How should she respond? His comfort eased into every ache of her soul, but should she allow this? Wendell was forward and could get the wrong idea easily. "There wasn't much reaction," she finally said. "But I did speak with him for a few minutes."

"That's important," Wendell said. "They say unconscious people can often hear us even when we think they can't, and once they're awake they speak of what a comfort that was."

"Do you think John will awaken soon?"

Wendell didn't answer for a moment. "We must pray for the Lord's will," he finally said. "But our heart can still ask, I suppose. You're wishing, then, for a touch of the Lord's hand on John?"

"*Yah*," Laura whispered.

Wendell smiled. "Medical miracles do happen."

"But divine ones?"

Wendell shrugged. "The Lord works through the doctors usually, but we can pray. King David prayed for his sick son who was at death's door, even when the Lord Himself had smitten the lad. Perhaps the Lord will change His mind. That's what King David told his servants."

"You believe the Lord has smitten John?" Laura didn't hide the horror in her voice. All of the guilt from that day rushed back, and her face paled.

Wendell let go of the green corn sheaf and reached for her hand. "I heard of what happened that day, Laura, but you must not blame yourself. We don't understand why John slipped or even why the beam shook so much. To claim that we do would be foolishness." His hand tightened on hers. "And to blame yourself is to say that we *do* know, even though we don't. We can only ask the Lord for mercy on John's condition."

"Would you pray then?" Laura's words leaped out, and Clare pulled in a sharp breath from the other side of Wendell.

"Certainly," Wendell said. He closed his eyes and whispered the words, "Dear Lord in heaven, Ruler of the universe, look down and comfort Laura's heart. Look down and see John's distress in the hospital room. If possible, heal him and restore him fully to the strong man he once was. Amen."

"Thank you," Laura whispered. "Thank you so much."

No one had prayed like this with her before, but she didn't dare say so. Wendell might think her too forward. Already he must know about the moment she and John shared behind the little shed, as apparently most of the community did. That thought brought a deep blush to her cheeks.

Wendell's hand was still on hers. A few young people had glanced their way, but no one seemed to think Wendell's presence beside her inappropriate. No doubt they knew she needed the comfort, and Wendell was the grandson of the bishop. *Yah*, he had pursued her before she dated John, but so far none of Wendell's words had given her cause for alarm. Maybe Wendell had a kinder side than she was aware of, or perhaps she'd just never noticed it before. Tonight Wendell's intentions had only been *goot*.

Laura leaned against his shoulder and whispered. "Thank you

again for praying with me. You have strengthened my heart in this dark hour."

"It is dark," Wendell agreed. "But not so dark that the Lord's light cannot reach us."

"Thank you," Laura whispered once more. She had begun to sound foolish, but not a word of her gratitude was faked. Wendell spoke words that she desperately needed to hear. Words no one else was saying.

Wendell smiled. "Well, I had best be moving on now, but don't lose heart."

He stood and didn't wait for an answer before he moved into the crowd of young men.

Clare moved closer to Laura on the bench to whisper, "That took a lot of nerve."

"He spoke *goot* words," Laura said.

"But praying with you like that?" Clare's eyes were round.

"He's the grandson of the bishop," Laura said, as if that answered any and all questions. Why was Clare alarmed if she wasn't?

"I suppose we need all the prayers we can get," Clare allowed. "Still…"

Laura glanced at Clare. "You don't object to a miracle for John? I thought you said the family was praying for John each day."

"*Yah*," Clare said, "but only as the Lord wills. We don't know what His will is. Surely Wendell knows this too and was just playing you along, Laura. So that in case…" She gave Laura a knowing look.

"Really! Do you think so?"

"*Yah*, I know so!" Clare's voice was sharp.

Laura looked away and pressed back her tears. Why was there such opposition? *Mamm* wanted an end to her relationship with John. John's *mamm* was angling for the same thing, and now Clare didn't like the comfort and hope Wendell had offered.

Laura stilled the protest inside of her. Bitter words were never right.

"I know that nothing makes sense right now," Clare said. "I'm sorry if I was a little harsh. In my heart I could wish that I knew the Lord's will and ask a miracle of Him, but I don't think that would be right, Laura. That's all I'm trying to say. But I also know that it's hard not to hope for something like that."

After a moment, Clare leaned over to give Laura a hug. "We'll have to hang together, okay? We must allow this to remain in the Lord's hand. Miracles are best left to the Lord's will."

Laura smiled but remained silent. She didn't wish to argue, but she would not let go of the hope in her heart. The Lord reigned on His throne even in the middle of man's chaos. She knew that. But why could she not ask for a miracle anyway? There was no wrong in that. If the Lord said no, she would submit, but she would ask while hope remained. Wendell might be false in his sympathies, but the Lord was true. She would never stop believing that.

Chapter Ten

Teacher Nancy hid behind her living room drapes to peer into the darkness outside. There were no headlights on the road, and she hoped there wouldn't be. She had told Charles to park well down on Ward Road and to walk in. Nancy took another long look out the window before she moved away and began to pace the hardwood floor again. This was madness, pure foolishness, and yet the idea had made perfect sense earlier. What if she invited Charles to her own home for a meal? Perhaps he would see how impossible their situation was and would vanish from her life. He would see that they lived worlds apart and could never come together.

This was desperation, of course, but she couldn't think of another way out. She had already told Charles, "I can't see you again! I already face enough questions from Deacon William with what happened at the barn-raising. I can't have your people recognizing me in public like that."

Her plea had been passionate, but her heart hadn't been in the words—and Charles knew it. He no doubt also suspected that love for him was blossoming in Nancy's heart. Not since her relationship with Yost Mast all those years ago had she been so desperately in love. Now she had fallen for a man unavailable to her by all the laws of her religion—an *Englisha* man. She shouldn't have spoken with him the day he had visited the schoolhouse, but the look in his eyes, their blueness, the sorrow that lingered from his own loss, had all been there in that first glance. What she had seen since had only deepened her respect and love for the *Englisha* man.

Nancy paused in front of the drapes to draw them together as fearful thoughts raced through her mind. Deacon William might even drive in with his buggy tonight. But was that likely? The deacon had seemed satisfied with her answers on the evening of the barn-raising. His only instructions had been, "Don't learn any more medical stuff from the *Englisha*, Nancy."

The deacon hadn't imagined the existence of Charles in his wildest dreams, but neither had Nancy. All of which would change quickly enough if she was caught tonight entertaining an *Englisha* man with supper in her house.

Nancy jumped when a soft knock came on the back door. She crept through the small house and her hands trembled as she pulled open the door. Charles's lengthy frame was silhouetted against the stars on the small stoop.

"Am I welcome?" his soft voice teased.

"Come." She grabbed his arm and pulled him inside.

"So this is an Amish home," Charles said, looking around.

"*Yah*, of course," she answered, taking his hand and leading the way into the living room.

"An Amish home," Charles repeated, glancing at the kerosene lamp on the table.

"*Yah*, I wanted you to see how we live. How I live." Nancy stumbled over the words, but got them out.

Charles chuckled. "The London blackout is more like it. It's dim in here."

Nancy didn't answer. She knew about the famous London black-out, but she probably wasn't supposed to know—at least according to Deacon William. But this wasn't entirely her fault. She had once planned to wed Yost Mast and raise a family full of *kinner* with him, not spend her life with her nose in book after book.

"I didn't offend you, did I?" Charles asked.

"Of course not. Come, I have the food ready." She took his hand again.

She had refused to settle for second best after the relationship with Yost had ended. That part of this evening was her fault. She could have married an Amish man a long time ago, but she had turned down all suitors. Now nature had struck back over her refusal to bow. There could be no other explanation.

As she led him into the small dining room, Charles's gaze swept over the round table with its silverware set out, but no food in sight. "I thought this invitation was for a meal," he teased again.

Nancy let go of his hand. "Just wait. I have everything on the stove, since I didn't know exactly when you would arrive. And the drapes are drawn in case someone stops by unexpectedly. I guess I'll have time to stick you in the closet." She attempted a smile.

Charles chuckled again. "This *is* the London blackout, but it's okay. I just didn't expect..."

Nancy nodded. "That's really my point. See now how impossible it is? We can't..."

He stopped her. "I love you, Nancy. You know I do. I never went looking for this, but we must not tell God no when He says yes."

"How can you say it was God who brought us together?" she gasped.

Charles smiled. "Surely you believe we were led together by a divine hand. How else do you explain the..." Charles glanced at the kerosene lamp and took Nancy's hand. "The unlikeliness of you and me meeting as we did...at just the right time, at just the right place so we could be alone and speak? You are just the right woman for me, Nancy. I firmly believe God is in this. He has given me love again to comfort my heart after the loss of Nichole."

Nancy changed the subject and headed for the kitchen. "I'll get the food on," she said. "I know you're hungry."

Charles held tight to her hand. "I'm coming to help," he said, and she held on to his fingers to lead him into the kitchen. By the dim light of the kerosene lamp Nancy lifted the lids on the prepared dishes.

"A plate and a spoon for tasting?" Nancy motioned toward the utensil drawer.

Charles disappeared from sight for a moment, and she reached for the spoon when he came back.

"No, let me," he said, dipping out a small portion and holding the spoon to her mouth. Nancy gripped his arm above the spoon handle and sipped.

"How is it?" he asked.

"I can't taste anything," she managed.

He smiled. "May I?"

"Of course."

He dipped the spoon back in the pot and moved it to his lips. "Delicious," he proclaimed. "Absolutely delicious!"

"Oh, Charles," she whispered.

"But you already knew that," he said with a grin.

She looked into his eyes briefly with an urge to tell him how much she loved him, but the words wouldn't come.

He stared down at the large soup container. "That's a lot of soup for two people."

"We don't have to eat it all. I usually cook enough for more than one meal."

"That's Amish too, I suppose."

She looked away and didn't answer. He picked up the pot of soup and led the way back to the dining room. Nancy followed with the soup dipper and hot pads, and laid them out before Charles set down the pot.

He gave the drawn drapes a brief glance. "What happens if they catch me here?" he asked.

"Not *goot*," she said.

"And yet you asked me over?"

She sighed. "I didn't know what else to do, Charles. I never can explain this fully. Not even if I try."

He inclined his head toward the drapes. "Perhaps they are drawn to scare me off?"

Nancy winced. "No, not exactly. But I admit I've wanted you to see how far apart we are in the ways we live. It makes…a relationship between us quite unworkable."

"I see," he said. But he didn't understand, and that was plain enough to Nancy. How could someone who was born *Englisha* know what it was like to have the eyes of the community on you, and all of the time? There was no place where eyes were not watching. Somehow, someone always found out. Nancy shivered. She could hide Charles for a while, but not forever. No one before her had managed to cover up such deeds, and neither would she. There was an *Englisha* man in her house for supper, and the light of the community's day would find it out sooner or later.

Charles's hand found hers. "I'm sorry if I don't understand, but I do love you. That I do understand."

She managed to smile, but could say nothing.

As they sat to begin their meal, Nancy paused awkwardly. "Will you pray?" she asked.

"Of course," Charles said. He bowed his head and offered a brief word of thanks.

As Nancy dished up the soup, he said, "Tell me about the accident at the barn-raising. I'd like to know."

"A young man named John Yoder fell from a shaking beam and was seriously injured." Her voice trembled. "What is there to say but that another young girl's heart is broken?"

"There are always tragedies, and someone innocent usually suffers. I'm sorry it happened."

Nancy gazed at the darkened drapes. "John and the woman who is to be his *frau*, Laura Mast, were so young and so full of life."

Charles was silent a moment and then gave her a soft smile. "Well, this is excellent soup. All the more so eaten by candlelight, or its equivalent—a kerosene lamp." Charles laughed. "That's quite romantic."

"I can get candles." Nancy returned his smile.

"No, this is fine," he said. "I just want to be with you. By candlelight or kerosene lamp, you're lovely."

"Charles, don't," she said. "I mean, I'm already enjoying the evening too much, and it was supposed to mark the end...not..." Nancy's voice faded away.

Charles lay his hand on hers again. "I understand, but there's nothing you can do that will chase me away or make me change my mind about you."

She pulled her hand back but didn't look at him. The topic of conversation had to change. "So tell me. How did you overcome your loss with Nichole?"

"Through the help of God," he said. "As I assume your young

couple will. I only wish I had been on call that day and could have helped with the boy's accident. It would have been good to see you in action in your natural habitat."

Nancy stilled the sudden intake of her breath. "You can never do that, Charles. Surely you sense the seriousness of my situation. If you had recognized me at the barn-raising, I can't imagine what would have happened. Deacon William was already full enough of questions. Can't you—"

Charles stopped Nancy with a touch on her arm. "Dear heart, I'm sorry to push the point, but if we want to continue our relationship, the time must come for a change. You know that, don't you? I can't join your community. That's not the way God has made me."

"And you think the Lord has made me *Englisha*?" The words burst out of her.

"God has made you a woman I can love." His voice was gentle. "Beyond that, I'm sorry if I'm asking something of you that I can't do myself."

"Charles, I was in love once before," she replied. "And I know that love is not enough."

Charles leaned closer. "Tell me about that. I've been very open with you about Nichole."

"I can't. He's Amish, and he's still alive. He's still part of this community."

"I see. Do you still love him?"

"No, of course not. But it's made me very careful about ever loving again…at least loving like that. All or nothing."

A slight smile played on Charles's face. "Does that mean you have feelings for me?"

She looked down into her lap, but could say nothing.

Charles's smile broadened. "I'll take that as a yes."

Nancy fiddled with her spoon. How unlike her Teacher Nancy persona she was behaving right now. She had forgotten what love did to her senses, to her balance, and certainly to her *goot* sense.

"Charles, the invitation tonight was to show you that this has to end," she whispered.

"I agree," he said. "It ends with our wedding. If you will say yes, we can have this whole thing wrapped up next month."

She met his gaze and her hands trembled.

"Please, dear, marry me," he said.

"I can't." Her voice shook.

"You don't want to? Is that what you are saying?"

"No! It means I *can't*. I want…" She bit off the words. "Tonight never should have happened, Charles. We are not from the same world."

"But we are also a man and a woman."

"It can't be, Charles. It can't be!" Her voice rose. "Please leave before I begin to cry. Don't you know how very hard this is for me? If you truly love me, you'll go."

He surveyed her for a moment as tears filled her eyes.

"I'll go," he said, standing. "But I will see you again. And next time it will be on my turf…with no drapes drawn."

He touched her arm before he slipped out the back door.

Nancy stared at the darkened drapes and the now-cold pot of soup on the table. She was cursed in love—there was no other answer. The Amish didn't believe in such things, but she was cursed. She simply was.

Chapter Eleven

Early Monday morning, Lydia stood behind the counter of Uncle Henry's small roadside stand on Highway 184. A pale sliver of the moon hung just above the horizon, and the sun would be up in a few minutes to flood the world with brilliant light. What better sign of the Lord's favor could there be? At the moment she needed all the signs she could get. Back home Laura's tragedy with John was still gripping the household in sorrow, and here on Uncle Henry's farm, they mourned with Laura.

Yesterday at the service in Uncle Henry's district, the discussion of John's accident had been on everyone's lips.

"They say there's little change in him," a woman had said. "He's still up at the Ogdensburg Medical Center."

"Drifting in and out of consciousness," another had added. "With little hope of recovery."

In the meantime Lydia was sure Laura was clinging to the hope that John would make a full comeback. That would not happen from the sound of things, but neither would Laura listen to advice. Especially from *Mamm*.

"John's condition is what it is, and you'll not be wedding him," *Mamm* had told Laura more than once before Lydia moved over to

Uncle Henry's place. But *Mamm*'s efforts to awaken Laura to reality fell on deaf ears. Laura's faith seemed to rise out of her sorrow, and Lydia was in awe of her twin. All of Laura's dreams of love had been brought to an abrupt halt with the accident. Lydia would not blame her twin for her stubbornness, as some did. If Milton were laid up in a hospital bed, she, too, might hang on to hope past any reasonable expectations.

Lydia sighed and looked up and down the empty road. It was too early for customers, yet she was out here on Uncle Henry's orders. Milton had been right. Uncle Henry was a bit of a slave driver. Yet she had been happy to comply. They were all eager for success on opening day. Now the hour had arrived.

Lydia knew she could be thankful *Mamm* hadn't forbidden this venture at the last minute with how busy things were at home. Laura had to visit the hospital at least twice a week. If it had been left up to Laura, she would visit John every day, but *Mamm* wouldn't hear of it. *Daett* had remained silent about Lydia's planned move to Uncle Henry's place, but he would have intervened again on her behalf if *Mamm* had come up with new objections. She'd be gone from home until at least Christmas. Her family would be okay, Lydia told herself. No one was indispensable—as the accident with John had clearly showed. She'd be back in the home district this Sunday for her baptism, and she could visit after that if the need arose.

"We can't let you get homesick now," Uncle Henry had teased her yesterday after the service. She had ridden with Uncle Henry's family in their buggy and back again after the noon meal. The truth was she hadn't been homesick in the least, but it was best not to say so too plainly. *Mamm* might be offended if the words came back to her, which they would. Uncle Henry always said exactly what was on his mind.

Hopefully Uncle Henry hadn't seen Milton smile at her after the service. Uncle Henry already knew too much of what there was to know about Milton and her. Milton was friendly, but things hadn't moved any further. They talked to each other around the farm, but that also seemed more like business than romance. If truth be told, she still felt shy about Milton and her feelings for him.

Laura, on the other hand, hadn't cared if the whole world knew about her relationship with John. Hadn't Laura kissed John in public on the day of the barn-raising—well, almost in public? Lydia could never do that. Love was a private matter kept in one's heart. She'd probably swoon with Milton's first kiss—if there ever was one.

Soft footsteps came up behind Lydia and she whirled around.

"Thought I was sneaking up on you?" Milton teased.

"*Yah*, because you were," Lydia shot back.

Milton wasn't fazed. "Penny for your thoughts on this fine morning?"

Heat flamed into her face, and Lydia looked away. Thankfully the darkness was still a cloak.

"Cat got your tongue?"

"I can speak perfectly well," she said. "Just don't go sneaking up on a girl when she's alone."

Milton gave her a wicked grin. "I was walking along the road like a normal human being, and there you were, all dreamy-eyed. No doubt thinking sweet thoughts of someone special. Who would the lucky man be?"

Lydia took a deep breath. "That's none of your business."

Her face was fiery red again, she was sure. She had to work around Milton until Christmas, so she had to get used to him. Somehow!

He was sober-faced now. "I'd be greatly honored," he said, "if it was me you were thinking of."

She said nothing in reply. She certainly wouldn't admit her feelings. It was bad enough her face was red.

"It is a nice moon," he said with a nod toward the horizon. "I guess you don't have to tell me who the man is, but…"

"I do agree, the moon is nice." Lydia grasped for the escape route, but Milton wasn't thrown off his trail.

"I know one thing, Lydia. The moon and you make me dream things." He looked toward the horizon again as a shadow crossed his face. "But life doesn't always let our dreams come true, does it?"

Did he mean John and Laura? She wasn't sure.

"I think you understand," Milton said, his gaze still on the horizon. "Beautiful dreams can fade away, can't they?"

"Do you mean John's accident?" Lydia ventured.

Milton shrugged. "*Yah*, that was bad too."

Clearly he meant more, but what?

"You do understand," Milton said.

Only she didn't. What did he mean?

"Even my sister has caught on to the changing times," Milton continued.

"Teacher Nancy? What about her?"

Milton glanced at Lydia. "You wouldn't believe what Nancy is up to."

Lydia tried to smile. "I'm sure Teacher Nancy can stay out of trouble. We all think the best of her."

Milton gave a little laugh. "Nancy's already in plenty of trouble, and I kind of admire her for it, but…" Milton gave Lydia a long look. "Are you really going through with your baptismal class next Sunday?"

"Of course!" The exclamation burst into the silent air. "Why don't you join the new baptismal class this fall?"

Milton laughed again. "That's exactly what I'm talking about. Why don't you come back and enjoy your *rumspringa* time a little more?"

So that was it. Thankfully an *Englisha* car appeared in the distance and slowed down.

"Looks like your first customer has arrived. Should I stay around and help?" Milton said.

"I can manage." She gave him a nervous smile.

"I'm staying all the same," he said, moving to the back of the stand where he shuffled around some empty boxes.

Lydia greeted the lady who climbed out of the car. "*Goot* morning."

"Good morning to you, and what a fine day," the lady responded. "I thought I'd get out early and begin my day like you Amish do. I was sure you'd be open already." The lady gave Lydia a big smile. "I figured that Henry Miller's stand would be a sure hit again this fall. I know by midday the lines will be long, and I hate waiting."

"I hope so," Lydia agreed. "Do you live close by?"

"Up toward Heuvelton." The lady smiled again. "I'm sorry. I didn't introduce myself. I'm Mrs. Langhorne. We might be seeing a lot of each other this fall. That is, if you—"

"Oh, I'm here till Christmas," Lydia hurried to say. "And I'm Lydia Mast. I'm sure my Uncle Henry will be delighted that he already has a regular customer."

"Yes, that would be me," Mrs. Langhorne said as she placed some apples and fresh cabbage in her handbasket.

"We have some just ripened tomatoes," Lydia offered.

"Oh yes," Mrs. Langhorne said. "Let me have three, and I think that'll be all for today."

Lydia tallied up the purchase, and Mrs. Langhorne paid. With a wave of her hand she was off. "Ta-ta! See you soon."

"You are a natural at this," Milton said once the car had disappeared.

"Thank you," Lydia replied. She allowed the compliment to seep all the way through her.

"Surely you understood what I was getting at before," Milton went on.

Lydia sighed. "No, I don't think I do. You're not talking sense."

"Well, then I'll just tell you plain. My sister Nancy is seeing an *Englisha* man."

"Teacher Nancy?" The words exploded out of Lydia's mouth.

Milton winced. "*Yah.* I saw them together myself last Friday night when I stopped by Nancy's place. Nancy had the drapes drawn." He shrugged. "I peeked in anyway. She's my sister and I have a right to know. They were eating supper at the dining room table."

"That can't be!" Lydia stammered. "Not Teacher Nancy! An *Englisha* man?"

His smile was thin. "Things are changing, Lydia. You should think twice about being baptized on Sunday. You should think of something else, just like I am. If Nancy doubts the faith, then…well, I've had plenty of doubts myself, and now…"

"Then it is true about you?" She took him by the arm. "You're planning to jump the fence, aren't you?"

"I didn't say that," Milton said in defense. "But I might."

Lydia trembled and let go of Milton's arm to grab the wooden stand in front of her. "I don't believe you about Teacher Nancy," she said. "You're making up all of this to justify your own rebellion."

"I tell you, I saw them," Milton said. "I'm not making anything up. I just want you to think long and hard before your baptism. Because after that, well…"

"*Yah*, I know. But I'll never leave the community. And if you're smart, you won't either." The blood returned to her face and she stood up straight. Her knees no longer buckled.

"But there's a whole world out there to explore, Lydia," Milton said. "We could travel together with some other young people, maybe to Europe, or at least out West to California. We'll never get to see the world if we just stay here. The only thing to do in the community is to settle down, marry, have *kinner*, and grow old." Milton's voice was bitter.

"We will not speak of this anymore," Lydia ordered.

She used *Mamm*'s tone of voice, which was awful—but she couldn't help herself.

The grim look grew on Milton's face. "I suppose you'll become a submissive Amish woman then. But that explosion a minute ago didn't sound very meek and quiet to me."

"Don't throw my words back at me!" Lydia snapped.

Milton appeared hopeful. "I don't believe you're Amish at heart, Lydia. You're hungering instead for adventure and the big, wide world."

"I am not."

Milton smiled. "'The lady thou doth protest too much, methinks.' That's what the bard says, according to Nancy."

Who's the bard? Lydia almost asked, but Milton was only baiting her. She was sure of that now. Was the man more than half-serious? How could he be with those tall tales about his sister? No doubt Milton wanted to see if he could shake her commitment to the community, which would justify how he had been tempted by the *Englisha* world. Well, she told herself, she would give him no justification.

"It is true about Nancy," Milton said, as if he could read her thoughts.

With that, he turned and headed up Uncle Henry's lane, the notes of his happy whistle drifting through the trees. Lydia listened and willed the pounding of her heart to still itself. Milton had asked her to tour the West with him. In almost the same breath he claimed Teacher Nancy had entertained an *Englisha* man for supper in her own house. It simply wasn't possible. Yet why would Milton lie? He might stretch the truth, but this had to be more than a stretch. And if Milton *had* told her what he had really seen, no wonder he was confused. What if it was true? If so, Lydia would have to pray for Teacher Nancy to see the error of her ways.

Lydia pulled her coat tighter around her as another *Englisha* car appeared. It slowed down, and she pasted a smile on her face. No matter how strangely this first day at the roadside stand had begun, she would believe that the Lord was with her. Somehow this would all make sense someday. Maybe she had been sent into Milton's life to counter the temptations he faced and to build her own resolve. He had opened up to her this morning in a way he never had before. But in so doing, he was asking her to jump the fence with him.

Lydia pushed away the vision of Milton's handsome face, and greeted the man and woman as they approached the stand with a cheery, "*Goot* morning."

Chapter Twelve

On Sunday morning as the clock ticked toward twelve o'clock, Lydia was in Bishop Ezra's living room along with the other members of the fall baptismal class. Together they sat on a special bench set up close to the ministers' seats, with Laura seated on Lydia's left. Lydia kept her head down and her gaze on the floor as Bishop Ezra addressed the room.

"We have here a row of young people who wish to make their commitment to the Lord and His church today. They have been instructed by our ministers all summer and have prepared their hearts and souls for this holy moment. Our prayers and best wishes have been with them since the beginning of this instruction class. We know that temptations abound in this present evil world. The devil goes about as a roaring lion seeking to devour the Lord's holy flock. Our flesh is weak, and the Lord knows this. He sends many angels to strengthen us and keep us close to Him, if we but yield our hearts to Him as these young people have done. They are truly an example for all of us. We pray the Lord will protect everyone, as these young people have been protected the past few months."

Bishop Ezra paused, his eyes sweeping over the congregation.

Lydia dropped her gaze again as the bishop continued. "Now let us come to the Lord in prayer and beseech His further protection on these baptismal applicants as they go forth after their vows into the work of the Lord's vineyard. Many of them will soon say further vows, those of marriage perhaps, and begin to bring up *kinner* in the fear of the Lord."

Visions of Milton's face faded in and out in front of Lydia's eyes. The grains of the bishop's hardwood floor took the exact shape of Milton's smile, but they were gone a moment later. Lydia blinked and stared. This was not real, she told herself. Milton's words on the first day at the roadside stand had been real. She was sure he had said them and meant them, even though he had mentioned nothing further. *Yah*, he still smiled and greeted her brightly each day, but what passed between them could only be described as the most casual of conversations—the words of two people who weren't in love with each other. How had things turned far south so quickly?

Her heart had throbbed with pain all week. Why would Milton ask her to postpone her baptismal vows? Had Milton become a temptation rather than a legitimate love pursuit? Was this what Bishop Ezra referred to with his words of warning? But how could the bishop know? Bishop Ezra hadn't been there to hear what Milton said, and Milton was sitting this morning in the unmarried men's section as if he planned to stay in the community forever.

"I'm coming to your district for the services Sunday," Milton had told her on Friday evening before she left Uncle Henry's for the drive over to Lead Mine Road.

"But it's my baptismal," she had gasped. "I thought…"

"I still want to be there," he had said, and then he smiled and walked off.

Milton had smiled at her again this morning when the class had come down from their last instruction time with the ministers.

Milton acted as though he fully supported her decision, which made things all the more difficult. Why did the man her heart was drawn to bring her such confusion? Was this love? She had never imagined love to be this way. She was thoroughly befuddled.

The worst part was she couldn't talk to anyone. Laura had her own troubles, and Lydia wouldn't have dared anyway. What Milton had said about his sister Nancy was too explosive for anyone else's ears, which meant that Milton had trusted her greatly when he shared the news.

The bishop's voice broke into Lydia's thoughts. "Let us pray," he said. She gathered up her dress as the congregation knelt with the row of baptismal applicants to the sound of shuffling feet.

While Bishop Ezra led out, Lydia prayed her own silent prayer. *Help us all, dear Lord. Times are so confusing that we can hardly see our way. Yet we know that You have promised to be with us—if we surrender our wills to You. You have given us Your Word to believe in, and You have surrounded us with the comforts of home and of those who believe as we do. Bring us through these difficult times. Help us keep our faith, and help Milton make sense out of life. Help me to say the right words if he speaks with me again, and help me to be true to the vows I will make today. Amen.*

Lydia waited as Bishop Ezra finally pronounced the amen, and the shuffle of feet again filled the house. When everyone had seated themselves, Bishop Ezra faced the row of applicants. "Will all of you please kneel to say your vows?"

Lydia slipped downward as Laura did the same. A soft sob escaped Laura's lips, and Lydia reached over to hold her twin's hand. She knew why Laura was crying. John couldn't be here today to witness this important occasion. Only yesterday John's family had brought him home from the hospital, but he was still bedbound. According to the doctor's advice, John should have stayed longer in Ogdensburg, but the bills had mounted ever higher—and as with everyone in the community, they had no insurance. Already thousands of dollars had been spent, all of it money that no one in the community had. The Yoder family would pay eventually, but with the hope of John's recovery almost gone, enough had been enough.

Laura had spent yesterday at the Yoders' house, while Lydia had come home to help around the house in preparation for her baptism. There would be family over later in the afternoon to visit.

"They've brought him home to die," Laura had sobbed when she returned in the evening, their horse Maud hitched to the buggy.

Mamm tried to encourage her daughter. "We must accept the Lord's will."

Laura had rallied with those words and declared, "The Lord will heal him. I know He will!"

That wasn't exactly what *Mamm* meant, but no one had contradicted Laura. The Mast family had been over this ground too often in the past weeks.

The shuffle of Bishop Ezra's feet came closer, and Lydia forced herself to focus. This was a most holy moment, and she didn't want to miss a second.

Lydia glanced sideways to see a dribble of water falling from Laura's head. Another stifled sob came from her twin, but Bishop Ezra didn't seem bothered by her display of emotion. No doubt the bishop thought that Laura's piety had overcome her.

Lydia held her breath as the bishop's black Sunday shoes appeared in front of her. She stared at them. The bishop's questions came from far away, but she must have answered *yah* at the proper places. The bishop's hands settled on her *kapp*, and three short splashes of water from Deacon William's pitcher followed. Moments later, the two wives, Elizabeth and Rose, offered their hand to her and helped her rise. With great solemnity each woman kissed her on the cheek and whispered, "Welcome to the church, Lydia. We wish you all of the Lord's *goot* blessings."

Only then did the tears come, but Lydia wiped them away. She was not given to emotion in public, unlike Laura, who was still sobbing openly. Elizabeth came back to take Laura in her arms and whisper further words of encouragement to her. What was said, Lydia couldn't hear. The actions of the bishop's *frau* were comfort enough. The sisters were a part of the community now, and someone would always care.

As the last song number was given out, Elizabeth returned with Rose to the women's seating area. Lydia reached over to hold Laura's hand while the singing rose and fell around them. With the song over, Bishop Ezra dismissed the service. Laura remained seated and Lydia stayed beside her. *Mamm* hurried over to sit on the bench on the other side of Laura.

At least Laura's sobs had ceased, though her face was still pale and drained. Unless the Lord gave extra grace, the Mast family wouldn't be able to stand much more of this sorrow. That, or John's sufferings would soon end with his passing. If that happened, Laura would be grief-stricken, but she could also begin to heal. So far there had been only hope denied, and they all were feeling the strain.

"Come, Laura," *Mamm* whispered. "They need these benches to make tables for the meal."

Lydia nodded and stood with *Mamm*'s grip firm on her arm. She stepped back to give the two room to pass. Laura was better off in the kitchen, where she could help with tasks that didn't require many steps. Lydia would volunteer to help serve the married men's table as she always did here in the district. Some things never changed.

Before Lydia could move on, several of the married women walked over to shake her hand and offer their encouragement.

"Welcome to the family," the first one said, and they all gave her a quick kiss on the cheek and wished her the Lord's blessings.

Lydia moved again when Teacher Nancy appeared in her side vision. Lydia took a quick breath.

"Did I startle you?" Nancy asked with a soft smile.

"*Yah*, I guess so." Confusion raced through Lydia's mind. All she could hear was Milton saying, *"My sister Nancy is seeing an* Englisha *man."*

Lydia forced herself to focus and smile.

"Are you okay?" Nancy's hand was gentle on her arm. "I had to come and welcome one of my beloved students to the church family."

"Thank you," Lydia whispered. "I have no regrets."

Nancy looked at her strangely. "I should hope not. That would be a shame after such sober and solemn vows."

Milton doesn't know what he's talking about, Lydia decided. There was no way Teacher Nancy could have been eating in secret with an *Englisha* man. Someone who did so would never say such words to her. Lydia forced another smile. "I have *wunderbah* memories of our days in your classroom. I shall never forget what you taught us."

Nancy nodded. "That's nice to hear, and the feeling is mutual. I have loved you and Laura as if you were my own *kinner*. Teaching has been one of the blessings the Lord has allowed me to bear."

Lydia managed to laugh. "I'm sure we were a burden."

"You were the sweetest things," Nancy said, "but come. You should have a special place at the first table today, I'm thinking. We only take the baptismal vows once in our lives."

"Oh, no!" Lydia recoiled in horror. "I'll wait to eat at the unmarried girls' table on the second round. I was getting ready to serve the men's table as I always do."

Nancy hesitated but gave in. "Always the humble servant you

are, but that's how it should be. The ways of the community are the best, I'm thinking."

Lydia's head spun. Nancy was saying some strange things today. And where had the idea of her taking a special place at the tables come from? Maybe Deacon William did have cause for concern with all the new ideas Nancy came up with for her students. And maybe Nancy had slipped even further? Otherwise, why would Milton have made up a story about his sister?

"Are you okay?" Nancy's questions came again. "Are you ill?"

Lydia forced herself to look up and meet Nancy's gaze. "Is it true what Milton told me? You had an *Englisha* man in your house for a meal alone?"

Nancy's mouth opened as if to speak, but no words came out.

Lydia trembled. Then it must be true. Milton had not invented the story. *But how could you?* she wanted to scream. *You are so many things, but not this.*

Nancy turned pale and motioned for them to move off to the side.

"I'm very sorry that you know this," Nancy said when they had seated themselves. "I would try to explain, but I guess there is no explanation."

"Do you plan to wed him?" Lydia dared to whisper. "Do you plan to jump the fence after all these years of faithful service to the community?"

"I don't plan to," Nancy protested. "But of course I hadn't planned any of this."

Lydia clutched Nancy's arm. "Then why? What happened?"

"We cannot speak of this here," Nancy said, a bit sadly. "It's not proper. I will make things right with Deacon William once you tell him, but I cannot go myself."

"You were my teacher," Lydia whispered. "I'm telling no one."

Relief crept into Nancy's face. "You won't?"

"*Nee*, but you must—" Lydia stopped. Who was she to lecture Nancy? This was all too much to comprehend. She would not reprimand her elders, regardless of what they had done.

"You must pray for me, Lydia. And for Milton." Nancy glanced at her. "Please."

"*Yah*, I will," Lydia managed. "We can always pray."

Nancy slowly turned and moved off without a backward glance. Lydia braced herself against the living room wall. No wonder Milton had thoughts about jumping the fence, considering the confusion in his family. She *would* have to pray—often and with her whole heart.

Chapter Thirteen

Early Monday morning, Laura drove her buggy toward the Yoders' home on Cooper Road again. Maud lifted her head high in the brisk air and blew her nostrils wide with each stride. White streams of breath hung briefly in the air before they vanished.

Laura reached up to wipe away a tear. She was not going to cry today in front of the Yoders. She would be brave—no matter what. She had prayed fervently for John to recover ever since the accident, but the Lord had not answered yet. At the same time, *Mamm* and Hilda had tried to prepare her for John's possible passing, but she had refused to pay any attention. This was not in stubbornness or in defiance of the Lord's will. She knew that the Lord did what He wanted, but she also knew the Lord heard the cries of the heart. Surely He would hear hers.

No doubt Deacon William would counsel her to be submissive to the Lord's will. And she was submitted. Had she not been baptized yesterday? Of course, Deacon William would mean something else by his words, namely that she stop her prayers for John's recovery. But she couldn't do that while there was breath left in him. She simply couldn't.

And what had Wendell Kaufman meant yesterday after the baptism when he had said, "We must pray for the Lord's will"? She no longer trusted him after that evening at Bishop Ezra's corn-husking. The man spoke out of both sides of his mouth, and his words yesterday doubtless contained a hidden message. Of course Wendell would pray for the Lord's will. They all did, but His will had not been made known yet. She would not assume what the answer was until the way was made clear, and neither should Wendell or anyone else.

Mamm must have known her thoughts because before Laura had left this morning, *Mamm* had warned, "Your heart is clouding your vision, daughter. Let the man go. You must face the truth."

Laura turned her face into the wind. "I love him," she mouthed. "And I will marry him. I will not have that stolen from me." A sob escaped her. "Unless the Lord wills," she whispered. She would have to accept the worst if that happened, but not before.

Laura struggled to calm herself with her hands firmly on the reins. There had been something in Wendell's eyes when he spoke with her yesterday. There had been an interest that Wendell had tried to hide, but she had recognized that look from the past. Wendell once again had designs on her. Not only that, he meant to get his foot in the door while her heart lay wounded. What else could explain his continued attentions and his mixed signals about John's healing?

Laura took a deep breath. Here she went again in her emotional state. She must not imagine things or hold anything against Wendell. He might simply be sympathetic toward her and nothing more. At least she could give the man the benefit of the doubt. Wendell knew she loved John. He had to know that. Nothing had changed there.

Laura pulled back on Maud's reins as the buggy approached the Yoder driveway. Maud lifted her feet high and almost pranced up to the barn. "Stop it," Laura spoke to the horse. "It's inappropriate." But of course Maud paid her no attention.

John's *daett*, Herman, came out of the barn before she could climb down.

"*Goot* morning," he greeted her, his voice subdued. "Brisk, isn't it?"

"*Yah*, Maud's all into it." Laura tried to smile. She took the buggy step with care and began to unfasten the tugs from the buggy shaft.

"John's still the same," Herman said, but he didn't look up. "It's nice of you to come over though, and so early."

"I had to," Laura said. "I…"

"It's okay." Herman's smile was kind. "I'm thankful for the love you've shown my son. Few women would have stood by his side the way you have—through all of this, and with what might still lie ahead. May the Lord bless you for your efforts."

Laura dropped her gaze. Now she was going to cry, and she wasn't even in the house yet. Had she finally found a kindred soul in John's *daett*?

"The Lord will do what is right," Herman continued, his hand resting lightly on Maud's bridle. "I guess you'll be staying most of the day." He offered his kind smile again. "I'll see that Maud's well taken care of." He didn't wait for an answer, but led Maud toward the barn.

Laura collected her bag and made her way up to the front door, where Hilda was already standing. "*Goot* morning," she said. "I've been expecting you."

"*Goot* morning," Laura responded. Her gaze had already moved to the hospital bed set up in the living room.

"There's not been much change. Not like we had hoped for those first few days after the accident," Hilda said. But Laura hardly heard. She hurried to John's bedside and reached for his pale hand.

"John," she whispered, but there was no response.

"I'll be in the kitchen if you want me," Hilda said, her steps fading away.

Laura was alone with John. It wasn't like the other times they'd been together, but still, her heart beat faster. John was here, even if he couldn't respond. Surely he must be able to hear her. She had to believe that. What John needed was sunshine. Laura glanced toward the living room window. Bright streaks of light were streaming past the drapes to fall across the hardwood floor. The hospital bed was on wheels. Did she dare?

Laura hesitated. She had best ask Hilda for help. Laura tiptoed over to the kitchen doorway, and Hilda glanced up with a smile on her face.

"Could you help me?" Laura asked. "John needs…" She stopped. Nothing sounded right. She couldn't order Hilda around in her own house. "The sunshine," she managed. "I think John would enjoy it. Can we wheel him over? He must…" Laura bit off the words and waited.

Hilda's smile had disappeared, but she proceeded to dry her hands on her apron. "I guess the sunshine would do him *goot*. But you know that there is little hope, Laura. John's in a body cast with his back broken in three places, and the swelling in his head still hasn't gone down. And he is unconscious most of the time."

"I know." Laura looked away. *But the Lord can hear our cries*, she wanted to say, but she must be respectful. Hilda loved her son, so her reaction was understandable.

"Come." Hilda's face had softened. "You have a kind heart, and we must not quench your spirit, even when things look hopeless."

"Thank you," Laura whispered. She followed Hilda back to the hospital bed where Hilda unlocked the wheels. With a quick nod from Hilda they began moving the bed slowly toward the living room window. The iron frame creaked and John groaned softly. Hilda gave him only a brief glance and continued on.

"He's okay," Hilda said, as if she read Laura's worried thoughts. "He makes worse sounds than that in his sleep."

They wheeled the bed into the full strength of the morning sunlight. Once the motion stopped, Hilda stepped over to adjust the drapes so that John's face was shadowed. Laura said nothing, but took John's hand again.

"There. That's better," Hilda said. "Call me if you need anything." She then headed back to the kitchen.

Laura squeezed John's hand as the sunlight streamed across his body. Sunlight was *goot* for the soul and for the heart. It must be. Was not the Lord Himself described as the light of the world? He was, and right now they could use plenty of light.

Laura glanced toward the kitchen, where the soft sounds of Hilda's cooking rose and fell. She should offer to help Hilda, and she would soon, but John came first this morning. There would be plenty of time for household duties afterward.

Laura knelt by the bed. The cold in John's hand crept all the way through her, but she pressed on and began to pray. "Dear Lord, I know that I have wronged John and You by my carelessness and intemperate ways. I should never have distracted John that day of the barn-raising, no matter what reasons I thought I had. I said I loved John, and I wanted him to hold me in my arms, and *yah*, I wanted his kisses. Now I have nothing. I have no right to ask for all of that back again. I should have waited for Your proper time and place and for Your will. You know my heart needs cleansing, but please don't take Your anger out on John. Forgive me. Give me another chance. Give me another opportunity to live with John as I ought. I promise to love him always. Please let John walk again. If that's not in Your will, bring John back and I'll still love him. Just let him come back to me. I know that's awful selfish to ask, but please think about my plea. I love him. I really do."

Laura paused as a sob choked her. Soft steps came up behind her, and Laura tried to stand. A hand on her shoulder kept her down. "Don't get up," Hilda's voice said. "Let me pray with you."

Laura buried her face in the quilt as Hilda slid to her knees beside her. The hard cast on John's chest pressed into her face, and the tears came. Hilda was going to pray with her when she had expected a rebuke instead.

Laura reached for Hilda's hand, and she didn't pull away. "Have mercy on my son," Hilda spoke distinctly. "Have mercy. Have mercy, dear Lord. Don't allow my son to linger in this state of suffering. Heal him or take him. Look upon our sorrow and don't give us more than we can bear. John was once so full of life and happiness. We…" Hilda stopped and slowly stood to her feet. "Come, dear. We have said enough. The Lord does not appreciate many words spoken into His ear."

Laura smiled and whispered, "Thank you for praying with me. It means so much."

"You are welcome." Hilda looked away. "Herman prayed for him this morning at the family devotions. Still, we must be prepared to accept what the Lord does."

"I know," Laura agreed.

Hilda wasn't as coldhearted as she seemed at times. She wouldn't have prayed with Laura otherwise. "I'll come help you in the kitchen now," Laura offered.

Hilda's smile was tender. "No, you stay here and spend more time with John. I think you do him *goot*."

As Hilda left for the kitchen, Laura took John's hand again. This time, the warmth startled her.

"John!" she exclaimed. She touched his face. "John!" she repeated. "Can you hear me?"

"Is something wrong?" Hilda asked from the kitchen doorway.

"*Nee.*" Laura looked up. "He just seems a little better."

Compassion filled Hilda's face. She stepped closer to slip her arm around Laura's shoulder. "My dear, that's the danger in praying for what we want. We think it's going to happen, when the Lord may have other plans."

"But his hand is warmer," Laura insisted. "And so is his face."

"He's in the sunshine," Hilda spoke softly. "That's *goot* for him, but we must not allow our faith to falter even when things don't get any better. John's temperature changes all the time."

Hilda gave her another quick hug before returning to the kitchen. No matter what Hilda said, John had improved right before her eyes. The Lord had given her a sign she could hang on to. Just a little sign, but this was a sign. She would not believe otherwise.

"I know you're in there," she whispered near John's ear. "I love you, and you're going to get better. The Lord can heal you if He sees fit. Pray with us, John, and ask. I'll be here for you when you come back. I promise. I'll stand with you. Regardless! I love you, and I'll never stop loving you. Never!"

Laura pulled away and studied John's face. His lips were moving slowly. She bent closer and listened. There was no sound, but she was sure John was praying, just as she asked him. He must have heard her. The Lord would also hear, and He would answer. She would always believe that. She must believe that!

Chapter Fourteen

Later that week Laura was home washing the dishes, taking her time until *Mamm* glanced at her. "You can't take all evening, Laura. *Daett* will be having prayer time soon."

"I know," Laura said. She tried to hurry, but her mind wouldn't stay on her work. This was how things had been all week. With Lydia gone, the house seemed empty and lonely, and on top of that, John hadn't shown any improvement today when she visited him. She had been so sure the Lord had given her a sign on Monday.

"How was John today?" *Mamm* asked, as if reading her thoughts.

"He will be well soon," Laura said, her head down.

Mamm sighed. "Are you sure, Laura? Are you surrendered to the Lord's will? I don't think you are. In fact, you're coming close to questioning the Lord. Think of what danger that places you in."

"The Lord doesn't want John to lie there like a vegetable and never walk again!" The words exploded out of Laura's mouth.

Mamm stepped closer to slip her arm around Laura's shoulder. "Come, daughter. Let's go pray with *Daett*. We can finish the dishes later."

"But the water will be cold," Laura protested.

"It's already cold," *Mamm* said. "You can add hot water when we come back."

Laura nodded and dried her hands. *Mamm* was right. She did need prayer. Just like John did.

"Come," *Mamm* said, giving Laura's arm a gentle pull. Laura gave in as *Mamm* led the way into the living room, pausing at the stair door to call up, "Nelson, Lester, prayer time."

Laura found a seat on the couch while her brothers' footsteps thundered down the stairs. At least someone in the house had energy left to spare.

Lester flopped down in his chair with only a brief glance in Laura's direction. Nelson sat beside her on the couch and smiled her way before announcing, "Oh, by the way, Wendell's coming over tonight."

Laura gasped, and everyone ignored her, which meant they all knew of Wendell's plan. Wendell wasn't coming to see Nelson. Of that she was sure. Was this the real reason *Mamm* had hurried her out to the living room for prayer time?

"Let's pray, *Daett*," *Mamm* said.

Daett hesitated for a moment before he knelt by his rocker. With her throat constricted, Laura couldn't speak, so she abandoned her protest and knelt. *Daett's* voice rose and fell as he recited the familiar German words, but Laura's mind raced with the startling announcement of Wendell's arrival this evening. What did the man want with her? Whatever it was, she must maintain her dignity.

When the prayer was completed, she would demand to know what excuse Wendell had used for his visit. Wendell had no right to intrude on her life. He had lost out to John, and now he should accept reality. John was going to walk again and get better. Her heart was not available. She had loved John from her school days, and Wendell had never stood a realistic chance with her even before she dated John. Wendell knew all of this, which could only mean he considered John's case hopeless and perhaps even fatal.

Laura suppressed a sob about the same time *Daett* pronounced the amen.

Nelson was on his feet in a flash, but Laura still caught his elbow near the stair door. "What is going on with Wendell?"

"Not here," he whispered. "Up there." He motioned with his head.

Laura bit back her words and followed him up the stairs. Nelson opened the door of her bedroom and stepped inside to wait until Laura followed. She turned to confront him by the dresser. "What does Wendell want with me? The nerve of that man!"

"Calm down," Nelson ordered. "Wendell's not coming with any ulterior motive. He wants to talk with me about hunting strategies this fall."

Laura didn't back down. "You know you could talk about that after the Sunday service."

Nelson's grin was lopsided. "Maybe, but then others might hear. We want the biggest buck we can find kept to ourselves."

Laura glared at him. "Then why will this evening include time spent speaking with me?"

Nelson shrugged. "You don't have to talk to him."

"You are pushing the limit," Laura told him. "All of you are. And for the record, John *will* get better, and he *will* walk again. So let me be clear. Even if Wendell manages to corner me tonight—with your and *Mamm*'s help, of course—I will not change my mind."

Nelson looked at her with pity. "Okay, but just remember, Wendell is a decent man...and he's healthy and available."

Laura kept silent. Was she wrong to be praying for a miracle? The human heart could easily be exalted if the Lord answered her prayer. Everyone knew that. Didn't Bishop Ezra remind the congregation often of this danger? Better to keep one's requests few and the heart grateful for what was given. But she had dared to ask, and not only ask, but ask for the best. No wonder her family was concerned, along with all of John's family. When Laura visited today, Hilda had worn the same look on her face as *Mamm* often had. The two mothers had already accepted what she couldn't. In the meantime John wasn't any better—but at least he hadn't passed.

Laura retraced her steps down the stairs, and *Daett* glanced up to give her a warm smile. "Come sit," he said, motioning toward the couch.

"But *Mamm*…" Laura protested. "The dishes…"

"*Mamm* understands," *Daett* said with the same smile.

Laura winced but took the side of the couch nearest *Daett*. This must be *Daett*'s version of speaking-to-my-stubborn-daughter time.

"How is John?" *Daett* asked in his kind tone.

"Not well." Laura didn't look at him. "But he will get better."

Daett cleared his throat. "Laura, surely you know that the Lord has His own plans in these matters. Are you hanging on too tight? Perhaps hoping for things that cannot happen?"

"The Lord can do anything He wishes," Laura declared. Who could find fault with that statement?"

"*Yah*," *Daett* agreed. "He can, but it's our hearts that are the problem. Pride is so easily acquired. I hear you have asked for a miracle from the Lord."

"Well, I don't know if it would be called a miracle," Laura said, "but I have asked that John would get better. What's wrong with that?"

Daett appeared troubled. "You take too much upon yourself, Laura. Is this because of how the accident happened? Do you still blame yourself for distracting John?"

Laura studied the hardwood floor. The truth was she didn't know what to say anymore. Everything about this affair was blurred and ran together.

"I heard that you led John away from his work and kissed him behind the shed only moments before he fell," *Daett* continued. "But you've always been impulsive, Laura. You've always reached for the best, and for what you've wanted for yourself. I don't fault you for kissing John, but it's how you do things. Could you also be out of line with your prayers right now?"

"John's *daett* is praying with me," Laura declared, unable to think of anything else to say.

"Herman?" *Daett* looked astonished. "Herman has been praying with you?"

"*Nee*, of course not," Laura said. "But from the few words he's spoken with me, I know his heart is with me."

Daett appeared skeptical. "I have heard no such thing. Herman's words to me at the services have been completely surrendered to what the Lord wills."

"And so are mine. I will accept what the Lord gives." Laura didn't know what else to say, so she stood and said, "I'll go help *Mamm*."

Daett didn't object.

As she entered the kitchen, *Mamm* met her with a hopeful look. "It didn't do any *goot*," Laura said.

Mamm's face fell. "You have us all so worried, Laura. Why can't you be sensible about this?"

"Hoping for John to get better is being sensible."

Mamm didn't respond but motioned toward the fresh hot water she had run in the sink. Soapsuds rose above the dishes, and Laura plunged her hands in. From outside, she could hear the sound of a buggy in the driveway followed by Nelson's quick footsteps down the stairs. Laura rattled the dishes as if in protest, but that wouldn't help. She would have to speak with Wendell. Her family would see to that.

As if *Mamm* had the same thoughts, she hurried out of the kitchen. Laura soon heard murmuring in the living room. Nelson must have brought Wendell inside. Laura ignored them and kept her back turned to the kitchen doorway. Maybe she was mistaken and Wendell would soon go upstairs to speak with Nelson and not bother her. She desperately hoped so.

Laura rinsed a dish and lifted it onto the drying rack. The dish clicked against the others, the sound loud in the still kitchen. A man behind her cleared his throat and Laura jumped.

"Sorry to startle you," Wendell said. "But your *mamm* told me I could find you in here. She suggested I could speak with you here and…" His words trailed off.

Laura forced herself to turn around and greet him. "*Goot* evening."

"*Goot* evening. And how are you doing?" His smile widened.

"Okay, I guess. Nelson said you were coming over to talk about hunting for the biggest buck in the community."

"Oh, that." Wendell grinned and took a seat at the kitchen table as if he belonged there. "I'll be chatting with Nelson in a little bit about that big buck, but first I…" He stopped, apparently unable or unwilling to state the obvious. "How are things going with John?" he finished.

"Not *goot*," she said. "But I'm praying for the Lord to heal John, just like you once prayed with me." There! She might as well come right out and say it.

"That's a little *Englisha*, isn't it?" he asked, and they both knew the answer to that question. "I was a little out of hand that night," he went on. "I was overwrought like everyone else was at the beginning, but my *goot* sense has prevailed now."

"Maybe Amish people can also experience miracles." She gave him a sweet smile. "Maybe John will wake up fully and walk again. I love him, you know."

Wendell didn't appear worried. "I don't doubt that you do. You have a large heart, Laura. You'll make some man a *goot frau* someday, but you must accept things for what they are. You must come to your senses like I did after that first evening. The Lord has His own plans, you know."

Laura busied herself with the dishes. She didn't have the energy for another of these conversations. They would go nowhere anyway.

"I want you to know that our prayers and concerns are with you, Laura," Wendell finally said. "The whole community is involved in this, and with John's family. They hope only for the best."

"Thank you," Laura managed. What else was there to say? She couldn't act stuck-up.

"The Lord is working His will, you know," Wendell continued. "Maybe not in ways that you think, but over half of John's hospital bill has already been paid. As you probably know, Deacon William sent out letters to the other districts and to the home community in Wayne County. We expect the Lord to supply fully for the need before long, and the hospital has agreed to a sizable reduction in their fees. That can only happen with the Lord's help. Those are the kinds of miracles our people believe in."

"I suppose so," Laura said toward her dishwater.

Wendell nodded. "I'm glad to hear that your heart is open to instruction, Laura. I know your parents have already told you this, but perhaps it's easier to hear from someone else. You have to place John's care in the Lord's hands and leave him there. John may pass away soon, and if he doesn't, he likely will never walk again or get out of bed. That will mean some adjustments for you, which should begin sooner and not later. That's what I have to say, and hopefully you will take it to heart."

"I will seek to surrender my will to the Lord's," Laura forced herself to say. She managed a weak smile, more to get rid of the man than anything.

Wendell rose and offered a final warning. "The heart is deceitful above all things, Laura. I'm grateful the Lord has granted me the privilege of guiding yours through this difficult time. I'll be in touch again."

Laura didn't protest. That would have started Wendell up again. She wanted this conversation to end. She wanted to slip upstairs and crawl under the bed quilt and cry herself to sleep. She wanted…

With a quick nod Wendell was gone, and Laura dipped her hands in the water and washed a dish slowly, going around and around and around until she was using only her fingers to finish the task.

Chapter Fifteen

Darkness was falling on Saturday evening as Nancy slipped out of her back door to glide across the yard. With a quick look in each direction she hurried south. When moments later the headlights of an *Englisha* automobile lit the woods around her, Nancy held her breath, but the car didn't slow down. Few buggies drove on her road at this time of the evening, and if one did pass by, she would wave and smile. From all appearances, she was just the community's Amish schoolteacher out for a late night stroll. No one could know her real intentions or see her heart caught in an impossible situation. Twice now she had been dealt this hand in love.

First with Yost Mast all those years ago, when he decided that another woman fit his needs better. She couldn't fault the man. Look at the splendid *kinner* Lavina had given him. Yost had two sons and two daughters, and the daughters were lovely twins. She could not have done half as well.

Now there was Charles, the *Englisha* man she had met. Charles was impossible. Charles was forbidden. Charles could not be, and yet she was drawn to him as she had been to Yost. Why had this happened to her twice? Why would love be denied to her again?

Nancy forced herself to walk faster. Perhaps if she hurried she would regain her *goot* sense and return to the house where she belonged. Maybe then Charles would eventually take her no for an answer. Surely he was a man who respected heartfelt feelings, even when he didn't understand them. If she could muster the same necessary courage to tell him not to call on her again, all would be well.

On the other hand, Charles clearly knew of the love that had sprung up in her heart for him, and he might not give up his marriage proposal that easily. But how could she accept him? Deacon William would visit the Saturday evening after the news broke, and she would be in the *bann* before two more weeks had passed. Could she stand that? Was her love for Charles enough to weather such a storm?

Nancy set her face. If she knew the answer to that question, comfort might settle in her heart. Could she trust a man again? She had been in love before, and that had not been enough. Yost had often held her hand back in those days when they dated and walked together, side by side. Yet he must have known from the beginning that their relationship wouldn't work. Yost had led her on. For two long years she had been driven home in his buggy on Sunday evenings, trying to convince herself that Yost would soon propose, but deep down she had known that he would choose someone else.

When Yost broke off the relationship, he had been kind. She could still remember his words. "I have loved you, Nancy, and your presence has been enjoyable these evenings we have spent together. I want to thank you for them. I respect you highly, but I think the Lord has someone else in mind for you—someone who can be a better husband than I would have been. Don't you agree?"

She had nodded, but that had been more to hide the tears than anything else, and to shelter the gaping wound in her heart.

"I will always remember our time together," Yost had said. But of course he hadn't. How could Yost have remembered if he went on to marry someone else? She had never been able to take that step, even when other men had asked to take her home from the hymn singing. "I'm committed to school teaching," she had told them with a gentle smile.

Only that wasn't the truth. She was committed to a memory of what once was. Or perhaps of what could have been. Nancy lifted her face toward the sky and wept. How could she ever trust a man again? The sweep of the stars overhead stung through her tears, and she looked down at the shadowy blacktop again. She would go back to the house. Charles had given up his chance tonight. If he couldn't be on time, it was best to end this. She couldn't trust this rush of emotion, this love that swelled up in her heart, just as it once had done for Yost. Only the avalanche was worse this time, as if to make up for all those lost years.

She would harden her heart and do the right thing. Wasn't that how duties were done? One clenched one's teeth and performed. She would perform tomorrow at the Sunday service. At least she would have a clear conscience for once. Wouldn't that be a relief? She could offer Deacon William a steady handshake and a sincere smile. The man knew she had strayed in her heart. She was sure of that. But Deacon William had no evidence, and he certainly didn't imagine the depth to which she had fallen.

Nancy quickened her pace back toward the faint outline of the small house in the distance. Soon the winter's snow would blast across the countryside, and she wouldn't be able to take these long evening walks. But what did it matter? Nothing mattered when the heart was broken.

Moments later headlights filled the woods on either side of Nancy, and the sound of an *Englisha* vehicle rumbled behind her. She stepped to the side of the road and kept her head down. The car slowed. Nancy held her breath as her mind raced. What if Charles had come after all? Why else would the vehicle stop? And this after all her resolutions. Why didn't she run for the house and lock the door? Charles wouldn't pursue her. He was too much of a gentleman for that.

"Nancy!" Charles's firm voice rose above the noise of his pickup truck. "Get in!"

Nancy let out her breath and reached for the door handle. She opened the door and climbed in quickly.

"I'm sorry for being late," Charles said. "But looks like I made it just in time." He grinned and didn't wait for an answer as he sped off past Nancy's small house.

Nancy looked out through the windshield, where the headlights bounced wildly on the passing landscape.

"I'm sometimes a little late," Charles continued. "I always try to make it on time." He laughed. "I'm glad you're with me tonight, Nancy. I've looked forward to this all week."

Nancy kept silent. He knew her feelings and why she was hesitating.

"So where shall we eat tonight now that you are on my turf?" Charles asked.

"Somewhere far, far away," Nancy muttered.

Charles chuckled. "How about in Potsdam? Is that far enough?"

Nancy nodded, but didn't look at him.

"No buggies there," Charles teased. "You can relax, dear."

Nancy took a deep breath and reached for his hand. "Charles…" she began, but stopped. It was of no use. She couldn't get the words out.

Charles tried to comfort her. "You'll feel better once we're out of Amish country."

Nancy glanced at him and tried to relax. Now that she was with

Charles, the worst was over. No matter where they went tonight, the fact that she was in Charles's pickup truck—if the news ever reached Deacon William's ears—would be trouble enough.

"Maybe you'll enjoy the evening a little," Charles said, his tone hopeful.

She gave him a soft smile, and his grin spread from ear to ear. "That's better. I knew you'd come around."

Nancy looked away. To enjoy an evening with Charles, she must forget about everything else—Deacon William and the community and her past with Yost. She was with Charles, and she did love the man. Why not act like it tonight? She had already transgressed seriously. A few smiles and kind words shared with Charles couldn't make things any worse. Maybe she could even believe that a miracle might happen and she could marry him someday.

Charles remained silent as he navigated the back roads and drove through the town of DeKalb. She had rarely come this far east. She only drove to Canton when it was absolutely necessary. Potsdam was beyond that and would be well out of the community limits. But she would not think about such things tonight—at least until Charles dropped her off at home later.

"So how was your week?" Nancy asked, once Charles had turned onto Highway 11.

He smiled. "About the same. Quiet for this time of the year. How's that boy from the accident? The one who fell."

"John Yoder is his name." Nancy gazed out into the night. "Not too well, but he's still alive, which is a miracle. They have him home now."

"Really? This soon with his injuries?"

Nancy frowned. "We don't carry insurance, and the bill was high enough already. Without hope offered by the doctors, why stay any longer in the hospital?"

"But he's getting better?"

Nancy winced. "He's not dead, if that's better. Many from the community think it would be best if John passed rather than spend his days a cripple or worse. His girlfriend, Laura, stays close by his side when she can. That's probably what's keeping him around, which may not be for the best. But who are we to know what the Lord wills?"

"Love can do strange things," Charles mused. "Don't ever underestimate it. Look at me, for example. I…" He stopped. "Sorry, I won't go there right now."

Nancy reached for his hand and held it tightly. "I know, but—"

Charles hushed her. "Don't say it. Let's just enjoy tonight."

So they were of one mind on that subject at least. Nancy held her grip on Charles's hand. She wanted to hold on and never let go, but that was impossible, even if she agreed to marry the man— which she couldn't. She simply couldn't. Nancy forced the words out. "It's kind of you to take me all the way up to Potsdam, Charles. You don't have to."

"Of course I have to." He grinned. "Your very breath is my command."

Nancy allowed a smile to spread across her face.

Charles squeezed her hand. "I knew this would do you good."

Nancy said nothing, but his close presence swept over her. She felt safe here, even though she wasn't. How could one be in such severe danger and also be at peace? But then again, maybe she wasn't in danger at all. Maybe the community had things all wrong, and Charles's world was the right one. The thought brought Nancy's head up with a start.

Charles glanced over at her. "Did I say something wrong?"

"No!" Nancy stilled her rapid breathing and looked away. "I just…"

"I was only teasing," Charles told her.

"I know."

Charles's voice was gentle. "It's okay. I understand."

Nancy sat up again. "You are so…" She hesitated.

"Charming and softhearted?"

Nancy smiled. "*Yah*, and I'm the one who is the problem."

Charles stopped her. "Remember! Just you and me and the world passing by tonight. Let's not think about anything else."

The pickup slowed as Charles approached Canton. He stopped at a light and smiled down at Nancy. "I know it's difficult and that I haven't been too helpful. I'm sorry about pushing things too fast when you asked me over the other night for supper. You gave me such an important piece of your life, and I took advantage of the moment in haste. I hope—"

"It's not your fault," she interrupted. "But let's not talk about us. Tell me about your work this week."

He grinned. "Okay. Let's see. We had that run into Heuvelton for an accident. A guy drove a little too fast into town and couldn't stop for Highway 812. Clipped his neighbor's car, but no one was hurt."

"Older fellow?" Nancy asked.

Charles nodded. "The state police wrote the fellow a ticket, I think. The judge will probably pull his license, but then again, who knows when one is too old to drive the roads? We'll all get there eventually, I suppose."

"I know," Nancy agreed, and her mind drifted. She could see herself old and decrepit in her buggy. Her teaching days would be past by then, and she would be alone. There would be no grandchildren gathered around her, because she had never…

"Penny for your thoughts?" Charles teased.

Nancy hid her face and Charles laughed. "There is still time to marry me, Nancy. All you have to do is say yes."

"I thought we weren't talking about that tonight," she whispered.

"Sorry," he said. "There I go again." He accelerated out of Canton toward Potsdam. "But the offer still stands."

Nancy took his hand again. Charles was a gentleman, and she was in love with him. Why else did she take such great risks? Maybe the Lord would work some miracle so she could accept Charles's gracious offer. But how? She couldn't imagine.

Chapter Sixteen

On a Monday morning in early October, Lydia opened up Uncle Henry's stand at the first blush of dawn. A hush hung over the woods as the sun's first rays pushed skyward and birds chirped their cheerful songs along the wood line.

Lydia rubbed her hands against her cheeks until warmth crept back into her fingers. She was ready for the first sale of the day. The locals who frequented the stand came early in the morning to make their selections. Mr. Ferris stopped by before he left for his office in Ogdensburg, so he was due any minute. Mrs. Chambers came about the same time on Mondays and Wednesdays. Between the two of them, they made large purchases that made Uncle Henry happy when he stopped by to check on sales.

"I knew I picked you for a *goot* reason," he told Lydia. "You bring in the bees like the apple blossoms in spring."

Lydia stretched her arms toward the sunrise. She was no apple blossom, but Uncle Henry was kind to say so. The truth was, she had plenty of problems. The worst was her continued desire for Milton's attentions in spite of his attempts to lure her into jumping the fence with him. To complicate matters even more, the longer they worked together, the further her heart turned toward the man.

And Milton was showing every sign of having the same feelings for her. She used to dream and long for this day. *Mamm* had wanted her to find a man she could love and marry. She should be on her knees thanking the Lord for this gift, only she wasn't—not with his talk about leaving the community.

Why were her heart and head in such conflict? This wasn't supposed to happen to her. In her wildest dreams she had never imagined that she would fall for a man who so openly planned to jump the fence. Maybe this was what had overcome Nancy. What else could explain Nancy's becoming infatuated with an *Englisha* man? If Nancy, who was so solid and faithful, had fallen so far, what danger was Lydia in?

Lydia shivered and drew her coat tight around her. The brisk air had braced her a moment ago, but the chill seemed sinister now—as if its hand could penetrate the warmest coat and the most steadfast heart. Here she had been worried about Nancy when she should have prayed for her own safety.

Lydia sent a quick prayer skyward. "Help me, dear Lord."

Around the bend of the road the headlights of an *Englisha* automobile appeared. The vehicle slowed to a stop, and Mrs. Chambers scrambled out with a large basket in each hand.

"Good morning," the woman shouted before she had shut the car door.

"*Goot* morning," Lydia replied with a quick wave. "You're out bright and early."

"And what about you?" Mrs. Chambers said with a laugh. "You Amish restore my faith in mankind. Makes me feel like a spring chicken too." Mrs. Chambers shifted her baskets. "Puts the vim and vigor back into these old bones to see you young ones taking on the burdens of the world so willingly. Why, more than half the earth is still asleep at this time of the morning."

"Mr. Ferris will be along soon," Lydia offered. "He's another early bird."

Mrs. Chambers snorted. "That old codger. I tried to beat him here this morning. He always takes the best pickings." Mrs. Chambers set down her baskets and began her selections. She conspiratorially leaned closer to Lydia. "But don't be telling him that. He will do his best to beat me on Wednesday morning if he smells a whiff of competition in the air."

Lydia chuckled. "Looks like that's happened already. Here he comes now."

Mr. Ferris's automobile bounced to a stop in front of Mrs. Chambers's car. This elicited another snort from Mrs. Chambers. "He had to park there, just like a man. Never can be in second place for anything."

Lydia hid her smile. Mrs. Chambers was quite fond of Mr. Ferris—unless Lydia missed her guess. She had picked up from bits of conversation that neither of them had partners at present.

"Good morning!" Mr. Ferris cheerfully waved when he got out of his car. He shut his door with a loud bang.

"*Goot* morning," Lydia shouted over the grumbling. "How are you this fine morning, Mr. Ferris?"

A pleased look spread over his face. "How could I be anything but very happy with such a cheerful face to greet me at the produce stand? I do declare you are practically sparkling this morning, Lydia. You've never looked prettier."

"Don't you be trying that silver tongue of yours on a young Amish woman," Mrs. Chambers snapped. "She's not falling for it— are you, Lydia?"

Lydia laughed and didn't answer. The banter was not intended for her. Mrs. Chambers wanted Mr. Ferris's silver tongue directed toward her. That was more likely.

Mr. Ferris chuckled. "You're looking mighty fine yourself, Elsie. I see you beat me here, so is there anything left?"

Mrs. Chambers beamed. "At least you're now trying your charm on someone who knows you well enough."

"And with as little success," Mr. Ferris quipped.

"That's right," Mrs. Chambers agreed, but she was clearly pleased.

"So what *is* left for me?" Mr. Ferris turned his attention to Lydia. "You know I didn't mean to offend you earlier."

"You did nothing of the sort," Lydia assured him. "Your words were kind. You know I'm comely enough."

"Now I've heard everything," Mrs. Chambers said. "The girl is a beauty, and so modest."

"You should try modesty yourself," Mr. Ferris told Mrs. Chambers with a sideways glance.

"I will take that tactic under advisement when I have more worthy objects to try it on." Mrs. Chambers glared at him.

Mr. Ferris laughed roundly. "You would think she hates me, Lydia, but she adores me. Absolutely adores me."

"Men!" Mrs. Chambers muttered. "They could not be more conceited."

"Why don't I help you with those baskets?" Mr. Ferris offered, seeing Mrs. Chambers digging in her purse for money to pay Lydia.

"Here, then. Hold this," Mrs. Chambers said, handing the man her full-to-the-brim baskets.

Lydia hid her smile as she totaled the amount on a small tablet under the countertop. She submitted the total when she finished, and Mrs. Chambers paid with cash.

"Shall we put these in your trunk?" Mr. Ferris asked, leading the way to her car.

"Yes, that's right," Mrs. Chambers said, her face glowing.

Lydia watched in amusement as Mr. Ferris set the baskets in her trunk. He used great care, she noticed, all while keeping up a steady stream of conversation. She couldn't hear what they said, but the words seemed to come easily enough. Mrs. Chambers even stood by her car door, and the two continued to talk after the trunk was closed.

Lydia's attention turned to the sound of Milton's buggy rattling into view, his horse sending streams of white breath into the morning air.

Lydia waved as Milton pulled to a stop near the stand. He leaned out of the buggy to shout, "*Goot* morning, Lydia. You sure look mighty cheerful this morning."

"And a *goot* morning to you," Lydia shouted back.

Milton's smile grew. "You *are* cheerful this morning. Does it come from being around such high-class *Englisha* people?" Milton motioned toward the car with his head.

"I'm just glad to see you," Lydia said. "I think those two are in love. Just think about that. Perhaps Uncle Henry's produce stand brought two lonely people together who would otherwise have passed each other by."

Milton laughed. "That's a nice thought, but you could be dreaming. Do you want to guess what I did this weekend?"

"I wouldn't dare." Lydia lowered her voice. "I do know you should be in the baptismal class that's coming up this fall, Milton."

Milton groaned. "Come on. Don't lecture me, Lydia. It's not becoming, especially on such a cheerful morning."

"Sorry," Lydia muttered.

"You still haven't guessed what I did over the weekend," Milton said.

She forced herself to look at him. "Okay, tell me."

"I bought a car," Milton whispered. "An *Englisha* car. It's just an old junker, but it runs. Our neighbor's boy had it for sale for the longest time, sitting in his yard, and I finally made him a deal. I think he was glad…" Milton paused. "Don't look at me like that, Lydia. I'm in my *rumspringa* and can buy a car if I want to."

"But…" She bit off the words. They wouldn't help anyway.

"I can do what I want," Milton repeated. "And you'll be going for a drive with me soon. You'll enjoy yourself, Lydia. I can even bring my junker over tonight after dark. Could you sneak out of your uncle's house for an hour?"

Lydia forced herself to breathe evenly. "I will do no such thing, Milton. I was baptized. You know that. You were there, and you should be joining the baptismal class this fall yourself instead of buying a car."

"You already said that," Milton said as he unloaded his buggy. "You know I'm not ready to settle down, and neither were you."

"I was baptized," Lydia protested. "What do you think that means?"

Milton appeared unrepentant. "Even so, I still say you're not ready to settle down. I know you better than you know yourself, Lydia."

Her hands trembled, but Lydia steadied them on the rough-hewn boards of the stand. Milton's words stung. She had always thought herself sure and unshakable when it came to the ways of the community, but her heart had ways of its own. Hadn't it fallen in love with Milton of its own accord, and wasn't it now persisting in that direction? Maybe she *would* give in by the time the day was over and sneak out for a ride with Milton in his car tonight.

"Do you have a driver's license?" she asked.

Milton grinned from ear to ear. "Who needs a driver's license for these back roads? I'll stay on the main drag for only a few miles."

Lydia opened her mouth to protest, but Milton jiggled the reins and dashed back up Uncle Henry's lane with his horse and buggy.

"Boyfriend of yours?" Mr. Ferris asked, and Lydia jumped. He chuckled. "I didn't mean to startle you, dear, but I have my things ready."

Lydia's face reddened. She had totally failed to notice Mr. Ferris, wrapped up as she had been in Milton. Thankfully this was Mr. Ferris and not a new customer who would gain a bad impression of the service at Uncle Henry's produce stand.

"He looks like a nice young man," Mr. Ferris said as Lydia hurried to add up his total. "He works here, doesn't he?"

Lydia tried to smile. "*Yah*." She gave Mr. Ferris his final sum.

Mr. Ferris seemed quite sympathetic to Lydia—as if he understood young people and life in general. "I thought so," he said. He paid and left with both arms filled with produce. Once at his car he set the bags in the backseat, and with a quick wave he climbed into his car. When he pulled out on Highway 184, he paused as a buggy driven at a rapid pace approached from the other direction. He waited until the driver had turned in Uncle Henry's lane before he continued north.

Lydia studied the buggy. It was Deacon Mose from Uncle Henry's district. *What is he doing out here this morning?* The deacon hadn't even waved to her as he raced by the stand and into Uncle Henry's driveway.

Another car, followed by another, pulled in and distracted Lydia. As she hurried about to serve everyone, a soft touch on her arm brought her up short. Uncle Henry cleared his throat beside her.

"I'm sorry!" Lydia exclaimed. "I didn't hear you come up, but we had lots of customers this morning, and—"

Uncle Henry's sober face stopped her. "Come, Lydia." Her uncle tugged on her arm. "Come over here and sit down."

She noticed Deacon Mose in the shadows of the produce stand, standing with his eyes downcast. Lydia reached for the planks on top of the stand to steady herself. Surely something awful had happened. Had John died?

"I don't know how to break this to you," Uncle Henry said, "but Deacon Mose just brought me the news. My sister—your *mamm*... you must come." Uncle Henry's grip loosened on her arm. "You'll go with us. Millie and I are driving over right now."

"But, but..." Lydia tried to find the words. "What happened?"

Uncle Henry hung his head. "Come with us. Deacon Mose will take care of the stand until others can arrive, and Milton's here to help. We must go, Lydia. Your *mamm* didn't awaken this morning from her sleep. She passed on in the night. She complained of a severe backache last night, and your *Daett* gave her a back massage. They thought that took care of the problem, but it obviously didn't. Your *mamm* must have experienced a heart attack."

Lydia clung to Uncle Henry's arm as the world around her spun. *Mamm* was dead! That wasn't possible! And yet Deacon Mose wouldn't bring such news if it wasn't true.

"I'm sorry for your loss," Deacon Mose told her as they walked toward the lane, but Lydia barely heard the words.

Chapter Seventeen

"Whoa there," Uncle Henry called to his horse. He pulled the buggy up beside the Mast barn, where several other buggies from the community were already parked. On the ride over, Lydia had imagined they would arrive and everything would be normal. It would have been a false alarm. But now, seeing the buggies, she knew it was true. But how could it be? How could *Mamm* be gone, and so quickly?

Uncle Henry slowly climbed out of the buggy with Millie and Lydia following him.

"I'll go with you into the house," Millie whispered to Lydia.

Uncle Henry nodded his approval as they left him to unhitch.

As she walked up to the house with her aunt, Lydia's mind raced. This was her home—she had been born here and played on this lawn all of her childhood. *Mamm* had always been around some-where. Now *Mamm* was gone. *Mamm* would never see any of her grandchildren on this side of eternity. The tears came for the first time, and Millie put her arm around Lydia. Someone opened the front door for them, and they entered the house. All was silent in the living room, where people were seated on chairs along the wall.

When Laura appeared in her vision, the two embraced to weep silently.

"I'm sorry I wasn't here," Lydia whispered into her twin's ear.

"You couldn't help it," Laura replied.

They moved to one side of the room and stood side by side in silence as the clock ticked loudly on the living room wall. Several of the gathered women also came forward to embrace Lydia.

"We're so sorry about this," Bishop Ezra's *frau*, Rose, said. "Your *mamm* was such a sweet woman and a blessing to all of us."

"You're not the only one who mourns," Deacon William's *frau*, Elizabeth, added. "We have all suffered a great loss today, but heaven has gained a saint. We must submit to the will of the Lord."

"*Yah*," Lydia agreed, though she didn't feel submitted right now. Hopefully that would come later. All things must be given into the Lord's hands. She knew that. How could they live otherwise?

"Come." Laura tugged on Lydia's arm. "Let me show you the bedroom."

"But *Mamm*'s not here yet, is she?" Lydia asked.

"No," Laura said. "Her body will be brought back later. I wanted you to see…" Laura's voice caught.

Lydia followed without resistance. Laura wanted to spend time with her where their *mamm* had last been on this earth. She should have thought of this herself. Lydia reached over to hold Laura's hand as they walked through the bedroom door. Stillness hung heavy in the room. The quilt looked as if it had been tossed back on the bed in a haphazard fashion. Lydia reached out to straighten one end.

"Leave it as it is," Laura said. "It looks like our lives now, *fahuddled* and confused."

Lydia pulled back her hand to stand beside Laura again. A creak on the hardwood floor behind them announced the entrance of

Elizabeth and Rose. The two women stood on each side of the twins and slipped their arms around them.

"We must weep, but we must not question," Rose reminded them.

"Amen," Elizabeth agreed. She glanced in Lydia's direction. "You should go see your *daett* in the barn. Nelson and Lester are out there with him. He's taking this hard and blames himself. He thinks he should have gone for help last night when your *mamm's* back pain came on her."

"I was here and didn't think of it being a heart attack," Laura said. "He did nothing wrong."

"We should still go see him." Lydia motioned her sister toward the door.

Laura came with her willingly through the living room. Bent heads and a few sad smiles from the women greeted them as they made their way outside, where some men were clustered around the barn door. Out on Lead Mine Road, Deacon William was directing traffic as more buggies poured into the driveway. Lydia hurried on, and the men nodded their condolences as the sisters passed by. Bishop Ezra stepped away from the others to open the barn door for them. He gave them a weary smile, but said nothing.

From near the horse stalls the sound of a man's sobs rose and fell. Laura whispered, "What are we to say to him? I've already said what I could."

"We'll just be with him," Lydia replied. The sound disturbed her, as it had disturbed her sister. They had never heard *Daett* weep like this before. Nelson and Lester looked up to greet them as the two girls approached their brothers.

"You have come," Nelson said, standing and motioning toward *Daett's* bent figure in one of the far stalls. Both girls hurried to their father, and Lydia cried out, "*Daett.*" His sobs ceased, and he slowly raised his face.

"It's not your fault!" Lydia and Laura sat down on either side of him.

Fresh tears formed on *Daett*'s face. "I bear plenty of blame, Lydia. I should have known it was more than a simple backache. But now your *mamm*'s gone."

Lydia slipped her arm around *Daett*'s shoulders, and Laura did the same. There was nothing more to say. *Daett* would have to mourn in his own way. They could be a comfort simply with their presence. That was the way of the community.

How long they sat there, Lydia didn't know. *Daett*'s cries eventually subsided. Lester finally cleared his throat and said, "I have some chores to finish." When he moved away, no one objected. Lester would find out soon—if he didn't already know—that someone else would take care of chores and whatever needed doing until after the funeral. But likely her brother needed time alone. They all needed time alone, which would come soon enough. But for now, *Mamm*'s burial lay ahead of them.

Daett struggled to his feet. "I had best wait inside until…" He extended his hand, unable to finish his thought, and then found his way slowly across the barn floor. Lydia stayed with him until they reached the door, where she turned back to wait for Laura. The two followed *Daett* a few steps behind him. Several of the newly arrived women joined them for the walk back to the house, and then stayed with them once they were inside the living room again.

There wasn't much that could be done while they waited for the body to be returned. Lydia wanted to busy herself so the moments would pass quicker, but her duty at the moment was to the customs of the community. They existed for a reason. She must stay still and mourn. Work could be a cover-up for sorrow and hinder the Lord's extended grace for their family's grief.

Deacon William soon appeared at the front door and motioned for them to come outside. Lydia stood up before *Daett* did and helped him rise. He would be strong again once this was over, but today she would help him. Life would go on. It had to. Lydia almost whispered the words to *Daett* as she helped him out the front door, but his attention was fixed on the black hearse parked in the driveway. *Mamm's* earthly remains had been brought home.

Daett tried to hurry forward but stumbled. Lydia caught his arm, and Laura appeared on the other side to help. Together they held *Daett* while the men slid the wooden coffin out of the hearse. The *Englisha* man who had driven the hearse was dressed in a dark blue suit, and he whispered to Deacon William as the men carried the coffin. Lydia couldn't hear what the two said, but Deacon William must have assured the man that everything would be handled from then on by the community. The *Englisha* caretakers in the area were not always used to the customs of the Amish. Usually they didn't object once they had fulfilled their legal duties.

"Thank you very much," Deacon William said aloud this time. "If you send the bill to me, I'll see that the family takes care of it."

The *Englisha* man nodded and moved off. Lydia held *Daett's* arm as the coffin moved past them and toward the house. Thankfully Nelson and Lester appeared to take over, and Lydia and Laura stepped back. Laura walked beside her sister as they followed their brothers and *Daett* back to the house.

The coffin was moved straight into the bedroom, and the bed was slid to one side. Once the coffin was set up and the lid unfastened, Deacon William swung it open. He leaned in to adjust something. When he finished, Deacon William motioned toward the bedroom door, and everyone except the family stepped outside. Nelson and Lester helped *Daett* forward. He struggled out of their grasp, and the boys waited as *Daett* approached the coffin. After his grief in the barn, *Daett* now stood with a bowed head in front of the body, apparently wept out. He reached inside for *Mamm's* hand, and they all waited as *Daett's* lips moved silently. When *Daett* finished, Lydia nudged Nelson's arm. He stepped closer. Lester did the same, and they all gathered around the coffin.

Daett began to speak aloud. "You have been a *goot frau* to me, Lavina. You loved me as only you could. I never had any complaints, not even one. Maybe that's why you were needed over on the other side. You were a saint even while you walked on this earth, and yet…I wish…oh, if only I had known what the problem was last evening. Maybe the Lord would have given us a few more years together on this earth."

Lydia held on to *Daett's* arm and pulled him close. Laura did the same on the other side. Nelson and Lester hung their heads as *Daett* prayed again. "Thank You, dear Lord, for my short days and years with Lavina. She has given me *kinner* and brought them up to love You as I do myself. She was a kind *mamm* to them. Lavina stood by my side in sickness and health as we promised each other that long-ago day. Thank You, dear Lord, for those few years of blessing. You have truly given, and now You have taken away. I mourn and I blame myself, but I also know that all things are in Your hands. I should have known better last evening, but perhaps You blinded my eyes so I could not see. You must have wanted Lavina by Your side for Your own purposes, which can never fail. Tell her that I mourn, but I also hope we can meet again someday in that land where tears and sorrow never come."

Daett finished his prayer, and Lydia glanced at her brothers— both of whom had tears in their eyes. She would say her own prayers tonight once she was alone in her bedroom. There would be little sleep until the funeral. They would stay awake as much as possible and watch with *Daett* over *Mamm*'s body. But the shock would eventually wear off. Tomorrow would be another day, but nothing would ever be quite the same without *Mamm*. Yet the Lord's will had been done. They must submit themselves to His strong hand and believe that He knew what was best.

Daett turned to leave, and Nelson and Lester followed him. Lydia stayed by the coffin, as did Laura. They stood arm in arm and wept without words until a measure of peace settled on them.

Chapter Eighteen

Two days of mourning at the Masts' house on Lead Mine Road had passed. Two days of relatives who came and went and who now had gathered for a morning funeral. Laura climbed up the buggy step and settled on the seat beside Lydia. The glare of the sun pained her eyes, and her whole body ached. She wanted to crawl under the quilt in her bedroom and wrap the pillow over her head. Her tears were all cried out, but sleep would bring sweet relief—unlike the final trip to the graveyard they were about to make.

But she must not falter, Laura reminded herself. She must be strong alongside the rest of her family. Lester filled out the surrey seat on the far side of the buggy, with Nelson and *Daett* in the front. All three men were grim-faced. Silence hung over the Masts' front yard, broken only by the creaking of harnesses as the buggies took their places in the funeral procession. The open buggy that contained *Mamm*'s casket stood at the end of the sidewalk. The two drivers had their faces bent into the wind, and one of the men lifted his hand to steady the coffin. *Mamm*'s body was in *goot* hands today, as they all had been from the beginning of this tragedy. The community had rallied around them. Laura could still feel the touch of the women's hands on her arms before the service had begun today. The scene would be repeated when they arrived at the graveyard. Everyone did what they could to bring comfort and to pray that healing would come quickly for the Mast family.

Laura's heart had suffered and somehow survived a double blow. First John's accident, and now *Mamm*'s death. Maybe this was why the Lord had not taken John. If she had lost both of them, the sorrow might have been too much. She hadn't seen John since the Saturday before *Mamm*'s death, but John's *mamm*, Hilda, had whispered in Laura's ear this morning, "He's awake most of the time now."

Hilda must have known Laura needed all the comfort she could get on this day. That John had progressed this far was a miracle in itself. Why the Lord chose to take one and leave another was part of His mysterious will. The Lord knew best, and if Laura had been forced to choose, she wouldn't have wished for John to leave her instead of *Mamm*. That was an awful thought to have on the day of *Mamm*'s funeral, but she couldn't help herself. Lack of sleep and a deep weariness brought on strange emotions and ideas.

Laura tightened her grip on the buggy door as the procession began. They lurched out of the driveway and turned toward the cemetery. Behind them the long line of buggies followed. The *Englisha* cars that approached the procession of buggies slowed or pulled off to the side of the road. None of the buggies paused after the first stop sign. If they had had to cross one of the state highways, it would be different. But the Amish graveyard lay in a quiet spot on Gilbert Road. They would be there in a matter of minutes.

"The Lord has given us *goot* weather in which to bury *Mamm*," *Daett* said from the front seat, his voice weak. "His grace is still with us."

"*Yah*, it is," Nelson agreed.

Laura glanced over at Lydia, who tried to smile back at her. This hadn't been easy on Lydia either. Why the Lord hadn't given Lydia a man to love was beyond her. Lydia should have been snatched up before Laura had been, but Laura had benefited from all the options. Meanwhile Lydia was stuck over at Uncle Henry's produce stand with Milton, who never asked to take her home from the hymn singing—all because Milton planned to jump the fence into the *Englisha* world, according to Lester.

Now *Mamm* was gone. Both sisters had mourned, and they would both move on, but why couldn't Lydia find a man to love? It would surely ease the pain of loss. This had been *Mamm's* biggest concern before she passed. Perhaps *Mamm* would have her prayers answered now that she was with the angels. Laura gave Lydia a kind smile and focused on the road again.

As they bounced into the open field beyond the graveyard, Laura grabbed onto the buggy door handle again. Only a dozen gravestones stood in the small plot of ground. The community was young compared to the older Amish communities in Wayne County, where most everyone had come from. *Mamm's* gravestone would tell of another soul that had left their earthly sorrows behind to enter the joys of heaven. Laura comforted herself with the thought that in glory, *Mamm* would never sigh or worry about her *kinner* again.

When Nelson pulled to a stop, Laura climbed down the buggy step and slowly walked around the back of the surrey. Lydia followed her and they waited with the men while *Mamm's* casket was unloaded. With great care the box was transported to the open grave and placed in position. *Daett* took his place in front of the casket and stood with his head bowed, while buggies poured into the field behind them. Not until Bishop Ezra took his place beside *Daett* would the graveside service begin.

Laura shifted from one foot to the other, her black shawl hanging down almost to the freshly dug dirt under her feet. The crowd of relatives began to press in all sides of the open grave. They soon parted to allow Bishop Ezra to approach. The bishop gave *Daett* a brief nod and then cleared his throat.

"Dearly beloved, we are gathered again on this day for the last time," he began. "Before us is the body of our dear sister Lavina Mast, whose soul is now in the hands of the Lord. Our hope is strong on her behalf. We trust as those who have reason for our confidence. Our faith is built on the grace of the Lord Jesus Christ, who shed His precious blood. We have seen what that grace wrought in the life of our sister Lavina, who chose to live that grace before us all. She demonstrated her faith for the entire world to see. She was humble and willing to obey the commands of the Lord. She loved her husband and entertained strangers in her home. She brought up godly children. All of them are here with us today." Bishop Ezra paused to glance over his shoulder. "For this we are grateful. Children raised in the fear of the Lord are no accident. Many prayers are needed as we strive to live a life in obedience to the Lord's ways. In this, sister Lavina has shown us the way, and today she rests in the arms of the Lord, where she is sheltered from all the toils of her labors. Her family sorrows, but someday they will see their mother's face again in the land of glory, which lies beyond the river."

Laura kept her eyes fixed on the bishop's face as he continued to speak. His words comforted her, but she was glad they were not being spoken over John's casket. She would continue to comfort herself with that thought tomorrow, and the day after, until John was well again. She also had reasons for a solid hope, as the bishop had for *Mamm*'s eternal well-being. Namely, she trusted the Lord's mercies. Had not the Lord shown John compassion up to this point? So why should that not continue? She must go to the Yoders' house and see John this afternoon—if such was possible. Would anyone object now that *Mamm*'s funeral was over? They wouldn't, Laura assured herself. She bowed her head along with everyone else as Bishop Ezra led a closing prayer.

After the amen, Laura stepped back with Lydia while the men helped close the grave. Elizabeth and Rose stood on each side of the sisters, their arms around Laura's and Lydia's shoulders until the last shovel of dirt had been thrown. *Daett* didn't move while the crowd slowly made their way back to their buggies. The sounds of horses' neighs and the rattle of wheels filled the air, but *Daett* stood there with his family around him.

"*Gott im Himmel,*" *Daett* finally prayed, his head lifted toward the heavens. "We commit Lavina for the final time into Your hands. Give us grace as we go back home and carry on without her. Be not angry with our stumbles. Our hearts do ache greatly. Be merciful to us in life, as You have been to Lavina in death. In Jesus' name. Amen."

Daett dropped his head and turned to go. Silently they all followed him back to the surrey and climbed in.

"Can I go see John this afternoon?" Laura asked on the way home.

"I don't know why not," *Daett* answered. "We have mourned, and now life must go on. May the grace of the Lord go with you, daughter."

"Thank you," Laura whispered. A ray of light seemed to enter her heart with *Daett's* words. Maybe there would be *goot* news at John's home to offset the sorrow they had experienced today.

"I'll go with you," Lydia said. "Unless you don't want me to."

Laura allowed a smile to fill her face as Nelson turned into their driveway. "You know you're welcome."

Lydia smiled back as they climbed down from the buggy.

"I'll go get your horse," Lester said before Laura could move toward the barn. "Wait here."

"Thank you," Laura called after him, but Lester was already in the barn.

She jerked her head up when a buggy came in the driveway behind them. Lydia nudged her. "Look who's followed us home."

Laura grimaced as she caught sight of the face inside the buggy. "Not him again!"

"Perhaps he's come to offer his condolences now that everyone has gone and he can have peace and quiet with you."

"I'll chase him away," Laura declared—only she knew she couldn't. Her family would see to it that Wendell was welcomed.

"Hello, Wendell," Laura said as he brought his buggy to a stop and climbed down.

At least Wendell was properly sober-faced. "I'm so sorry for your loss, Laura," he said. "And for yours, Lydia." He nodded in Lydia's direction. "I wish with all my heart that this had never happened."

"We all wish that," Laura retorted.

"The Lord gives and the Lord takes," Wendell continued. "We must remember that lest a great confusion grips our minds and hearts. We must trust the Lord to bring things out for the best in the end."

"*Yah*, that's what *Daett* says," Laura said.

Wendell nodded. "And your *daett* would be right. The heart often doesn't understand the Lord's doings. We must resist the urge to doubt and must carry on with the path that is open before us." Wendell gave them a slight smile. "I've watched your family these past few days, and I can say that I've seen a proper submissive and contrite spirit expressed by everyone. I imagine this trial was not easy—losing a *mamm*—and yet you have taken it with great trust and grace in the Lord's hand. I hope you continue to walk in that grace."

Is that what you came to say? Laura almost asked, but she already knew the answer. Wendell was here to make his presence known to her so that she wouldn't forget him.

"I'm going to see John this afternoon," Laura said boldly.

Wendell's face became stern. "On the afternoon of your *mamm*'s funeral?"

"You stopped by on the afternoon of my *mamm*'s funeral!" Laura shot back.

"Laura," Lydia chided.

Wendell appeared ready to say something, but he didn't. Maybe he figured Lydia's rebuke was sufficient. One thing was for sure—the man had no shame.

"Wendell, it's kind of you to stop in," Lydia added.

Wendell's face lifted, and he nodded. "I came to offer you and your family my heartfelt sympathy. I hope that offends no one..." He let the sentence hang until Lester appeared in the barn door with the twins' horse, Maud. "Howdy," Wendell greeted Lester. "I'm sorry about your mother."

"*Yah*, thanks," Lester muttered. He twirled Maud about as Lydia lifted the buggy shafts. Wendell stood alone by Laura's side while the others hitched Maud to the buggy.

"You really should think long and hard about your *Mamm*'s wishes for you," Wendell said out of the corner of his mouth. "Especially now that she's gone."

Laura pressed her lips together and said nothing. Wendell didn't have to mention what that was. They both knew.

"The will of the Lord is often expressed by doors that are open," Wendell continued. "The Lord desires that everyone in the community do their part for the future generations. We are to bring *kinner* into the world the way your mother did, and rear them in fear of the Lord—unless the Lord expresses His will otherwise, which in your case, Laura, He hasn't. Why are you walking into this barren

situation with your eyes wide open? This is the day to change the
course of your life. I am willing to bring you home from the hymn
singing when you are ready."

"You have some nerve," Laura whispered. "How dare you?" She
pressed back the tears. "Is it not enough that I have lost my *mamm*?
Must you also use that to try and get your own way?"

"It's not my own way," Wendell retorted. "I pray that you will
see that soon."

Laura looked away and waited for more, but instead she heard
Wendell walking toward his buggy. The sound of his horse's hoofbeats soon carried out of the driveway, but she kept her eyes shut
until Lydia spoke. "Are you ready to go see John?"

Laura opened her eyes and nodded. She didn't dare speak at the
moment. Wendell's words stung because she knew what he meant.
John could never bear children—not with his present injuries—yet
she planned to marry him anyway.

Laura whispered a quick prayer. "Help me, dear Lord. Please
help me."

Lydia looked at her strangely but said nothing.

Chapter Nineteen

A chilly afternoon breeze blew through the buggy as Laura drove Maud toward the Yoders' place. Lydia sat silently beside her, and the steady clip-clop of Maud's hooves on the pavement had been the only sound to fill the buggy since they had left home.

Laura pulled the buggy blanket up higher on her lap, and Lydia did the same. As usual they were of one mind. But did Lydia side with her when it came to Wendell? Not that it mattered.

Laura glanced at her twin. "I suppose I should tell you what Wendell said."

"If you wish." Lydia attempted a smile. "But I can about guess."

Laura looked away to hide the tears. "I doubt that. He had the nerve to tell me that John and I could never have *kinner*. Not with John in his present condition."

Lydia gasped. "That was plainspoken, even for Wendell!"

"And the truth, of course! Which is why it hurts! But it doesn't change my mind. The Lord can give us what we need, even *kinner*."

"*Yah*, He can," Lydia agreed. "But that's asking a lot. Even hoping for John to get better is asking a lot. I hope you won't think I'm a traitor when I say that maybe you *should* consider Wendell now that *Mamm* has passed. He might make you a decent husband."

"*Mamm*'s passing changes nothing," Laura shot back.

"You know it does."

"Like what?" Laura hung on to the reins as she pulled into the Yoder driveway.

"Deaths always change things," Lydia said. "They increase our duty to the community and the faith. On that, Wendell is correct."

"I'm being faithful to my love for John and his for me," Laura countered. "That's also one's duty. And *Mamm*'s death makes me stronger in my love for John."

Lydia shrugged. "I'm just saying it seems like we've both landed in a mess with the men we love."

Laura sat up straighter. "Sorry. I've been too wrapped up in myself, but you're right."

"That's okay." Lydia offered a tender smile. "You can't do anything about Milton anyway. Milton likes me, I think, and he wants me to jump the fence with him."

"That *is* a mess," Laura agreed. "I guess we both need miracles—which the Lord will surely supply."

"I'm not as confident as you are," Lydia said. "But there's no question we need the Lord's help. Me with Milton, and you with John. If the man can't walk or work, you know you can't marry him. There's this little matter of support. John's parents will care for him if John doesn't marry, but if he does marry, you'd be on your own."

Laura pressed her lips together. What was there to say? What Lydia said was true, but still…

"And there's John to consider," Lydia continued. "If John *does* come around—and that's still up in the air—he might not take you as his *frau* if he can't walk. John knows he has to support you, and so do his parents."

Laura kept her voice steady. "The Lord will help us."

This she hadn't thought of. John was an honorable man. He could easily see her as a martyr or some such thing. He might not believe that her love was deep enough to travel this valley and come out safely on the other side.

"Dear Lord, help Lydia and me," Laura whispered as she pulled up to the Yoders' barn.

"Amen," Lydia echoed. She hopped out, and Laura followed her to begin unhitching Maud from the buggy.

John's *daett,* Herman, appeared in the barn door and hurried toward them. "You have come on the day of your *mamm*'s funeral? You should not have."

Laura managed to smile. "It has been a while since I've been here. And life must go on, must it not? I need to see John."

Herman grunted and appraised Laura with a long look. He finally nodded and took the tie rope from her hand. "Okay, go on in the house. But you're not unhitching your horse from the buggy. I'll tie her up. You and your sister need to leave before long."

Laura dropped her gaze and stepped back. The submissive gesture should please Herman. As her future father-in-law, she needed him on her side. Placating Herman was the least she could do at the moment.

"Come." Lydia took her arm.

"I'm not a *bobbli*," Laura protested once they were out of Herman's earshot. Lydia kept her hand on Laura's arm until they reached the front porch.

Hilda opened the front door for them. "*Goot* afternoon, girls." Hilda's smile was gentle. She motioned them on inside. "John's awake. He must have known you were coming."

Laura tried to breathe evenly. "How is he?"

Hilda's face clouded. "He doesn't drift off into unconsciousness as he did before, and he seems to know we're here, but…"

Laura left Lydia with Hilda and hurried toward the bed. John's white face turned on the pillow toward the sound of her footsteps.

"John!" she called out. "I've come again. I'm so glad you're awake."

A trace of a smile crept across his face. "*Yah*," he whispered. "You have been here often, I think. Or was it only in my dreams?"

"I've been here!" she exclaimed, grabbing his hand. "Oh, John, you seem better. Much better!"

His face darkened. "I don't know about that. There's still a lot wrong with me." He stopped and turned his face toward the ceiling.

"I know, John." Laura clutched his hand in both of hers. "But I love you. I always will."

She waited, but his head didn't turn back to her. She wanted to touch his face and pull his gaze back toward her, but Hilda and Lydia were behind her.

"John," Laura repeated. "I love you. With all my heart. I always have, and the accident changed nothing. Even if you can't walk again, I don't care. The Lord will help us. Our love hasn't changed. Wouldn't I have stayed true to you if we had already said the wedding vows?"

John's face turned toward her with a solitary tear on his cheek. "But we *haven't* wed, Laura, and…there's something I need to tell you that you don't know."

"It can't be that bad," Laura said. "The only thing you could say that would make a difference is that you don't love me anymore."

"Of course, it's not that," John said. He hesitated and then squeezed Laura's hands. "The truth is…I can't see. I've waited for a long time to say it, hoping this blindness would go away, but it hasn't. I can't see you. Not a thing. The world is black to me."

The room seemed to tilt on its axis, and Laura grabbed for the side of the bed. Had she heard correctly? "John." She bent toward him. "What did you say?"

"I'm blind," he repeated. "I haven't been able to see a thing since I've been awake. That's why I tried to drift off again so many times. I hoped my blindness would go away or that I would..." He stopped. "Laura, you can't love a blind man who can't walk."

Laura didn't move as quick footsteps came up behind her.

"What he did he just say?" Hilda asked.

Laura kept her gaze on John's face and remained silent.

"John!" Hilda spoke directly to her son. "What did you just say to Laura?"

"I wanted to tell Laura first," he finally said. "I'm blind, *Mamm*. I've been blind since the accident. I've wanted to die because of it. I'm just so useless this way."

Hilda reached over to loosen her son's hand from Laura's grasp. She wrapped her arms around his thin frame and held him close, as if he were still a small boy who had come to her with news of his scraped knee.

"You had best go," Hilda said to Laura. "You heard what John told you. It's over, dear. You can't marry a blind man."

"But I can!" Laura exclaimed. "This is no worse than not walking. I love him, and he loves me. Ask John if you don't believe that."

Hilda shook her head. "Laura, you have to let go. This cannot be. John is paralyzed and now blind."

"I'm not leaving!" Laura declared. "I'm his promised one, and this could improve. He could get his eyesight back again. And why would the doctor not have said something if John was blind?"

"They sent him home with no hope to offer. Remember?" Hilda lay John down on the bed again. "Now please go, Laura."

Laura didn't move. "Ask John if he still loves me. I want to hear it from his own lips." Laura paused. "If John says he doesn't love me, then I'll go."

Hilda's gaze moved between John and Laura. Finally she sighed.

"I already know the answer, but his love notwithstanding, we have to do what's best for the both of you. This can't go on, Laura. Surely you know that. Marriage is a great responsibility. John won't consent to marry you no matter how much he loves you. Not if he's blind and can't walk."

Laura pushed past Hilda's arm until her face was just above John's. She spoke slowly. "Do you love me, John? Enough to marry me regardless of what happens? Regardless of this? Because it all make no difference to me. The Lord will still be with us."

The moments ticked past until in a faint voice John said, "I do still love you."

"See?"

"It's plain enough," Hilda admitted, "but that still doesn't make it right."

Laura leaned forward to hug John. Hilda would have to think what she wished. A great victory had been won, and John had dared to speak his heart. Laura would always love him for that. John could have dismissed her out of his agony. The pain of his blindness could have driven the man to insanity, but John had not sent her away. He had left the door open for the Lord to work. Even if it took a miracle.

"Come, it is enough for one day." Hilda placed her hand on Laura's shoulder. "You buried your *mamm* only a few hours ago. Go home and rest, Laura. Maybe things will look different in a while."

Laura loosened her hold on John's neck. She wanted to kiss him, but that would have been indecent with Hilda and Lydia in the room.

"Thank you for still loving me," she whispered in John's ear.

John's hand grasped hers in a tight grip. He didn't say anything, but tears trickled down his cheeks.

"I'll be back again soon," she said, moving away from the bed.

Lydia also had tears in her eyes as she took her sister by the arm.

The two made their way out to the porch. Herman wasn't in sight as they went down the steps and approached the buggy.

"Get in," Lydia ordered. "I'll untie Maud."

Laura silently obeyed. Lydia untied Maud and tossed her sister the reins. As they pulled away, the barn door opened and Herman stepped out to give them a wave of his hand.

When they were out on the road, Lydia turned to her sister. "You know you have a long, hard road ahead of you," she said.

"This is true," Laura agreed, "but I love him, and John had the courage to stand true to that love this afternoon. He is a man regardless of what has happened to his body."

"Maybe the Lord will walk with us and help us both," Lydia suggested.

Laura smiled and reached over to slip her free arm around Lydia's shoulder. "I know He will."

Chapter Twenty

Nancy Beiler peered out of her kitchen window at the buggy that had pulled up to her barn. Who would drive in her lane on a Saturday afternoon? Perhaps one of her students had stopped by to discuss a problem? Nancy pulled her head back and thought for a moment. That was hardly the answer. Things were going well at the schoolhouse, and everyone knew their lessons. This visit wasn't related to schoolwork, but more likely to her personal life. She had planned to meet Charles tonight after dark. No doubt, that was where the problem lay.

Nancy leaned forward for another look. Sure enough, Deacon William was stepping out of his buggy. This could not be *goot*. Had she been found out? But how? She had taken such care, and so had Charles.

Nancy pulled her head back as Deacon William glanced toward the house. The deacon's face was somber, but he always looked that way when he made house calls for church problems. That's what she had become. A church problem. She might as well face it. This was what happened when a person tried to act in secret. Eventually the truth came out. She had reminded herself of this last week at Lavina Mast's funeral, but nothing had changed. She even had managed to catch a few moments alone with Charles on the evening of the funeral.

Perhaps it was for the best that Deacon William had discovered her transgressions. At least the matter would be out in the open, where judgment and condemnation could fall upon her. Maybe that was what she needed to correct her ways—if she wanted to correct them. That, of course, remained the question.

Nancy's mind raced as she forced herself to open the front door and meet the deacon with a smile on her face. "*Goot* afternoon."

"*Goot* afternoon," he responded. "Do you have a few moments, Nancy?"

"*Yah*, of course." Nancy forced her smile to broaden.

Deacon William wasn't smiling, but he took the chair she offered him. Nancy closed the front door and took a seat on the couch. She was so used to dishonesty by now that she could act cheerful even when she knew something was dreadfully wrong. How low she had fallen. What if she had been in Lavina Mast's place and the Lord had called her home? Lavina had been ready, but could Nancy say the same for herself?

"How are things going at school?" Deacon William asked.

"Okay, I guess." Nancy forced her eyes to meet his. "I mean, none of the parents have complained. I've been trying to heed your words—and not teach them *Englisha* things."

"And have you been learning new things yourself from your contacts with the *Englisha* world?" the deacon asked.

Nancy blinked. What a strange question. Was Deacon William toying with her? But that was unlike him. "I don't know what you mean," she finally said.

Deacon William regarded her with a steady gaze. "Something is going on, Nancy. You're not the same anymore. Elizabeth has noticed, and so have some of the others. You seem distracted at the Sunday service…even distressed. Have you been making contact with the *Englisha* people in some way that your conscience is bothering you? Perhaps they have told you things that trouble you greatly. Has your faith been shaken? The Lord has called us to a simple and humble life. The knowledge these people have can easily unsettle the spirit and bring doubts into the strongest soul. Is this what is happening to you, Nancy?"

Nancy's mind spun. None of this made the least bit of sense. Had she been seen with Charles or not?

"I…" She tried to speak, but no words would form.

Deacon William appeared troubled. "I take your hesitation for guilt, Nancy, so let me make this easier for you. One of the parents saw an *Englisha* man stopping by the schoolhouse last week. This has to stop. I know you think it might be harmless, but we can't have this influence coming into the community. We believe the Lord uses the medical field to heal, but it is not for us to learn how. We leave that in the hands of others who have been given more grace than we have." Deacon William sighed. "I told you this at the barn-raising when John Yoder was injured and you tended to him. I thought you would listen, but maybe I should have spoken with you again to make sure you understood. You hold an important position in the community, one we all respect, but you can't act like this, Nancy. Having *Englisha* people in the schoolhouse is totally unacceptable."

"But…" Nancy began again.

Deacon William leaned forward. "You know this is true."

She nodded. What else was there to say? By her silence, she was lying. Nancy forced herself to focus as Deacon William spoke again. "The parents have complained, so we must do something. Can I at least have your promise that this will stop once and for all, and at the next communion time, maybe you can make a confession?

Discreetly, of course. That should satisfy most people, and I can tell anyone who speaks to me before then what the plan is."

Nancy knew this was her way out. No one need ever know what had happened before this. She could tell Charles tonight that she would never see him again, and they could...But Nancy stopped herself. No, she could not live like this. She could not!

"Is that agreeable?" Deacon William attempted a smile. "I'm trying to make this easy for you, Nancy. Surely it's not that difficult to respect the wishes of the community. You are one of us and always have been. I want to assure you of that. No one is trying to make things miserable for you."

Nancy's hands trembled, but she had to speak. "I can't do this anymore," she said. "I can't deceive you and the community any longer. The Lord already knows that I have transgressed greatly."

Deacon William tilted his head. "You have done what?"

"It's more than you know," Nancy managed, and the rest of the words burst out. "The *Englisha* man you refer to. His name is Charles Wiseman. I've been dating him for some time. He wants me to marry him. I love him, I really do. But I can't marry him, but neither can I stop seeing him. It's all a horrible mess!" Nancy closed her hands so tightly the nails dug into her palms.

Deacon William could not have appeared more astonished. "You, Nancy? Our schoolteacher? Dating an *Englisha* man? Pretending that nothing is going on? How can this be?"

"You heard right," Nancy said. "I have been seeing an *Englisha* man. I haven't been honest with you from the start." She lifted her chin higher. "You'll have to excommunicate me, I suppose, and find someone else to teach on Monday morning, because I—"

Deacon William silenced her with an upraised hand. "Stop, Nancy. Start at the beginning. Tell me the whole story."

"There is no beginning," she muttered, "and no ending, apparently.

Charles stopped by the schoolhouse one day—that's all. And we fell in love. I don't know how else to say it. Maybe my heart was ready after all the years of sorrow I've been through with Yost's rejection of me, but I know that's no excuse. I fell in love with him. How else do I say it?"

"Are you…?"

Nancy winced. "No. Charles isn't that kind of man, Deacon William. I'm the problem—that and my heart. I've lived a *goot* life, *yah*, but apparently there was a flaw in me that I didn't see. After Yost rejected me, I never got over the hurt. Deep down there was still the desire to have a husband I loved and to bear *kinner*. When the Lord didn't provide, I found my own way. That's what it looks like to me."

"But you had offers of marriage in the community, Nancy. Or at least offers to date!" Deacon William exclaimed. "Is this not true?"

Nancy kept her gaze fixed on the floor. She really didn't want to discuss this with the deacon. She had already said enough. "I'm expecting my punishment," she said. "I'll make no objections. I'm sure you can find someone to fill in at the schoolhouse on Monday. Teachers aren't that difficult to find."

Nancy pressed back the tears. At last she had finally spoken the truth. However painful the road, this was better than the one she had been on. Now she could marry Charles, even with the turmoil in her heart. He would be overjoyed when she told him.

Deacon William stood to pace the room. "This is not acceptable. I've known you all of my life, and we can't lose you like this. Not our best schoolteacher—to an *Englisha* man. Of all things, Nancy. Think…and stop this madness. There is still time."

She shook her head. "There isn't, Deacon. I wish there was, but there isn't. I can't do this on my own."

He pounced. "See! But you wish you could, so there is hope."

She shook her head.

"*Yah*, there is!" Deacon William declared. "We will not stand by while this happens. I know your heart, and I know what is right."

"What are you going to do?" Nancy asked. "I'm meeting Charles at the schoolhouse later this evening. I'll invite him here and tell him that I accept his offer of marriage. From what he tells me, he's willing to wed me quite soon. I don't need many frills. I was raised Amish, I'll tell him. Just a new *Englisha* dress is *goot* enough, and we can live here after the wedding if he wishes."

Deacon William stopped his pacing and said, "You speak out of your head, Nancy. I'm going to Bishop Ezra's place right now. He'll support me on this, and we'll take care of everything."

"What do you mean?" Nancy asked, but the deacon was already out the front door. Moments later his buggy tore out of her driveway and disappeared rapidly up the road.

Would she be excommunicated tonight? That didn't seem possible. Even with her strong words there would be discussions, further warnings, and counsel taken with the whole community at a Sunday service. Nothing could be done tonight. Deacon William must have gone to Bishop Ezra for moral support. No doubt the two would be back to give her further directives in only minutes.

Nancy busied herself in the kitchen. Charles would be here later for supper, and she should prepare something more than soup for their engagement celebration. She would keep up the preparations, even when Bishop Ezra arrived with Deacon William. That would demonstrate to both of them her determination—if there remained any doubt in their minds.

Nancy slipped down the basement stairs and found two large potatoes and a jar of canned corn. She took both back upstairs and wrapped the potatoes in tinfoil. There was no time for mashed potatoes, so baked would do. She lit the stove, and twenty minutes later the corn was steaming in the bowl.

Nancy was still working when she heard the sound of buggy wheels coming into the driveway. Deacon William didn't knock but came straight in with Bishop Ezra and his *frau*, Rose, behind him. No one said anything, and Nancy kept busy until she heard their footsteps leaving again. She glanced up to see Rose seated by herself at the kitchen table.

"Where have the men gone?" Nancy asked as the sound of buggy wheels went out the driveway.

"You can guess," Rose said. "I'm here to stay for the night. Ezra will pick me up tomorrow morning, and we'll follow you to the services."

"But, I—" Nancy protested.

"No ifs, ands, or buts," Rose said. "Someone is staying with you until you come to your senses. And that *Englisha* man won't be bothering you again. You have nothing to worry about, Nancy. The Lord can heal your heart and make things right again."

Nancy gasped. "The men are talking to Charles?"

Rose nodded. "When he comes they'll be waiting out on the road. It's for the best. Now let me help you finish supper, and we can eat it together—just the two of us with the Lord's grace."

"I…" Nancy tried again.

This she had not expected, but it was useless to protest. She should try to reach Charles first, but Bishop Ezra and Deacon William wouldn't allow it. Nor would Rose allow her to leave. Nancy steadied herself on the counter with both hands, and Rose stood up to slip her arm around Nancy's shoulder.

"It's for the best," Rose repeated. "Just remember that."

Nancy didn't know if it was or wasn't, but she didn't feel anything either.

"The potatoes," Nancy managed.

"I'll check them." Rose opened the stove door, and warmth

rushed out to fill the room. "They're not ready," Rose said, closing the door again. "What else is there to do?"

"Nothing. But I don't think I can eat anyway."

"Oh *yah*, you will," Rose chided.

And she would, Nancy knew. She would obey because there was nothing else to do. She knew how to obey even when her heart was dead.

Chapter Twenty-One

Lydia stood rearranging the pumpkins at Uncle Henry's road-side stand, placing the smaller ones in front and the larger ones toward the back. The first rush of morning customers had purchased well over half of what she had put out only a few hours before. Uncle Henry would be pleased. Halloween fell on Monday next week. With the stand closed on Sunday, that left only a few days to sell these pumpkins and the ones still on the vine.

"We'll sell them all this year," Uncle Henry had declared at breakfast. "We have to, with all this high-priced help we have around here."

Uncle Henry had been teasing, of course, but Lydia believed he was right—especially after this morning's rush. For her, the feeling of satisfaction was enough of a reward. Since *Mamm's* funeral, her work seemed like an island of sanity amid raging seas. Maybe this was why the Lord had allowed her to work for Uncle Henry this fall. She wouldn't do well at home with *Mamm* gone. Laura could handle the empty house and was the optimistic one who had great faith that the Lord would walk with them through their trials.

Lydia paused to straighten her back. After the funeral she had supported Laura in her belief that everything would turn out right. But she wavered often, while Laura did not—and Laura's faith had been rewarded in part. *Yah*, John was still blind, but his back had mended beyond the doctor's wildest expectations. Now Laura wasn't giving up hope for John's eyesight. Her twin prayed every day, but did the Lord still give sight to the blind? The thought seemed impossible, and perhaps Laura didn't think such a thing would happen either. The truth was, if John could walk, Laura planned to marry him even if he remained blind. Laura would consider his walking a miracle and claim victory.

Laura was an inspiration. There was no doubt about that. But for Lydia, taking the practical attitude was so much easier. This was why she had encouraged Laura to consider Wendell's offer of a date. In a way, she was glad Laura had refused. If Laura had faltered, what hope would there be for her own situation with Milton?

Lydia sighed at the thought. *Yah*, Milton would take a miracle too. She couldn't bring herself to tell Milton once and for all that their situation was hopeless. But neither could she consider jumping the fence with him. But if Laura continued to believe in the Lord, maybe she could do the same. At least her courage was stirred that an answer might come. What that answer would be, she couldn't imagine.

Yet miracles were that way, were they not? Miracles were impossible situations that the Lord solved for helpless human beings. The thought took her breath away. Could she one day be Milton's *frau*? Could they both be happy and settled in the community? This question put Laura's courage in a whole new light. The mountain looked even taller when she placed the obstacle in her own life. How brave Laura was.

In the meantime, her heart pined for Milton's affections. There was no question about that. This clouded her judgment. She wouldn't have dared continue to hope, except for Laura's example. Her sister was setting a worthy example for her to follow, even if hardly anyone else in the community agreed.

Lydia sighed and searched the road in each direction for any sign of approaching automobiles. She needed a steady stream of customers to sell her pumpkins, but maybe the Lord also knew that she needed a few moments to catch her breath and think about Milton. He hadn't said anything lately about his new *Englisha* automobile. Maybe the shock of her *mamm's* passing had given Milton a more sober outlook on life. Maybe the miracle from the Lord was already at work? The choice that Milton should make seemed so simple to her. Why couldn't Milton set his heart on continuing in the community instead of jumping the fence?

The sound of a buggy came up the driveway from Uncle Henry's house, and Lydia quickly rearranged a few more pumpkins. She must look busy when Milton drove up. The last thing she needed was for him to know how much she cared. Milton had to know that she liked him, but not…

Lydia stood upright as Milton drove the open buggy loaded with fresh pumpkins out of the woods. He drove with a wild dash toward the stand, and Lydia watched him with an open mouth. At the speed Milton was traveling, it was a surprise any of the pumpkins remained on his buggy. But that was Milton for you. He lived recklessly, as if there were no consequences. She could almost imagine how he would drive that forbidden *Englisha* car of his. What she couldn't understand was why she was so attracted to such a man.

Milton brought his horse to a stop in a small cloud of dust.

"*Goot* morning, lovely one," Milton sang out.

Lydia pulled up her coat collar to hide the heat creeping up her neck. Milton wouldn't dare say such things if Uncle Henry was around. But since they were alone, Milton took advantage of the situation. Of course, she didn't object, which was an awful thing, but…

"Cat got your tongue on a cold morning?" Milton teased. He sailed off the buggy with one effortless bound, landing lightly on his feet.

"I'm quite able to speak," Lydia squeaked.

Milton laughed heartily. He obviously knew way too much.

Lydia tried to scold him. "It's the way you come tearing up the driveway with pumpkins on the back of your buggy that chills my bones. What if you spilled them and split them wide open? Uncle Henry didn't pay you to help raise them only to see you lose them."

Milton grinned from ear to ear. "Isn't that a mouthful, even for you?"

"You should behave yourself," Lydia chided.

Milton stepped closer, his grin growing wider. "Well, are you going to help me unload these pumpkins or not?"

Lydia tried to breathe. Did all girls melt like butter in his hands?

Milton lifted the first pumpkin off the wagon and regarded Lydia with a sober face. "I'm sorry for my teasing. You must still be mourning your *mamm*'s passing. I should be more…"

"It's okay," Lydia said. Now she wanted to cry. Milton could change directions on a dime and still be perfectly on target. "I've been thinking of her."

Milton lifted another pumpkin off the wagon. "Losing one's *mamm* couldn't be easy."

"But the Lord allowed it."

Milton's lips tightened. "*Yah*, I know."

Lydia still hadn't moved. "You're not losing your faith, are you?"

"I don't know much about the Lord's doing. I just try to live each day at a time, and let things happen as they will." Milton transferred another pumpkin.

"But, we must—"

As Lydia spoke, a car pulled up and a man got out. Lydia turned her attention to the new customer.

"Mighty fine pumpkins you got here," the man said, taking an apprising look at the display. He tapped several of them with his knuckles.

"My Uncle Henry raises the best," Lydia told him. "And besides the pumpkins, we still have our other produce as well." Lydia gave a quick wave of her hand across the well-stocked shelves behind her.

"I see," the man replied with a smile. "But pumpkins it is for me this morning. I'll take four of them."

"Which ones would you like?" Milton asked from behind Lydia. "I'll carry them to your car."

The man grinned. "I'd like to choose from your wagon, if you don't mind. Straight from an Amish farm to my front lawn. I like that." The man laughed. "You should use that as your slogan."

Milton laughed along with the man, and followed him over to the wagon. The man chose each pumpkin carefully while Milton waited and chatted with him. When the last pumpkin was loaded into the car, the two were still laughing. Milton was right at home with *Englisha* people. Lydia had noticed that before, but Milton was also right at home with most people—including her.

Milton chuckled when he returned to the stand. "Maybe I should learn how to carve pumpkins."

"You should not," Lydia said. "You've learned enough *Englisha* ways already."

Milton gave Lydia a long look. "You should lighten up, girl. There's time enough to settle down in the community."

"So you're planning on joining the baptismal class soon?"

Milton's laugh was dry. "Not likely! Not after what's happening to my sister."

"Nancy!" Lydia gasped. "What has happened? Surely she hasn't…"

Milton grunted at the heavy pumpkin in his arms. "Aren't you going to help me?"

Lydia forced herself to move. How could Milton be so blasé about such an important question? But if she wanted him to speak, she'd have to wait. Milton didn't respond well to pressure.

"I didn't expect Nancy to fold so easily," Milton finally said. "She was an inspiration to me, but now…" Milton let the words dangle in the bright sunlight.

Lydia unbuttoned her coat and remained silent. Milton picked up another pumpkin before he asked, "Haven't you heard?"

Lydia tried to hide the tremble in her voice. "I don't know what you're talking about."

Milton grunted again. "I suppose you've been too distracted with your *mamm*'s passing, but that may be another reason Nancy gave in. Didn't my sister almost marry your *daett* way back when?"

"Would you talk sense, Milton?" Lydia said with exasperation.

"I am talking sense! My sister was in love with that *Englisha* man, and now she's given him up. Deacon William just took over Nancy's life, and now…" Milton threw both hands up once he'd set the pumpkin down. "Nancy just gave it all up for a boring life in the community."

Lydia kept her lips pressed together. Was this *goot* news? She couldn't tell from Milton's rambled account.

"Deacon William came right over and told Nancy she had to give Charles up," Milton continued. "Of course the deacon would say that, but Nancy didn't have to give in. Now they have someone staying with Nancy all the time. They even have one of the younger girls helping at the schoolhouse. Nancy's never alone. I guess they'll keep this up until your *daett* marries her." Milton sent Lydia a glare.

"That's what I heard is next in the plans. They want the old wounds healed."

"I know nothing about this," Lydia protested. "No one has told me any such thing."

"Well, I think it's wrong," Milton said. "Just plain wrong. One should be able to leave peacefully if one wants to. Nancy was in love. I know she was."

"So Nancy isn't leaving the community now?"

Milton only grunted as he unloaded the last pumpkin. Lydia hadn't helped him yet, but Milton didn't seem to mind. "Will you go for a ride with me this weekend?" Milton asked.

Lydia willed the rapid beat of her heart to still. "I don't know…" she managed.

Hope lit up Milton's face. "But you'll think about it? I would love to take you for a spin into town. I can pick you up right here, tomorrow night around ten. No one need know."

"You know it always leaks out."

"But you *might* come?" Milton still had hope written on his face.

"You want me to come that badly?"

"*Yah.*" Milton stepped closer. "You know I like you a lot, Lydia. I'd love to have you with me for a night on the town. Surely you can do that without anyone catching you. And if someone did, what would you have to do? Uncle Henry would understand, don't you think? I'd take all the blame for carting around a baptized girl."

It was wrong, and Lydia knew it. Besides, if she gave in to this, what else might she give in to? Jumping the fence? "I can't do it," Lydia said. "I wish I could, but I just can't."

Milton shook his head and turned away. "Why is all the resolve on the other side? Why couldn't Nancy have had this kind of determination?" Milton stared down the road as another *Englisha* car slowed down. "I have to be going," he said, climbing back in his buggy. He clucked to his horse and whirled back up the lane with even more dash than he had displayed when he appeared.

"That's a nice horse," the lady approaching the stand said. "And a handsome young man too."

"*Yah*, he is." Lydia tried to smile. But everything was ice inside. Why couldn't she give in to Milton just a little bit? But that was not the Lord's way. She must not doubt. There was always harm done when one gave in to temptation.

"So what can I do for you?" she asked the lady.

The lady smiled and pointed. "I think I'll take that large pumpkin over there, please."

Lydia's mind spun as she took the pumpkin to the lady's car and collected the money. What was this about *Daett* and Nancy? Did *Daett* plan to wed Nancy now that *Mamm* was gone?

Chapter Twenty-Two

The golden rays of an Indian summer sunset hung in the sky that Saturday evening. Inside Uncle Henry's farmhouse, supper time was not its usual boisterous affair. They were all tired, but their weariness was caused by something deeper than physical labor. The reality of *Mamm's* death still haunted them during these quiet moments.

Uncle Henry looked up from his plate and smiled. "We have had a *goot* week of pumpkin sales. I want to thank you for the *goot* job you've been doing, Lydia. Without your charming face out at the stand, I'm sure half of our customers would have shopped elsewhere. And you did that with the sorrow of your *mamm's* passing still heavy on your heart."

"*Yah*, I am sorrowing," Lydia agreed. "But you grew the pumpkins. I didn't do much other than greet customers and take their money—"

"You're as modest as your *mamm* was," Uncle Henry interrupted, "and you're as much of a jewel too. She was a great *frau* to your father and a *wunderbah* sister to me. May the angels in heaven minister to her tonight."

Aunt Millie reached across the table to hold Uncle Henry's hand.

He tried to smile. "Tomorrow we rest and refresh our spirits at the Lord's house. Bishop Jonas might even have a rousing sermon for us all." Uncle Henry chuckled, and Lydia and Millie joined in. They all knew that old Bishop Jonas from this district hadn't done a rousing sermon in years. The aged bishop used to preach up a storm in his youth, but he had slowed down in recent years. The words were still the same, but now they were delivered in a voice that barely carried through the house.

"He's still a *goot* man," Millie said. "And I can always hear him fine from where the married women sit."

"*Yah*, his heart is in the right place," Uncle Henry agreed, then turned his attention to Lydia. "How are you doing, dear? Seems like we're so busy I rarely get a chance to ask."

"Still mourning, I guess," Lydia said. "I miss *Mamm* a lot, but life moves on."

"*Yah*, it does," Uncle Henry said. "That reminds me. I spoke with Milton this afternoon."

"Oh?" Lydia jerked her head up nervously.

Uncle Henry grinned. "I thought that might interest you, Lydia."

Lydia covered her face with her hands. Why had she let slip her feelings about Milton?

Uncle Henry laughed and went on. "Milton wanted to know if it would be okay if he stopped by later this evening." Uncle Henry glanced at the kitchen clock. "Actually in thirty minutes or so."

"Why?" Lydia almost choked on the word.

Uncle Henry chuckled. "I thought maybe you'd have some idea about that."

Is Milton bringing his Englisha car here? The words almost slipped out. But Milton would never dare make such a bold move.

Uncle Henry winked. "He wants to bring his buggy over to take you for a ride. It's not exactly a date…but you never know."

"In his buggy?" Lydia bounced to her feet. "I must get ready then." Had her miracle happened? Had Milton decided to stay in the community?

Millie waved Lydia back down again. "You look fine, Lydia."

"*Yah*, you should finish eating," Uncle Henry said with a smile. "I should have said something sooner, but then you might not have been able to eat at all."

"Oh, I can eat fine!" Lydia demonstrated by taking a bite. Somehow she had to regain her dignity.

Uncle Henry eyed Lydia. "So you two must be getting serious about each other."

Lydia took another bite as an excuse to say nothing.

Uncle Henry was still looking at Lydia when he asked, "You've heard about his sister, haven't you?"

"*Yah*, some of it," Lydia said.

"I don't suppose you're worried that Milton might do the same sort of thing…like jump the fence?" Uncle Henry asked. "Do you have doubts about Milton because of Nancy?"

"*Yah*, maybe a little," Lydia allowed.

Uncle Henry nodded. "I can see where that might be a problem, but the ministers are taking care of Nancy. I think Milton's okay. But your concern speaks well to your favor, Lydia."

"Milton told me about his sister," Lydia said. *But please don't ask more questions*, Lydia prayed.

"That's *goot*," Uncle Henry said, as if that answered all things. "At least he's being honest."

Lydia wouldn't tell Uncle Henry the whole story. Milton *wasn't* being entirely honest. She mustn't let on what Milton's opinion was of his sister's treatment by Deacon William.

"Well, let's pray and give thanks so Lydia can leave," Uncle Henry said.

They bowed their heads and Lydia offered her own silent prayer. *Help me, dear Lord, and thank You if this is a miracle from You. If not, help me to still be thankful. Just please help me.*

"Amen," Uncle Henry said to conclude the prayer. Lydia jumped up again and began to clear the table, but Millie stopped her with a shake of her head. "Go up and change, if you must. Milton will be here any moment."

Lydia nodded and whispered her thanks. Seconds later she was up the stairs and in her room. She selected a Sunday dress first, but placed the dress back in the closet at once. She had to calm down and not overdo things. A clean work dress was all she should wear.

By the time Milton drove into Uncle Henry's driveway, Lydia was taking measured steps down to the living room, giving Millie a little wave as she passed the kitchen doorway. Uncle Henry noticed from his rocker and grinned. At least the mood of the evening had changed. Life did indeed go on, even with *Mamm* gone.

Lydia took a deep breath and stepped out on the front porch. The last of the sunset had vanished from the sky, and Milton's buggy stood silhouetted against the barn. With slow steps Lydia approached.

Milton's voice from the open buggy door greeted her. "*Goot* evening, Lydia."

"*Goot* evening, Milton." She searched the darkness for his face.

As if he knew, Milton leaned out of the buggy. "Were you surprised when you heard I was coming over?"

"*Yah*, I was," Lydia admitted.

"Well, I wanted to see you, and since you wouldn't go for a ride in my car…" He grinned. "I thought you might go for a ride in my buggy instead. I couldn't pass up a chance of being with you."

Lydia didn't answer. Instead she hurried around to the other side and hopped up the step to bounce onto the buggy seat.

"Getup!" Milton hollered, and off they went down the lane, past the remaining pumpkins in the fields. The stand was closed tomorrow, so Uncle Henry would still have pumpkins left over on Monday evening. But Lydia didn't want to think about pumpkins right now. She was seated beside Milton in his buggy, and they were off for an evening drive. Who would have thought this would ever happen?

"Are you happy now?" Milton asked.

"*Yah,* but you didn't have to do this."

"I wanted to," Milton said, driving past the dark frame of the roadside stand. "So where would you like to go?"

"We could just drive," Lydia suggested. "But could you tell me what changed your mind? You didn't seem interested after I turned down your offer of a ride in your car."

"Like I said," Milton said, "I just wanted to be with you. In a setting other than work."

"So you've changed your mind about…" Lydia stopped. She shouldn't say too much.

Milton squeezed her hand. "Let's just enjoy our evening together. We don't have to speak of anything else." Milton let go of her hand to wave toward the darkened fields. "I just wanted to show you that I'm serious, Lydia. About you and me and the future. I'm not so stubborn that I wouldn't consider staying in the community. But let's just leave that be. Okay?"

Lydia nestled against his shoulder. The gesture seemed natural enough, almost as if she belonged here—which she did. Her heart said so at least. "Thank you, Milton," Lydia whispered into the darkness. "This means a lot to me."

"And to me," he said before silence fell between them. The lights of the *Englisha* houses passed by the buggy. Here and there, a few of the living room windows twinkled with Amish gas lanterns and kerosene lamps. Lydia held Milton's hand and stayed close to him. The lights from the cars on Highway 184 illuminated the interior of the buggy as they passed. When the next one came, Lydia glanced up at Milton's face, and he smiled down at her. They drove on in silence again.

The lights of Heuvelton were soon visible on the horizon. Perhaps she should give way at least a little tonight. It wasn't right that Milton should make all the sacrifices, especially since he was still on his *rumspringa*. But what could she do that would still pass any questions Uncle Henry might ask tomorrow morning?

"The town of Heuvelton has their trick or treat tonight," Milton said, as if he could read Lydia's thoughts. "We could go buy a few bags of candy and pass them out at a street corner from the buggy. Wouldn't that be fun?"

Lydia sat up straight. "You would do that?" This would pass Uncle Henry's questions and everyone else's. "*Yah*, let's."

He chuckled and drove straight toward the small supermarket on the edge of town.

"Stay right here," Lydia ordered when Milton pulled the buggy to stop. She didn't wait for an answer but raced inside. Thankfully she had brought her purse. She would pay for this with her own funds. Milton had suggested the idea, and she would pay.

Lydia entered the double doors and headed for the candy section. The selections were slim since this was trick or treat night, but she found a large bag of small Snickers and various flavors of wrapped gum. This would be sufficient, Lydia decided. She took her selections and paid at the counter.

The clerk handed Lydia the bagged candy. "Enjoy yourself."

"Thanks," Lydia said, rushing out again.

Milton leaned out of the buggy with a grin on his face. "There's a perfect corner right over there!" He pointed, his arm highlighted under the bright streetlights. "I've been watching it, and the children are pouring past."

"Let's go then." Lydia climbed back into the buggy. "And thanks for a great idea."

"My pleasure." Milton's face beamed.

Lydia focused on the street ahead of them. Milton was right. This was the perfect spot. Was this the beginning of a new life for them? Who said things had to go exactly the way they did for other couples in the community who ended up happily married? They were unique and their journey was unique, but she would not think of the future right now. This was the present, and Milton was with her.

He pulled to a stop, and they both hopped down from the seat. Already children were headed toward them with gleeful grins on their faces.

"A buggy out trick-or-treating," they hollered.

Lydia smiled up at Milton as they stood together and passed out the candy. Surely her heart would soon burst from happiness.

Chapter Twenty-Three

The dim November sunshine crept past the drapes of the upstairs bedroom where John lay. Laura knelt beside the bed and reached for John's hand. John hadn't spoken or looked at her in the ten minutes since she had entered his room. When she arrived at the Yoders' home, John's *mamm* had sent her up the stairs with a weary smile but without any delay.

"John," Laura whispered again. "I love you."

John kept his head turned away from her, his lips silent.

"I love you," Laura repeated. "Nothing about our love has changed. Remember how we…" Laura stopped. Perhaps it was best not to remind John of their last kiss.

John finally spoke softly. "How can you love me with Wendell after you?"

"How do you know about him?" Laura asked. "I don't care about Wendell. Surely you know that."

John turned toward her, his sightless eyes pale. "So it is true? Wendell wants to court you?"

Laura gripped the side of the bed with both hands. This was not *goot*. She couldn't lie. John already knew.

John turned his face back toward the wall. "You had best leave now, Laura. I can't be a proper husband to you if I can't see. You should accept Wendell's affections."

"But I don't love him!" Laura reached for John's face and turned it toward her. "Look at me. See in my eyes how much I love you?" At once, she realized how foolish her words were. "I'm sorry!" she said. "I wasn't thinking…"

"You should go now," John said softly as he turned his face away from her again.

Laura leaned across the bed. "But you love me, John. I know you do. What else matters?"

His shoulders shook but silence filled the room.

"Tell me you don't love me," she demanded.

Laura touched his shaven cheek. John blinked but didn't turn toward her. "Our love was given to us by the Lord," she whispered. "We can't let it slip away just because the road has become difficult." A tear slipped out of John's eye, and Laura continued. "Do you really want me to date and eventually marry Wendell, even while I still love you? And while you feel the same? What kind of life would that be? I'd see you at the Sunday meetings and know that we could have been wed. Meanwhile I would have to live with another man simply because he still has his sight. Do you want me to live like that, John? For all the years until the Lord calls me or Wendell home?"

John's face twitched and he opened his eyes. "How can we ever be happy when I can't see? When I can't work? I will not live on charity, Laura. My hospital bill is enough of a burden to the community. I won't saddle them with a foolish marriage when I can't support a wife and maybe *kinner*. The Scripture says such a man is worse than the heathen."

A soft knock on the door was followed by Hilda entering the room.

"Do you need anything, John?" Hilda asked.

"No, I'm okay," John said. "We were just talking."

Laura kept her gaze on John's face, not looking at Hilda. No doubt Hilda's entrance was a signal that it was time for Laura to leave. She knew John's parents wished she wouldn't show up to visit. Hilda's weary smile when she had arrived said that plainly enough. But how did they know what the right thing was for John and her? They loved John, but not the way she did.

The bedroom door closed softly as Hilda left.

"Kiss me," Laura whispered. "Quickly, before she comes in again."

"*Mamm* is not against us," John muttered. "My parents only want the best for me."

"But you love me. You know you do," Laura said, pulling him close. His lack of resistance told her that nothing had changed between them. She knew it hadn't, and now John knew. His hands reached for Laura and traced the outlines of her cheeks. From there John's fingers moved to her nose and the bottoms of her ears.

"See, this is how we will love each other," Laura whispered. "Nothing has changed!"

John groaned and pulled his hands away. "You are forbidden to me now, Laura. I am smitten of the Lord." His face darkened.

"No you aren't! We will walk through this valley together and come out on the other side still holding each other's hands. For as long as the Lord gives us the breath of life."

John shook his head. "It's too much to ask."

"We can plan our wedding this fall," Laura insisted. "We can still set the date for the end of December. That's late in the wedding season, but people will understand. And that will give us time to find a place to stay, and maybe find some work that you can do." Laura rushed on. "The Lord will provide. Marriage is from Him, John, and He honors love. We won't have much, but I don't need much if I have you!"

His face softened for a moment.

"It can be!" Laura almost shouted. She muffled her voice with a quick clamp of her hand over her mouth.

Something like the old grin played on John's face.

"You can have me as your *frau*, John." Laura clutched his hand in both of hers. "I don't want to say the vows with Wendell or any other man."

A hint of joy filled John's sightless eyes. "You don't?" His hand tightened in hers. "It can be like before? When I could see? When I was a man?"

Laura didn't hesitate. "You *are* a man, John. Nothing has taken that from you."

John shifted in the bed. His hands reached for hers. "Let go," he said, his voice soft. "You must see what I really am—a blind man."

Laura was wide-eyed. "But you can see the light!"

A soft smile filled John's face. "How did you know that? I never told anyone."

"Because I love you, and love knows."

"*Yah*, you do," John whispered. He held out his arms. Laura embraced him, and they clung to each other.

John finally let go. "Somehow I will walk again—I know I will."

"And we love each other," Laura added.

John smiled. "Since we're going to dream then, let's dream about our wedding."

"Oh, John!" Laura sat beside him. She had won the battle. John would wed her this fall.

"We need to find a place…" John began, but stopped. "No, all

I want to think about is you, and the sounds of our wedding day. I will hear Bishop Ezra's voice as he preaches the main sermon, and you'll be beside me—well, across the aisle on the chairs in front of your living room. I will think of how the house appeared once, and of your face, and I will know that I will touch your eyes that night. I will feel your presence all day, even if I don't—"

"I know you will see," Laura interrupted. "Just differently. We will be the same people, and the Lord will help us."

"I can almost believe." John hesitated. "You've always inspired me to believe, even before this happened." His hand lingered on his sightless eyes. "Did I love you too much, Laura? Is that why my sight was taken from me?"

"No one can love too much," she told him.

John didn't appear convinced. "I do love you. Tell me what the girls will wear in the wedding party."

Laura took a deep breath. She had believed, and now the Lord had given. This was like a dream. "A dusty blue," she said, "and a dark blue for me. That will be appropriate. We don't want to draw attention to ourselves."

"*Yah*," John agreed. "There are many who will wonder, and we shouldn't offend them."

"We won't offend them," Laura assured him. "But don't think about the community right now. Think about us. December will come quickly, and we have many plans that must be made."

John seemed lost in thought, but his smile hadn't faded. "I will take up harness work. I can do that. Uncle Junior has a shop north of the community, and I can learn there. I once heard him say that he never has time for all the detailed embroidery that the *Englisha* want done for their show horses. With my sight gone, I can learn patience. I can work with my hands, and it pays well. Uncle Junior said so."

"You see the positive!" Laura exclaimed, wrapping John in

another tight hug. "The Lord is already speaking. He will supply a small house where we can live and raise our *kinner*. We don't need much or anything fancy." They were silent for a moment. "We must tell your *mamm*," Laura said.

John looked toward the window. "I had best tell her, and *Daett* as well. You shouldn't be in on this."

"But I am soon to be your *frau*."

John didn't back down. "I will speak to them myself." He almost looked like the John of old with his resolute face.

Laura gave him a quick hug. "As you see best then. I guess it's time to act like you'll be my husband soon."

A hint of a smile crossed John's face. "*Yah*, it is best," he agreed. "There are things I must tell *Mamm* and *Daett* alone, since they have spoken such strong words against us already and…" John paused, but the resolution on his face didn't fade away.

"You'll say the right thing." Laura's arms tightened on his shoulder. "I'll go now," she said.

"You have been so sweet today," John told her before she left the room.

At the bottom of the stairs, John's *mamm* looked up with concern, but Laura didn't stop.

"See you soon," Laura called as she stepped outside and walked down the porch steps.

Chapter Twenty-Four

On Friday evening Laura was washing the supper dishes by herself. Nelson and Lester were upstairs while *Daett* relaxed in the living room reading his weekly *Budget*. She should have insisted that Lester help dry the dishes, but he always made such a fuss over women's work that it wasn't worth the effort. John wouldn't act that way, Laura comforted herself. He was kind and gentle, and once they were wed, he would love to help her with the dishes. John's miracle of walking again would come true. They would work together and linger over the kitchen sink in the winter hours of the coming year. John might be blind, but he could feel with his hands and especially with his heart. She could imagine John pausing to give her a hug as he wiped the plates dry.

Laura smiled and twirled a dish in her hand. She should have told *Daett* tonight about their wedding plans, but she hadn't. She had tried right after supper, but the words had stuck in her mouth. Perhaps it would be best if she brought John over to the house once he could walk, and they could tell *Daett* together. Maybe John's parents would even consent to come along, since this was an unusual case. They could all talk together about the future and prevent any further uncertainty between the families.

"The Lord will work it all out," Laura spoke aloud.

She must not doubt now. Not when John had finally believed and agreed to wed her. Laura picked up a plate and paused as she caught a glimpse of a buggy in the kitchen window. She leaned over the sink for a closer look. The buggy had stopped by the barn, and John's *mamm*, Hilda, was climbing out, followed by his *daett*, Herman. Laura pulled back from the window, and the plate slid from her hand and into the soapy water with a splash. Why were John's parents here? Had they come to help plan the wedding of their own initiative?

Laura took another peek out of the kitchen window. There was no sign of John of course, and his parents were already on their way up the walk. This was not *goot*. It could only mean one thing. John's *mamm* and *daett* had come to speak with *Daett*. She should have forced herself to tell him at supper, but now it was too late. Laura dropped the washcloth and raced into the living room, but *Daett* was already out the front door and standing on the porch with a perplexed look on his face. She wanted to reach out and pull *Daett* back into the house, but that wouldn't work. How foolish she had been not to force the words out of her mouth at supper.

Laura tried to still the rapid beating of her heart. No doubt John's parents had come to express their disapproval of the wedding plans. Deep down, she knew and had known all day. That was why she hadn't been able to speak with *Daett*. But she must pray and believe, no matter what happened next. "Dear Lord, please, oh please, do something," Laura whispered.

Daett now stepped off the porch to approach Hilda and Herman. She couldn't hear their voices, but *Daett* was smiling. Whatever Herman had said, it wasn't about a forbidden wedding. Laura ducked behind the drapes before she fled into the kitchen. She should be at work when Hilda and Herman walked in. That would make the best impression. She would appear innocent, even if she wasn't. John's parents knew by now that she had persuaded John to plan the wedding. How foolish she had been to leave the Yoders' house before she had spoken with Hilda about the matter. Instead she had left riding a euphoric cloud of emotion because John had consented to a wedding. She could have refuted any objections Hilda had before they were set in stone. Now she would have to speak with great deference with so many parents present.

Laura finished the last of the dishes and draped the wet cloth over the dryer rack. She could hear the voices clearly rising and falling in the living room.

"We thought we'd come over to speak with you about a matter," Herman was saying. "But I suppose Laura already told you the basics."

"No, she hasn't mentioned anything unusual," *Daett* said. "Has Laura done something she shouldn't have?"

The voices were lowered, and Laura couldn't hear their response. But *Daett's* voice was soon plain enough. "Laura. Come here."

Hilda smiled when Laura walked in the living room, but there was sadness tinged around the edges of her face.

Daett didn't beat around the bush. "What's this I hear about you planning to wed John this fall?"

"*Yah*," Laura managed. "I was going to tell you, but…" There really was no excuse, and *Daett* knew so.

"But with *Mamm* gone, how did you think we could manage?" *Daett* exclaimed.

Herman cleared his throat. "I think the objections are a little more serious than that, Yost. We don't feel our son should wed your daughter at all. Not in his condition. He has already been enough of a burden on the community's compassion. There's no way John can take care of a *frau* in his state, let alone *kinner* if the Lord should give any to this union—that is, if this miracle of walking should happen. But even without *kinner*, there are heavy responsibilities associated with a marriage."

"This is true," *Daett* said. He looked straight at Laura. "Surely you know this, daughter?"

"The Lord will help us," Laura whispered. "We love each other. Why would the Lord give us this love if we are not to marry? Please try to understand, *Daett*."

Hilda's smile was gone. "It cannot be! I don't want to sound cruel or harsh. We were in favor of John and Laura's marriage before the accident, but much has changed since then. We simply can no longer give our blessing to this union. Even if John walks again and even learns a trade, that still won't build a home or buy a farm. John cannot pay the bills and support a *frau* and *kinner* as a blind man."

Daett looked at Laura again. "*Yah*, this is true. You should know this, Laura."

"The Lord will help us," were the only words that would come out of Laura's mouth.

"We appreciate Laura's faith," Herman said. "But we must be practical and use the wisdom the Lord has given us. To walk blindly into an impossible situation would be against His will. We don't think John should take Laura as his *frau*, or anyone else for that matter. We think our feelings are validated by what we know of Wendell's interest in your daughter. That is a sign from the Lord, we feel, that John should give up his engagement to Laura. Wendell is quite certain he can win Laura's love if John will not interfere. Such things are"—Herman cleared his throat—"well, they are tender subjects, but we think that Laura's rejection of Wendell's offer out of hand is not wise. We have spoken with both Deacon William and Bishop Ezra about the matter, and they agree with us."

"You would have me marry Wendell when I don't love him?" The words burst out like a storm.

Hilda gave Laura a sharp look. "I think this is a subject for the parents. Young people are not known for their wisdom in these matters."

Laura kept silent. She had to control herself.

"We have made ourselves plain enough, I think," Herman said. "Laura is to call off her wedding plans and not come over to our house to see John again. Beyond that it is up to you, Yost, but we think it best if Laura considers Wendell's offer seriously. The least she can do is date the man for a few months. How else can Laura know if she loves him or not?"

"Because I love John, and I won't stop loving him." The words exploded again.

From the look on Hilda's face, Laura had just sealed her doom. Hilda probably no longer wanted her as a daughter-in-law even if John could see with the vision of a hawk.

"You have a *goot* evening then." Hilda forced a smile, rose from her seat, and headed for the front door ahead of her husband.

Daett hurried forward to see them out, but Herman waved him back. "Keep your seat, Yost. We're old enough to find our way out."

They all chuckled at Herman's words, and Laura fled to the kitchen. How could they take this so lightly? John loved her, and she loved him. She should be weeping and wailing right now, filling the house with noise. Instead she collapsed in a kitchen chair and buried her face in her hands as the Yoders' buggy left the driveway. Moments later *Daett* appeared in the kitchen doorway and seated himself beside Laura. "I can't say that I'm surprised. I know you loved John, but Herman and Hilda are right. And you can't marry the man if his parents object—let alone Bishop Ezra and Deacon William."

"I do love him!" Laura wailed. "Why can't you be on my side?"

Daett thought for a moment. "There's nothing wrong with loving. But sometimes there are considerations other than love."

"If I can't wed John, then I will never wed anyone else," Laura declared. "Never!"

"Now, now," *Daett* said with a tender smile. "The Yoders mean well, and I happen to agree that you and John have no business beginning a married life together this winter."

Laura grasped at straws. "Then next year?"

Daett thought again before he answered. "I think the Yoders are also right that you should accept Wendell's offer to date you. A girl I knew once froze her heart after she couldn't have her way in love, and things never…" *Daett* looked away and fell silent.

"You don't have to tell me about Nancy," Laura said. "I already know about your past with her. But I'm not cutting off my relationship with John."

"You don't have much choice." *Daett* regarded her. "You are not welcome at the Yoders' any longer."

"And you think that's right?"

"What I think is that you need to learn obedience, Laura," *Daett* said. "This attitude of yours in unbecoming for a daughter of the community. Maybe if you hadn't been so headstrong at the barnraising the accident would never have happened."

Laura looked away as tears formed. "You really feel that way?" She had almost forgotten that she had blamed herself for John's accident. And now *Daett* had brought it up.

"I don't really know," *Daett* said. "John was distracted. There is no question about that. Why else would the man fall? John has always been an expert on the barn beams."

Laura leaped to her feet, but *Daett* grabbed hold of her arm. "Sit, daughter. Running away isn't going to help."

Laura sat slowly and lowered her head in her arms again. *Daett* tugged on her shoulder. "I know this is difficult to see, but the Yoders are right."

Laura raised her head to face *Daett*. "Why would you want me to leave the man I love, just because he is in trouble? Doesn't the community believe in standing by each other through thick or thin, for better or worse, and now you want me to abandon John?"

A smile played on *Daett's* face. "Is this the sermon you gave John? No wonder he was persuaded to marry you."

Laura looked away. After a moment of silence, she bounced to her feet and said, "I'm going over to see Wendell right now!"

"To accept his marriage offer?" *Daett* asked. "That's a little forward, even for you."

"No. I'm going to tell him to get lost," Laura snapped. "Maybe that will put some sense in everyone."

"You will do no such thing," *Daett* said. "You're staying right here. And when Wendell next asks you for a date, you are accepting."

Laura gasped. "But I can't. I'll never love Wendell. Never!"

"*Yah*, you can. I think Wendell is quite a catch. He comes from a *goot* family, and they have their farms paid off. There isn't a reason in the world why you can't date the man."

Laura stared at the floor. How was she to obey this order? She couldn't, but she must if she wanted to remain in *goot* standing with the community. Trouble with Deacon William or Bishop Ezra was the last thing she needed. But dating Wendell? How could she?

"You *can*," *Daett* said, as if he could read Laura's thoughts. "You don't have to think about marrying him yet. Being around another man and getting your mind off of John may be exactly what is needed. Now go to bed and get some sleep. We have to get up early tomorrow morning for our Saturday work and preparations for the Lord's day."

Laura stood and left without a backward glance. Nelson stuck his head out of his room when she reached the top of the stairs. "What's going on?" he asked. "Awful lot of fuss down there."

"Trouble!" Laura said, rushing past. She didn't want to insult Nelson, but if she tried to explain, the tears would gush. That she didn't need.

Nelson shrugged and reentered his bedroom before Laura closed the door behind her. She flopped down on her bed and let the tears come. Long moments later, she stood and walked to the window to look up at the stars. They twinkled in the heavens in all their fall glory.

"Somehow we will make it," Laura said out loud. "Even if I have to see that horrible Wendell once or twice. Maybe that's the only way to demonstrate to the man that I feel no love for him. Surely he won't wish for a *frau* who doesn't have feelings for him."

Laura took another look up at the stars before she slipped under the quilt and fell fast asleep.

Chapter Twenty-Five

Amid the chill of the evening, Nancy stepped out on her front porch to listen to the distant sound of a horse's hooves on the pavement. Was someone on their way to visit her? If so, who? Deacon William's daughter, Betsy, was in the kitchen. Betsy was staying with Nancy all the time now, even at the schoolhouse. There was no moment when she was alone, so Deacon William would have no cause for a trip to her house. But maybe he wanted to check on how things were progressing. The deacon wasn't one to take his information secondhand, even if his daughter was the source.

Nancy listened again to the beat of the horse's hooves as they drew closer. She still wrestled with what she had accepted as the will of the community, but perhaps the option to leave the community to marry Charles no longer even existed. Charles might have been deeply offended by whatever Deacon William had told him, and their relationship might have been ruined beyond repair. But deep down she knew this wasn't true. Charles was a patient and kind man. He probably knew how her situation was playing out. Charles would take her back with open arms. Hadn't his truck drifted past the schoolhouse several times in the past few days? Betsy always noticed and made a point to show her face at the door before Charles drove in. Nancy could have hurried out of the schoolhouse, jumped in his truck, and left her current life behind, and Betsy couldn't have stopped her. Yet she hadn't. She had sat still and waited. But for what?

Nancy sighed and slipped back into the house. Maybe the buggy would go on past. If it didn't, she would see who had arrived soon enough.

"Visitors?" Betsy asked when Nancy walked back in the kitchen.

"I'm not expecting anyone," Nancy replied, but that went without saying. Betsy knew her routine well.

Betsy nodded. "*Daett* said he would stop by sometime this week, but he didn't say when."

"Then maybe it's him." Nancy busied herself with the last of the supper dishes.

Moments later Betsy exclaimed, "It's not *Daett*! It's Yost Mast!"

Nancy caught her breath. In a way she had expected this. Even after all these years.

Betsy regarded her with a strange look. "Why would Yost be here?"

Nancy didn't respond. What was there to say that a decent teenager would understand? Instead, she left the kitchen and went out the front door. Yost stood beside his buggy, as if he wasn't sure what step to take next. She might as well face this head-on.

"Yost." She greeted him as the distance closed between them.

"*Goot* evening, Nancy," Yost said. "Can I come in?"

"Maybe on the porch." Nancy motioned with her head. "Betsy's inside."

"I know," Yost said. "Deacon William told me."

Nancy led the way to the porch, their footsteps the only sound in the quiet evening air. She climbed the steps and sat down.

"Can I sit?" Yost motioned toward the open seat beside her.

"There's still room." Nancy didn't look at him.

"I haven't gotten roly-poly in my old age," Yost cracked. "At least not yet."

"*Yah*." Nancy managed to smile. "You have aged well."

"And you too," he returned.

Nancy looked away. Not that long ago, such words from Yost would have been most inappropriate, but things had changed with the death of Lavina. Nancy could still remember sweet words from Yost after all those long years. Words he doubtless gave Lavina many times since then. The only problem was, Nancy's heart no longer beat faster at his words. She clasped her hands and looked down at the porch floor. Yost would have to state what he wanted. She would not help him broach the subject.

Yost finally filled the silence. "It's a beautiful evening. How long is Betsy staying with you?"

"Perhaps you know that since you no doubt spoke with Deacon William!" The sharpness of Nancy's words hung in the air.

"Sorry, I didn't mean anything." Yost laid his worn hands on his denim trousers.

"Did Deacon William send you?"

Yost shook his head. "I came of my own free will. I'm sorry if my visit offends you after all these years. But when Lavina passed, I knew that I should...the community wants us to heal the past, Nancy." Yost paused. "Anyway, with that in mind, I thought of you, and of our time together years ago. I know that I took another direction, which I understood as from the Lord, but now Lavina's gone and we are both still here. And there is that other problem."

"So this is how it will be?" Nancy met his gaze. "All matter-of-fact? No explanation for why you cut off our relationship and chose another woman? Not that I blamed you. I have plenty of faults, and Lavina has given you fine *kinner*, but..."

Yost laid his hand on Nancy's arm. "I'm clumsy, Nancy, and I do need to explain. I guess that's what I've been avoiding."

Nancy waited while Yost stared off across the open fields, where long shadows stretched toward the horizon.

"The truth is I don't know," Yost finally said. "We were seeing each other for some time when Lavina caught my eye. I know that was probably wrong, but I told myself that we weren't married, and…" His voice trailed off.

"So even though I loved you with my whole heart, you walked away?" Nancy's tone turned bitter.

"I'm sorry, Nancy." Yost hung his head. "That's all I can say. Lavina was a *goot mamm* to our *kinner*, and a *goot frau* for me, but the Lord has taken her home. You are not without your own mistakes, I'm thinking. So perhaps you shouldn't be too hard on me."

Nancy gasped. "Are you referring to Charles?"

"I didn't mean more than I said, so don't be offended. But I'm impressed greatly that you're still here. That much can be said in your favor. You could have left with the man. Others have done so before you, but you haven't."

"You think maybe I've been waiting for a marriage proposal from you?"

Yost laughed. "You wouldn't be like that, I'm thinking. You've always been dedicated to the community and to our way of life. That's why I trust you."

"But what if I don't trust you?"

Yost regarded Nancy for a moment. "We're supposed to heal this wound, you know. Do you expect me to do the same thing twice, to cut off our relationship—if we have another one?"

Nancy didn't answer the question. "So do you want one?"

Yost grunted. "Why else would I be here? You are a fine woman."

Nancy shrugged. "Maybe I should marry you. If nothing else to get Betsy out of the house and regain some peace and quiet at the schoolhouse. I'm not used to having someone breathing down my neck all day."

Yost didn't appear too pleased. "I thought Deacon William told me you were taking this well."

Nancy laughed. "Did you expect to find me where you left me, Yost? Did you think all those lonely years would leave me unchanged? You know how I used to feel about you, but you married someone else. And now you show up once your *frau* passes, and you want me to dance and sing for joy. Is that it, Yost?"

"I guess I wasn't thinking of it that way," Yost replied. "I am wrong again, it seems."

"Am I the kind of *frau* you want?"

Yost smiled. "I'm back at your doorstep for the second time. It seems the Lord has His plans better figured out than I do."

Nancy looked away. "Do you know the tears I cried over you? I wept my eyes out after you cut off our relationship. And to add insult to injury, you began dating Lavina not three weeks later. How do you think that made me feel?"

Yost ran his shoe around in circles on the porch floor before he answered. "Rotten, I suppose."

"*Yah*," Nancy said. "And then some."

"Why did you never marry?" Yost seemed to feel the need to change the subject. "In the community, of course," he added.

"Maybe the Lord was saving me for your second marriage?" The bitterness returned to her words.

Yost shook his head. "We can go around in circles all evening, Nancy, and still get nowhere. The past is the past, both yours and mine. I know the hurt is there. I can't change that I said the marriage vows with Lavina, and you couldn't help that your wounded heart fell in love with an *Englisha* man. But let's move on now. I need a *frau*, and my *kinner* could use a *mamm*. Laura especially is going through a lot right now. I think you could help her."

Nancy bit back another bitter response. Perhaps somewhere in there was the Yost who used to love her. She had to wonder if that was true. He wasn't here for practical reasons alone. She cautiously reached for his hand. How often had she done that in Yost's buggy when he drove her home from the Sunday evening hymn singings?

A smile crept across Yost's face as he wrapped his fingers around hers. He did remember. This was exactly how Yost used to respond. Nancy leaned her head against his shoulder and allowed herself to drift back through the past. She could almost hear the whir of the buggy wheels under her, and envision Yost's young, handsome form seated beside her. She looked up at his face. He was still handsome but definitely older. As was she.

"So how do we do this?" Nancy asked.

Yost chuckled. "I guess we'll have to take things a step at a time. I could start by taking you home again on Sunday evenings, like old times."

Nancy sat bolt upright. "You would drive me home from the hymn singing again?"

Yost appeared puzzled. "Well, I thought we could pick up where we left off."

Nancy shook her head. "I'll leave those times in my memory, thank you. I'm sure they wouldn't be the same. But you can come over on Sunday evening if you want. We can talk and I can make popcorn."

"Isn't that like old times?" Yost teased.

"Maybe," Nancy conceded, "but no buggy rides home from the hymn singing. We're too old for that."

Yost gave in easily. "Okay. Whatever you want." He stood to leave. "I'll see you next Sunday night then. Say, six o'clock or so?"

"That's fine." Nancy gave him a sheepish smile. Her eyes watered, but thankfully Yost didn't seem to notice.

He stopped to wave before he climbed into his buggy and drove out the lane. Slowly Nancy felt her way back inside the house. Betsy looked up from the couch with a smile. "So is that what it looked like it was?"

"It is," Nancy replied. "He's coming back next Sunday evening for a date."

"He's a handsome man," Betsy said with a sly grin.

Nancy allowed a smile to fill her face. "That he is, indeed."

Chapter Twenty-Six

A week before Thanksgiving, Lydia shooed two loose turkeys they used for a display back into their crates. Uncle Henry knew how to create a buzz for his roadside stand, all while making a handsome profit. The pair had become quite the pets in the past weeks. She couldn't bring herself to sell them, even after Uncle Henry had suggested gently this morning, "Best to let them go soon, Lydia."

"I let the children pet them, and that increases sales," she had begged.

Uncle Henry had grinned, and said no more. They would settle the fate of Brisket and Bucket, as she had dubbed the pair, later. She only said the names out loud around *Englisha* people. Both Uncle Henry and Milton would laugh at her for naming turkeys, but she didn't care. Giving the turkeys names had also helped sales.

The roadside stand had been turned into a turkey market two weeks ago. The turkeys, all in their prime, were kept in a fenced hay field behind Uncle Henry's farm. There they grew even fatter on choice feed hauled in from Heuvelton and natural, tasty morsels like grasshoppers. They were sold live, but for a small fee, they could be made oven-ready.

What that entailed, she didn't want to think about. Milton took care of the orders. Men could handle such things. Lydia turned her thoughts to her duties. There was an hour of daylight left, and there would likely be a hard frost overnight. The clear blue sky all day and the brisk northern wind coming down from Canada forecast that clearly enough.

"We're moving everything inside for the night," Uncle Henry had informed her an hour ago. "Got to keep these turkeys and vegetables in *goot* spirits for another week." Uncle Henry laughed. "Milton will be out with the wagon to help you soon."

Even now, the snort of Milton's team could be heard in the trees. Lydia brushed dust off her apron and waited as Milton drove up.

"Why haven't you sold everything?" Milton teased before leaping down from the wagon.

"Because you chase away all the customers with the awful things you do with those turkeys," Lydia shot back.

Milton laughed. "I think my fine turkey preparations have the whole county impressed. Clean! Fast! Efficient!"

"You are so conceited!" Lydia said, but she couldn't help but join in Milton's laughter.

Milton lifted the first box of produce and slid the carton onto the wagon bed. "I hear my sister is dating your *daett*."

Lydia's mind tried to adjust. How could it be? "*Daett* dating Nancy?"

Milton grinned. "You're behind the times, girl."

"I've not been home much lately," Lydia responded. "So tell me."

Milton shrugged. "They're seeing each other, and that's all I know. There's not much to it. If I don't miss my guess, they may yet be married by Christmas."

Lydia tried to still the loud beat of her heart. Was this the miracle she had prayed for? If Nancy married someone from the community instead of the horrible *Englisha* man, Milton's recent reforms might last.

"Don't you approve?" Milton stopped with a carton in his arms to stare at her.

"Of course I do." Lydia forced herself to bustle about. "This could be an answer to prayer in so many ways."

"*Yah*, I suppose…" he said. Yet Milton appeared puzzled.

Lydia wasn't about to explain or express her doubts to him. That might make them come true. Milton hadn't brought up the subject of his *Englisha* automobile lately, even though she was sure he still owned the vehicle. In spite of this, Milton hadn't mentioned jumping the fence once since that *wunderbah* evening they had spent together in Heuvelton passing out candy. Of course, Milton hadn't mentioned anything else either, but he was just taking his time, Lydia assured herself. She knew Milton was still wavering between two worlds, but she could live with that. This gift from the Lord had already moved much further and faster than she had dared hope. Maybe some of Laura's faith had indeed rubbed off on her.

"Do you want to go out tonight again?" Milton asked, as if he was reading her thoughts.

Lydia didn't miss a beat. "Of course, I'd love to. As long as—"

"*Yah*," Milton cut her off. "I'll behave myself. No stopping in at the *rumspringa* gatherings, and no *Englisha* automobiles." He sounded just a touch bitter.

"I wish you'd get rid of that car of yours and join the baptismal class," Lydia said.

Milton grinned and ignored her comment. "I'm thinking a nice buggy ride into Heuvelton should be just the thing for tonight. Maybe we'll have a pleasant surprise."

"Maybe," Lydia allowed. "That was a sweet time we had on Halloween."

Milton's grin broadened. "Sweet is right…with all that candy we gave out."

Lydia rolled her eyes. "Oh brother!"

Milton laughed. "Well, then, here's to a pleasant evening. Do you want to ride up with me right now?" Milton grunted as he loaded the last carton.

"I'll walk, but thanks," Lydia chirped. "I have to put some of these empty boxes away."

"Then I'll stay and help you for a few minutes. We'll have the place spick-and-span in no time."

Lydia regarded Milton for a moment. "That's nice of you."

"Hey!" He held up both hands. "I'm always nice."

Lydia laughed. "You don't have to put on airs, you know."

Milton responded with a humble and fallen face.

Lydia laughed harder. "That's also airs, though you do look quite repentant."

"That's me," he said, busying himself with the last of the boxes.

She loved the man. There was no question about that. Whether Milton loved her enough to not jump the fence was the question. But she must not despair. So far his offer of rides into town had been signs that pointed in the right direction.

"Okay, clean enough," Milton announced. He surveyed the stand as if to check on himself.

Having tidied the stand, Lydia hopped up onto the wagon seat, and Milton followed her. "Getup!" he hollered to the team.

Lydia clung to Milton's arm as they bounced down the dirt lane. "I hope we have a smoother ride tonight," Lydia said.

Milton chuckled. "I guess we could take the wagon into town and make a hayride out of the evening."

"Really?" Lydia exclaimed. "Did you just think of that?"

Milton winked. "I'm quick on my feet, you know."

"And full of yourself." Lydia nestled against him on the smooth stretch past the house. If Uncle Henry or others of the family saw her, she wouldn't care. She may as well let the whole world know that she loved Milton.

"Whoa there!" Milton brought the wagon to an expert stop by the barn door. "Let's take your Uncle Henry's children along for the hayride. We can stop in at several of the Amish families' places along this road, and we'll have the wagon filled with children in no time." Milton grinned as he hopped down from the wagon. "Would you like that?" he asked over his shoulder.

"You know I would," she said, climbing down slowly to unload the boxes. They unhitched the team of horses when they finished, and Milton took them inside for water and feed.

"I'll leave their harnesses on," Milton said when he returned moments later. "They'll make the perfect team for our hayride tonight."

"I can't wait," Lydia said, smiling up at him. "You know, you can be really sweet when you want to be."

Milton glowed. "Now that's a compliment coming from you. I'll store that up for many pleasant memories in the cold days ahead this winter."

"Stop teasing," Lydia chided. "You know I like you."

"And I like you." He looked down at her with a pleased expression. "Then a hayride it will be. How's the moon tonight? Do you remember?"

Lydia's mind raced. "I think it's been cloudy the past few nights, but I wasn't really paying attention."

Milton glanced at the sky, where a lone star twinkled in the east above the horizon. "It'll be cold, but the moon's coming up around nine or so. I think it'll be clear."

"You pay attention to such things?" Lydia asked.

"I do when you're around," he said.

Lydia tried to ignore the compliment. "This hayride is such a great idea. Right up there with passing out candy for trick or treat. I don't understand where your great ideas come from."

"From right here." He tapped his chest. "You do *wunderbah* things for me, Lydia."

Lydia looked away as heat rose into her face. Thankfully Uncle Henry appeared in the barn door and she didn't have to answer.

"Sold everything today?" Uncle Henry asked with a quick look at the empty wagon.

"I tried," Lydia said. "But no, we put the unsold things in the storage bin as always."

"The heat from the barn animals should keep things from freezing," Milton added.

"So what are your plans for tonight?" Uncle Henry asked. "I see the horses still have their harnesses on."

"Oh, Uncle Henry," Lydia gushed. "Milton has come up with a *wunderbah* idea. He's taking me and the children for a hayride tonight, and the neighborhood children as well. Whoever lives on this road who wants to."

"If you'll let me use the team?" Milton hastened to ask.

Uncle Henry smiled. "You have hit on a perfect idea, Milton. We should do things like that more often. Lydia, you might want to go in and help Millie with supper. That'll move things along so you kids can get started."

"*Yah*, of course!" Lydia hurried off toward the house with great joy. The Lord was continuing to send signs her way that His blessing was on their love. Uncle Henry approved fully. She was sure of that, and now there was Nancy and *Daett*. How many more signs of assurance did she need?

Aunt Millie looked up from the stove when Lydia rushed into the kitchen with a smile on her face. "What's the hurry?"

"Milton's taking me and the neighborhood children for a hayride tonight," Lydia said. "Uncle Henry said I should help with supper."

"*Goot* thing I'm on time then," Aunt Millie said. "This will be a great joy for the children."

"And for me!" Lydia said, wondering if she had just admitted too much.

Aunt Millie laughed. "There's nothing wrong with being in love, dear. We all go through it."

Lydia busied herself setting the table and didn't respond.

"Why Milton doesn't clinch the deal with you is beyond me," Aunt Millie said quietly. "His sister's straightened up her act now, and there should be no reason for any hesitation on Milton's part. He's such a nice man."

"*Yah*, he is very nice," Lydia whispered, but Aunt Millie didn't hear. She had gone to call the children down from upstairs. Lydia didn't repeat herself when Aunt Millie returned with two of the school-age children in tow.

Aunt Millie looked down at her two children and announced, "Lydia has some *wunderbah* news for you."

"We're going on a hayride tonight with Milton!" Lydia responded on cue.

Astonished looks turned into glee. "Really? Tonight? A hayride?"

"Right after supper," Millie said.

All the food was on the table when Uncle Henry and Milton appeared fifteen minutes later. The last of the children came downstairs, and everyone took their places at the table.

Uncle Henry bowed his head in a prayer of thanks, and Lydia did likewise—but not before she snuck a quick look at Milton.

He grinned back and mouthed the words, "You're sweet." Or so it appeared. She couldn't tell for sure, but a warmth filled her.

Lydia forced herself to focus on Uncle Henry's prayer. "Now unto the God of our fathers, we give thanks for this evening. We give thanks for Milton and his *goot* idea, and for Lydia who has come to help out with the roadside stand. Bless them both, Lord, and protect everyone on the road. In Jesus' name, amen."

Lydia snuck another look at Milton as she passed the food, and he smiled back broadly. Clearly he was enjoying himself, and not just because of the food. He was looking forward to spending the evening with her. Lydia's throat tightened at the thought. She filled her own plate and somehow chewed and swallowed.

"Eat plenty," Uncle Henry hollered out, as if they needed encouragement. "Brisk evenings outside burn up lots of energy."

"We should all go along," Aunt Millie said, apparently caught up in the excitement.

Uncle Henry seemed to ponder the idea. "Maybe we should. If Milton and Lydia don't object."

"That would be great," Milton said. "After all, it's your team of horses we're using."

"We'll sit in the back with the children," Uncle Henry decided, a twinkle in his eye. "Milton and Lydia will be undisturbed up front on the wagon seat."

"Then let's give thanks and be on our way," Millie said. "This is getting better all the time."

Uncle Henry bowed his head again and moments later announced the amen. Lydia jumped to her feet and began to clear the table.

Aunt Millie tried to stop her. "This can wait until later."

"I'll work on it while you get the children ready," Lydia said.

"I'll help her," Milton added.

"Well!" Aunt Millie exclaimed. "Then I will hurry."

She disappeared into the living room with the children in tow. Uncle Henry left by the washroom door to bring the wagon up to the house.

"This is so sweet of you," Lydia whispered in Milton's direction. He began to move the plates to the counter and seemed to know where things went.

"Not as sweet as you are," he whispered back, a wicked grin on his face.

She wanted to hug him and hold him tight right there. This was what Laura must have felt for John. No wonder her sister was so determined to marry the man.

Aunt Millie reappeared in the kitchen doorway. "Time to go!"

"That was fast," Milton said. He tugged on Lydia's arm as she tried to clean another dish. "Time to go, your aunt said."

Lydia thought she saw him mouth the word *sweetheart* to her, right there in front of everyone. Only Milton would dare such a thing, even at a whisper.

"You have some nerve," she told him on the way out, but with a smile.

His grin was all the confirmation she needed. Milton had called her his sweetheart.

Lydia clung to his arm as they approached the wagon, only letting go to climb into the front seat. Uncle Henry, Aunt Millie, and their children climbed onto the seats in the back, which Milton and Uncle Henry had set up while Lydia helped Aunt Millie in the kitchen before supper.

Milton took the reins and hollered, "Getup!"

As the wagon bounced out the lane, Uncle Henry began to sing a hymn and the others joined in. The music hung under the trees along the lane and wafted into the open air toward the stars as they approached Highway 184. Lydia leaned against Milton's shoulder. Milton sang along with the hymn, but she couldn't make the slightest sound come from her throat at the moment.

They went north to Kokomo Corner and then turned left to stop at the first Amish house. Uncle Henry jumped down to pound on the front door. "Anyone up to a hayride tonight?"

Astonished faces appeared, followed by a rush for winter coats and a scramble of legs and arms as children climbed up on the bales of hay. The parents joined Uncle Henry and Aunt Millie in the back on the next stop. By the third home, they were full and heading south on West Road, singing hymns until the moon lifted its smiling face above the horizon.

"I told you the moon would be up," Milton crowed above the singing.

Lydia didn't answer. She buried her face in his coat until her tears had dried.

Chapter Twenty-Seven

Early on Thanksgiving morning, the sun sent streams of light over the distant horizon and shrouded Milton's buggy in a soft glow. Lydia nestled herself under the buggy blanket with Milton beside her. His horse, Red, blew great breaths of steam into the brisk air. They had been on the road for half an hour already, headed home toward the Masts' place for Thanksgiving Day. Lydia hadn't said much so far, and neither had Milton. The wonder of his presence beside her was enough. From all appearances the Lord had given Milton's love to her.

Lydia leaned her head against Milton's shoulder and thought of the *wunderbah* hayride they had been on last week. Today would prove just as blessed, she was sure. Milton was with her, and he loved her. What else could she want? Lydia snuggled deeper into the buggy blanket and searched for Milton's arm.

Milton turned his head to smile down at her. "A little chilly, isn't it?"

Not with you in the buggy, she wanted to say, but she wasn't quite bold enough. Not yet. Instead she smiled up at him. "Thanks for taking me home today."

"It's my pleasure," Milton said with a smile.

The warmth under the buggy blanket crept through her, and increased the beat of her heart. Some morning she would believe that Milton had fully made up his mind not to jump the fence. She would also believe that Milton planned to join the baptismal class in the spring. He had never said so, but surely that was on his list of must-do things if he planned to wed her. Wasn't that where love eventually led, and wouldn't that be the natural result of the *goot* times they had spent together?

After a few moments Lydia dared to glance up at Milton again, but he seemed distracted as he watched the passing trees. "Does Laura still have her mind set on marrying John?" Milton asked.

"*Yah.*" Lydia struggled to sit up straight under the buggy blanket. "As far as I know."

"Maybe you can speak to her today and persuade her otherwise," Milton said. "John's parents have made their wishes clear enough, even if John has managed to sit up in bed a few times and move his legs. They still won't let her marry a blind man. She really needs to accept Wendell Kaufman's offer of a date. All the man wants is a chance to see if the relationship will work."

Lydia forced a laugh. "That's not quite my impression of the man. He's no meek and mild fellow like John. And I know that's what Laura wants."

Milton shrugged. "I'm just saying. Your sister shouldn't marry a blind man. On that I agree."

Lydia gasped. "Why are you suddenly so interested in the subject?"

"I'm not." Milton said. "I don't know Wendell that well. I just want what's best for you and your family."

"I'm standing with Laura on this," Lydia said. "If John is sitting up in bed and moving his legs, he'll walk eventually. She's already been given one miracle. Who's to say that she won't be given another one?"

"You think John will see someday?"

"I don't know about that," Lydia admitted. "But why can't they find a way to love each other and make it in spite of his blindness?"

"It would be very hard to make it work," Milton said, jiggling the reins. "I guess this is a touchy subject, isn't it?"

Lydia nodded, and they rode the rest of the way in silence until *Daett's* farm came into view ahead of them.

"Still looks the same." Milton grinned.

"*Yah*...home," she managed.

Daett must have heard them coming and was outside waiting. He called out, "*Goot* morning, Lydia! If it isn't my long-lost daughter herself!"

Lydia hopped down to fly into *Daett's* arms. "It's so *goot* to see you," she said.

Milton chuckled. "You have a lovely daughter, Yost. She's doing an excellent job at the roadside stand. I declare we wouldn't have moved half the things we did, if Lydia hadn't been out there with her smile and friendly greeting."

Daett grinned. "I'm sure you're right. Here, let me help you unhitch while Lydia heads on into the house. Nelson and Lester are upstairs relaxing after the chores, but I'm sure Laura can use help in the kitchen. The poor girl has been aflutter all morning."

"Of course!" Lydia exclaimed. She gave Milton a quick glance, but he was already busy unhitching.

Lydia hurried up the sidewalk. What a joy it would be to see Laura again. Now that she was here, the longing to see her sister swept over her. How she had missed her twin.

Lydia entered the familiar front door, and Laura appeared from the kitchen draped in a white apron, her face stress-filled. Lydia rushed toward her to wrap her in a tight hug.

"You've come!" Laura said, as if she couldn't breathe.

Lydia let go to study her sister at arm's length. "You look awful, Laura. What's been going on?"

"I'll be okay." A tear trickled down Laura's cheek. "It's just everything, I guess, but at least you're here now."

"But just for the day." Lydia studied her twin again. "Maybe I should come back home to stay, and take care of the house and *Daett*. Is that what the problem is?"

Laura shook her head and managed to smile. "You know work has never bothered me. It's John, I guess, and the fact that no one seems to understand us. But let's not talk about that right now. We have dinner to prepare, and—"

"We *will* talk about it!" Lydia declared. "We've always been able to work and talk at the same time."

A hint of a smile appeared on Laura's face and they entered the kitchen together. "It's so *goot* to have you home, Lydia. You have no idea how much. And you understand, don't you? About John? *Daett* tries, but he's wrapped up in his own world. Not that I blame him with *Mamm* gone and…"

"I want what is best for you," Lydia replied. "As I told Milton this morning, now that John is sitting up and moving his legs, he will surely walk again, and then you will have received one miracle that no one thought would happen. Why couldn't you receive another one and have things work out somehow?"

Laura's face glowed for a moment. "You say the sweetest things, Lydia. How can you have such faith when no one else does?" Laura's countenance darkened. "But I don't want to blame anyone. I'd probably say the same thing if I was in their place."

Lydia shook her head. "No, you wouldn't. You've helped me tremendously with my own faith. Milton has…" Lydia paused. Now was not the time for *goot* news when Laura was so down. "So what are you going to do about Wendell?" Lydia asked instead. "Milton said on the way over that…" Lydia stopped again. Laura didn't need to be burdened with further outside opinions either.

"What can I do?" Laura said. "I can't marry John if no one will marry us. John's parents have forbidden me from coming over again. You know what happens if I disobey. Bishop Ezra will take that as a mark against my character and won't marry us for sure, and John wouldn't want me to…" Laura's voice drifted off. She measured flour into a bowl as if the concentration took all the energy she had.

Lydia reached over to pull her sister close. "The Lord will give you your first miracle and maybe your second one. We have to believe that it will happen."

"We don't always get what we want," Laura said, measuring out another cup with great care.

Lydia took a deep breath. "The Lord has been giving me Milton's love of late. Isn't that a miracle? If that can happen, why can't your miracle happen?"

Laura brightened. "You and Milton? I knew you cared for him, but I figured he brought you this morning because you both were working at Uncle Henry's place, and because his sister will be here today."

Lydia smiled. "It's more than that. We've been having some *wunderbah* times together. Milton comes up with these ideas, and he's…"

"Has he mentioned joining the baptismal class?" Laura asked.

Lydia looked away and didn't answer.

Laura's voice was gentle. "I believe the Lord gives us great miracles. I guess I also believe in impossible things at times."

"It's hard, isn't it?"

"*Yah*, I don't know what you should do," Laura continued. "But I'm afraid there is only one course open for me. I can't rebel, and maybe once Wendell sees that I can never love him, he'll come to his senses. Surely he won't want a *frau* who doesn't love him. He's not that kind of man. Maybe after that…" Laura stopped and stirred the bowl with quick strokes.

"What are you saying? You wouldn't…"

"*Yah*." Laura bit her lower lip. "I guess I'm giving in. At least for a little bit in the hopes that—"

"But there must be some other way," Lydia tried again. "You could pray and you could—"

Laura stopped her with a raised spoon. "Just comfort me today, Lydia. Don't tell me of sweet things, or of *wunderbah* times you shared with Milton. I'm trying hard enough to forget those moments with John. The thought of Wendell, and of him kissing me someday…" Laura turned pale. "Only the Lord can give me the strength to bear such a thing, or to escape that fate. That's all the miracle I can hope for right now."

"Then you hope Wendell won't marry you once he knows that you don't love him?"

Laura nodded. Lydia wrapped her arms around her twin, and they clung together until a knock at the front door pulled them apart.

Laura wiped her eyes. "Who could that be? *Daett* and Milton wouldn't knock."

"Maybe Nancy," Lydia suggested.

Laura leaned over the kitchen sink to peer out the window. "It's her buggy," she said in a whisper. "And here we are all tearstained."

"Well, she might as well get to know the family!" Lydia declared. She left Laura to answer the front door. At least *Daett* had the right touch in love. After all these years of *Daett* being married to *Mamm*,

Nancy was apparently taking him back. Love had returned quickly between Nancy and *Daett*.

Lydia pasted on a smile as she opened the front door. "*Goot* morning," she said in greeting.

"*Goot* morning," Nancy responded. "I hope I'm not intruding this early in the morning, but I thought I'd come and offer my help."

"We need all the help we can get." Lydia forced a laugh.

Nancy joined in, but her face said plainly enough that she could see the deeper meaning behind the words.

As they walked to the kitchen, Nancy said, "I hope that we…" She seemed to search for words. "That me dating your *daett* isn't a problem."

"Of course not!" Lydia exclaimed. "We have our other problems, but not that."

"I guess we all do." Nancy's voice was kind enough. "But I didn't come to meddle. Just to help with the food. What can I do?"

Laura was standing at the sink when she turned to greet Nancy. Nancy hurried forward to hug her.

With Nancy's help they would have dinner prepared in record time. The whole family would sit down to eat with smiles on their faces, and chatter about everything except what ached in their hearts. That's what was wrong about this day and about their lives right now. They tried to make the right choices, but underneath…

Chapter Twenty-Eight

Laura stepped out of the washroom door at Bishop Ezra's home and scanned the line of buggies. Nelson and Lester had left moments earlier, but Wendell hadn't driven up yet. Did he intend to humiliate her further? He hadn't looked or smiled at her once all evening. The young folks' volleyball game had ended twenty minutes ago, but Wendell had lingered, engaging several of the young men in the barn in conversation. Maybe he wanted to impress upon her that he had everything under control—including her. Well, he didn't. She shouldn't have agreed to this ride home in the first place, but now she was committed with Nelson and Lester gone.

Laura waited beside the washroom door. Two girls came out arm in arm, glancing at Laura before they climbed into one of the waiting buggies. There was still no sign of Wendell. She should go look for him and help him hitch his horse to the buggy, but she couldn't. Not yet, at least.

Laura moved forward slowly. Was she being foolish? What if Wendell had left already? That would be a scandal all in itself. She could hear the whispers. *Laura's pretty messed up with all her miracle talk, and now Wendell's got cold feet and left her sitting at the volleyball game.*

But no. Wendell was too invested in this evening to leave without her. He should know that if he left her, she would never agree to another ride home with him. But then again, knowing Wendell and his boundless confidence, maybe he thought he had her firmly in hand. After all, he had been able to convince her to leave with him tonight.

Laura sighed. She might as well walk toward the barn to find Wendell. But she would not help him hitch his horse to the buggy. Her walk out to the barn was the limit. She'd climb inside Wendell's buggy and let him experience what he'd been giving her all evening—the cold shoulder.

Laura approached the last few buggies parked beside the barn. Several men were still milling around, their forms indistinguishable in the dim darkness of the lanterns. Several horses were hitched up and snorting as the owners made their last-minute adjustments. One of them took off with a start and dashed past Laura, but it wasn't Wendell's buggy.

Laura pressed on until she was almost at the barn. Wendell's buggy was parked on the far side, but the man was nowhere in sight. Should she climb in or return to the washroom door? This had become an intolerable situation. Wendell couldn't have been detained in the barn. This slowness to leave was of his own making, but for what reason?

Laura turned to leave, but she paused when the barn door opened. Wendell appeared with his horse and a triumphant look on his face.

"*Goot* evening," Wendell called to her. "I see you're waiting for me."

"Where have you been?" she retorted.

Wendell grinned. "I had to straighten out some plans with Ben Yoder for next week. We're both…" Wendell motioned toward the buggy shafts with his head. "Can you pick them up, please? Makes it easier, you know." His grin broadened. "Isn't this how you treat your boyfriends?"

"I've only had one," she snapped.

"It's never too late to learn, I guess." Wendell waited with his hand on his horse's bridle. "Glad I made number two at least."

You're not making anything, Laura almost shot back. But Wendell was enjoying her anger way too much. She bent down to pick up the buggy shafts instead. Here she went again, giving in to the man.

Wendell brought his horse underneath with a quick twist of his wrist, and Laura busied herself with the tug on her side. Apparently all her resolutions were for nothing. If only she could find her faith again…but that hope seemed far away, lost in the ironclad prohibitions of John's parents. That was a mountain she had no strength to climb. John had taken his first hesitant steps this week, but her miracle was lost in the mist of the valley.

Wendell peered over the top of his horse. "We shouldn't fuss like this, you know. These little games are unbecoming of mature adults. The Lord invites us to live together in peace and harmony, even when things don't go the way we had planned."

"You didn't have to humiliate me," Laura said.

Wendell's laugh was soft. "I wasn't trying to humiliate you, Laura. I'm not even sure what you mean by that."

Laura kept her mouth shut. Any explanation would only make things worse. Laura finished with the tug and hopped in the buggy. Silence was the right answer at the moment.

"That's *goot*. You're a submissive and quiet woman, I see," Wendell said from the other side of the shafts.

He smiled in the soft lamplight and then tossed her the lines— the same way John used to. Laura clung to the reins. She must not sink into utter despair. The memories of John would always be there. Laura held her breath when Wendell pulled himself up and sat beside her. He was so close that when he took the reins from her, one of his hands lingered on hers. Laura stayed frozen in place. This evening couldn't get much worse.

Wendell hollered out of the buggy window, "Getup, there!"

His horse took off, and they dashed past the sidewalk where several of the girls were still waiting for their rides. Laura caught sight of their smiles as the buggy sped past. Why did everyone approve of Wendell and her as a couple? Couldn't they see the pain in her heart? All everyone saw was John's blindness. The community would have rallied around them if the accident had happened after they were married, but with them unmarried, everyone thought it was tempting the Lord to expect happiness for them. To marry a blind man who couldn't support himself and his future family was simply unthinkable.

Wendell smiled down at her as they cleared the lane. "So how was your Thanksgiving?"

"We had a *goot* time," Laura allowed. "Lydia came home with Milton for the day, and Nancy was there."

"The Lord's will is being done," Wendell said, as if that summed up everything perfectly. "Did Nancy have some *goot* advice for you?"

Laura winced. "Lydia and I have been close to Nancy since our school years, but Nancy isn't our *mamm* yet. I didn't ask her about you, if that's what you mean."

Wendell grunted. "At least Nancy's doing the right thing. I'm hoping that rubbed off on you. Either way, I'm happy that you've come to your senses. It's about time."

Laura stared straight ahead.

Wendell gave her a sharp glance. "Maybe you should have a long talk with your sister about Milton. I hear he has no plans to settle in the community. Did Nancy say whether her choice has changed her brother's mind? Surely you spoke of such an important matter?"

"It was Thanksgiving," Laura whispered. "We're still a grieving family, Wendell. *Daett* and Nancy have just begun to know each other again after many years. We are thankful for what we have without trying to improve things we have no control over."

Wendell snorted. "That doesn't sound like you at all, Laura. You were so sure that John would walk again and everything would go back to normal."

"And John *did* walk, didn't he?"

"You know my feelings on that." Wendell let out a strangled chuckle. "And the community agrees with me, which is why you're in this buggy. I'm not a monster, Laura, because I want to wed you. What man wouldn't? You're quite a catch. Everyone knows this, as I've known since way back when. My question for you is, why didn't John know? He didn't ask to marry you until you lured him behind the shed at the barn-raising and charmed the question out of him."

"That is not true!" Laura shouted. Wendell's horse suddenly sped up.

"You don't have to scare him with your yelling," Wendell chided.

"What you said is not true!" Laura repeated in the same tone of voice.

"That you didn't kiss John, or didn't charm him?"

Laura pressed her lips together and didn't answer.

"You know it's true," Wendell continued. "You kissed John *and* charmed him."

"And you are both awful *and* horrid!" Laura pulled away from him on the buggy seat.

Wendell didn't appear fazed. "Someone has to tell you these things, Laura. You may not like to hear them, but you will thank me someday. I'm a faithful soul. I'll stick around even considering the problems your family might have."

Laura bit her tongue.

Wendell ignored her silence. "I hope everyone continues to walk in the Lord's will, but I also know that bad habits are hard to break. Nancy had drifted pretty far with her transgressions with that *Englisha* man, and your *Daett* is now seeing her. I know the whole community is overlooking the problem, and I hope they are right, but still...then there's your sister, of course. Milton may follow his sister's example. In light of all that, I'd say my love for you goes very deep, Laura, to risk so much. Don't you agree?"

Laura still couldn't answer.

Wendell didn't wait. "In the meantime, I am here and in love with you, Laura. I'd make you an excellent husband, if I have to say so myself."

Laura choked on her words. "I don't know where you get your information, Wendell, but it's all wrong. Lydia would not leave the community regardless of what Milton does, and *Daett* knows what he's doing. Deacon William and Bishop Ezra are both involved in Nancy's situation. Surely they know more than you do."

Wendell grinned as he slowed for the Masts' lane. "I know you mean no disrespect, Laura. You're just feisty, and I like that in a woman. I would even commend you for being high-spirited. Especially after everything you've been through lately. I know you've suffered a great loss with your *mamm*, and to a lesser extent John, but the Lord has been with you. And He will be with us—if you surrender your will to Him." Wendell smiled as he brought the buggy to a stop beside the hitching post.

"You can just tie up," Laura said before she climbed down.

He hesitated. Wendell knew what that meant. He couldn't be

staying long if his horse waited outside in the cold rather than in the warm barn.

"Just tie up," Laura repeated.

Reluctantly he pulled a horse blanket from under the buggy seat and draped it over the horse's back.

Laura didn't wait. She was halfway up the walk when Wendell caught up with her and took her hand firmly in his. Laura almost pulled away, but the effort was too much. Wendell didn't let go until they climbed the porch steps and approached the front door, where the soft light from the lamp inside spilled over the wooden floor.

"Someone left the light on," Wendell commented. "A nice welcome home, I'd say."

Laura didn't look at him. He would see the tears on her cheeks if he cared to look. What would John say if he knew she was with another man tonight? But John likely knew. Someone would have told him, and he would approve. Wasn't that what John's parents had told her? John wanted her to go on with life.

"Are you keeping me on the porch all night?" Wendell finally asked.

Laura forced herself to move. "Come." She opened the door and stepped aside.

Wendell followed to look around. "Do I get anything to eat now that I'm here?"

Laura pointed toward the couch. "That's where John used to sit. You can wait while I get something from the kitchen."

"I'll come with you," he said. "Did John ever help you prepare tasty morsels?"

Laura froze again. She didn't want Wendell in the kitchen, but he wouldn't go back even if she told him to. And of course John had never helped her in the kitchen. They had spent their time snuggled on the couch in sweet conversation, with plenty of food to eat.

She entered the kitchen to point at a chair "Sit there!"

Wendell smiled and took the seat as Laura picked out several fresh chocolate chip cookies from closed canisters. She laid them out on a plate and filled two glasses with milk. As she took a glass and a plate in her hands, Wendell jumped up and accepted them from her. She took the other glass of milk and plate of cookies and led the way to the living room.

As she sat down on the couch, Wendell seated himself beside her and took a bite out of a cookie. "Hmm," he said. "These are *wunderbah*."

"Thank you," Laura mumbled.

"And so are you."

She didn't respond.

"You know, this is going to work, Laura." He finished another bite of cookie. "It will just take time. Some things come quickly and some things come slow, but the ones who take their time will stay. Think about that."

"Since there is plenty of time," Laura said, faking a smile, "you can leave pretty soon, don't you think?"

Wendell's smile waned. "That's not quite what I meant."

"Your horse is cold," she reminded him.

"I'll put him in the barn the next time," he said, throwing her a glare.

Laura almost laughed but stifled the emotion. Wendell noticed and didn't appear pleased. How long would he put up with her attitude? Did Wendell really think he could win her over? Apparently he did.

His *goot* humor soon returned. After he finished his third cookie and washed down the crumbs with the rest of his milk, he rose slowly and said, "Well, then I'll see you two Sunday evenings from now, after the hymn singing if not before." He paused at the front door to look back.

Now was the time to tell him no, but she was frozen in place again.

"See you then." Wendell left with a smile on his face.

A few moments later, his buggy lights flashed past the living room window. Laura stayed seated for another fifteen minutes before she could move. She must find her faith again. That would mean defying *Daett's* advice and going against the consensus of the community, but better that and life as an old maid than this. She had always considered herself strong, but maybe she had been carried about by her emotions. Look where the despair of losing John had taken her. She had just endured a ride home with Wendell and had scheduled another date with him. What had happened to her?

Laura stood and stared out the living room window. Wendell's buggy had long gone from sight, and the only lights on the road were the occasional beams from an *Englisha* automobile.

Laura bowed her head as the sobs racked her body.

Chapter Twenty-Nine

The following Thursday evening, Laura was sitting on a bale of hay in Bishop Ezra's barn. The other young people from the district sat in a half circle around the room. Toy parts lay all around them in boxes on the swept barn floor. Laura had laid the instructions for her toy out in front of her, and she tried to focus as a train set slowly formed in her hands.

Bishop Ezra sold toys for Christmas from his small shop, and the young folks had come in for the evening to help him assemble them. Sales were better than expected this year, and the bishop was behind in his orders. At least that's what Wendell claimed, and being the bishop's grandson, he ought to know. He had been seated beside her on the hay bale until Bishop Ezra asked for help with carrying in more boxes. Of course Wendell had volunteered, but with reluctance. His emotions were hidden behind a cheerful smile. She had noticed his demeanor, and so had Bishop Ezra.

"You can come right back," Bishop Ezra had teased. "There's the rest of the evening, you know."

Laura trembled. She had been trying to fortify herself for the upcoming date with Wendell on Sunday evening, but she had

forgotten about the youth gathering this week. The man was clinging tighter to her than a bee to a spring flower. At least Wendell
hadn't asked to drive her home again after the gathering. There were
limits to what she could take. Things were not supposed to move
this quickly, but Wendell clearly intended to wed her soon.

The cheerful voice of Deacon William's youngest daughter, Miriam, interrupted Laura's thoughts. "How are things going tonight?
Can I sit with you?"

Laura didn't hesitate. "*Yah*, of course."

"At least until Wendell comes back." Miriam laughed, and sent a
quick look over her shoulder. "Are you two going steady yet?"

Laura frowned. "No. We've not even had an official date."

"Well, you're both older, so…" Miriam smiled as if that said it all.
"Things can go fast, you know."

Laura concentrated on the toy train.

"It's for the best, you know." Miriam's hand touched Laura's gently. "But I imagine it can't be easy."

Laura pressed back the tears and kept her head down.

"I'll pray for you," Miriam said. "Maybe things will get easier
soon. Wendell's a nice man, and everyone approves."

"I know," Laura managed. She forced a smile and finished the last
string in the toy with a flourish.

"That's the spirit," Miriam said. "You're such a sweet girl. It's no
wonder Wendell fell in love with you."

Thankfully the barn door creaked open again, and Laura didn't
have to answer Miriam. That would be Wendell returning with
Bishop Ezra and the boxes, she was sure. But Miriam, seated beside
her, made no effort to rise.

Laura lifted her eyes and gasped. John had been brought in seated
on a wheelchair. She leaped to her feet and would have dashed forward, but Miriam grabbed her arm and pulled her down.

"You can't go to him," Miriam said sharply. "That's not proper anymore."

"But he's…" Laura stopped. She couldn't breathe, feeling a heavy weight descending upon her chest. She hadn't seen John since she'd been forbidden, and now here he was at the youth gathering. She should have known this would happen eventually, but…

"Just focus on another toy," Miriam said. "Wendell will be back soon."

As if that helps, Laura almost said. John was on his feet now, a little unsteady but able to walk. The miracle she had prayed for was on display in front of everyone, and yet she wasn't by John's side. What a cruel fate! Victory had been snatched from her hands! But how could she defy the community's wishes? And John's? And John's parents' wishes? And *Daett*'s?

"One piece at a time," Miriam said kindly. "And here's Wendell back with Bishop Ezra."

Laura kept her gaze on the barn floor. Wendell's form soon appeared in front of her, but she still didn't look up.

"I've been keeping your seat warm for you," Miriam chirped, bouncing to her feet.

"Thank you," Wendell said, but he didn't sound happy.

Laura dared sneak a peek at Wendell's face. He looked like a thundercloud. A thrill ran through her at Wendell's discomfort. He also hadn't imagined that John would reappear. Yet what Wendell felt could be nothing compared to the sorrow that gripped her heart. She was so near yet unable to speak to the man she loved.

Laura heard the sharp intake of her own breath when John glanced their way—as if he knew where she was seated.

"Control yourself!" Wendell said out of the corner of his mouth.

"I loved him—I still love him," Laura whispered. "With my whole heart."

Wendell's face grew grim. "That was then. This is now."

Laura stifled her protest. What was the use? Yet she couldn't take her eyes off of John, who was now being led to a seat by Bishop Ezra himself. Bishop Ezra whispered something in John's ear, and John sat down slowly on a bale of hay. Bishop Ezra straightened himself and seemed to ponder what his next move should be.

John lifted his head and said something, and a questioning look filled the bishop's face. He soon bent down to hand one of the simpler toys to John, a game that required the attachment of posts and strings around the sides. John ran his hands over the assembled parts several times, while the bishop laid the necessary pieces in front of John. The point was obvious. John planned to put the game together, or at least try.

"Stop watching him," Wendell ordered, loud enough for the couple next to them to look their way.

Laura didn't break her gaze from John's hands. They moved slowly at first as John carefully sought out the parts of the game. He consulted the assembled toy repeatedly and seemed to have found his way.

"Stop it!" Wendell ordered again.

"He's doing it," Laura whispered back, her voice full of joy. John's spirit was exactly what she expected.

Wendell's voice was a quiet whisper now. "Stop looking at him! Do you hear me, Laura?"

Laura turned toward him. "Okay, but I'll never stop loving him. That's the way it is, Wendell, even if I can never marry him."

Wendell swallowed, and his Adam's apple bobbed. "It takes time, these things," he said, more to himself than to her. "The heart is strange in its way. The Lord owns it and brings it back to His own will, even if the road is difficult and uncertain. Of that we can be sure." Wendell focused on Laura's face. "Do you hear me?"

Laura looked away. She wasn't about to respond. Wendell knew the answer to his question. "I'm going to speak with John," she said instead.

Wendell reached for her, but Laura eluded him to stand. Suddenly a wave of weakness flooded through her. What was wrong? She had to speak with John, but she couldn't make a move.

Wendell grabbed her arm. "Sit, Laura," he ordered.

Laura pulled her gaze from John's face, as she seated herself again. Everything and everyone was against her! She wanted to pray, but what was the use? Did the Lord even hear? A groan escaped her. Wendell looked the other way, and busied himself with a toy train set. As long as she didn't get up to speak with John, Wendell would be happy. The tears began to form, but she didn't dare wipe them away. There had been enough scenes from her tonight. All around them people sent sympathetic glances her way. At least they cared—unlike Wendell, who was concerned only with what he wanted.

Why had she consented to another date with the man? The logic escaped her at the moment. Something about wanting Wendell to see that she could never love him. But he clearly already knew that and didn't seem to care. The rest of the community thought she had given in to what they saw as the will of the Lord. If she rejected Wendell, her decision wouldn't change the minds of John's parents. They'd entrenched themselves deeper into their decision that their blind son would not marry. Spinsterhood certainly lay ahead of her.

Laura hung her head, and Wendell gave her a quick glance. He must have decided it was best not to give orders or even engage her in conversation. Laura lifted her head enough to finish another toy set. Wendell also kept himself occupied, but he seemed distracted by John—who had successfully assembled his first toy.

Bishop Ezra came over to inspect the attempt when John waved his hand for help. The look on Bishop Ezra's face turned from a question into surprise, followed by a smile. John didn't smile, but he set himself to work on the next toy with determination on his face.

"This relationship is over," Laura said in Wendell's direction.

He jumped as if stung. "What do you mean?"

"You know what I mean," she said.

"Do we have to do this in front of everyone?"

"No one has to hear if you don't make a scene." Laura faked a smile. "They'll think we're finally having a friendly conversation."

Wendell winced. "If you think you can marry John just because he can put a simple toy together, then guess again." A satisfied look crossed Wendell's face. "You might as well give up, Laura. I thought you had, but I see that further struggles lie ahead. You had best accept the Lord's will."

"I already have," she said.

"No you haven't," he shot back.

Laura took a deep breath. There was only one way out of this. She had to embarrass Wendell so deeply that he would never bother her again. Of course, her own reputation would suffer in the process, but what did she care? And what was wrong with speaking with John tonight, or sitting beside him? Nothing! Maybe she could never marry John, but she could speak kind words to him tonight, and let the sticks fall where they would.

"Laura!" Wendell's tone was sharp.

Laura ignored him and stood. She could not falter this time. Her legs had to hold her. Slowly she forced them forward one step a time. John must have heard her step because he looked upward.

"It's me. Laura!" she whispered, seating herself on the hay bale beside him. "You're doing so great, John, as I knew you would."

"You shouldn't be here," John said, his face turned toward her.

"I'm not leaving," she replied. "Please don't chase me away."

The struggle on his face was intense. "I can't marry you," he said.

"You don't have to," she said. "But you can't stop me from loving you."

"What about Wendell?"

"What about him?" she said. "Who's Wendell?"

John's grin spread across his face. She wanted to lean against his shoulder, grab his hand, and kiss him, but she only smiled. Somehow he could see her. How? She didn't know, but surely he could.

"How are you doing?" she asked him.

"Okay, I guess."

Laura felt Wendell's stare digging into the back of her neck, but she ignored him. She had finally done the right thing. Beyond that she had no idea what would happen, but she didn't need to know. Having John beside her was sufficient joy for the moment.

Chapter Thirty

It was early Saturday morning, and Nancy Beiler was driving her horse, Floe, through the streets of Richville. She hung tight onto the reins as Floe flared her nostrils amid the heavy traffic. She had hoped to miss the traffic rush, but the Christmas holidays were approaching and the *Englisha* were out in force. Nancy kept her eyes on Floe's every move. Her horse usually didn't act up in town, but lately she had been jumpy for no apparent reason. Likely Floe was reflecting Nancy's own jittery feelings, or maybe Floe knew the real reason for their trip into town. Nancy planned to call Charles.

After another night of agonizing, she knew the time had come. She must meet with him. Yost Mast would likely make a formal marriage proposal soon, perhaps tomorrow after the Sunday service. Unless something was done she would go along with his plans, and a date would be set. Yost would want an early spring wedding, if she didn't miss her guess. She must make her move now. Today! Regardless of what that might mean.

The truth was, she had tried to make a go of things with Yost, but it wasn't working. Her former feelings for Yost had not returned, and neither had she seen the glint in Yost's eyes that he once had at the sight of her. She could remember that look well, but the years had taken their toll. Yost had seen her sitting in church as a single woman for too many Sundays, while he lived with Lavina and raised his family. One couldn't change such things. Some habits were too deeply ingrained to change just because the circumstances had.

They had been in love once. *Yah*, this was true. She had no doubt about that, but Yost was now looking for a *frau* to comfort the ache in his heart. In so doing, he was looking to the past, but he wasn't looking with love in his eyes. He was simply planning to settle for second-best. Though he was okay with that, she would not be. Especially when she had the real thing within arm's reach. She couldn't go into marriage with Yost when her heart belonged to another man, no matter what the community thought. If she married Yost, she would always wonder what her life could have been if she had chosen another path. She had to find the courage to choose the right road now while there was still time.

It was a road that led into darkness, *yah*, and into the *bann*— into the life of an outcast and a thousand other things that made her hands tremble. But the choice also included the love of a man. A true love! A love that bound a heart to a heart. How could she help it if that man was an *Englisher*? Was she to blame for Yost's decision all those years ago? Yost had chosen another woman, and now her heart had chosen another man.

"I hope you understand that I didn't try to fall in love with Lavina," Yost had assured her again last Sunday evening.

"It's okay, Yost," she had told him, but later she knew why he had said the words.

Yost finally understood how much his actions had hurt her, and he figured she hadn't healed from the wound. Only she *had* healed.

That was the surprise. Yost's explanation wasn't needed anymore. She no longer pined for a marriage with him. Not since Charles had come into her life. The Lord had sent healing in His own time, and Yost had returned to a heart that was already in another man's power. *Yah*, she loved Charles, and no actions or words from Deacon William or anyone else had changed that. Even her own surrender to the community's judgment hadn't accomplished the desired result. She still loved Charles, and if he would have her after all that had happened in the past weeks, she would marry him.

"There it is," Nancy said out loud at the red light.

Floe pranced on her four feet as if she, too, couldn't wait to arrive at the outdoor pay phone. The hardware store had one that was used mostly by the Amish, which was why she had come early before the store opened. Things would be easier if no Amish man wanted to use the phone while she made the call. Normally she would be allowed her privacy, but with her recent past, there would be reason to question.

"Lord, help me," Nancy muttered as she pulled back on the reins and parked Floe at the far light pole. There was a hitching rack near the hardware store, but the spot seemed too conspicuous. Here she could be seen, but she might avoid a conversation with any Amish people who arrived. Nancy climbed down and tied Floe to the pole, and then she moved quickly to the pay phone halfway across the parking lot. Nancy glanced around one more time before she dropped in the coins and dialed the number she knew by heart. Charles had given her his cell phone number early on. She had committed the number to memory but never used it.

What would he say when she called? Maybe he wanted nothing more to do with her after whatever Deacon William told him. If that were the case, at least she would have her answer and could make the best of things. Yost need never know she had strayed before she accepted his proposal of marriage.

Nancy dialed the number and waited. She felt like a nervous teenager again. But wasn't that how people acted when they were in love? Even older people? The heart apparently never changed.

"Hello?" Charles's voice was crisp.

Nancy trembled. "Hello, it's me, Nancy."

"Nancy," he said. "*You're* calling *me*?"

"I have to see you, Charles," she managed. "If you're still willing...I mean, to see me."

"But Nancy..." He hesitated. "Are you sure? This can cause you trouble and—"

"I want to see you, Charles. It's my choice, not theirs." The phone shook in her hand. "Will you please see me?"

"Where?"

"At my house. I'm at the pay phone in Richville, but I can be back home in thirty minutes."

"Nancy! You'd best wait where you are. I'll be there in a few minutes."

When she didn't answer, he asked, "Okay?"

"Okay," she whispered and hung up the phone.

What did that mean? Nancy leaned against the side of the phone booth and tried to regain her strength. She was the strict Amish schoolteacher who was about to jump the fence. She was determined but knew the journey wouldn't be easy. Old habits learned over a lifetime didn't die at once. Surely Charles would understand and have patience with her. He loved her, didn't he?

Nancy turned from the phone booth and walked to her buggy. Floe looked at her as if she knew Nancy was guilty, but highly approved anyway. Nancy laughed out loud, the sound approaching hysterical. The pressure had affected her mind, Nancy told herself.

Horses didn't know anything about jumping the fence—even smart horses like Floe. But at least Floe was still her friend. By tomorrow morning she would need all the friends she could find. That was if Charles didn't reject her offer. With all she had put him through, she couldn't blame him if he did. There were many women among the *Englisha* who would make a better *frau* for Charles than she would.

Nancy looked up as a buggy pulled into the parking lot and stopped at the hitching post. Emil Helmuth, a married man from the community, climbed out and waved to her. She waved back but didn't move. She ought to go inside and buy something she needed, but she couldn't remember what that was. And she might miss Charles. She couldn't take any chances. If Emil saw her with Charles the whole community would know by nightfall. They would deal with her accordingly. Deacon William had been kind to her once, but that would end with a second serious transgression.

Thankfully Emil went on inside, and moments later Charles's pickup truck pulled into the parking lot. Nancy gripped the buggy wheel for strength and waited. Charles parked beside her and opened the door.

"Come," he said softly, motioning toward the other side of the pickup truck. A faint smile filled his face.

She didn't answer but climbed in the truck.

"So," he said. "What is this about?"

"I'm ready to come into your world," she said. "If you will still have me."

"You will marry me?"

"*Yah*," she whispered. "If you wish."

His smile grew. "I've wished for nothing else for a long time. How often did I ask you, but you—"

"I know," she interrupted. "But I'm ready now. I can't live like this anymore. I owe it to myself and to you. I want to follow my heart, Charles. You are a decent man. I'm in love with you, and if you still love me after what I've put you through…" Nancy let the words hang in the air.

Charles nodded. "Strange things have happened lately, I agree. I've never been lectured by a deacon before, but he was kind enough about it. He simply told me you had made your choice, and there was no going back." Charles's face darkened. "Have you really changed your mind? You know I love you. I've made that plain enough, but I'm older, not as elastic as I once was."

"Oh, Charles." She caught her breath. "I'm so sorry. I never should have agreed to Deacon William's plan, but it's hard coming out from the community. It seemed easier, somehow, just to go along and give up. But in the end, I realized I can't marry a man I don't love. Not while I still dream of you. I owe that to myself, and to you, and to the Lord. You want everything that I want, Charles. I know you do. You can't help it that you're *Englisha*, and I can't ask you to become Amish. My duty is to come your way, not the other way around."

He reached over to touch her face at the very moment Emil walked out of the hardware store and glanced their way. Even so, Nancy forced herself to forget about Emil, and she gave in to Charles's embrace.

"You really will marry me then?" Charles asked.

In answer, Nancy moved closer to him and lifted both hands to tenderly cradle his chin. He must not have shaved today, because the telltale bristles filled her palms. He smelled of cologne, and of the *Englisha* firehouse, and a hundred other things forbidden to her.

"Kiss me," she whispered.

He didn't hesitate, and as soon as their lips touched, she relaxed in his embrace. She kissed him without guilt. After a few moments, she let go and straightened herself on the pickup seat. She caught sight of Emil again. He was standing still, looking their way. Charles turned his head and noticed the man for the first time. Alarm filled his face.

"Don't worry," Nancy assured him. "They need to know."

Charles chuckled. "Wow. You have definitely changed."

"*Yah*, definitely," Nancy agreed.

"You will marry me today then?"

Nancy smiled up at him. "Give me some time. I have to take the proper steps. Say my good-byes and let the community go through their process. But in a few weeks I'll be ready."

Charles didn't appear convinced. "Are you *sure?*"

Nancy gave him her best smile. "*Yah*, I am. In the meantime you can stop in whenever you wish. Does that convince you?"

Charles glanced at Emil, who still hadn't moved. "I suppose so. You did kiss me in front of that Amish man. You've never done that before."

"See?" Nancy climbed out of the pickup truck. She turned before she closed the door. "And there's another kiss waiting for you when I see you next."

"Is that a promise?"

"A promise," Nancy said.

She closed the pickup door and waited until Charles pulled away. She waved and was ready to climb in the buggy when Emil hurried up to her.

"Who was that?" he demanded.

"Charles Wiseman," she told him. "My future husband."

Emil gasped. "You were kissing him right here in public. *You*, Teacher Nancy!"

"*Yah*," Nancy said. "Kissing is common, isn't it, when two people plan to marry?"

"Does Yost know about this?" Emil glared at her.

Nancy shook her head. "But I'm on my way to tell him now."

She untied Floe and climbed in the buggy. Emil stared after her as she drove out of the parking lot, but she ignored him. She had other things on her mind. Like the conversation ahead of her. She must speak with Yost and his daughters. The talk would not be easy, but she was determined. As determined as she had ever been about anything.

Chapter Thirty-One

Later that Saturday morning, Lydia swept the last of the crumbs from under the kitchen table in her family home. Breakfast had been served well over an hour ago. Laura had helped with the dishes, but she had fled upstairs at the first opportunity.

At the breakfast table, Lester had joked, "Looks like somebody has a lot of Saturday work ahead of her."

No one had laughed. They all knew Lester wasn't referring to their regular Saturday housework, but to Laura's humiliation of Wendell Kaufman at Bishop Ezra's this past week. That Laura had dared to openly sit beside John had caught even Lydia by surprise when the news reached her at Uncle Henry's.

Uncle Henry had proclaimed at once, "You need to go home for a weekend visit, Lydia. Be with your sister."

She had known that dark days lay ahead of them, but this? To defy Wendell so openly? Her twin, who had spoken so bravely of the Lord's hand at work, had resorted to brazen actions that couldn't help in her quest to marry John.

Laura indeed had plenty of work ahead of her if she wished to repair Wendell's wounded pride—but she really didn't. They hadn't discussed the issue yet, but she would have to approach Laura soon. What should she say? Should she encourage Laura to apologize?

That had been *Daett*'s advice when Lydia had met him out by the barn. "Tell your sister to straighten things up with Wendell, Lydia. She can start by going over tomorrow and telling the man she's sorry. By herself, preferably, but you can go with her if you wish."

Uncle Henry likely meant the same thing when he spoke to Lydia before she left the roadside stand yesterday afternoon. "You can help your family, if anyone can. A little humility expressed by your sister will go a long way, I'm thinkin'."

Even with the rush of the busy Christmas season upon them, Uncle Henry had insisted that she go home for the weekend and help bring Laura to her senses. But she was the wrong person for the task. She should have been honest and told Uncle Henry that she was on Laura's side—at least when it came to Laura's hope for a miracle. But the words had stuck in her mouth, and Uncle Henry had taken her hesitation to mean that she didn't want to leave the roadside stand in the middle of a busy time.

"We'll manage," Uncle Henry had assured her with a kind smile. "Sometimes there are things in life more important than business."

So now she was home. But how she was to help was beyond her. She could comfort Laura and maybe suggest that she could have chosen a subtler way to cut off her relationship with Wendell, but that advice was a little late.

The truth was, Laura had taken a serious step. One from which there probably was no going back. John's parents had forbidden the relationship between their son and Laura. Brash actions like this from Laura would only cement their determination. Things had become dark and difficult indeed. If ever Laura needed help from the Lord, it was now.

But there was no indication any such aid was forthcoming. One comfort at least was that Lydia's relationship with Milton was still on an even keel. They hadn't progressed further or fallen back.

The dustpan shook in Lydia's hand as she deposited the crumbs in the oven. A burst of flame licked out of the round opening before Lydia slammed the oven lid and hung the wire holder back on the wall. How explosive things were in life, especially in human relationships—and in love, of course. Laura had followed her heart again and likely destroyed any hope she had of marriage. Wendell would see to that. No unmarried man would dare ask for Laura's hand—at least not until this current crop of single men had found partners. From there the only choice would be some widower who dared launch his ship into her sister's emotional waters. Laura would have to settle for second-best, but then again, Wendell had been second-best.

Lydia sighed and replaced the broom in the hall closet. The time had come for a long talk with Laura. She might make things worse and drag her own spirits down, but Laura was still her twin sister. If only *Mamm* were here, or even Nancy. Maybe she should make a trip over to Nancy's and bring her soon-to-be *mamm* back with her. Nancy might know where to go from here.

But she wouldn't bother Nancy this morning. Instead, she slowly made her way up the familiar stair steps. She didn't knock on Laura's bedroom door, but walked on in. When Laura looked up, woe was written on her face. Lydia sat on the bed beside her and slipped her arm around her.

"We need to talk," she said.

"About what? I did what I did, and I don't regret it."

"But maybe you shouldn't have," Lydia ventured.

"Do you really think so?"

The words stuck in Lydia's throat and she could say nothing.

"See then? There is nothing to speak about," Laura said.

"You know there is," Lydia insisted. "*Daett* and Uncle Henry have opinions about it, and there is the future, and what will happen to you, and what Wendell will say, and…"

Laura forced a laugh. "Let him say what he wishes. I'm *not* going to wed him. I'm going to marry John."

Lydia pressed her lips together.

Laura's voice was firm. "I'm going to marry John. If I have to wait a hundred years and am old and withered and haggard." Then Laura giggled. "You should have seen Wendell's face, Lydia. I didn't look back but once, and it wasn't funny then, but it's funny now."

"It's *not* funny now," Lydia told her.

"But you should have been there, Lydia. I got to sit beside the man I love, even if it was only for the rest of the evening. I got to remember what once was. How John used to look at me with such passion in his eyes, such joy, such…Oh, Lydia, I want to feel his arms around me again. I want John to hold me and tell me everything will be all right. That we will build new memories together. Blind people have their ways, I've heard. Other senses develop. We certainly wouldn't have to learn to love again, because we already know how. John wanted to reach for my hand the other evening. I could tell, but he barely dared speak to me. I just sat beside him and helped him work on his toys."

"I can imagine," Lydia said.

She could see the scene clearly even now. Tension would have been thick enough in the old barn to cut with a butter knife, yet no one would have said a word. What could they do—drag either John or Laura away? Even Bishop Ezra hadn't said anything. He was a wise man, and he hoped Laura would come to her senses without a further public display of humiliation.

"I *will* marry him," Laura repeated.

Lydia pulled her sister close. "Maybe we should both stop

dreaming and face reality." Her heart sank at the words, but she had to say them. This was what *Daett* and Uncle Henry expected of her.

"We? Has Milton rejected you?" Laura gasped.

"No! But you know there are dark days ahead for me too, Laura. Milton hasn't joined the baptismal class, and…" Lydia stopped. She could say no more.

"Dear heart. You must keep up hope. Miracles still happen. I know they do. Hasn't John started walking? I should never have allowed Wendell to take me home from that youth gathering or agreed to a date. I only made things worse. I tore John's heart to pieces. I wanted to explain everything the other evening, but I couldn't speak plainly with everyone around us. But he understood, Lydia. I'm sure he did. Why else would I have gone to sit with him with Wendell right there in the room? John's blind, but he knew Wendell was there." Laura glanced at Lydia as the sound of buggy wheels came from the driveway. "That must be Nelson leaving for town, or perhaps *Daett*."

Lydia shook her head. "That was a buggy coming in, not leaving."

Laura sat up straighter. "You don't think…?"

Lydia got up to look out the window. "It's Nancy. She just drove in, and she is talking with *Daett* by the barn door."

"See?" Laura's face brightened. "That's a *goot* sign. Nancy has been given her miracle after all these years."

Lydia didn't take her eyes off the two figures beside the barn door. "*Yah*," she agreed, "but *Mamm* had to die for it to happen."

"Don't be so negative," Laura chided. "The Lord makes *goot* things come out of even bad things. Look at me and John. How much better would life have been if John hadn't fallen? But he did, and we still love each other. That's a miracle in itself. I wish *Mamm* hadn't passed, but she did, and now Nancy has her chance at happiness."

Lydia glanced at her sister. "I can't imagine Nancy sitting around waiting for *Mamm* to…" Lydia stopped. The words were too awful to say. Of course Nancy hadn't waited for *Mamm* to die. Nancy had fallen in love with an *Englisha* man. Everyone seemed determined to sweep that truth under the rug.

"She'll be our *mamm*, even if she doesn't feel like our *mamm*," Laura said. "Nancy will be something different, but a miracle nonetheless." Laura came over to stand beside Lydia. "See, they love each other. Look at them talking."

"By the way *Daett*'s waving his arms around," Lydia said, "it looks like Nancy is giving him bad news."

"Oh, that's just love," Laura said before she went back to sit on the bed.

Lydia looked out of the window again. Nancy and *Daett* were now coming toward the house, but they didn't walk close together as lovers should. She was right, and Laura was wrong. Nancy and *Daett* had run into a rough spot. Maybe Nancy had some doubts about the wedding and had come over to discuss the matter. *Daett* would not take well to a postponement of their wedding date. *Daett* wanted a *frau* in the house soon, and a *mamm* for his daughters.

"They're coming in," Lydia said.

Laura bounced up from the bed. "Oh, and we haven't cleaned!"

"Nancy won't blame us for talking instead of working," Lydia said. "But we should get busy."

The two girls made their way downstairs and found Nancy near the front door with a slight smile on her face. *Daett*, however, was nowhere to be seen.

"Have you come over to help us out for the day?" Laura chirped. "We were just upstairs talking, but we're getting busy now."

Any hint of a smile on Nancy's face faded. "I'm afraid not. I need to speak with you girls. Can we sit on the couch?"

"Sure," Laura said, seating herself. "You can have the rocker." She motioned with her hand.

Nancy took the offered seat, but Lydia stayed on her feet behind the couch.

"This is going to be hard to say, girls," Nancy began, "as it was to tell your *daett*. But I wanted you to hear it from my own lips. I won't be marrying your *daett* after all."

"You won't?" Laura half rose to her feet.

"No, I won't," Nancy said. "I'm sorry. I had hoped things could be worked out, and I wanted to tell you that I haven't been pretending these past weeks. I tried to love your *daett* the way I used to. I did truly plan to marry him—but in the end, I can't. Sometimes you can't recapture the past."

Nancy paused and the hint of a smile returned. "There was a time when your *daett* and I loved each other deeply. At least, I loved him in that way. But he chose to marry your *mamm*—which I don't hold against him. On my part I stayed single because my heart wouldn't open to another man." Nancy stared out of the window for a second. "But now a man has reached my heart, but it isn't your *daett*. We've all been avoiding the subject, hoping the feeling would go away. But my love for Charles Wiseman hasn't gone away. I know the community thinks this doesn't matter, that I should marry your *daett* anyway, and that love would grow between us again. But I can't leave what I truly love for what I hope might happen. I'm not asking you to understand. I just wanted to tell you myself that I'm going to marry Charles."

The floor spun in front of Lydia's eyes. She hung on to the back of the couch as Nancy stood. Laura jumped up to give Nancy a hug, but Lydia couldn't move. This was the end of her miracle. Now Milton would leave the community along with his sister. This was the nudge he would need, since he was already teetering on the edge of the fence.

"I'm so sorry, Lydia," Nancy said, as if from a long distance away.

Lydia couldn't move, but she nodded. The front door opened and closed. Lydia was still clutching the back of the couch when Laura returned to embrace her, and the two clung silently to each other.

Chapter Thirty-Two

Late on Christmas Eve, Lydia climbed into Milton's buggy. Uncle Henry had closed his roadside stand in the morning, and she should have left for home after lunch when they had brought up the last boxes for storage in the barn. Aunt Millie would have driven Lydia home if she had asked her to, but she hadn't. Instead she had asked Milton to drop her off on his way home.

Lydia settled into the buggy seat but avoided looking at Milton. "Getup!" Milton called to his horse, Red, and off they went down Uncle Henry's lane and out onto Highway 184.

Lydia gazed at the scenery as they drove past the familiar fields. She had begun this season with such hope in her heart, and much had happened at Uncle Henry's this fall—both *goot* and bad. A lump formed in Lydia's throat. She wouldn't be back after Christmas, and neither would Milton. Would he then slip away...into the *Englisha* world? If so, she could not, would not, go with him. In which case, she saw her life slipping away as well. How could she hang on? Somehow she must get Milton's attention. But how did one grasp at hope when things were dark? Laura believed in miracles, and she was inspired by that belief. But Milton no longer seemed possible, nor did his love seem attainable.

"It was nice working for your uncle," Milton said.

Lydia looked away. She couldn't speak. Thankfully Milton seemed to understand as he let out the reins again. Red settled into a steady trot on the blacktop.

"Thanks for taking me home," Lydia finally managed.

Milton's smile was thin. "It's a pleasure. Don't think twice about it."

That's all he has to say? The question eating at her heart made her want to cry out in protest, but she stifled the urge. There was no sense in making a scene.

"I suppose you heard that Nancy's excommunication happened last Sunday in your home district," Milton said, his voice bitter. He didn't look at her.

"Did you go?" Lydia asked.

"She's my sister," Milton said, as if that answered everything.

Lydia took a deep breath. "I could be bitter too," she said. "Our family has its own troubles, you know. My *daett* had planned to marry your sister. Now with Nancy marrying an *Englisha* man, *Daett* will take a while to get over that blow."

"But Nancy loves Charles! What else was she to do?"

"I'm sorry. I didn't mean to imply...That was just my way—"

"It's okay," Milton said, cutting her off.

She didn't respond. Milton didn't expect her to. They were two hearts wounded in their own ways. That was clear enough. Cautiously she slipped her hand around Milton's arm. He gave her a gentle smile, and Red's hooves beat a steady rhythm on the pavement.

Was there hope for them yet? Milton didn't pull away from her touch. Did he also miss the close times they had once shared and wish things could be different? How could Milton have shared such precious moments with her, only to forget all about them?

Lydia ventured a quick look up at his face. "Did you know about Nancy's plans?"

"Not before anyone else did," he said. "I thought she was settled on your *daett*."

Lydia's heart raced. Did she dare ask? She had to. "Haven't you missed our times together at Uncle Henry's, Milton? You planned such sweet things for us to do this season. Can't we go on the way we once did? You and I?"

His arm twitched. "I'm sorry, Lydia. Things change."

"But why?"

He didn't answer for a long moment. "Because I'll be leaving the community soon. With Nancy excommunicated, I can't stay. And unless I miss my guess, you aren't coming with me." He hurried on without waiting for an answer. "So I might as well take the big step right after Christmas. I have my car now, and I can get a job in Ogdensburg. I'll get an apartment and leave all this old stuff behind for a new life."

Lydia didn't move. Her hand was still in his arm, but her whole body was weak. Milton wanted her to come with him? She had suspected that, but to hear him say it…

"*Would* you come with me, Lydia?" He looked down at her. "I mean, eventually? I wouldn't expect you to leave home at once or get your own apartment in Ogdensburg, but we could see each other secretly in the meantime."

His meaning was plain enough. He wanted her as his *frau* in the *Englisha* world, away from the community she loved. But out there, she would have Milton. Wouldn't that be her miracle? The very thing she had prayed and longed for?

"Would you?" Milton repeated. "You can take all the time you wish to answer. I won't rush you, but we could see each other whenever we get a chance. I don't know how that would all work, but if you're willing, it's possible. Nancy will be married to Charles before long. It's not as though you wouldn't know anyone out there." Milton waved his arm vaguely toward the open buggy door. "Nancy's your old schoolteacher and almost *mamm*, so to speak. Surely we can't go wrong if Nancy has done the same thing?"

Lydia reached for the dreaded words. "But that's *jumping the fence*. I'm a baptized member, so I'd be excommunicated." She looked up at him. "It's easier for you. You wouldn't have to go through that."

"It wasn't me who joined the baptismal class," Milton chided. "I would have told you not to if you had asked."

Lydia sat up straighter on the buggy seat.

"Please," Milton begged. "I know this isn't the way things are usually done, but these aren't normal times. How often does a sister turn down a request to marry her old lover and instead marries an *Englisha* man? I'd say that's a pretty strong sign which way the winds blow. We ought to take our chance, Lydia. We can be happy out there. The whole wide world awaits us. We can travel. We can see things, all without the stifling arm of the community wrapped around our shoulders."

"I like the community," Lydia whispered. "I have always liked it."

"But there's more," Milton insisted. "And Nancy's out there. You wouldn't be alone."

"I'd be very alone."

"You'd have me," Milton said.

Lydia's chest hurt, but she looked up at him. He was so handsome, so near, so bold, and so full of himself. Milton hadn't changed. He still planned to jump the fence. And she had failed to change his mind.

"I can't do it," she said.

"I didn't think so," Milton said. "But tell me why not. You'd get used to the *Englisha* ways right quick, Lydia. Their women have washers and dryers and microwaves and all kinds of fancy things in the house. You could live on easy street compared to how we live now. Think about that before you say no."

Lydia stifled a sob. Milton missed the point entirely, and she couldn't enlighten him. How could she? *It's about my love for you, and your love for me, and our love for those who love us.* How could she say that?

Milton jiggled the reins, and Red increased his speed. Was Milton eager now for the ride to end? She had rejected his offer, had she not? What man wouldn't be hurt and disappointed? Lydia stifled another sob.

Milton gave her a glance but didn't say a word. What was there to say? He had offered his best, and she had turned him down. But it wasn't too late. She could have him if...

"I can't do it!" Lydia repeated. "I'm sorry. I want to, Milton. I love you, I really do. I've wanted this for so long—you don't know how long. Oh..." Lydia covered her face with her hands. Her words were a pathetic cry now. She had completely embarrassed herself.

Milton tugged on her arm until she looked at him. "Can't you come with me, Lydia?" he asked again. "What do I have to do—get down on my knees? Do I have to stop the buggy and crawl in the dirt? I want to be with you, Lydia. I want to date you properly like you deserve, and someday provide a home for you—if you'll have me, of course. But we don't belong in the community. I've tried to convince myself otherwise, but it hasn't worked. I can't stay, but that doesn't mean I don't want you. You are so much fun to be around, Lydia. Why can't we walk through life together? You bless me, Lydia. You warm my heart. You bring out the best in me, like no other girl ever has. Let's not throw that away."

Lydia wiped her tears. "But jumping the fence *is* throwing it away."

Milton groaned. "I wish you wouldn't be like this. I wish you would trust me. Isn't a man supposed to lead his family in the right way, as he sees it?"

Pain racked Lydia's whole body. How was she supposed to answer that question?

"Isn't that right?" Milton insisted. "We've heard that preached all our lives. Haven't we? And what do you think Nancy is doing?"

Lydia forced herself to breathe. This was all so wrong, yet she had said enough. Milton was a man. That she couldn't follow him was her fault. The pain around her heart was so intense that she couldn't speak even if she had wanted to explain.

"It's still no, isn't it?" Milton said.

Lydia focused on the passing fields outside the buggy door and didn't respond. She would always remember this Christmas Eve as the day their love had died.

When Milton shook the reins, Red ran faster. The Mast driveway appeared in front of them, but Milton didn't slow down until he was almost there. Red stumbled on the turn, and they dashed up to the barn door for a sudden stop. Lester's face appeared for a moment in the barn window.

"Here we are," Milton announced. He made no move to climb down from the buggy.

Lydia forced the words out. "It's good-bye then?"

"I guess so," he said. "Unless you change your mind. I won't wait forever."

Lydia slowly lowered herself to the ground. All she needed on top of everything else was a spill down Milton's buggy step. Once on solid ground, she walked up the sidewalk without a backward glance. Milton's buggy wheels whirled on the driveway behind her, but Lydia pressed on. When Laura opened the door with a bright smile, it faded at once.

"Oh, Lydia!" Laura exclaimed.

Lydia sobbed as they embraced, and she didn't quiet down until Laura led her to the couch. There the story spilled out in a great rush.

"We must believe in the best!" Laura declared at the end. "The Lord can still make miracles happen. Doesn't John walk?"

Lydia didn't protest. She was too numb. And what did it matter? Tomorrow was Christmas. They would be alone at home, with everyone in a difficult mood. *Daett* wouldn't want to leave the house after Nancy had refused him, and he wouldn't recover from his humiliation for a long time. Now Lydia had her own heartache to nurse. Only Laura seemed hopeful and full of joy.

"We'll have breakfast by ourselves tomorrow," Laura said. "But the Lord will still be with us."

She would not disagree with that truth, Lydia decided. Even in the darkest trials of the night of one's sorrows.

Chapter Thirty-Three

The first serious snowstorm blew into the North Country the week after New Year's Day. Blasts of wind tore off tree branches and left behind drifts piled three feet high in places.

The morning after the worst of the storm, Laura drove out of the Mast driveway with Lydia seated beside her. Laura held on to Maud's reins with both hands as she navigated around the drifts, which had crept into the road since the last snowplow had driven through.

Laura set her chin and took a tighter grip on the reins. An *Englisha* pickup appeared in the distance and roared past them, spraying snow on Maud. The horse slowed to a walk to shake her head, and Laura let her take her time. She would let nothing dampen her spirits this morning. Nothing! This errand was too important. If the plan didn't work, the Lord would lay another one on her heart. She would not give up until she said the marriage vows with John. Wendell's attentions had done the exact opposite of what Wendell had hoped. She was more committed than ever to a wedding day with John.

"We should have stayed home until this snow clears up," Lydia muttered.

"No, we shouldn't have," Laura said. "Now is the right time to set out. I'm convinced of it."

"But to Deacon William's place? What will the man think?"

Laura kept the smile on her face. "He knows me. He's probably expecting me to show up. The man likely wonders what took me so long before I asked for his help."

Lydia grimaced.

"Anyway, you're with me, and that's enough for now." Laura settled back into her seat. She was more nervous than she admitted to Lydia, but Deacon William would hear her out. The man had a tender heart. Hadn't he given Nancy every chance to correct her mistakes? Laura fixed her gaze on the next snowdrift ahead of them. Maud shook her head again as the snow blasted across the road.

"I wish I had your nerve." Lydia said. "Maybe then I could jump the fence with Milton. That's what he wants—a woman with spunk and courage. But I just can't. On that count, I'm a failure, Laura. A total failure."

"Don't say that," Laura chided. "You know that's not true. Not jumping the fence with Milton was the only decision you could make. He probably respects you even more by now. Milton knows you're a principled woman who won't give in to the wrong thing to get what she wants."

Lydia groaned. "I don't have your cheerful outlook, Laura. There's nobody waiting for me the way Wendell waited for you—not to mention a dozen other unmarried men who would snatch you up at a moment's notice. No one has looked twice at me, even during the time I spent in Uncle Henry's district. Milton—"

Laura stopped Lydia with a quick pat on her arm. "Don't run yourself down. I know the quality person you are, and if the men can't see that, it's their fault. Milton will come around. Just keep hope alive in your heart."

She didn't fault Lydia's gloomy outlook in the least. The truth was, she'd shed plenty of tears on her pillow over the hopelessness of her own situation.

"I'm not giving up," Laura said out loud. "Not yet."

Lydia's smile was sad, but at least she was supportive, even amid her own pain and despair.

Laura pulled back on the reins as Deacon William's place came into view. Maud seemed to sense their destination and plunged into the lane, right though a drift blocking half the driveway. The buggy bounced sideways but settled down on the other side.

"See, even Maud knows we should be here," Laura said, hanging on to the reins as Maud made a wild dash for the warm side of the barn.

Deacon William's face appeared in the barn window as Laura climbed down from the buggy. By the time she had the tie rope fastened, the deacon had hurried up to them.

"What brings you girls out on this wintry morning?" he asked. "Is something wrong at home? Your *Daett* is—"

"No, everything's fine." Laura gave the deacon a weak smile. "Of course *Daett* is struggling, as you can imagine, but he'll be okay. The Lord will give him strength for…" Laura stopped. She had said enough.

"*Yah*," Deacon William agreed. "The Lord's will must be done, but it is not *goot* for a man to be alone. I will pray for your *daett*, and I will speak with him at the next service. He should not take Nancy's rejection to heart. We all did what we could, but a person must still make their own choices, and Nancy has made hers."

Laura nodded toward her sister. "Lydia was kind enough to come along with me this morning for support."

"*Goot* morning." Deacon William acknowledged Lydia's presence but then turned back to Laura. "Did you wish to speak with me in private? We can go into the house where it's warmer. Elizabeth is baking bread, but I'm sure she'd welcome Lydia's help."

Laura gave him another smile. "I'll take you up on that. But Lydia and I have no secrets. You can speak freely around her."

"That's even better." Deacon William beamed. "In fact, Elizabeth might have a few moments to spare from her kitchen work. She could sit with us, if you don't mind?"

Laura didn't hesitate. "Certainly! But if Elizabeth is in the middle of bread making, we can help her first. Lydia and I have all morning."

"Then let's go find out," Deacon William declared, leading the way to the house where he held open the front door. Elizabeth hurried out from the kitchen to greet them and take their coats.

"We don't want to disturb your work," Laura said. "In fact, we can help if you need us."

"The bread's rising now," Elizabeth said with a smile. "And regardless, whatever brought you girls out this morning must be worth a little of our time."

"Then let's be seated." Deacon William waved toward the couch. He settled into the rocker himself, and Elizabeth smoothed her apron and sat beside him on hers. They both looked expectantly toward Laura, who gathered herself.

Now that the moment had arrived, all her thoughts had fled away. This was so important, these next few seconds, if she ever wanted to wed John. Tears gathered in Laura's eyes and she lowered her head.

Elizabeth got up to slip her arm around Laura's shoulder. "Oh, you poor dear. Is this about John?"

Laura nodded. "I suppose you've heard what I did at the youth gathering a while back?"

"*Yah.*" Elizabeth stood by her side. "You've always had plenty of spunk."

"But I had to! I couldn't stand it one moment longer. There I was with Wendell, trying to show him that I would never love him, but John was over there, and I felt I should have been with him. It's so wrong. All of it! We should already be wed by now." Laura caught her breath. This outburst was not going to help. Deacon William might be open to a humble and broken cry, but this sounded like an outraged woman. But she would not despair. She couldn't. "I still love John," Laura continued. "With all of my heart, and I know the Lord wishes for us to be wed. It cannot be otherwise. Won't you please speak with John's parents and tell them how wrong this is?"

Elizabeth said nothing and returned to her rocker. Deacon William stared out the front window at the snowdrifts for a moment before he responded. "You know, Laura, that the church doesn't get involved in these matters. We don't tell people who to marry. John's parents are the ones who oppose this. It's not the church's business to tell them they're wrong. And how would you support yourselves, Laura? John must agree with his parents on the matter. Why else has he not pursued you further?" Deacon William's voice was gentle. "Even when you've made your interest so plain to him."

"And to everyone else," Elizabeth added. "Not that I'm scolding you, Laura, but maybe we can help you to face things. Wendell Kaufman is a very decent man. Maybe William can still speak to him and things can be patched up between the two of you."

Laura pressed back the tears. She had blown her one chance. That was clear enough. Lydia must have agreed, because she reached over to comfort her. Laura held Lydia's hand while she collected herself.

"I don't know how to explain myself properly, I guess," she finally whispered. "I come across too strong right now and probably appear as if I'm not being submissive to the Lord's will. But the truth is that I wouldn't ask this of you, Deacon William, if I didn't feel it was the

Lord's will that I wed John. I know in my heart that John feels the same way. He loves me. That hasn't changed. I know you want John to make more of a fuss, but that's not John's way—especially now that he's blind. That has broken his spirit. He's too *wunderbah* a man to claim his right to a *frau* if he can't see—especially if his parents are against the union. John needs some reason to believe that he still has a right to take his place as a husband at my side, and perhaps later, if the Lord wills, as a *daett* to his *kinner*. You could explain that to him, if anyone could, Deacon William. I know you could."

A thin smile spread across the deacon's face. "I admire your courage, Laura. John is blessed indeed to have such a dedicated woman who gives her love to him, but I must say that Wendell would likewise be worthy of your devotion. I haven't spoken with the man since the..." Deacon William cleared this throat. "But I would be willing. I think Elizabeth is right. Even if Wendell's pride was deeply wounded by your actions, pride is something we all must lay down. I'm sure Wendell can see this and will be willing to forgive you."

"There's nothing to forgive," Laura said, slowly rising to her feet. "I'm sorry I've taken up your time this morning. I'm sorry for the poor impression I've made, but I will continue to pray for the Lord's will. In the meantime, I have no love in my heart for Wendell, so—"

"Just think about what we said," Deacon William interrupted. He stood up to place his hand on Laura's shoulder. "That's all we ask, and the church's blessing will be with you regardless. Because I know you won't do anything foolish, Laura. You're not like Nancy—for whom I express my deepest regrets." Deacon William paused, and Elizabeth nodded from her rocker. "Maybe once that shock has worn off," Deacon William continued, "things will be different around your house. Spring will soon be here, and perhaps Wendell's offer will appear more attractive with the trees in full bloom."

Laura shook her head. "Nancy said she tried to help me, but I don't know how she could have, even if she had wed *Daett* like she planned to…"

"The Lord's will is our answer," Deacon William said. "And we must not look to man's help, even from people we love. Think about what we said, Laura. Pray, and we will do likewise." Deacon William held the door open, and Laura slipped out with Lydia right behind her. Neither of them said a word as Deacon William hurried ahead of them and untied Maud from the hitching post. Laura and Lydia climbed in the buggy, and Deacon William gave them an encouraging smile before he tossed them the reins. He stood aside and watched them leave until they had cleared the huge drift across the end of his driveway.

"Well, that didn't go well!" Laura declared, once the buggy had settled down.

"At least we're still alive," Lydia muttered.

"And we still have the Lord!" Laura said. "He really is our only hope now!"

Chapter Thirty-Four

On a Saturday afternoon two weeks later, Laura awoke with a start. She shouldn't have dropped off to sleep in the middle of cleaning the upstairs, but the thought of what she would go through tomorrow morning at the service had been too much. John would be sitting in his usual place along the back wall, seated on a rocker brought out especially for him. His sightless eyes would stare straight ahead, though he would know Laura was seated among the row of single women. Their connection was still there, still strong, but John wouldn't turn his head. Meanwhile Laura would struggle not to cry out from the pain.

Laura sat up straight on the bed when *Daett*'s voice called up the stairs. "Laura!"

How did *Daett* know she had fallen asleep? Most of the time he walked around the house as if he was in a dream. And hadn't he gone out to the barn right after lunch?

"*Yah!*" Laura called out, jumping off the bed. She pressed out the wrinkles in her dress with both hands. *Daett* would understand, even if he noticed that she had fallen asleep in the middle of a busy Saturday afternoon workday.

Laura opened the bedroom door and peered around the corner. *Daett*'s concerned face was framed in the open stairwell at the bottom.

"I need to speak with you," he called up the stairs. "Can you come down?"

"*Yah.*" Laura gave her dress a few more swipes before stepping into the hallway. When she came out of the stairwell, *Daett* was seated in his rocker.

"Please sit," *Daett* said, trying to smile. "Deacon William spoke with me last Sunday. I've been meaning to speak with you about…" *Daett*'s voice drifted off.

"I'm sorry. I just—"

"It's okay," *Daett* interrupted. "I'm the one who should be sorry. Maybe you would have come to me if I hadn't been so…" *Daett* looked away. "I'm just sorry about everything."

"You don't have to be." Laura reached over to touch his hand. "I understand. Did Deacon William speak ill of me? I know I probably shouldn't have gone over to speak with him, but…"

A thin smile crossed *Daett*'s face. "He was more concerned about me than you. Deacon William seems to think you'll come out okay. It's me that he had words for."

"Words for you?" Laura said, feeling relieved.

"One of his concerns is that I need to pay more attention to my daughters," *Daett* went on. "And that I find another *frau*, and soon. That's part of paying attention to my family, apparently."

"I—"

Daett silenced her with a wave of his hand. "Don't be blaming yourself for anything, Laura. I just wanted to let you know that I plan to follow the deacon's advice. In fact, Deacon William suggested that I consider his cousin, a widow by the name of Sherry Yoder. She will be visiting from Wayne County this week and staying at Deacon William's place. The deacon has already spoken with her on the matter. I wouldn't be surprised if that's why Sherry made the trip up to the North Country, so the woman must be willing to wed quickly." A wry smile played on *Daett*'s face. "Anyway, I have agreed to drive her home from the hymn singing tomorrow evening. You can tell the others, if you don't mind. I don't really feel like telling Nelson and Lester. You or Lydia would be better at that. If Sherry is agreeable, we'll have the wedding in the spring I suppose. I should settle down quickly and get a proper *mamm* in the house again."

Laura sighed. "But don't you think it's a bit early to be talking about a wedding to someone you've never met?"

Daett waved the protest away. "I know that it's unexpected, and that we...well, we have no history, but it's not like we need one. We're both older, and the community has its expectation, as does my family. I need to set my house in order."

"But you might be settling for..."

Daett nodded. "I know. She might be overweight and sharp-tongued." *Daett* smiled again. "But love will come. It always does when we walk in the will of the Lord. It's time I set an example for my daughters."

Laura gasped. "Is that what Deacon William said? That his cousin might have a few flaws, but that you could *settle*?"

Daett grinned and didn't answer.

"You don't have to marry a woman you don't love because of me," Laura said. "I'm sure Lydia feels the same way."

"You should get your feet on the ground, Laura, and out of those clouds you live in. I know I've not paid much attention to my children lately, involved as I was with *Mamm*'s death and then my planned marriage to Nancy..." When he choked on the words, he looked away.

"You really don't have to do this." Laura reached for his hand again. "The Lord will provide in His own time. I know He will."

Daett looked strangely at her. "Those are *goot* words, Laura. I've heard you saying things like that around the house for a long time. I know what you mean by them, but you can't hang on to John's love forever. The Lord has spoken on the matter, and you are not to wed him. You can't change that by your positive attitude, just as I can't change the Lord's decision to take your *mamm* home, or Nancy's decision to jump the fence. I can choose to make right choices, and so can you—but living with one's head in the clouds isn't the right way. You should see Wendell again, Laura. Let him bring you home from the hymn singing. Let Deacon William speak with him. Wendell had his feelings hurt, but he can overcome that. I know you would make him a decent *frau*. You have a heart of gold. Wendell could use a *frau* like that."

"And so could John!" Laura exclaimed. "Even more so. John's blind, but Wendell can pick up any girl he sets his mind to. He doesn't need me."

Daett appeared troubled. "Is that what this is about? Are you still driven by guilt because you feel you were partly to blame for John's fall?"

"No!" Laura protested. "This isn't about guilt. It's about love."

"You have no obligations to John, Laura. You don't have to punish yourself by marrying a man who isn't up to supplying for his family. Just think how impossible it would be for the two of you. Where is the money going to come from for you to set up house? No bank will loan to a blind man, not if he hasn't established himself, and John has no record of any business success."

"He's trying," Laura blurted out.

She caught her breath. She had no proof that John was working on anything, but his character would demand such a thing. She couldn't imagine John sitting around the house doing nothing.

Daett shrugged. "I did hear that John is working at a harness shop, but that's still a long way from being able to supply for a family. And *kinner* may come soon after the wedding. You know that. How would the two of you pay for that expense, even if the bank would loan you money for a small place?"

The Lord will provide, Laura almost said, but she sat quietly instead.

Daett seemed to take her silence for agreement. "It will be a long, long road back for you, Laura. You will doubtless be humbled by the Lord as you admit to Wendell that you shouldn't have behaved the way you did, but you should begin the journey at once. Humbling is *goot* for the soul. Look what I will have to admit to Sherry Yoder. That the Lord took my *frau*, and that the woman I wanted to marry left me for an *Englisha* man. But that's all part of spiritual growth. So if you agree to settle things with Wendell, I can tell Deacon William tomorrow that he may speak with the man and put this all behind us. I'm sure that Wendell will consent to bringing you home from the hymn singing again."

Laura stood up and stared out the window.

"This isn't that difficult, Laura," *Daett* said. "Wendell's a decent man. Look how…"

"A buggy just pulled in," Laura whispered. "I think it's John's parents…with John."

Daett shot to his feet. "What would they want?"

Laura didn't answer. She had no idea. They had forbidden her from seeing John. What worse news could they bring?

Behind them the basement door opened, and Lydia called out, "Someone's here. Shall I go see?"

"I'm going," *Daett* answered, grabbing his coat and his tattered wool hat from a hook beside the stove. With a strange glance at Laura he hurried out of the house.

"Who is it?" Lydia asked.

"John's parents," Laura said. "I'm going upstairs."

Lydia's words stopped her. "You are not! You'll wait for them."

Laura took a deep breath and forced herself to walk over and stand beside her twin as they looked out the window. They saw *Daett* in front of the buggy, in animated conversation with John's *daett*, Herman. Moments later they moved toward the house with John right behind them. He seemed to follow the sound of the footsteps on the snow, because no one paid him any special attention. Laura's heart beat heavily in her chest. Why was John with his parents? And why had they come to visit?

"Why are they here?" Lydia asked aloud.

"I don't know," Laura managed.

"Maybe I should go back to the basement."

Laura stopped Lydia this time. "Whatever they want, you should be here for it. Stay. Please."

"But..." Lydia began, but she stopped and seated herself on the couch instead.

Laura stayed at the window until the last minute. She took slow steps toward the front door and opened it. Her face had no feeling in it, and her hands were cold.

"Hello, Laura," Hilda said in greeting. "I hope we haven't surprised you too much on a Saturday afternoon."

"Well, *yah*, a little," Laura stammered.

John looked toward her from the back of the group. He wore his old smile but didn't speak. The snowy floor of the porch spun before Laura's eyes, and she clutched the side of the doorway.

"I'm sorry for the suddenness of this," Hilda said. She took

Laura's hand and led her toward the couch. Lydia stood to help, and between the two of them Laura was lowered onto the seat.

"Well, this is quite a surprise!" *Daett* declared, taking his seat on the rocker again. "Why don't you tell Laura what you told me outside?"

"What is this about?" Laura squeaked.

"Quite a sudden turn of events," Herman said, peering at Laura. "Have you been praying a lot lately about you and John?"

Laura didn't hesitate. "Of course! I still think we—"

Herman stopped her with a shake of his head. "There's no sense in going into all that again. You know why we objected to the marriage between you and John, and those reasons haven't changed. But the situation has changed. Quite changed!" Herman stopped to clear his throat. "But why don't you tell Laura, Hilda. This is more of a woman's thing. I don't explain sudden changes very well."

Hilda gave Laura a gentle smile. "Herman makes things sound too complicated. What has happened is that last week, we began receiving letters from other Amish communities. Most of them are from the parents of schoolchildren, but also some from their grandparents. All of the letters contain money, and a few have large sums in them. We went to Deacon William about the matter in the middle of this week, and he checked the story with several schoolchildren in his district. It seems that Teacher Nancy—before she left, of course…" Hilda paused to glance at *Daett*. "I'm sorry, but it's a part of the story I can't leave out." *Daett* nodded and Hilda continued. "Anyway, Teacher Nancy had her schoolchildren write to all of their relatives and friends explaining the accident and how John and Laura couldn't marry since he was blind now, even though they still loved each other. The schoolchildren asked if anyone would be willing to help the young couple with startup funds so they could continue their relationship and eventually marry."

"Enough money has come in to buy a small farm, with some left over," Herman said. "We take this as a sign from the Lord that He is indeed blessing the union."

"And the letters are still coming," Hilda added.

The living room was swimming before her eyes, but Laura forced herself to listen as the murmur of Hilda's voice continued. Something about the sum of money and what could be done with the amount, and how settled they would be with a farm all paid for.

With shaky legs Laura stood, and John rose to his feet to meet her. Laura rushed forward and almost fell into his arms. John was everything she remembered. He was strong, and tender, and handsome. She looked up into this face and stroked his smooth chin. He still smelled of lye soap, wool shirts, and hay in the barn. Only the smell of leather was added. She buried her face in his chest and wept silently.

Chapter Thirty-Five

A fresh snowstorm had blown in on the evening before Nancy's planned wedding. She peered out the living room window of her small home to see the drifts gathered in her driveway. Thankfully the worst of the storm had passed.

She looked out onto Ward Road and saw a snowplow working its way northward. That would clear a path on the blacktop, but it would do her driveway little *goot*. How would Charles pull in to pick her up for the ride into Ogdensburg?

Deacon William usually brought down a team of horses and a homemade snow scraper to open both her driveway and the school's out on Highway 184. If Deacon William couldn't see to the job himself, he always sent one of his cousins. But no one from the community had been by since she had made her decision to jump the fence. They certainly wouldn't arrive to help out on her wedding morning.

She would have to traipse through the drifts in her wedding dress. The predicament was all her fault. The wedding should have taken place in December, the way Charles had wanted. But she had made him wait another month. Why? So she could catch her breath before she made the final plunge into the *Englisha* world.

Charles had tried to understand. He was that kind of a man. He would also patiently bear the bad weather this morning, even with snowdrifts in her driveway, and even if she had to march through them in her wedding dress. Maybe she should wear her everyday dress and change at Charles's house in Ogdensburg?

But she had asked Charles for enough. After all, he could have chosen an easier woman to marry. But he hadn't, so she would cling to that thought and be thankful. Charles loved her and she loved him. Her heart raced when he was with her, more than it ever had when she dated Yost.

Back then they had both been young, and the whole world had lain before them. Now she was considerably older…but young enough that there might still be time for *kinner*. Though Charles had a daughter, Lisa, who would live with them, he would be open to *kinner* of their own. She hadn't dared bring up the subject with him, less she turn all sorts of colors. She knew the *Englisha* were more open to discussing such subjects, but she wasn't *Englisha*…yet.

By tonight she supposed she would be considered *Englisha*. She would be Charles's *frau*. This morning was the last she would see of her home, or even think of it as home. She hadn't packed any of the dishes yet, but there was no need to. Charles had a well-stocked house in Ogdensburg, so they would deal with her things after the wedding and the honeymoon. Together. As man and wife. She would place the small farm in Charles's name before they tried to sell it. It was in the middle of Amish country, but the community wouldn't buy from her. They would buy from Charles—after thoughtful deliberations and plenty of grumblings, of course. She knew her people, and in the end they would buy the property if it was in Charles's name.

Nancy slipped into her kitchen with a smile on her face. She had been right about Laura Mast and John Yoder. Deacon William couldn't help being impressed with the letters she had helped the schoolchildren write to their relatives. Especially considering the results. Even in her wildest dreams she hadn't expected that much of a response—but she had known her people were compassionate and tenderhearted. And now Laura and John were in the middle of wedding preparations. She didn't know for sure, but she could predict that Laura would push for a wedding soon, likely this spring. Nancy wouldn't be invited, but she had been involved. No one could change that, but neither must she obsess over her past. She couldn't always be the ex-Amish woman. She would be Mrs. Nancy Wiseman by tonight. Thankfully her German accent was toned down from her years of teaching school.

"You will pass as my wife easily," Charles had assured her. "You already sound like an educated woman."

She had smiled and given him a hug. "I'm not sure about that," she had said.

Charles hadn't pushed the point further. "I love you, Nancy. Just remember that."

She had melted in his arms, and held on to him for a long time. By tonight she would be his *frau*, snowstorm or no snowstorm, drifts or no drifts. And the past would be the past. She would manage the future somehow. In the present she should shovel a path from the house to the barn and from there out to the lane. If she began at once, she could finish, clean up, and be presentable by the time Charles picked her up at 11:30. Amish life had always been about hard work. She might as well go out with the routine she knew so well.

Nancy hurried into the bedroom and changed into her chore dress. The rips and tears had been patched multiple times. But who would see her this morning? The dress would stay behind when she'd leave with Charles in a few hours, as would all her Amish clothing. The break would be clean. She was determined and had taken the time to prepare herself. Once Charles saw her full transformation, he would appreciate the late wedding date.

Nancy removed her warmest winter coat from the hook in the closet and slipped it on. She found the snow shovel in the corner of the washroom. With a gentle nudge she opened the front door. A cloud of snow drifted down from the eaves of the house, and Nancy wiped her gloved hand across her face. The wetness of the flakes stung. She paused for a moment to clean off the steps in front of her.

A loud "Whoa there!" jerked Nancy's head up.

Deacon William and his team of horses were in her driveway.

"*Goot* morning," Deacon William hollered out. "The Lord has given us a beautiful snowstorm."

Don't you know this is my wedding day? Nancy almost hollered back. But of course, Deacon William knew. She had been wrong. The deacon was here to heap coals of fire on her head with his kindness. That was the community's way with people who were in the *bann*. She should have remembered that.

"You have come to help me," Nancy called out.

"*Yah*," he said warmly. "We'll have the driveway open in no time."

He waved and shook the reins of his team. They blew long streams of steam from their nostrils and laid into the harness. Snow flew as Deacon William made another round. She should go inside and make hot chocolate for the man, but he wouldn't drink the offered nourishment. Not from her hand. That was also the community's way. They could give but not take from excommunicated members. So she might as well work on the sidewalk. Deacon William wouldn't bring his team up this far.

Nancy shoveled the snow and kept track of Deacon William's progress. She wanted to thank him when he was done, and she knew he might leave without further conversation if she didn't catch him in time. On the other hand, if she went out to speak to him, he might embark on a final lecture. He'd feel obligated to reach out one last time before she became Mrs. Charles Wiseman.

Deacon William finished before Nancy reached the end of the sidewalk. He let the reins hang limp over the homemade snowplow and made his way across the untouched snow. "Let me help with that." He held out his hand for the shovel.

Nancy gave him a warm smile. "I can do this much after all that you've done. I'm very grateful, Deacon William. Thanks. I didn't know how I was going to get out in my wedding dress."

A cloud crossed Deacon William's face. "You'd not be reconsidering now, would you, Nancy? The Lord must be mighty disapproving of your choice for Him to send a snowstorm the night before your wedding."

Nancy forced a laugh. "That's because I didn't marry Charles in December like he wanted to. I had to take a few more weeks to prepare myself properly for the jump into his world."

Deacon William's face fell even further. "That's a very lighthearted attitude for the awful step you're taking, Nancy. Once wed to the man you are his *frau* before the Lord and the church. You can't come back again, even when you see the error of your ways. And that day will surely come. There's great wickedness lying out there, Nancy. Only the Lord knows the full extent of man's evil heart. You're very innocent, I'm thinking. You've been sheltered here all of your life."

She wanted to change the subject. "How's Yost doing?" Argument was useless. They had been over all these points before.

A slight smile crossed Deacon William's face. "My cousin came up the other weekend—Sherry Yoder. Yost took her home from the hymn singing, and I'd say they hit things off okay. Might even wed this spring, I'm guessing."

"I don't know her," Nancy said, looking away. "But I'm glad to hear that Yost has found someone."

Deacon William gave Nancy a pointed look. "I didn't mean to encourage you in your ways, Nancy. But if Yost found someone so quickly, I'm sure the Lord will provide for you—once you're back in *goot* terms with the community. I'll make things as easy for you as I can."

"You never give up, do you?" Nancy tried to give him a warm smile, but the pain still shone through. The deacon wasn't making things easy this morning, but neither would she turn aside from her determination. "I'm not coming back. But thanks for your concern and for clearing my driveway. I'd offer you hot chocolate, but…"

"*Yah*, I know." Deacon William nodded. "It is the way it is. Will you be living here after the wedding?"

Nancy shook her head. "I'll be selling…well, Charles will. I'll sign the farm over to him, and the people can deal with him."

Deacon William smiled. "I'll have to think about that, you know."

Nancy returned his smile. "You will, but in the end I'll be right, as I was with Laura and John."

Deacon William's smile broadened. "You do seem to have a decent touch, Nancy. Thanks for helping out with them." Then his smile faded again. "Why aren't you staying, Nancy? Think of all the *goot* you could have done as Yost's wife and the mother of his children."

"I have done what I was supposed to do," Nancy said. "Well, almost. I still have one task to do…"

"You'd best not tell me."

Nancy lowered her head. "I suppose so, but now I must get changed. Charles is due any moment. He's usually early, in fact."

"I'll be going then." Deacon William tipped his hat, and climbed back on the homemade snowplow. He jiggled the reins and turned the team toward Ward Road. With a wave of his hand he was gone. Nancy finished the last few feet of the sidewalk before she dashed back into the house. She hadn't hung her coat up in the mudroom before Charles pulled in the driveway and parked beside the barn. She rushed into the bedroom. He would have to wait, but didn't men often wait for their women?

Nancy changed while the front door opened and closed. Charles would be on the couch when she came out. A shiver of delight ran all the way through her. Was this how Amish brides felt on their wedding day? She would never know. The tipping point had come and gone while she had been occupied with clearing the snow.

Nancy opened the bedroom door and stepped out. The dress was simple enough. She had insisted. The white lace was still pronounced and drawn across a similar colored background material. The train stopped at her shoes, but billowed out a foot or so behind her. Charles stood when she stepped out of the bedroom door, a grin filling his face.

"You are more beautiful than ever," he whispered, his grin growing into a full smile.

She wanted to leap into his arms and feel them around her, but she held still instead. He came closer and took her hand. "Come," he said. "It's time to go."

"It is," she agreed.

"No regrets then?" He paused to scrutinize her face.

"None," she said, lifting her face to his.

"Did someone clear your driveway this morning?"

She nodded. "Deacon William."

"I thought…"

"Let's not talk about that," she said. "There's only us now. You and me."

His smile grew broader and his grip on her hand tighter. Charles led her along the path, where he helped her into the car and closed the door. They said little on the drive to Ogdensburg. Snowplows passed them with the traffic thin.

"The preacher will make it," Charles said, as if there was doubt. She hadn't thought about that. Amish buggies weren't stopped easily by snowstorms, but this was another world.

"I'm sure he will," she agreed. "For someone like you."

"You mean you," he said.

Nancy didn't respond as they stopped in front of the red brick church. The rounded stained glass windows of the First Baptist Church had little snowdrifts at their bases. The sidewalk was cleared though, and several cars were parked along the street. This was her church now. She'd come here for a women's Bible study next week. Charles had told her about the planned activity when she asked how she could be involved.

They walked up the sidewalk and through the doorway beyond the high arch. A few of Charles's relatives and his daughter, Lisa, were in the front rows. Milton was also there, a big grin on his face. Lisa stood to face them with a bouquet in her hand. A simple one. Everything about the ceremony would be simple. Nancy had insisted on that. The preacher was waiting ahead of them. Charles kept her hand in his until they reached the front.

The questions were simple too, and there was no sermon. Nancy said yes instead of *yah*. That effort was also easy. And then she was his *frau*, and Charles kissed her right there in front of everyone. Nancy's face glowed until she appeared redder than the roses in her bouquet, but no one seemed to care. She was *Englisha* now. She was Mrs. Charles Wiseman, and she loved the man. More than she could say.

Nancy clung to him on the walk back down the aisle and outside, where Charles helped her into the car. She took his hand again after he climbed in on his side, and she didn't let go when he accelerated rapidly up State Street. There was the weeklong honeymoon ahead of them, but she was on her way home—her new home where love and happiness lay.

Chapter Thirty-Six

February's short days were almost past, with no sign of spring in the air. Lydia told herself that was to be expected. Winter was known for its long, cold grip on the North Country.

Lester was driving Maud on the way to the youth gathering at Deacon William's place. Ever since they had left home, Lydia and Laura snuggled warmly under the thick buggy blanket as Lester and Laura chattered nonstop about the planned evening of ice skating.

"You'll be hanging on John again tonight," Lester teased. "When I know *good* and well you can skate like an angel."

"I'm not an angel," Laura said. "And John needs me. He's quite the brave man to venture out on the ice without his sight. That's a man for you, if you ask me—strong, confident, and so handsome in his dark blue stocking cap."

"You should do a few twirls on your own," Lester insisted. "You'll lose all your skills before long."

"I have all the skills I need," Laura shot back. "I have John."

Lydia smiled, but she didn't join in. She usually didn't succumb to the blues, but she was teetering on the edge at the moment—and had for the past few weeks. Laura had been given her miracle, but

Lydia's had not appeared yet. Why was the Lord withholding her miracle? Laura had two miracles now: one when John walked again, and another when Nancy's pleas through her schoolchildren had brought in tons of money.

John and Laura would be set for at least a full year, if not longer. Unless, of course, some unforeseen tragedy struck. But Laura's faith would see them through whatever difficulties lay ahead.

Even *Daett* was apparently receiving his miracle. His relationship with Sherry Yoder was in the letter writing phase. Sherry had charmed *Daett* completely. She had been neither overweight nor sharp-tongued, as they had once joked. Four years had passed, *Daett* said, since Sherry's husband had died.

"Sherry's been kept single by the Lord to comfort my soul!" *Daett* declared. *Yah*, this was *Daett's* miracle, for sure. Would Lydia be left out? All signs pointed in that direction. She didn't have Laura's boldness to stir the pot and pursue Milton. What else could she do? Milton had offered to date her if she joined him in jumping the fence, but she couldn't. Milton wouldn't be persuaded to change his mind. Not with Nancy married to Charles Wiseman. The newlywed couple had set up housekeeping in Ogdensburg. Nancy's old place was up for sale and would be perfect for Laura and John.

"John ought to put in a bid for the place," *Daett* had told them last night. "I hear Nancy put the deed in her husband's name. That's a little fishy, but I don't think Deacon William will complain if John's the one who wants to buy."

That would be another miracle for her sister, while she was still empty-handed. Had she made a wrong choice somewhere? Maybe she shouldn't have been so high-minded with Milton and accepted his offer. Nancy had jumped the fence, so why couldn't she? But that was an awful thought. She shouldn't even entertain the idea.

Lydia forced herself to think of more pleasant things. Milton was the easiest subject on hand. He'd be there tonight. He always came to the skating parties at Deacon William's pond. Milton was a whiz on skates. He was one of the fastest skaters in the community. To watch Milton twirl across the pond, first forward and then backward with equal ease, took her breath away. Milton was everything a girl would want, only she couldn't have him.

Lydia stopped herself again. This was a time of temptation. She often had to remind herself of that fact. She was at a low point in her life, where doubt and confusion easily reigned. She must not forget that, and yet she did. One look at Milton's handsome form out on the ice and she would forget everything but her desire to be his girlfriend and his future…

Lester's voice broke into Lydia's thoughts. "You're mighty quiet tonight. We're almost at the pond and you haven't said a word."

"I'm thinking," she deadpanned.

Lester laughed. "That must be some awful difficult thinking."

"Don't be hard on her," Laura chided. "Her heart is mourning right now."

Lydia looked away. Laura understood her at least, even if she could do nothing about the situation.

"I'm sorry," Lester muttered. "I didn't know."

"It's nothing," Lydia said. "You don't have to feel sorry for me."

"*Yah*, it is something," Laura said. "Stick up for yourself, Lydia. Milton's been as bad to you as Nancy was to *Daett*. I guess heartlessness runs in the family."

"No, he's got a kind heart," Lydia said in Milton's defense.

"He's kind of a rascal, if you ask me," added Lester. "So you must have it bad to stick up for him."

"She *does* have it bad," Laura said before Lydia could speak. "Just don't rub it in."

Lester shrugged. "Okay! Sorry anyways."

"You're a dear," Lydia said, managing to keep the tremble out of her voice.

Silence settled in the buggy as Lester pulled back on the reins and turned into the field behind Deacon William's place. There the woods broke into an open meadow, and the buggy bounced to a stop beside the long line of buggies that had already parked.

"We're late," Lester sputtered as he leaped out to secure Maud. Then, before Lydia's feet hit the ground, he had his skates out and slung over his shoulder and was on his way to the pond.

Lydia wrapped her skates around her wrists and trudged along behind her twin.

"He could have waited for us," Laura grumbled, slowing down to take Lydia's hand. Together the two made their way across the rough, snowy ground to the pond, where a bonfire had been lit. Wild flames leaped skyward, casting crazy shadows over the ice.

Laura glanced over at her unsmiling sister. "Lydia, you have to take courage. The Lord will supply your miracle. He gave me mine, and it looks like *Daett* got his too. Why wouldn't you get yours?"

Because I'm different! The words almost slipped out of Lydia's mouth.

Laura seemed to take her silence for consent as they sat down at the edge of the ice to lace up their skates. The forms of the young people mixed in with the shadows from the fire, filling the pond with erratic colors of red and black that danced between heaven and earth. Lydia caught her breath as she looked up from her laces to soak in the sight.

She would be out on the ice in moments. In the meantime, the anticipation supplied its own delight. Thoughts of Milton did the same. Lydia strained to make out Milton's form among the shadows with no success. He would be out there. Milton was never late for a skating party.

Lydia hurried with her laces as Laura stood. "I'm going over to John," Laura said, and skated toward a group of young people near the bonfire. Lydia had been too wrapped up in her own thoughts to notice John among them. But Laura had been right. John was on his feet, and without guidance he made a few slow circles on the ice. He seemed to return safely each time, perhaps guided by the warmth of the fire.

"John!" Laura called out, her voice filled with joy.

John stopped midstride and waited. He seemed to sense Laura's approach and took a few short glides on the ice toward her. Their hands met and lingered before Laura led John farther across the ice. That's how they would be all evening—together, in love, so in love, and still unable to believe that the Lord had allowed them this happiness.

Lydia focused on her last skate lace. The string was stuck with a knot formed in the second tier of tie straps. Lydia tugged, but it only made things worse. She raised her head for a long breath and stopped when one of the forms dashed out from the group and skated to an abrupt halt in front of her. Ice chips flew and landed in her lap.

"Milton!" The exclamation came before she could see his face. Only Milton would make such a daring gesture.

His laugh was confirmation enough, sending warm shivers up her back.

"What's the problem?" he asked.

She squinted up at him. "Skate lace. I can't seem to untangle it."

He knelt in front of her, one knee on the ice, and the other bent under his stomach. With his swift movements the string gave way and seemed to untangle itself.

"You're a marvel," she said.

He laughed again. "That's what I like about you. Come. The evening waxeth old."

Lydia joined his laughter as Milton helped her up. She could feel the strength of his fingers through his gloves.

"Are you okay?" he asked, his face wrinkled in concern. "It is a little cold out here. Do you want to move closer to the fire?"

I want to move closer to you, she almost said, but how inappropriate that would have been. Laura said such things, but she wasn't Laura.

"Let's skate," she said instead. "I'll warm up soon enough."

He smiled and took both of her hands. "Will you be my partner? They're getting ready for a couples race. I was waiting for you."

Lydia threw her head back and laughed out loud. "I would love that. *Yah*, I'll race with you."

He didn't act surprised by her exuberance. She should try such outbursts more often, even if she blushed worse than a ripe tomato in the summer's heat. But how could she change from what she was? At least Milton seemed himself again, so full of life and fun. Had he changed his mind and planned to stay in the community? Was that why he had sought her out and warmed her heart again?

"Over here!" a commanding voice called out from the edge of the pond. "Race is starting."

Milton pulled on Lydia's hand. "We'll win this race. I know we will."

"I'll try my best," she told him.

"You are the best," he whispered.

With a pounding heart Lydia took her place at Milton's side.

"You have to keep a hold of your partner's hand," the commanding voice instructed. Lydia couldn't make out his face, but he sounded like one of the older unmarried men. Maybe her cousin Benny Mast.

"Now on the count of three," the voice said, "skate all the way to the end of the pond. Touch the shoreline with at least one of the partners, and then back. Take care—and one…two… three!"

Milton pulled on her hand, and Lydia pushed down on her skates with all the strength she had. They sped across the ice and soon overtook the front-runners. Milton hung on to her hand with both of his at the end of the pond, and she bent down to touch the shore. They were off again in one quick swoop. None of the other couples executed the move with such smoothness, gaining Milton and Lydia precious seconds.

"You're a *goot* skater," Milton muttered in Lydia's ear as they raced back across the pond. Lydia hung on to Milton's arm as he slowed down with several final twirls on the ice. Her heart pounded in her ears, and laughter rose up from deep inside of her. They had won. She had not held back Milton, the best skater among the young unmarried men.

Was this her miracle? Or the beginning of her miracle? What else could it be, but a sign from the Lord to comfort her heart?

"We won," she managed, once Milton had finished his last twirl.

"*You* won," he said. "You really were *goot*."

She held on to him, wanting to never let go. But of course that wasn't possible. Another race was being organized.

"Winners can't be in this one!" someone shouted.

There was laughter and general agreement. Lydia didn't have the strength left anyway, which gave her a few moments alone at Milton's side. He didn't seem to mind as the next race was called out.

"Nancy's wedding was very beautiful," Milton said as he watched the skaters racing for the distant shore.

Lydia didn't respond. She couldn't speak. She had known this couldn't last, but for it to end so quickly…Couldn't the Lord have allowed her a few hours of hope?

"Did I say something wrong?" Milton looked down at her.

Lydia shook her head because he hadn't. She was the one who couldn't respond to his offer.

"We are so *goot* together, Lydia," he said. "You could still come with me."

Lydia closed her eyes and allowed the tears to run. She couldn't see anything when the skaters returned with another close call at the race's end. Milton cheered the winners, but she couldn't move, let alone cheer. She let go of his arm and skated back to the fire with arms outstretched. She felt frozen and needed the warmth.

She *was* frozen, Lydia told herself. Her heart was as cold as a spring calf caught in a snowstorm. She had no one and no shelter from this storm. She would never experience her miracle.

Chapter Thirty-Seven

Lydia was driving Maud slowly up Highway 11 toward Heuvelton early on a March morning. She had not told an untruth to either *Daett* or Laura this morning. Someone *did* need to make a trip into Ogdensburg.

"The plow tips need replacing before the weather breaks," Nelson had said at the breakfast table two weeks ago.

Daett had nodded. "The Ogdensburg store's the only one with those at a decent price. Maybe I can make the trip before spring gets here."

And so the inspiration had been born. Milton had supplied the details of where Nancy lived at the last skating event. He had carefully ignored Lydia since the disastrous moment when she had once more turned down his offer. So in the middle of the evening, she had discreetly found him in a dark corner near Deacon William's pond.

He could not have looked more surprised. "You want to visit Nancy?"

It's not what you think, she had wanted to say. But of course it was what Milton thought—that she might consult her about jumping the fence. Why else would she visit Nancy?

"*Yah,*" she had managed.

"Just down the street from the First Baptist Church," Milton had whispered back. "Can you remember the address if I give it to you?"

"*Yah,* of course," she had told him.

After committing the address to memory, she said nothing else and skated away.

"Be careful," Milton had called after her.

Yah, she would be careful. If Deacon William found out that she had visited Nancy now that she was excommunicated, there would be nothing but trouble. And to make things worse, she had led Milton to believe she might consider jumping the fence with him. She wouldn't, but that begged the question: Why did she want to speak with Nancy?

Lydia sighed and jiggled Maud's reins so that she trotted faster. The truth was, she needed to speak honestly with someone about the turmoil in her heart, or something would burst inside of her. Of course her sister knew she was troubled. Laura knew even amid her joy with John. *Daett* knew, because Laura had told him. She had heard the two whispering in the living room several times. They always fell silent when she walked in.

So this morning she had said to them, "I need some time away from the house, if you know what I mean."

Daett had agreed without protest. "I'll send along written instructions about the plow tips we want. Enjoy the long drive." He gave her a smile that showed he really meant it.

Lydia checked her dress pocket. The folded paper was still there. She needed instructions because fieldwork was one thing *Daett* had never taught his daughters. Some of the community girls learned, but *Mamm* had kept them busy with traditional roles—housework, canning, and a hundred other things related to their eventual marriage.

Did *Daett* suspect the real reason for her trip? She wasn't known for bold moves like Laura was. Instead, Lydia was reduced to sneaking around. That was all the courage she could muster. In her heart she was timid and uncertain about how to obtain what she desired—at least when obstacles stood in her way. Why Milton loved her, she couldn't imagine. He was so courageous and open about his intentions, and certain of how to accomplish them. He seemed to have no qualms about jumping the fence into the awful *Englisha* world.

Lydia winced and almost pulled back on Maud's reins. She should turn around right now and forget this whole thing. What if Nancy wasn't at home? Or what if Nancy advised her to make the choice she had made herself? Was that what Lydia wanted to hear? Would that give her the courage to jump the fence once and for all?

Lydia groaned. Milton still loved her after all the rejections she had given him. How could she walk away from such dedication? Milton could have jumped the fence on his own by now, but he was obviously waiting for her. There could be no other explanation. Milton could see past her firm words and into her heart. He was hoping she was wavering and might give in to what her heart longed for. How she did wish that Milton might be hers and that she might be his, as Laura was John's.

Lydia jiggled Maud's reins. If she didn't hurry her courage would fail her. She would return home without the plow tips and have to explain the whole thing to *Daett*. He might understand, but he also might not. Lydia continued to drive, past the signs on Highway 812 that pointed toward the Ogdensburg International Airport. The place seemed strange and impossible. How could there be a connection to the whole world so close to home? From here one could fly anywhere in the world, or at least to places that led to anywhere. Maybe that was the plan she should suggest to Milton.

They could both buy plane tickets and fly away, never to return to the community.

Lydia clutched the reins, and Maud slowed down. No, she could never go through with such a plan, even if Milton agreed. Where would they live once the plane landed? Where would they set up house? There must be money to spend, which required a job. There must be a wedding. The *Englisha* had preachers, like the one Nancy used to marry Charles. She had always imagined that Bishop Ezra would join her hand to the man she loved until death parted them. The way *Daett* had married *Mamm*, and all the generations before them.

Oh, if only she could forget Milton, or forget that she loved him, or that he loved her. But did she want that? Weren't those few evenings she had spent with him and that *wunderbah* time before Christmas at Uncle Henry's worth the pain? Even if she never wed him? Even if Milton became a memory?

At the intersection, Highway 812 turned right toward the tractor supply, and ahead of her was Nancy's street. She wanted to see Nancy first, but duty called. She would buy what *Daett* wanted, and then she would visit Nancy.

Lydia clucked to Maud, and the horse perked up her ears. "We're almost there," Lydia said to encourage her. "Just a little ways, and you can catch your breath."

Maud seemed to understand. She lowered her head and blew her nostrils.

As she turned into the store's parking lot, Lydia pulled back on the reins again and came to a stop. She jumped out to tie Maud to a light post. "I'll be right back." She patted the horse's neck. After a quick look backward, Lydia hurried into the store. A kind-looking older man with a store logo on his shirt appeared in front of her.

"Can I help you, young lady?" he asked. "I'm Ben."

Lydia smiled and handed him the piece of paper *Daett* had given her.

Ben grinned. "Got to get it right, I see."

"*Yah*, I don't know much about farming," Lydia told him.

"Come this way then." Ben moved toward the back of the store. The pieces he showed her were much heavier than she could carry, and *Daett* wanted four of them.

Ben read her face well. "Don't worry, young lady. I'll get these out for you, even with my old creaking bones. You can push the cart to help."

Ben didn't wait for an answer. He also didn't pay attention to her muttered protest. In moments he was back with the plow tips loaded in the cart. Lydia grabbed the handle and headed toward the checkout counter. The cart creaked and groaned beneath her as she pushed.

"Sounds about like me." Ben chuckled as he followed Lydia. At the counter she paid with the bills *Daett* had given her, and then she pointed the cart toward the front doors. Ben waited there and held them open for her. Maud turned her head their way and watched them come across the parking lot.

"Howdy there," Ben said to the horse, and turned to Lydia. "What's her name?"

"Maud."

"Nice name for a horse." He loaded the plow tips in the back as if he had done this before and knew where buggies hauled their cargo. "Nice doing business with you Amish people," he said. "Be sure and come back."

Lydia smiled her thanks to Ben, untied Maud, and climbed in the buggy. He waited to see her off, and she waved from halfway across the parking lot. He had pushed her cart back toward the store and paused to wave back. What a nice man Ben was. Maybe the *Englisha* world wouldn't be as bad as she had thought.

Lydia pinched herself and focused on the drive toward Nancy's. She didn't belong out here, and yet she wanted to speak with her former teacher. She was really confused. And here she had always thought she was the stable one, while Laura did sudden and bold things. How wrong she had been. Laura had turned out much more stable. That was plain enough to see.

Lydia turned Maud north at the next intersection, and the horse shook her head. "We'll be going home soon," she encouraged Maud again.

Nancy's street soon appeared, and the First Baptist Church was where Milton told her it would be. Lydia shivered as she drove past the building. The brick facade and the rounded arches seemed so cold compared to services held at Bishop Ezra's home. How did Nancy say her marriage vows with Charles inside that structure? Clearly there were nice people in the *Englisha* world, but it was still the *Englisha* world—strange and distant.

Lydia slowed down when the correct house number appeared. The color was what Milton said it would be, and the porches were huge. She could almost imagine a swing hanging from the ceiling if the brick steps hadn't spoiled the effect. No Amish home would have such an extravagance. Lydia pushed the thought aside and found a street sign to tie up to. She left Maud staring after her as she quickly walked up to the front door. There was a doorbell, and Lydia pressed the button. Footsteps came at once, and Nancy's face appeared—only the face wasn't quite familiar. And yet it was, but so much had changed. Nancy's dress and hair and...

"Lydia!" Nancy exclaimed. "I'm so glad to see you! Milton said you might visit."

"*Yah*, it's me." Lydia stared at the new Nancy before her.

"Come right inside. You're so welcome." Nancy held the door open.

Lydia managed to enter without tripping over the doorstep. Her feet seemed unwilling to move.

"I just finished the wash," Nancy said, "and I was ready to go downtown, so you got here just in time."

Lydia tried to breathe evenly. "I hope I'm not disturbing you."

"Not at all," Nancy assured her. "I'm so glad you came, although won't this get you in trouble?"

"They don't know I'm here." Lydia blushed. "I offered to drive to the tractor supply for *Daett*, and I wanted to get away from the house. Everything's so..."

Nancy smiled. "You don't have to explain. I understand, but I'm glad things worked out for Laura and John. I'm sure you feel the same way."

"Of course."

"This is about Milton and you, isn't it?"

Alarm filled Lydia's face. "Has Milton told you?"

Nancy shook her head. "Milton doesn't say much, but I know my brother and I know you. He wants the two of you to jump the fence, doesn't he?"

"*Yah*," Lydia whispered. "He's asked me a few times already, and I keep saying I won't do it. And yet..."

"I understand." Nancy gave Lydia a quick hug. "Do you want to jump the fence like I did?"

"In the worst way, no." Lydia looked away. "But..."

"There is Milton," Nancy finished. "How complicated things do become."

"I'd be excommunicated like you are," Lydia blurted out. "Is it worth it?"

Nancy's smile was thin. "You shouldn't look to me as your example, Lydia. We all have our own choices to make, and none of them are the same. There was a time when I would have given almost anything to have your *daett* wed me. I was in love, as much as a young girl could be, and look where I am now. I couldn't walk away from what the Lord had sent into my life, even for a chance to return to what I once had. By the time the opportunity arose again, I didn't even want it anymore."

Nancy paused for a second. "I hear your *daett* is getting along great with Sherry Yoder. I think that proves my point, doesn't it? We should never settle for second-best, Lydia. Only you know what is best in your situation. Ask yourself, 'Does my love for Milton and his love for me call us to accept what is second-best?' Because true love never asks us to step down, but to step up. If Milton isn't giving you what is best, then your love for each other won't make up for the lack. Nothing will." Nancy reached over to squeeze Lydia's arm. "Does that help?"

Lydia tried to smile. "That's a little deep, I guess. Did you learn those words from the *Englisha*?"

Nancy laughed. "Maybe, but I doubt it. I think they were always in my heart. Why else would I have dared marry Charles? Now shouldn't you be going before someone from the community drives past and sees your buggy?"

They both laughed.

"*Yah*, and with me, that could happen," Lydia added.

"Let me get a bucket of water for your horse," Nancy said. "We have one right in the closet here I can use. Maud's her name, right?"

Lydia nodded and waited while Nancy filled the bucket from the kitchen sink. Together they took the pail to Maud, who drank eagerly.

"Thanks," Lydia told Nancy. "That was kind of you."

"You choose what's best now. Don't forget that." Nancy stroked Maud's neck.

"Thanks," Lydia said as she climbed back in the buggy. Nancy untied Maud and tossed her the tie rope. With a wave of her hand Nancy let go of Maud's bridle, and Lydia was off down the street. When she turned to look back, Nancy had disappeared inside the house.

"What's best for me?" Lydia whispered to herself. "What's best for Milton and me?"

But she already knew.

Chapter Thirty-Eight

Dusk had fallen on Sunday evening, and Laura was sitting on the Yoders' living room couch with her hand clasped in John's. She had driven Maud home from the hymn singing with John seated beside her. In the old days John would have driven her to her house for their date, but this was no longer the old days. Many things had changed for them, but not their love for each other.

They had weathered every storm thrown at them, even when the Lord had willed that John should remain blind after the accident. Yet the Lord had chosen to give them each other. And was that not enough? From his smile, John seemed to think so, and Laura's heart was so full of joy she could almost burst. On top of that, their wedding lay in front of them this spring. Beyond lay years and years—if the Lord willed it—in which she would love John with all of her heart.

Laura smiled up into John's face. "You look hungry tonight. Shall I bring you something to eat?"

"*Yah.*" His smile grew. "*Mamm* has some brownies ready, I think."

"I brought chocolate chip cookies along," she said. "But they're still in the buggy."

"That's even better." John chuckled. "I thought I smelled them on the ride home."

"You did not," Laura chided. "But I'll go get them."

John didn't protest. He stayed on the couch, his smile undimmed as Laura ran through the darkness to the buggy and retrieved the plate of cookies from the back. She should have brought them in when she arrived with John, but she had been too distracted. John still did that to her. He overwhelmed her senses so that she couldn't see or feel anything else.

Laura paused to glance skyward. "Thank You for all this, Lord. You know I don't deserve what You've done. And now, please help Lydia. Things aren't working out between her and Milton. Please give us another miracle. Surely You have one up there in heaven to spare for my sister?"

Laura took her time as she went back up the sidewalk. She had prayed this prayer often in the past weeks. No answer had come yet, but she had waited months for John's restoration. The miracle would also come for Lydia. She was sure of it, but she kept her enthusiasm tempered in front of her twin. She could pray and she did, and that brought peace. Even Lydia seemed more peaceful lately. She had noticed the change from the day Lydia had taken that mysterious trip into Ogdensburg. Why *Daett* had allowed Lydia to drive up alone, she couldn't understand. For all they knew, Lydia might have planned to meet up with Milton and elope. That would not be a miracle in her book, but *Daett's* faith in Lydia had paid off. Lydia had returned when she was supposed to and had seemed calmer ever since. Lydia had even thrown herself openly into the spring wedding preparations, which brought up the matter of a date. It must be settled with John tonight. *Yah*, a final date must be set. Laura calmed herself and opened the front door again.

"I thought you got lost," John teased.

Laura laughed. "Just taking my time. It's a beautiful night out there, though a little cold. The stars are bright."

"I noticed you didn't take your coat," he said.

"You could see that?" Laura came close to touch his face with her free hand.

"I see more than you think," he said.

Laura pinched his cheek and set down the plate of cookies, and then she hurried into the Yoders' kitchen to fill two glasses with milk. When she returned, John's fingers brushed hers as he took one of the glasses, his gaze fixed on her face. Laura settled herself on the couch beside him.

"We need to talk about the wedding," she told him.

"Whose wedding?" he teased.

She slapped his arm lightly. "Stop it. I'm trying to be serious."

"Are you still sure about this?"

"John!" Laura chided. "Don't even ask that."

"I can't help but think I'm dreaming sometimes," he said wistfully. "All those months after the accident I thought you were lost to me forever. First my bedridden state, then my blindness. Yet here we are talking about our wedding." He found her hand, and his fingers tightened on hers.

"The cookies," Laura told him. "You should eat them."

"I thought you wanted to talk about our wedding," he said.

Laura leaned against him and they laughed together.

Laura sobered to look up at him. "Also, I think we need to buy Nancy's old place," she said. "And set a date for when we think the weather will break."

He nodded. "That means we should visit Bishop Ezra soon."

"*Yah*," she said, squeezing his hand. The cookies lay on the plate in front of them, forgotten for the moment.

"How's Lydia doing?" he asked. "You haven't said much about her lately."

"I really don't know." Laura sat up straighter.

"We should pray for your sister," he told her. He didn't wait for her to agree before his lips began to whisper, "Great God in heaven, look down in compassion upon Lydia as she struggles with submission to Your will. I know the cup You give is difficult to drink at times, and yet You have been merciful with Laura and me. Give Lydia that same grace. May she find Your will with Milton. May their hearts be led as You desire. Amen."

"Amen," Laura echoed. She gazed up at John's face. She adored the man. There was no question about that. He had never prayed like this before the accident. She would not have wished to go through what he had suffered, but there were compensations apparently. More than she had expected.

"I think it's time for cookies," John said, reaching for two of them. His fingers didn't miss the plate or drop crumbs as he took a bite and chewed slowly. "My milk," he said. "I forgot where I put it."

Laura led his hand to the floor. John's hand encircled the glass, and she lifted her hand with his to trace his face. Carefully she moved across his sightless eyes. He didn't resist or protest, his breath soft on her fingers.

"You know I love you, John Yoder," she said. "Very, very much."

He stopped her hand and whispered, "I could say the same, but you already know it."

"I want to hear it again," she said. "A thousand times a day."

He laughed. "Isn't that a little much? But I can say it once more. I love you, Laura. I love you."

"That was twice."

"I know," he said, and they laughed together again.

"We should stop being silly," she announced, sitting up primly on the couch.

"I'll never stop being silly with you, so get used to it," he replied.

"I guess we've had enough sorrow to allow for our silliness."

"I suppose so," he agreed. "But I guess we should be serious now. We have lots of plans to make. I know I want Lydia and Milton as the witness couple from your side of the family."

Laura dropped his hand. "Are you sure? Wouldn't that be meddling?"

"*Yah*, I'm sure," John said. "I think we should help them out. Call it meddling if you wish."

"We should wait and see," Laura said. "That's what I think."

"Ask Lydia tomorrow and see if I'm not right." His voice was firm.

She gave in. "Okay. I'll ask Lydia first thing."

Laura stared at his face again. Where had this new John come from? She didn't know, but she liked it. And if John's meddling helped bring Lydia and Milton together, she was all for that.

"We should go see Nancy's old place," he said. "In fact, let's go now!"

"But it's dark out," she objected. "And getting colder."

"Come on," he teased. "There are lights there for you, aren't there? I want to show you the place. I've waited too long already, Laura."

"But how do we get inside? Your parents, they—"

"I have the keys," John said. "I've spoken to Deacon William, and he took me out there the other day."

"You've been? But why was I not…?"

He stood up but bent over to kiss her cheek lightly. "Come! I want to show you the future, Laura—our future."

"I must at least tell your parents where we are going," she managed. "In case we get frozen to death and need help."

He laughed. "I'll wait. Go!" He waved his hand, and Laura dashed off to the kitchen table. She wrote out a quick note and laid the paper in plain sight with the kerosene lamp burning nearby. Hilda would find it easily if she wondered why the house had grown silent so early in the evening.

Laura returned breathless to the living room. John opened his arms and held her close for a moment. She took his hand and led the way out the front door. He climbed in the buggy by himself as she untied Maud and climbed up on the buggy seat beside him.

Maud took off on her own and turned the right way at the end of the driveway. John's gaze was fixed up at the sky. "I can still remember how the stars looked, but it seems a long, long, time ago."

Laura let go of the reins with one hand to hold his.

"You are a bright and shining star in my life, Laura," he said, his face still turned upward. He smiled and squeezed her hand as Maud plodded forward. The cold soon crept in, and John pulled the extra buggy blanket out from under the seat. Carefully he tucked the edges around them. "All snuggly now?"

"With you? *Yah*," Laura said.

When they laughed, the sound was soft above the crunch of the buggy wheels in the snow, and the soft thud of Maud's hoofbeats on the road. Nancy's home soon appeared in the starlight, a bare form sitting among the snowdrifts. The lane had been cleared, and Laura pulled Maud to a stop at the hitching post. A path had also been shoveled up the sidewalk to the front door.

Laura turned to look at John. "You had everything ready, didn't you?"

He nodded. "*Daett* and my younger brothers pitched in. I helped where I could, which wasn't much. Deacon William cleared the driveway. But I didn't know we would come down tonight." He grinned. "I like surprises when they involve you."

"John," she chided, climbing down to tie Maud to the hitching post. She took his hand and they made their way up the sidewalk with its dusting of snow. They stamped their feet on the porch rug and opened the front door after John had felt for and found the lock. Laura lit the kerosene lamp on the desk by the front door, and the flickering flames warmed the empty living room walls. This would soon be home, this place she had come to as a schoolchild when Teacher Nancy let them stop by on the way home. Nancy always had a tender spot in her heart for Yost Mast's children, and now she knew why. Nancy had once loved *Daett*, and Nancy had seen to it that John and she got the house. She was sure of that.

"It will be ours," John said. "Nancy knew how to handle things so that we could buy the place." His hands passed over the mantel above the cold stove. "It's already winterized. Nancy saw to that before she left. But we'll have it warm and hopping before the wedding day."

"It'll be springtime by then, John." Laura moved slowly around the room. "We won't need a fire."

"I want a fire in the stove on our wedding day," he said. "Maybe a small one, a sign of remembrance that our love was always alive in the winter of our soul."

"Oh, John." Laura wrapped her arms around him. "Then we'll make sure there is a fire in the stove on every anniversary date for the rest of our lives." She clung to him until he pulled away.

"Come," he said. "I know you've seen the house before, but I want you to see rest of it."

She held his hand and followed him as he carefully moved from room to room in the soft flickering light of the kerosene lamp.

Chapter Thirty-Nine

The day of Laura and John's wedding arrived, and the last of the snowbanks still clung to the side of the roads. Little rivers of water flowed in the ditches, driven along by the warm rays of the spring sunshine. Inside the Masts' home the benches were set up in the living room, and from there into the main bedroom and part of the kitchen. The dining room table was moved to the side, where it sat tight against the wall between the stove and the countertop. The murmur of the morning's last sermon ceased, and Bishop Ezra stood near the kitchen doorway looking out over the packed room with a slight smile on his face, his hands clasped over his chest.

Laura's whole body ached from the effort of not moving on the hard, backless bench. She wanted these morning hours of her wedding unsullied by any mistake on her part. There might be dust in some corner of the house that some sharp-eyed woman from the community would spot, but a fidgety bride she would not be. She would honor John with her composure and control in public. After their wedding vows were said, she could throw her arms around his neck tonight, and dance about all she wanted.

Bishop Ezra smiled and began to speak again. "And now we have come to this hour, when two will be made one. Our dearly beloved John Yoder and Laura Mast have sought out each other as companions for their journey through life. We all know the trials they have endured these past months, yet the two have not allowed trouble to turn them aside—either from their love for each other or from their love for the Lord and His people. For this we honor them, and hold them up as examples to our young folks. They have blazed worthy paths for those who come after them. So let us all take heed to the lessons they have taught. We do not know what trouble lies in front of us. No one is exempt from either the Lord's chastisement or His testing. This couple has been sorely tested and have been found faithful."

Bishop Ezra paused to look directly at the two of them. "You have been allowed to come to this day, John and Laura. I know the road has been difficult and the days dark, but you have arrived. We rejoice and are glad with both of you. May life give you great grace and great joy in each other. May your devotion to the Lord be rewarded, both in this life and in the one to come. And if the Lord grant you the gift of *kinner*, I am confident that you will bring them up in the fear of the Lord and in obedience to His will."

The bishop looked over the crowded living room. Laura was sure her neck was bright red from the bishop's plain talk, but she no longer needed to be embarrassed about such things. John would soon be her husband, and *yah*, she wanted *kinner*. She wanted many of them, perhaps a dozen if the Lord so willed it. Their whole house would be full of laughter and joy, and John would be a *goot daett* to all of them. She was sure of that. Look how John had won her and kept his love firmly planted in her heart. Love had stayed there even through the days when their relationship could have been ended forever by events beyond their control. There might be other such happenings lying in front of them. Who knew? But after the miracle of this day, she would never doubt the Lord's ability again.

Laura looked up as Bishop Ezra smiled down at them and held out his hand. "If the two of you still wish to exchange your wedding vows, please stand." Laura almost leaped up but stifled the impulse in time. She must wait until John rose and then follow him slowly.

John took his time, and Laura stood in front of him. His nearness loomed above her. Never had John seemed manlier or more handsome. The soberness of the moment only added to his dignity and strength. John might not see with his natural eyes, but his soul saw much more than anyone knew. His love reached across the space between them, and Laura allowed the warmth to fill her whole body.

Bishop Ezra's words reached her as from a great distance. "Will you, John Yoder, promise to love and cherish this woman until the Lord shall see fit to part you in death?"

John's *yah* came clear and steady.

Laura listened and managed to say her *yah* at the right place.

Bishop Ezra continued, and moments later he reached for Laura's hand and placed John's on hers. "And now may the God of Abraham, and Isaac, and Jacob, join this man and this woman in holy matrimony. As God has made them one, so let no man ever separate the union this side of eternity. And unto Him who has made all things, we commit this couple, both now and forever. Amen."

Bishop Ezra let go, and Laura waited again until John had taken a step back. She timed her movements so that she seated herself just after John had settled on the bench. John was her husband now. She looked over at him—her husband—as Bishop Ezra took his seat. As the last song was begun, John seemed to sense her gaze, and a slight smile played on his face. Warmth crept up Laura's neck and she looked down at the hardwood floor. Her boldness must not be on display today. Not even after she had said the wedding vows. John knew that she was a proper and submissive woman, but others might not understand her exuberance. John deserved to have his choice of a *frau* praised and not doubted by the many relatives who had traveled great distances to attend the wedding.

The last notes of the song ended, and John stood from the bench. Laura followed him to stand by his side. She took his arm as the wedding party moved down the narrow aisle toward the front door. People moved further back than normal to give John extra space. Laura smiled her thanks, but John could have navigated the path without a stumble—especially with her by his side. Right now they moved as one. They were made for each other.

Someone opened the front door, and Laura pulled back on John's arm. He seemed to know what she meant and lifted his foot higher to step across the sill. Laura's hand guided him, and John took the steps with ease. Behind them Lydia and Milton followed. Laura turned to give them a bright smile.

"Sorry if I've been ignoring the two of you," Laura told them. "I've been wrapped up in my own little world this morning. But we're married at last!"

"You have a right to be happy!" Lydia said. "You need to enjoy the day. And *yah*, you are married. I saw Bishop Ezra join your hands myself a few moments ago."

"I know!" Laura took a little leap into the air. "Breathe deeply, breathe deeply," she whispered to no one in particular.

John chuckled. "I see my *frau* is in a *goot* mood."

"Oh, John! I'm trying to behave myself. Honest."

"You're doing fine." John gave Laura's hand a quick squeeze.

Laura glanced over her shoulder again to give Lydia an encouraging smile. She wanted to give Milton a sharp rebuke for not having a wedding date set with her sister by now, but that would be out of line. Laura smiled instead at Milton and told him, "Thanks for helping us out today."

"Wouldn't have missed it." Milton winked as they entered the barn.

Daett had wanted to move the reception down the road a mile to their nearest Amish neighbors, but Laura had vetoed his plans.

"The barn can be cleaned, and it's just fine," Laura had assured *Daett*.

In the end *Daett* had given in, but not before he had ordered a new coat of whitewash for the entire first floor. That had brightened things up more than she had expected. Things were near to perfect now, which John deserved. She was sure John's relatives from Ohio would be impressed, even if the reception was held in the lower level of the bride's barn. Now if Lydia and Milton could patch up their differences today, her wedding would be truly perfect.

Laura guided John to the corner table, set up in front of the doors of the grain bin. The rough-hewn wood had been used to their advantage, serving as a rustic backdrop to the fruit arrangement Lydia had put together yesterday. Flowers were out of the question by the community's standards, but they had come close with a few bright green twigs with their freshly sprouted leaves placed at strategic spots. Her miracle looked like a miracle indeed.

"Now I wonder what we can do to help Milton and Lydia find happiness?" Laura whispered in John's ear as she helped him find his chair.

John seated himself before he whispered back, "How are they doing?"

"I don't really know," Laura said. "I've been thinking about other things."

John chuckled. He understood perfectly. John had also been

thinking about her and the vows they had exchanged. She could tell by the expression of deep joy written on his face.

"You're my *frau* now," John said. "My dear, precious *frau*."

Laura blushed deeply. "Someone might hear you."

From Lydia's smile she could tell that her twin had overheard the exchange. Thankfully Milton was deep in conversation with a cousin who had come up to speak to him.

Laura leaned toward Lydia and whispered, "I hope you don't despair today, regardless of how things turn out."

Lydia glanced at Milton before she answered. "You can pray for me. That's about all that can be done right now."

"Then you've not given up?" Laura lowered her voice when Milton glanced at the two of them. She smiled sweetly at him.

Milton smiled back and continued his conversation.

"He'll hear us next time," Lydia warned.

"You shouldn't give up."

"I guess I should tell you I went to see Teacher Nancy in Ogdensburg the other day," Lydia admitted.

Laura gasped.

"Teacher Nancy helped you and John in your dark time," Lydia explained. "Why wouldn't she know what I needed also? Especially since it involves her brother."

Laura pressed her lips together. "Nancy's in the…you know what. What if someone had seen you?"

"They didn't," Lydia said. "Nancy gave me *goot* advice. I will always be thankful for her wise words."

"What did Nancy say?" Laura leaned in closer to Lydia.

"I can't tell you here, but just know that I'll be okay," Lydia said.

John had obviously been eavesdropping and entered the conversation. "And so will you and Milton. You love each other, and love leads to the best outcome."

Lydia blinked. "You have a very wise husband, Laura."

"Thank you," John replied. "We'll be praying for you."

Lydia nodded and turned away, but not before a tear glistened in her eye.

Laura leaned against John's shoulder as Bishop Ezra stood up to lead out in the thanksgiving prayer for the meal. The Lord had given Laura a wise and *goot* husband who cared about her and her family. She had to follow His lead and place Lydia in the Lord's hands. She looked up at John's face and he smiled down at her. She had not forgotten that she was John's *frau,* and neither had John. Tonight a warm fire awaited them in Nancy's old house, which was now theirs. They would get down on their knees in the living room, and offer a prayer of thanks.

Chapter Forty

Nancy sat fidgeting in Dr. Hag's office. Why was this taking so long? And why was she so nervous? She hoped her instincts were correct, and that her prayers were answered, but she wanted confirmation.

Dr. Hag entered the office the second time and gave her a look she couldn't read.

"Well, was I right?" she asked with impatience. "Is it what I suspect?"

"Should be here in about seven and a half months." Dr. Hag broke into a smile but then sobered. "You know that complications can occur readily at your age."

"The Lord will be with me," Nancy said. "At least I won't be having a half-dozen children."

Dr. Hag chuckled. "I heard that you left the Amish community. Will you have support here in our world?"

"Charles, my husband, has many friends. I'm involved with him at the Baptist Church. Yes, we will have plenty of support...though, of course, I miss my Amish friends and family from the community."

Dr. Hag nodded. "That's understandable. Well, I'm certainly

happy for you and your husband. You're in good health, so we really don't anticipate any problems. Of course, we'll monitor your progress with regular appointments until your delivery."

Nancy dressed and paid the receptionist, Mrs. Brinkman, on the way out. The strangeness of writing the check as Nancy Wiseman still stirred her, but in a *goot* way. "Thank you," she told Mrs. Brinkman.

"And congratulations on the news," Mrs. Brinkman replied with a smile. "We'll see you next month. Here's your appointment card."

Nancy tucked the card in her purse and left the doctor's office. She drove out of Heuvelton toward Ogdensburg and soon pulled onto a side road. She parked by the edge of a small wood and climbed out of the car. Only a short trek into the woods was needed. There she found what she looked for: wildflowers in fresh bloom. With the snows almost gone and the days much warmer, she had been sure the trilliums were out, and her faith had been rewarded.

Back in her car Nancy placed the wildflowers carefully on the passenger's seat, and when she arrived home, she placed them just as carefully in the blue Ming vase on the dining room table. She bent low over the flowers and took a long breath. The wild fragrance filled her, and joy bubbled up from inside of her. She was carrying Charles's child.

Charles must be told tonight when he came home. Lisa had returned to college after the wedding, so only the two of them were in the house. She might as well act like the *Englisha* did. An announcement at supper would be perfect.

Nancy took another long breath of the flowers' fragrance. In spite of her joke to Dr. Hag about her half-dozen children if she had married an Amish man, this would likely be her only child either way. A woman in her forties could only bear so many children. She was blessed to be expecting one at all. To think that the Lord had given her love so late in her life—and now a gift that came from such love. She would bring the child to a healthy birth.

"Choose the best," she had told Lydia all those weeks ago.

Lydia had understood, although Lydia's choice would likely be different from hers. She had no regrets about leaving the community. Yost had been an attempt to recapture a love that had long since died. She had lived on a memory. The inspiration had been enough to fuel her love for school teaching and for the *kinner* of other parents. But the freshness and the newness were gone, like a trillium flower from twenty springs ago whose white blossoms had withered. Yost would have been satisfied with what was left, but she would not have been. Now Yost could experience a new happiness with Deacon William's cousin Sherry.

Charles had told her last week, "I ran into that deacon again, and he told me your old boyfriend is marrying in late May."

"Oh," she had said. "That was kind of Deacon William."

"Regrets?" Charles had teased.

"No regrets," she had said, followed by a kiss.

Nancy smiled at the memory and ran her fingers lightly over the tender white of the silky wildflower. Yellow bloomed from the center, reaching skyward with all the joy of spring written on its face. She was glad the wildflowers were in bloom. As a young girl she had gathered them often in her fingers, but knew it was useless to carry them home.

"You can plant some along the fence row if you like them so much," her *mamm* had told her. "But you can't bring them in the house."

Of course she could have taken them inside the house, but *Mamm* had meant she couldn't place them in a vase as the *Englisha* did. The community didn't subject what the Lord had made to such a display in their homes. Flowers brought pride too close for humans to resist temptation. But there was nothing prideful about this vase of flowers. There was only joy and laughter and hope and faith in the future. She would bear a child who would be here after she was gone. She would name her…

Nancy paused and smiled. Her child would be a girl. She was sure of that. She would call her Sunshine or Flower, maybe. Nancy chuckled in the still house. How wild her imagination had grown. Even among the *Englisha* such names weren't acceptable, and she wanted her child to grow up accepted. Her girl must feel at home. She must know she would be loved and appreciated. Charles had raised Lisa like that, and he would show the same consideration to her girl.

She had never been a *mamm* before, but the Lord would be with her. She would raise this daughter with the best of herself. With the Lord's help that would be sufficient. If they were given another child, the same grace would be supplied again.

Nancy took a deep breath. She must not expect too much. That she would be a mother even once was a miracle beyond anything she had dared dream only a few years ago. The community's teachings said that love came once the wedding vows were said, but she had risked all for a love that had come before the wedding, and her faith had been rewarded. It was not as the community saw fit, but her heart had seen the fingerprints of the Lord plainly enough.

Along with Charles had also come the opportunity to pursue her hunger for knowledge. The Lord had made the world, and her heart longed to see more of His beauty and glory in creation. Charles hadn't hesitated in supporting her desire to learn. A new computer was installed in the spare bedroom—a faster one, Charles claimed, than his old one. Fast enough to connect to the website of a Christian college in Virginia. She had never been to Virginia, but the wonders of *Englisha* technology had taken her there in spirit. The online classes were the best available, the website said, and Charles had nodded his agreement.

"It'll be a decent education," he had said.

To pay for it all, she had taken a part-time job at the tractor supply in town.

"That's not necessary," Charles had told her.

She had returned his smile and applied for the job, which mostly involved restocking shelves. She would be offered a higher position soon. She could tell by the approval in the manager's voice. She had planned to accept the promotion, which would mean more hours. Now with the child on the way she would have to postpone all that, but she didn't want to live off of Charles. She was his *frau*, but this was the *Englisha* world. Things were done differently.

Nancy took one last look at the white wildflowers and began to make supper. Thankfully, Charles liked her Amish cooking—which was good, since that was all she knew.

Nancy pulled dishes from the cupboard so that they clattered and banged. Those were the sounds of home, and she loved them. In the past, such sounds reminded her of the emptiness of her house— and life. But now when she was alone in the house, Charles's presence lingered. Charles was a husband to love, and he loved her.

Nancy gave the recipes only a quick glance. She knew them by heart. If she hurried the meal would be ready in time for Charles's usual arrival. The evening darkness would be upon them soon, but joy would fill their home tonight. Happiness was already in their hearts, but shared news, when it was *goot*, made the delight increase by leaps and bounds. She had always known this, but she had never shared such tidings with a man before. A man whose child she was carrying.

Nancy stirred the gravy as the scent of the wildflowers drifted past her. Behind her the timer went off, and Nancy dropped her stirring spoon to pour the hot water from the potatoes, leaving them in the sink to cool.

An hour came and went, and steam rose from the prepared dishes. Everything tasted like it should. The samples were taken in route to keep her confidence high. Not that she hadn't done this before, but there was news tonight. Charles would be home soon. A man who was her husband would eat the food she had prepared. That made a difference—a mysterious difference. She cared deeply, profoundly, in a way a hundred generations of women had done before her. She was part of a whole, a continuation of what had always been and what she would not complete.

All the dishes were on the table when the front door opened. Nancy stood by the table with the scent of the wildflowers stirred by the breath of air that moved from the open door.

"Hello?" Charles called out. "Anybody home?"

"In the kitchen," Nancy called back.

His footsteps came quickly, and he soon appeared in the doorway. "Flowers on the table? And you look lovely." He waited, taking in her odd smile.

"Something's up," he said. "What gives? What's the occasion?"

"Does there have to be an occasion?" she asked, stepping closer to kiss him lightly on the cheek.

"But there *is* one," he said. His arms pulled her tight for a moment. He knew her too well.

"Maybe," she allowed, "but the food is warm. Let's sit and eat."

He sat without protest and with bowed head, offered a blessing. Then he looked up and said, "Okay, now tell me what's up."

Warm flashes raced up her neck. She was *Englisha* now, but old Amish habits died hard. How would she share the news if this had been Yost? Certainly not here in the kitchen, even if there were no other ears to hear.

"Is something wrong?" His voice dripped with concern, and he reached his hand over to touch her face. The uncovered food steamed in front of them, but he ignored it.

Nancy smiled broadly. "There's nothing wrong. Everything's right. So right, in fact, that …" She paused and was surprised to feel tears emerging. "I'm carrying your child."

"You're *expecting*?" he said. "That's wonderful!" Then he saw her tears. "You did want this to happen, didn't you?"

"*Yah*." The old word slipped out. "With all my heart."

He reached for her with both hands. "Dear heart," he whispered. "What a wonderful woman you are, and now a mother—or soon to be. When did you know?"

"I've wondered for a week or two," she said. "But I went to Dr. Hag this morning to make sure."

Charles still smelled of his morning cologne, fresh and exotic—a scent she had picked out for him after the wedding. "It will be a girl," she finished. "I just know."

"The child will be precious either way." He held her close.

She pulled away from him. "You must eat. The food will be cold." She dished out the first portion for him.

When he had taken his first bite, she asked, "Is it okay?"

"You know it is," he said. "Like you. Perfect!"

She looked away as a waft of the flowers' fragrance drifted above the smell of the food.

He smiled. "Eat," he said. "For you and for her. For us and for our life together."

She nodded, unable to speak.

Chapter Forty-One

With the warm afternoon breeze on her face, Lydia slipped through the crowd of wedding guests in Sherry Yoder's front yard. All of them were strangers to her, as were most of the guests. Lydia had traveled down to Ohio from the North Country with a hired van for *Daett*'s wedding two days ago, along with Laura and John. Nelson, Lester, and several others from the community had also come with them. *Daett* had been here for a month to spend time with his bride and to help with the wedding preparations. The group would return home tomorrow with the hired van, while *Daett* and Sherry would follow in a week or so on the Greyhound bus.

The Mast house would feel empty when she returned home. Nelson and Lester would be there, and she would keep house for them. They would attend the youth gatherings and the Sunday services together, but nothing would be the same. Not with Laura married and living with John, and now *Daett* married too. Sherry would want things her way when she returned to the North Country with him—which was Sherry's right. Sherry would be the new *mamm* of the house. There might even be a young one arriving by this time next year. All of which meant that Lydia should make plans of her own…but what? Milton had vanished. He hadn't been at any of the youth gatherings that she had attended in the past month. She had no right to know how and where Milton spent his time. And yet…

Lydia climbed the front porch steps, where a group of young girls were lingering along the railing, deep in conversation. A few of them gave Lydia a quick glance and waved.

Lydia waved back and said hi, pasting on a smile as she moved closer to the girls. The porch swing was unoccupied. Everyone apparently preferred to stand after the three-hour church service and hearty meal afterward, but the seat appeared inviting to her. Lydia sat down and the chains squeaked.

One of the girls glanced her way.

"You're Lydia, aren't you? Yost's daughter."

"*Yah*, that's me." Lydia forced her smile to widen.

"I'm Esther, Sherry's cousin." The girl offered her own smile. "I hope you feel at home in Ohio."

"It's nice," Lydia said to be polite. "And Sherry's folks put us up well for the night. Even my two brothers didn't complain."

Esther's eyebrows rose. "Two brothers? I must have missed them in the bustle at the noon meal."

Several of the girls giggled. "Don't be so obvious, Esther."

"I'm sure they're quite handsome with a *daett* like Yost." Esther sent another smile Lydia's way. "Your *daett* got himself a decent *frau* this morning. Sherry's my favorite aunt!" Esther glowed with approval. "And your *daett's* quite a catch from the things I've heard. Sherry couldn't stop talking about him at the family gatherings these past months." She searched the gathered crowd on the front lawn. "How many of your community people came down with you besides your two brothers?"

There was choked laugher from the railing. "Why don't you just come out and ask the real question, Esther?"

Esther colored and Lydia hurried to answer. She knew what these insinuations meant. "A few," she said. "My brother Nelson brought his girlfriend Emily along, but Lester's still available. He's the tall one."

The laughter was more subdued this time.

"Looks like your *daett* started a trend, Lydia," one of the girls said from the railing.

"We should speak of something else!" Esther declared.

"Now you want to change the subject?" the girl shot back. "Maybe I'll be one of the lucky ones and be taken to the dinner table tonight by a North Country man."

The laughter was louder this time, and the conversation was soon buzzing again.

"What about you?" Esther asked Lydia. "You didn't bring anyone along?"

Lydia blushed deeply. "I don't have anyone."

Esther regarded Lydia skeptically. "Don't try to convince me of that."

"I don't," Lydia insisted.

"What about him?" Esther motioned across the lawn behind Lydia's back. "He seems quite interested in you. If I don't miss my guess, he's finally gotten up the nerve to come up and talk with you. I know he's not from around here."

Lydia looked in the other direction on purpose. This was not something she needed—unwanted attention from a strange man in Ohio. How would she deal with that?

"He's coming," Esther whispered. "He has to know you. How else…" Esther punched Lydia gently in the ribs. "Come on, look!"

The girls along the railing sent sly glances toward the man, but Lydia still didn't look in his direction.

"He's sure handsome," Esther whispered.

When Lydia snuck a look, the word burst out of her mouth. "Milton!"

"*Yah*, in the flesh." Milton's grin spread from ear to ear.

"So who is this?" Esther asked.

Milton didn't miss a beat. "Nobody, really. I've just come to chat with Lydia. Do you mind?"

Esther didn't move. "So how do you two know each other? I didn't see you at the service this morning."

"I was sitting on the wall like a fly," Milton teased, and laughter rippled down the line of girls.

Milton was at his best—bold, brash, and full of himself.

Lydia tightened her grip on the back of the swing but found nothing to say.

Thankfully Esther covered the silence for her. "You still haven't told us how you know Lydia, and why you're here."

"Are all girls in Ohio this nosy?" Milton chuckled. "Or only the pretty ones?"

Esther turned all sorts of colors, and Lydia found her voice. "Maybe you *should* tell us why you're here, Milton. Neither Sherry nor *Daett* gave you a wedding invitation that I know of."

Esther looked at Lydia as if she had lost her mind, but Milton had played with her heart for long enough. Now he obviously planned to embarrass her in front of these strange girls. If this continued, they would all know her history with Milton before he left.

"I'm sorry if I shouldn't be here." Milton gave Lydia his sweetest smile. "I know I'm not invited. That's why I wasn't at the service this morning, but I thought maybe you could get me an invitation for dinner tonight. Aren't you the bridegroom's daughter? See, I'm in strange country and homesick for the beauties of the North Country."

"But…" Lydia was at a loss to continue.

"And I thought you might accompany me to the table along with the invitation." Milton grinned. "If you don't mind, that is. I know I would enjoy the occasion very much."

"Well, I…" Lydia stammered. "*Yah*, I guess it'll be all right."

"I'll see you then," Milton said. With a smile he retreated across the lawn. Lydia watched him go, transfixed by his familiar form. He seemed to know lots of people and stopped often to shake hands as he moved through the crowd.

"So what other secrets do you have?" Esther asked.

"None!" Lydia retorted, amazed at the turn of events.

Esther's glance told her plainly that Esther didn't believe her, as did none of the other girls. They wore open admiration on their faces.

He's not my boyfriend, Lydia wanted to shout at them. *He just breaks my heart and plays with my emotions. He wants me to jump the fence with him.* But none of those words came out of her mouth. She wouldn't degrade Milton. He was a *wunderbah* man. She had tried to cast him out of her heart, and every time she thought she had accomplished the task, Milton showed up again. Not only did he show up, but he made some move that sent her heart all atwitter.

"You're a lucky girl," Esther said. "Maybe I ought to visit the North Country myself. Have you got any more like him stashed away up there? Or that available brother of yours, is he…?"

Lydia didn't answer as she stood to walk away. There was no answer needed. Esther's voice soon blended in with the buzz of conversation behind her. A hundred questions raced through Lydia's mind. Why was Milton in Ohio on the day of *Daett's* wedding? He must be here on business. So why come to the wedding? He had on his best Sunday suit. Did Milton want to surprise her? Shock her? Impress her? So she would finally consent to jumping the fence with him? If that was the answer, Milton had won the first round. She had accepted his offer tonight, because she couldn't resist the man. Her heart was fixed on him, still longed for him, wept silent tears inside while she kept her eyes dry.

Lydia made her way through the front door of the old farmhouse. She had to get away from the crowd. But where? People were still everywhere as they chatted about the awesome wedding meal Sherry's parents had served in their huge pole barn. Compared to Laura's wedding, this meal and setting had been…Lydia pushed the comparison out of her mind. Laura had been happy with what was available on *Daett's* farm.

"Let's keep the wedding small with *Mamm* gone," Laura had told *Daett*.

Lydia paused to look around before she made a quick dash toward the stair door. Milton would take her to the table in that huge pole barn this evening. The thought took her breath away—even if Milton had ulterior motives. Her heart betrayed her while her mind stood firm.

Lydia took the stair steps one at a time. They creaked like the ones at home, the sound a familiar one from her childhood. This was Ohio, a new community, but it was much the same. These people were her people. They had the same customs as her community did. Which stood to reason, since this was where most of the North Country community had moved from. Still…

Lydia found a bedroom door and knocked gently. There was no answer, so she entered. The quilt on the bed featured a star-shaped pattern, and the dresser was clean and newly polished. Lydia walked over to the window and looked down at the crowd on the lawn below. Milton's form materialized among a small group of men near the barn. The distance was too far to see his face, but he seemed perfectly at home. His arms waved about, as if he were in the midst of a story. As usual, he was the center of attention. He was so…

something. After all this time she still couldn't find the exact words to describe her attraction to the man. Lydia was unable to look away. He drew her, deeply, in a way no other man did.

The *best*, Nancy had said. She was to choose the best. Was Milton the best? Perhaps, but the path he wanted to walk with her wasn't the best. She knew that. The struggle raged again. Would she give in tonight if Milton asked her once more to join him in his planned jump into the *Englisha* world? What if he came right out and asked the question again? He might. Hadn't he marched right up to speak with her in front of a strange group of girls? What if Milton asked the words, whispering them quietly at the table? "Will you be my *frau*, Lydia? I'm ready to wed you when you are."

Could she resist that? What if he took her in his arms behind the buggies after supper? Could she still say no to jumping the fence while resting in Milton's arms?

Lydia wrapped her fingers around the dark drapes and gazed down at Milton's distant face. Would she betray her highest convictions? Her faith? On *Daett's* wedding day? Her heart pounded with the question. Her knees trembled as she held on to the drapes. She wanted to breathe a desperate prayer heavenward for strength to resist, but the words died in her mouth.

Chapter Forty-Two

Several hours later Lydia kept her gaze straight ahead as the long line of single girls approached the huge pole barn. Her heart was pounding, but at least she could hide her emotions well. That had always been a gift of hers—unlike Laura, who showed all of her feelings on her face.

A wave of a hand came from the crowd of married women gathered near the pole barn door, and Lydia caught a glimpse of Laura and waved back. Laura had wanted to know who was taking her to the dinner table tonight. She had refused to say who the man was, which had only added to Laura's curiosity.

Lydia dug her fingernails into the palms of her hands as Milton stepped out of the crowd of unmarried men. He held his head high and marched right over toward her. She couldn't take her eyes off of his face. He was so handsome, so sure of himself, so unafraid of the world. He was as comfortable here as he was in the North Country, while she struggled with the jitters amid unfamiliar circumstances.

"*Goot* evening," Milton whispered, his head bent low for a moment. "You're the prettiest of all the fair maidens tonight."

"Milton," she scolded.

"Come now," he teased. "Not even a *goot* evening for me?"

339

"Please, Milton," she begged. "I'm nervous enough."

He nodded, and Lydia didn't look at him again until they had seated themselves in the spacious pole barn. Servers stood at the end of the long tables ready to begin once the prayer of thanks had been offered. The smell of delicious food drifted out from behind the curtains, where the evening cooks worked. Sherry's parents had prepared only the best food in celebration of their daughter's marriage to *Daett*.

Lydia gathered her courage and asked Milton, "Why did you really come to Ohio?"

Milton grinned. "To see you, of course."

"Don't tease me," she pleaded. "I can't take it right now."

"I'm not teasing," he said. "I did have some business, but that could have been arranged some other time. I adjusted my schedule because I wanted to surprise you."

Lydia didn't dare look at Milton. Thankfully Bishop Monroe from the local congregation chose the moment to stand and announce, "Let's bow our heads and give thanks to the Lord for this *wunderbah* meal prepared for us."

Everyone bowed their heads down the long lines of tables. Lydia waited a few seconds after the amen to look up.

As expected, Milton was looking at her. "It's so *goot* to see you, Lydia," he said.

"Thank you. It is a pleasure to be with you," she managed.

"Wow. Look at the spread tonight," Milton said, surveying the trays carried by the servers. "Barbecued chicken, ham casserole, green beans...and date pudding. I hear that Ohio date pudding is unequaled anywhere."

"It is *goot*," Lydia agreed, giving Milton a suspicious glare. "You know you could have given me some warning you'd be here today."

"And have you turn me down before I even arrived?" Milton chuckled.

Lydia stilled her protest. He was more right than she cared to admit. This could well have been the only way she would have consented to seeing him again. How could she refuse him when Milton had cared enough to rearrange his business trip to see her? Her arms grew weak at the thought, and Lydia almost dropped the plate of chicken.

Milton came to her rescue. "Whoa there!"

It's your fault, she wanted to say, but she gave him a sweet smile instead. This might be her last evening spent so close to Milton. She wasn't going to give in to his renewed offer to jump the fence with him.

Milton heaped his plate high again as the trays of food made another round. "I haven't eaten all day." He glanced sideways at Lydia.

"You look well fed to me," she said.

He slapped his stomach. "I guess I did have breakfast, but that was so long ago…"

"You poor thing," she cooed, and he roared with laughter.

"It's nice that someone cares if I live or die," he said once he'd calmed down. With a quick swipe of his hand Milton piled fresh salad high in the tiny corner left on his plate.

"You shouldn't put so much food on your plate," Lydia chided. "They'll be passing around these plates of food for a few more rounds."

"You're sweet, you know, even when you scold," he teased.

"I'm sorry. I guess I shouldn't fuss when you're…" Lydia looked away. She couldn't say the words when this evening would be over much too soon. Milton would say nice things, followed by another plea outside the pole barn with darkness wrapped around them. She would say no, and that would be the end of that.

"When I'm what?" Milton asked.

"When you're *here*," she whispered.

Milton's voice was gentle. "I understand. More than you can

imagine. I've been doing a lot of things I shouldn't have, Lydia. Of course you're upset."

"I'm not upset," Lydia said. "I'm just…"

He gave her a quick glance.

"Well, maybe a little upset." A tear trickled down her cheek, but she didn't wipe it away. "Is this just another of those *wunderbah* things you come up with that we can do together, but nothing ever…"

Milton touched her hand under the table. "I'm the one who is sorry, Lydia."

He took a bite of his food and chewed slowly. His hand hadn't left hers under the table, and she didn't pull away. What a pickle they were in. Neither of them could leave the other, but they couldn't come to terms either.

The minutes ticked past, and Milton's plate emptied. Lydia could hardly touch her food, but she managed to eat enough to satisfy any curious onlookers. This was *Daett's* wedding and she should be happy, not close to tears. Laura's smile from her place across the room beside John caught Lydia's eye. Laura sent a little wave again. Laura saw by now that Milton was here. That much was obvious, and Laura would be hoping things turned out okay. John might even be praying, since Laura had surely told him about Milton's presence.

"I need to say something." Milton's hand moved in hers. "The words just come hard for me."

"For you?" Lydia exclaimed. "That's hard to believe."

He shrugged. "*Yah*, for me. The road back will be difficult and long. I still have a lot of progress to make, but Nancy has spoken with me."

She gripped his fingers under the table. "Did she…?" Lydia couldn't get the words out.

"Nancy didn't say anything to me about your visit," Milton said. "What we talked about was me and life out there." Milton paused.

Lydia didn't move. Why did Milton have to draw this out? The torment was almost too much.

"I want to join the community, Lydia," he said. "I think it's for the best."

"You want to?"

"I do," he said. "Nancy doesn't think I'll be happy out there. Not without someone I love very much with me, and probably not then." Milton gave Lydia a quick look. "You're always in my thoughts, Lydia. No matter how much I resolve to leave the community behind and start a new life, I can't do it without you. That's what it is. You've given me so many chances, and you've given me another one tonight when you probably expected I'd ask you again to jump the fence with me."

Lydia looked away.

He leaned closer. "I hope you can learn to trust me, Lydia. Especially after all the begging I did, trying to get you to go *Englisha* with me." Milton grinned weakly.

Lydia tried to breathe evenly. The date pudding bowl was almost to them on its first pass, and Milton hadn't even noticed.

"I'm serving you," she said, reaching for the bowl and placing several heaping spoonfuls on his plate. "Enough?"

He nodded.

Lydia dipped out several spoonfuls onto her own plate. The dark dessert laced with white whipped cream looked delicious. She passed the bowl on before taking up her spoon.

"To your journey back," she said, lifting her spoon.

He slowly comprehended, and he lifted his spoon to hers. As they ate, the smooth goodness melted in their mouths.

A smile crept across Milton's face. "You will be with me then— on this journey back?"

She nodded, her eyes locked with his.

"I've already told Deacon William I'm joining the baptismal class this spring," Milton said, looking down. "I know it's already started, but the deacon said he was sure an exception could be made. He'd teach me the missed information himself if necessary. For someone like you," he said.

"He did not!" Lydia knew her face was bright red.

"*Yah*, he did!" Milton chuckled. "Hey, you're even prettier when you're blushing. Did you know that?"

Stop it! she ordered with a look. Milton's soft laugh came anyway. Lydia forced herself to focus on the last of her date pudding. She couldn't taste anything, but it didn't matter. Milton was beside her, and he had said the words she had given up all hope of him ever saying. Thankfully the singing began a few moments later. Milton held the songbook with her, but they looked into each other's eyes more than at the page in front of them. The hour and a half passed for them like a moment of time.

"Come." When the singing concluded, Lydia pulled on Milton's elbow and drew him outside. She shouldn't do this. A kiss now would be much too early in their relationship. But on the other hand, she had known Milton for a long time, and she had waited for this moment for a long time too. Milton seemed to discern her intentions and made no objection when they slipped behind the buggies and out of the lantern light. Voices murmured around them as the crowd came out of the pole barn, but Lydia didn't hear a word. Milton was too close to her. She drew him closer and reached up for him, and they held each other.

"I wish this moment would never end," Lydia said.

"But it's only our beginning," Milton said in a whisper. Then he held her as if he would never let go.

Discussion Questions

1. Do you have any memories of receiving or writing love letters as is common among the Amish?

2. What is your experience with identical twins and their different natures? Could you identify with Laura and Lydia?

3. Where did your sympathies lie as Teacher Nancy's conflicted actions were revealed? How would you have responded if living in the closed community of the Amish?

4. Do you think Laura was to blame for John's fall at the barn raising? Should she have acted differently?

5. Have you ever believed for a miracle? How did the Lord lead you through the journey?

6. Wendell succeeds in making a pest out of himself. Should Laura have handled him any differently?

7. *Mamm*'s death is a shock to everyone, but opens the door to reconciliation between Nancy and Yost. Should Nancy have taken this opportunity? Explain the answer further.

8. What were your impressions of Milton and his eccentric ways? Was Lydia falling in love with him understandable?

9. Does anything in modern life correspond to the control and influence Amish parents have over their children's marriage choices?

10. What were your feelings on Nancy's behind the
    scenes impact upon Laura and Lydia's life. How do
    you think the Amish community felt?

**Don't miss the first two books in the
St. Lawrence County Amish series…**

A HEART ONCE BROKEN

*What happens when two Amish cousins set
their kapps for the same man?*

Cousins Lydia and Sandra Troyer and their friend, Rosemary Beiler, have always been close. The two cousins, however, both have eyes for handsome Ezra Wagler, leaving Rosemary to watch from the sidelines. But when the cousins' fathers face financial ruin, Lydia and Sandra make a deal as to who should have Ezra's affections…at which point Rosemary decides to make a play for Ezra herself.

UNTIL I LOVE AGAIN

Will a secret from the past threaten Susanna's future?

Susanna Miller's freedom during her *rumspringa* goes a bit further than she wants her family to know. A birthday sign innocently placed on a gas station billboard condemns Susanna as she realizes her relationship with the charming Joey Macalister, an *Englisha* man, has become far too close.

Her *daett* is not pleased, but what he hasn't told her is that he himself has regrets about events from his own *rumspringa*. Widower Ernest Helmuth knows Ralph Miller's secret, but he has said nothing as of yet. He plans on having Susanna as his bride no matter what.

With her baptism approaching, Susanna knows that time is running out to make her choice: stay with her family or hope she can find love in the *Englisha* world. With Ernest Helmuth watching, that decision might not be hers to make.

Is Susanna's faith strong enough to make the right choice?

About the Author

Jerry Eicher's Amish fiction has sold more than 700,000 books. After a traditional Amish childhood, Jerry taught for two terms in Amish and Mennonite schools in Ohio and Illinois. Since then he's been involved in church renewal, preaching, and teaching Bible studies. Jerry lives with his wife, Tina, in Virginia.